GENERATIONS

Noam Josephides

Praise for GENERATIONS:

Like the best of Science Fiction classics, Generations reminds us that the future is a canvas of our making, and with it — our definition of being Human."

"Generations' message hits hard, while being a fun and engaging rollercoaster of a read!"

"Thought-provoking, innovative and brimming with emotional depth!"

"A timeless tale of the dark side of ambition, and the courage to defy the evil it spawns."

GENERATIONS

By

Noam Josephides

First paperback edition April 2024

Book cover design by Daniel Kutz

ISBN 979-8-9886679-4-0 (hardcover)

ISBN 979-8-9886679-2-6 (paperback)

ISBN 979-8-9886679-3-3 (ebook)

U.S Copyright Registration: TXu 002-412-245

Library of Congress Control Number: 2024904311

www.generationsnovels.com

This book is accompanied by an optional

🎧 SOUNDTRACK 🎧

So slap-on your headphones, or crank up that HiFi system…
And let's embark on a journey through space!

Get your FREE SOUNDTRACK COPY here:

GENERATIONSNOVELS.COM/SOUNDTRACK

PART ONE

CHAPTER ONE

In a classic *me* move, the low doorframe hitting my head took me by complete surprise.

"*Kunye mala!*" I cursed. *Again, Sandrine?!* Girl, now you're *definitely* going to be late.

I darted a quick look back into the office to ensure no one had noticed my fumble. If any of my Archivist colleagues caught me running straight into the overhead nanoplast frame, the mockery would last them a *Parsec*.

I crouched to pick up the inksheets spread all over the floor. A tiny, dark-red circlet bloomed on one of the flexible sheets. I smeared it off and reached a finger to my forehead. It came back bloody. *Just perfect*, I thought. Not only am I late for a formal meeting with the number one citizen on this ship — the actual Primo of the Thetis! — now I'm about to take his deposition with a *kunye* bloody gash in my head, like a clumsy schoolgirl?

OK, focus. I backtracked to my desk and picked up a small MetaGel band-aid. I slapped it on and headed out to my already-late appointment. You got to hand it to those *Earthers Passados*. Building a multi-generation colony ship like the Thetis, flinging it across the galaxy in a glorious scientific triumph — only to neglect factoring for the 0.6g babies getting progressively taller with each generation?

Kinda makes you wonder what else the *Passados* forgot with the last-minute panic to initiate the launch back in those days.

Yet, eight generations and fifty-odd light years later the Thetis, admittedly, held quite intact. So one could only hope it would hold for the two final generations and get us to planetfall without any drama.

"You're late," Nyasha Woo, the Head Archivist — and my boss — commented as I passed by his desk.

"I know," I stopped and searched for his eyes. "Why send *me* up there?"

Nyasha didn't raise his head from the inksheet he was reading. "It's the Thetis Primo, Sandrine," he muttered, "who else would I send? Any of the Juniors?"

"You know how I am around politicians. What with my glorious history with the administration."

Finally, he met my gaze, then shrugged and gestured at the surrounding Archive office. "Well, you're part of that administration now. Maybe it's time for healing. And — you're late."

"Aargh," I growled. "So I suppose at some point you're going to tell me what's this deposition I am taking from Primo Anderson all about?"

Nyasha raised his glasses to his head, the small lenses almost disappearing in his short salt-and-pepper curls.

"This is a delicate matter," his deep brown eyes held my gaze. "You will not be taking Anderson's deposition. There will be a written one ready for you to pick up and hand over to the Archive. As in — to me. Discretely."

I didn't like that. "So if I'm only playing errand-girl here, maybe it *is* a task for one of the juniors. What's the point in sending a Sen—"

"—Sandrine," Nyasha interjected uncharacteristically. "I need a Senior Archivist I can trust there. And I need this done on-protocol, by-the-book, zero-corners-cut. Will you help me with that please?"

"How?" I leaned closer and whisper-shouted at him. "What book?

Which *kunye* protocol am I supposed to keep if you're sending me up there blind?"

Nyasha hesitated, his eyes reflecting the inner struggle he was going through. To me, Nyasha Woo was much more than just a boss. I knew him since being practically a teenager, and he supported me through the darkest time in my life. He fought for me and I knew he trusted me like his own daughter, which was why that sudden secrecy was so unusual coming from him.

After a few silent moments, I could see a decision forming behind his frozen expression. He pulled his glasses back over his eyes and rose from the squeaky office chair. With a gentle palm over my arm, Nyasha walked me toward the exit door and away from any curious ears in the large open space of the Archive.

"There was an extortion attempt," he blurted out flatly and handed me a stack of case file inksheets.

I stopped in my tracks. "A… *what?*"

Nyasha turned to face me, a head shorter and as serious as a hull breach.

"Someone is trying to extort the Thetis Primo. So now you know."

He turned away and started receding back into the Archive office, his inconceivable words hovering behind him like a trail of specters.

Chapter Two

My head was throbbing as I stepped out of the Archive and started toward the Ascenders. I stretched my neck in a slow, circular motion, re-centering myself as the sudden opening of space hit my senses. Level 13 was a double height level, which was a real perk considering they could have stuck the Archive at some industrial or administrative level in the single digits. That open space was mostly recreation parks, sports facilities and public speaking arenas. It had benches and CarboFoam trees with flowers that looked almost real. Even the air itself felt fresher here — quite the mental stretch, obviously, for a ship that hadn't had an outer seal cracked in a hundred and eighty years.

Extortion? The word felt alien in my mouth, like a stale piece of fruit that just won't go down. An extortion of the Thetis *Primo?* That concept was so utterly inconceivable, so out of place in the peaceful and cooperative society of the Thetis, that my mind had a hard time placing it in any reasonable context.

OK. Meeting. I took the diagonal path through the sports park, squeezing between loud groups of 8th Generation teenagers doing their morning kundalini sessions and skating and b-balling and all the fun stuff kids do in their pre-Contribution years. I started skimming though Nyasha's inksheets, trying to get a basic grip on the case details.

The park was busier than usual for a weekday morning. It was peak election season on the Thetis, which apparently stirred a lot of excitement in the rivaling supporter groups huddled on both sides of the path. Elections for Primo were a once in every twenty five years ordeal, so the last time that went on I was a mere three-year-old toddler and too young to remember. The supporters were a noisy bunch: on my right, advocates of the residing Primo Sebastian Anderson were waving signs bearing his signature motto, 'Stability and Unity'. On my left, a markedly younger group campaigned for Mrs. Athena Saugado, an up-and-coming albeit controversial contender, calling for the need for change in Thetis leadership.

The noticeable size difference between the opposing groups told the perennial human story — people just didn't like change all that much.

And anyhow, I was an Archivist — a representative of the Code of Law on the ship, and couldn't be associated with any form of political activity. So I just pushed through the hubbub and made my way to the closest Ascender platform.

I waited for the counter-traj — or "upward"— Ascender that would take me to the Primo's quarters on 34th, pressing the MetaGel band-aid to my forehead. With any luck, the seven minute trip would be enough to heal the head cut completely before my meeting with the Primo.

That would hopefully save me some embarrassment, which in my playbook would be marked as a good day, wouldn't it?

* * *

"So, is it no-helmets-to-work day today?" asked the Suit, pointing a lazy finger at my head-bump. "Level 13 ceiling not high enough for you?"

Kunye MetaGel band-aid, I thought. I've always been a slow skin healer. And now I was so self-conscious about the cut that I felt like a flashlight was beaming out of my forehead.

The Suit scanned me top to bottom with eyes so colorless they resembled dirty pucks of ice. And those eyes were decorated by white eyelashes which almost seemed unnatural.

"What are you, Generation 7?" He asked.

"Gen7, second cycle." *I'm tall, not OLD, wapa!*

He was clearly impressed, as much as a muscle-brain can be, I guess. "Well you're a rarity! Never heard of such a young Senior Archivist, am I wrong?"

"I'm smart," I faked a smile, hoping to discourage any further small-talk attempts.

The gray-eyed Suit raised a brow. "And polite, too."

I scanned my surroundings impatiently. "I'm here to pick up Primo Anderson's deposition. We done with the personality analysis, Suit?"

Did that come out too aggressive? I thought. I sometimes get that way when I'm super-nervous. I piled my deposition inksheets on the low, wooden coffee table. I always love to call them Suits to their faces. Mostly it's because I can't bother to tell them apart. But really it often throws them off balance, and you have a better chance of seeing beyond the inflated self-confidence.

Why would anyone even need to keep Suits for personal protection on the Thetis was beyond me — there hadn't been any violent or criminal breach of Code in four generations, and sporadic conflicts between individual Thetans are dealt by the Archive, which is where I work. Maybe it's a status thing for the Primo, I guess? Excessive, if anyone asks me.

The Suit held my gaze, obviously wrestling with how to react to my subtle challenge, then presumably decided I wasn't worth the effort. He shifted his eyes elsewhere and sat down on the chair near the entrance door, slightly deflated.

"He's going to be delayed. Upcoming elections make the Primo's schedule a bit chaotic these days." He shrugged. "Surprisingly, everyone wants something."

All this running to get here on time and he's late? Awesome.

Apparently my frustration was quite openly readable, as he added, "Sorry for that. No disrespect to the prestigious Archive."

I raised my head in surprise at the change of tune. He stepped closer and offered a firm handshake. "I'm not here for the Primo's protection," he said flatly. "Jericho Pakk. I'm handling communications for the Anderson administration."

"So not muscle — politician," I muttered, studying Pakk. "It *is* kind of the same these days, ne?"

He stiffened and pulled his hand back, backing off toward the door. His icy eyes kept an unflinching glare at mine. *Nice self control,* I thought.

"He's on his way up, Archive lady," he muttered and closed the door behind him.

Being in the Thetis Primo quarters felt eerily weird. I double checked the placement of my inksheets on the table, then took the chance to look around a bit. Primo Anderson's place was noticeably luxurious, which is quite a surprise when it comes to the Thetis. The habitat quarters on the ship were very similar to each other — simplistic, effective and humanly chaotic in a way. Everyone on the Thetis is part of a joint mission and is sharing in all resources equally.

Well, at least that's what they teach you in kindergarten, right? No rich or poor, no need for social climbing or turf wars. 'Where there's no competition, there's no status', the saying goes.

And where there's no status, there's no conflict. The core notion of stability along this multi-generation journey relies on the deep underlying concept of *Unity*. And even the Primo of the ship was a mere servant to this cause. Granted, an elected one by the Thetis population, but a servant nonetheless.

But this place was very different. It was... neat. And space-y. And somehow extraordinarily antiquated. Where all of us had CarboFoam slabs for tables, the one I was sitting at was definitely real wood. An even greater peculiarity, the entire square of soft, light-brown sofas placed at the centre of the lounge area was actual, biological *leather*. How those were perfectly intact more than a hundred and eighty years since Embarkment was a mystery to me — such delicate and degradable materials were avoided when building the Thetis. Especially as more durable, synthetic alternatives were so affordably available. *It does work its effect, though,* I admitted to myself.

A glimpse of my own reflection in the decorated wall mirror caught my eye. I stepped closer, ensuring I was in a presentable form for the meeting. I tucked a stray strand of hair behind an ear — my hairdo-of-the-month was straight, shoulder-length, and space black. Hairstyle experiments have been my most active playfield in the past year. Curly, shaven, asymmetric — I've done 'em all. Violet, my best friend and a therapist, could probably write a whole thesis about how that relates to my recent psychological rollercoaster, but whatever. I just liked the change. Beyond that — a strong chin, eyebrows Nyasha labeled "stubborn",and nice teeth. I wasn't by any stretch beautiful, but every now and then I had a moment where it all came together, I guess.

A rustle of feet approaching from the outer corridor startled me back to attention. The door slid open and Jericho stood in the threshold, gesturing in my general direction.

"Primo Anderson, Senior Archivist Sandrine Liet".

Here we go.

"Sandrine!"Anderson entered the large room with a brisk and confident stride, his wide smile accentuating strong cheekbones and firm jaw. It wasn't the first time I've seen the Primo, of course, but I have never actually met him in person. He was... impressive. You could tell the man immediately and effortlessly dominated every room he stepped into. He was just *perfect* for his position, from the custom-fit ultramarine suit which looked like he was born into, to his just-right tanned face and energetic, yet relaxed, body language.

The Primo took the sofa across from me and leaned forward, stretching a formal hand over the table. Not a single hair moved in his picture-perfect, short trimmed grey cut. "May I call you San?"

"I..." I felt suddenly off-balance. *Am I blushing?* "...the deposition document will designate me as Arc. Liet," I mumbled and shook his warm, steady hand. Anderson paused for a split second, and — in a way which seemed anatomically impossible — stretched his smile even wider.

"Yes, yes. Of course — protocol." He released my hand and straightened in his seat, the leathery material creaking slightly with the shift of weight. Anderson kept steady eye contact with me for another second or two. For a brief moment I thought I saw a glint of recognition there, but it quickly disappeared.

"Primo Sebastian Anderson," I started, "I don't want to take too much of your time. I was sent to formally receive your written deposition about the extortion complaint you filed — "

"You can call me Sabi," Anderson raised his palm in a friendly, apologetic gesture. "I'm so sorry to have dragged you all the way up here. It comes to nothing, really."

I paused and looked at him tentatively. "How so, sir?"

Jericho Pakk joined us on the sofa, laying a heavy palm on the stack of inksheets in my hand.

"The Primo would like to withdraw the complaint and strike it off the Archive records," he said quietly.

"It was but a simple mistake," Anderson kept smiling. "No reason to spend any more of the Archive's precious time on the matter."

I sat back in the leather sofa, my eyes tracing a triangle between both men and the pile of inksheets, trying to re-assess the situation.

"So, wait," I held the files mid-air in front of them, "this is a recorded formal complaint about a potential extortion of the Thetis Primo. You filed it, sir."

Both men flinched and exchanged glances. "Let's use the term *attempted unlawful influence*," Jericho said, still looking at Anderson.

"So, I assumed that the purpose of that deposition was to clarify the case details and determine further investigation?" I proceeded cautiously.

Jericho's body tensed and he was almost ready to jump out of his comfy sofa. Anderson put his palm over Pakk's arm, settling him down. He kept smiling at me.

"Let me show you something, Sandrine. Something very few people on the Thetis have ever — or will ever — see with their own eyes," he said. "Then we'll think together how to tackle this little unpleasantry. Te?"

Without waiting for my confirmation, Anderson rose with surprising lightness from the deep sofa and led me to the back wall of the big lounge. A line of framed photographs decorated the wood-covered wall, most of them of the expected public-figure kind: his inauguration day as Primo; some commencement speech he gave at the Academy; wearing safety-goggles at the helm of some factory machinery demonstration. Highlights of a politician's life. Several of the photos included Anderson's only son, Sam, alongside him. *They sure have the same smile in those photos*, I thought. *Same Genline, no doubt.*

But the Primo wasn't focused on the photos. He reached out and opened a wide drawer which slid out and extended from the wall. I immediately noted the unique shine of the drawer-safe inner plating. *Liquid diamond. This must be something important.*

Gently, Anderson pulled out a large picture-frame and held it to the light. It was slightly larger than a standard inksheet, and the frame was handcrafted brown leather, sewn with real thread. I immediately recognized the document framed behind the thick duraglass. I took a small step back in surprise. "Is this—"

Primo Anderson's smile and soft eyes took in my awe, as if he was revealing a magic secret to an enthusiastic child.

"Indeed, it is. The original Embarkment Certificate of the Thetis."

CHAPTER THREE

I had seen digital scans of the Embarkment Certificate, of course. Every Thetan studied it at one point or another at the Academy, and as an Archivist I naturally had the scanned versions available to me anytime I wanted to revisit them. But the real thing felt utterly different. The notion of the actual, tangible object that had been hand-signed almost two centuries ago, marking the send-off of our entire species into *generations* of space-travel — well, this was a piece of *history!*

And Anderson was holding it like it was the most mundane object in the world. Like he *owned* the thing.

"Would you like to hold it, Sandrine?" He positioned the frame in front of me.

"No, no, thank you Primo Anderson, I could never..." I took another step back, afraid to somehow infect the object with my clumsiness. *Let's practice crossing doorways for a while before handling delicate historical artifacts, won't we?* Still, the Embarkment Certificate mesmerized me. The material on which it was printed looked organic — *could this be... parchment, maybe?* — and showing slight signs of deterioration. It was probably a good idea to stow it away in that condition-controlled safe-drawer. That certificate should be preserved for eternity!

Although mainly symbolic and ceremonial in nature, the

Embarkment Certificate contained the foundational text of the Human race's hopes, values and defining tenets of the Thetis mission. It was hand-signed by the 21 mission directors who had led the hundred-year project to its conclusion. They were experts in fields varying from genetics to engineering to social planning and others.

My eyes drifted to the bottom of the page, where three neat rows of ink signatures named the giants who had devoted their lives to getting the Thetis to Embarkment. A devotion left unrewarded, as all twenty-one of them were eventually left behind on Earth, none of them selected to board the actual mission.

Why is he showing it to me? Why now?

"This is very impressive," was all I could come up with. Anderson's smile receded a notch to reveal a trace of concern. He laid a soft hand on my shoulder, gently walking me back to the leather sofa.

"Can I let you in on a secret?" His deep, brown eyes scanned my face. Anderson didn't wait for my reply — *I guess politicians sometimes ask questions not in search of an answer, but as a mean of focusing attention.*

"Why do you think I keep the Embarkment Certificate in my own private quarters, when it could easily be kept at the Archive?"

Is this some kind of test? "I don't know… Redundancy?" I tried, "keep scans in the Archive and the original up here, in case of any damage?"

Anderson sneered and shot a look at Jericho Pakk. "A typical Archivist answer. All the focus on the details, yet no regard to the grander vision."

He fixed his eyes back on me, his look softer now. "The answer, Senior Arc. Liet, is *perspective*." Anderson began painting imaginary circles in the air as he spoke.

"People often ask me: 'Sabi, what is the purpose of our generation?' And when people say 'purpose', they really intend to say 'meaning'. And let me tell you, Sandrine," Anderson raised a friendly brow, "not as Primo, but as a fellow human being, that for the mid-Generation Thetans, which were born in space far, far away from Old

Earth, and who will end their lives in space decades before we reach any of our potential destination planets — finding a meaning to one's life is no mean feat. Excuse the pun," he smiled.

I shrugged. "Maybe we're just killing time in transit between point A and point B. Trying to not mess things up until the Resettlement generation gets all the action and higher calling and stuff?"

"That's a very cynical viewpoint," the Primo shot back with an austere expression, looking at Jericho Pakk. "The demise of our species' origin planet and our quest for Resett on a new home don't mean we don't play a crucial role in this process. Otherwise, the *Passados* could have just cryogenically frozen the GenZero crew and sent them off on the two-hundred-year journey."

"Sure would have saved a ton of complications," I said.

"But that's the whole point!" Primo Anderson clasped his hands in excitement. "We are very different people than the ones who embarked on this journey. Almost a different *species* by now, I would dare to say."

I smiled. This reminded me of countless head-banging debates between me and Nyasha. He *loved* history, and the Archive provided unlimited data on subjects ripe to pick a friendly brain fight about.

"Imagine," Anderson continued, "an entire population of Earther humans waking up from a two hundred year stasis, expected to Resett successfully on a new planet. They're not used to the atmospheric composition and pressure. They struggle to handle 0.6g gravity. Their tolerance to locally-grown food, water, radiation, you name it — is extremely fragile."

The Primo stood up and started pacing about, brushing off Pakk's subtle signals to keep the speech on a time-leash. *I guess a politician in an election year is an untamable beast.*

"You see — the Thetis journey *itself* is part of the process preparing us for optimal outcome when we finally reach Resett, te?"

"So, that's our big purpose?" I asked. "I mean, 'we are the change?'"

Well, isn't that the election motto of every kunye Suit in the history of mankind.

Anderson paused his hand mid-motion in the air, a quick shadow of weariness crossing his smooth face.

"You're an Archivist," he blurted out. "You maintain the entire knowledge base existing on the Thetis. From pre-Embarkment data uploaded by the *Passados*, to every scientific, engineering and societal development made on the Thetis itself. The dots are all there to connect. It should be *obvious!*—" Anderson half-turned toward Jericho, "—isn't it obvious?"

"It does take a certain intellect to grasp," Pakk noted, eyeing me with a glint of triumph. *This is for earlier,* said his glare.

Sabi started counting on his fingers, like trying to get the most basic concept across to a dull child.

"Generation Zero," he touched his index finger, "meaning the Earthers selected to board the Thetis for Embarkment, up until Gen3, Gen4 even — they were the Shapers. They were all either planetfolk themselves, or had an Earther parent or grandparent, right?"

I nodded to the rhetorical question.

"That means they still had planetfolk mentality: values, society structure — even physical capabilities! — all created in millennia of Earth conditioning. Those traits were optimized for survival on Earth and, of course, irrelevant to life in space. So those generations had a very clear purpose: shaping a new society that could thrive on the Thetis, with its finite space and resources, population planning and disconnect from the random, chaotic nature of... well, Nature."

Anderson sat down again, and Jericho Pakk took the small sofa chair to my left.

"Those were the generations of *giants*, Arc. Liet! They knew they would never see another planet in their lifetime, yet were ready to reinvent everything that is Human to us today."

In the corner of my eye, Jericho shifted in his seat and spread out what looked like a bunch of legal forms on the table. Anderson didn't seem to notice him. He was absorbed in his own line of thought.

"What about Generations 8 — the teenagers running around the ship today, and Generation 9, who we eagerly expect in the coming Birth Year? Well, Sandrine, they will have a different purpose altogether. They will be the Builders. They will carry on their shoulders the biggest task the Human race has ever encountered — preparing for Resett of our species on a new planet! Preparations will begin with them so that the GenXers who will actually colonize it will be ready. You now begin to see, there is a multi-generational *process* at play here. And how might that process work, Arc. Liet?"

I shrugged. "On a technical level, there's the conditioning plan. The Thetis is programmed to slowly shift the conditions on the ship across the trip. Air pressure, temperature, humidity, season length, gravity pull — it's all slowly changing to match the destination planet conditions."

Anderson chuckled. "That's right — I bet a GenZero Earther would hardly be able to *breathe* on the Thetis as it is today!" His face sobered again as he considered his words. "But, as you said, that's just the technical part. The bit that worries me more is the societal part. The human tribe we will have become come Resett. Those generations will have to be prepared to adapt back to living on an actual planet. On *Terra Firma*. It will be categorically different than the Thetis."

"So where does that leave *us*, Primo Anderson?" I asked gently.

The Primo pressed both his palms together.

"My father was Gen4. He used to say that us Gen6 kids were the first truly modern, space-borne human generation. *Homo Infinitus*, he used to call us."

Anderson's eyes lit up as he was speaking about his father. *Didn't his father run the Archive at some point?* I recalled coming across the lineage of duty holders in the Archive files.

"Gen6, and that also stands for your Gen7, are where the problem began. By Gen6, most of the rapid changes of adapting to life in space had already occurred. The urgency of things started slowing down, and that posed the question of *purpose*. Are we the Waiting Generation? But if we *are* but a vessel, carrying our slowly-altering genes and bodies passively forward, then what value do we put on Life beyond procreation? Will childless people not have a reason to exist? Are we to regard them solely as consumers, rather than contributors? Will their life's value be their on-ship jobs and nothing more?"

Ouch. That hit close. My recent falling-out with the administration — the whole mess with my then-partner Kilian — resulted in my delisting from the upcoming Birth Year.

Revoking my right for procreation was devastating and unfair and eventually drove me and Kilian apart. I always assumed that despite Nyasha's efforts to help keep what happened as low-key as possible, Anderson *must* have known about it, or was even part of the punitive process. Now, I wasn't so sure anymore. Would the Thetis Primo trouble himself with a simple Archivist's parental aspirations?

"I'll spare you the drama." Anderson lowered his palms again and touched my hand gently. "We *do* have a purpose here. There *is* an all-important, underlying meaning we must all embrace. And that purpose can be summarized by two words: *stability* and *unity*."

"I'd vote for that," I chuckled. *Because this whole speech I am getting feels awfully like part of his election campaign.*

Anderson didn't smile. "I know, It may sound quaint or unfashionable. But the obligation lies with us to provide our children, and their own, with the perfect starting point for their conditioning plan toward Resett. This is not a task to be taken lightly. We will have been living in a confined shell travelling at a third of the speed of light for *two centuries* by then. At Embarkment, there were twenty-two thousand people aboard the Thetis. We're over fifty thousand by now. The upcoming Birth Year will push that number past sixty."

Anderson let the number sink in for a second. "It's getting crowded. It is our task, and I dare label it our official *purpose*," he looked at me intently, "to unite and maintain a stable society so that the generations ahead of us can establish a new home for Humanity."

As if on cue, Jericho Pakk stood and hovered over us, pointing at the inksheets spread on the table. Anderson looked at them doubtfully, a sigh escaping his mouth.

"I know I'm laying a lot on you, Sandrine," he said. "You didn't come up here expecting a history lesson or a moral speech, but it is highly relevant that you understand that I am operating from a very deep perspective on our mission."

And at that, Anderson shifted gears. His body stiffened and his tone retuned to a formal, official speak.

"And it is *precisely* that perspective that compels me to put my own inconveniences aside and prioritize the people of the Thetis. The people do not need another scandal, let alone with the elections for Primo held later this month. Being a true leader sometimes requires personal sacrifice."

Jericho Pakk handed me the inksheets. "Primo Anderson withdraws his complaint immediately. These are the Archival forms, already filled with the decision to close the investigation. Ready for you to sign, Arc. Liet"

What's going on here? I thought. "So there was no extortion attempt?"

Jericho and Anderson exchanged a silent glance. The Primo leaned toward me. "It's best to label it as a mere misunderstanding", he said in a low, controlled voice. "We believe what happened is that Jericho here took an independent initiative to consult with Head Archivist Nyasha Woo about a certain communication we've received. There was no intent to file a formal complaint about the matter. I believe Nyasha over-enthusiastically mis-read the situation. In any case, no need to further stretch this little mishap. No harm done and we have a lot to do for the good people of the Thetis today!"

Anderson smiled triumphantly and stood up in a quick, athletic movement. He buttoned his suit jacket and flattened an invisible wrinkle in his smooth polysilk trousers. The Primo looked as fresh and energetic as a Gen8er.

"It was a pleasure meeting you, Sandrine," Anderson concluded, then smiled light-heartedly. "I'll take you up on that vote! Embark and Prosper," he signed off with the traditional Thetan greeting.

"Terra Firma Espera", I tried to add a ceremonial touch to the customary reply, while struggling out of the sofa and to my feet. "It was my honour meeting you, Mr. Anderson."

I extended my hand for a formal handshake but Anderson was already halfway to the exit door. I watched him stride confidently out of the Primo quarters and into the hallway, joined immediately by two staffers pushing a pile of inksheets into his hands as their pace increased.

A quick tapping sound pulled me back to the moment. Jericho Pakk was standing over the table, his finger pointing at the blank space at the bottom of the official form.

"Your chip finger please, Arc. Liet," he demanded flatly.

Chapter Four

I felt slightly lightheaded when I left the Primo quarters and made my way towards the Ascenders. The cryptosigned inksheets were burning a hole in my hand — *Let's just get those filed at the Archive as quickly as possible,* I told myself. A conversation with the Thetis Primo was about all the excitement I could hope for this day. *And the original Embarkment Certificate!* To an Archivist nerd like me, that was a genuine *treasure!*

I walked all the way to the far side of Level 34 and onto the magnetic Ascender platform. I started the descent in the translucent box that would take me back to 13, gazing through the duraglass pane. A sense of calm began to settle back within me as the alternating views of the various levels passed before my eyes.

The levels on the Thetis were torus shaped donuts piled on top of one another, creating the towering projectile shape that was our ride through the universe. An array of vertical Ascenders, spread evenly around the outer circumference, offered an open view of each level as they crossed it on the way up or down. A second, smaller array of Emergency Ascenders was built around the inner circumference of the donut — those were intended for ultra-fast nonstop travel and were deliberately located as far as possible from the outer shell of the ship. As Senior Archivist I naturally had full access to those as well.

Wouldn't it be fun, just for once, to pull rank and slide one of those armored boxes all the way down to 13 in no-time? After all, I *am* holding an important signed document from the Primo... but, Emergency Ascender usage was logged and, well... just unnecessarily flashy. On the Thetis, no matter who you were — you walked and traveled like everyone else.

At the center of each level's torus, behind triple layers of shielding separating us all from outer space, was a wide gap — an enormous tunnel, half a mile in diameter, cutting through the Thetis from top to bottom. That was the IDB, the Ionized Debris Beam (or as most Thetans preferred to call it — the "Trash Tube.")

As the Thetis travelled through interstellar space at thirty percent the Speed of Light, even a tiny spec of dust colliding with it would create the impact of millions of fusion bomb detonations. To avoid such disastrous occurrences, the Thetis shoots an ionizing beam forward to disintegrate any potentially harmful object in its way, then magnetically collects the resulting ionized particles like a sinkhole into the IDB. The result is a terrifying torrent of particles flowing through the wide gap in the middle of the Thetis, then dumped back to space behind it.

Stick your hand in the Trash Tube — and it would disappear within milliseconds. Good thing the ship planners placed no hatches or access doors into it in the general level areas — or you bet some *kunye* Gen8er kid would find it a worthy prank.

As the Ascender entered the 20s, my heart expanded. I spent most of my childhood running around the school and academy complexes of 27th, and my Genmom still lived at one of the old-school districts of 24th. She was teaching at the academy for the past thirty years, so it made sense for her to stay close. But us Gen7ers? We couldn't have fled fast enough to the newer, stylistic neighborhoods of 19th the moment we were assigned out of the schooling cycle. Still, passing through the 20s always felt more like *belonging* than any other place on the Thetis to me.

The lower 20s were very different than the geometric, efficiently planned living quarters above them. Those were home to a vast network of crop fields, agriculture districts and food processing plants.

Here were the hydro farms, algae humidors, NanoDrip protein replicator facilities and raw material processing factories. I've suffered through several summers of doing my tours of duty in the agri levels during my teen years. Even now, through the duraglass partition of the Ascender, I could feel the familiar, cold humid breeze flowing through those levels. *Looks like the Thetis is initiating another winter cycle,* I thought. *Has it been a full year already?*

As the thoughts and views of the Thetis filled me with the warm familiarity of the one home I'll ever know, a new realization suddenly surfaced in my mind:

Everything that just happened was pure *bafunye*.

Having sufficiently cooled off outside of Anderson's charm-bubble, looking back at the past hour his charade couldn't be clearer.

For starters, why was I asked to sign the complaint withdrawal forms on the spot? Isn't it supposed to be the other way around — the plaintiff (in this case, Primo Anderson) signing first on his complaint withdrawal request, and only *then* the Archivist signing for approval?

But the forms were already pre-filled and pre-signed before I even came in. Did Nyasha know about this and approve this unusual process? I'll need to verify with him at the Archive.

The Ascender passed Level 19, and all I craved was jumping off the carriage, crawling back to my small single-occupancy hab and hide away. But that, regrettably, would have to wait till much later in the day.

As we kept descending down the levels, I began to feel increasingly stupid and naive. *What was the deal with me getting the grand tour of Thetis Vision from the kunye Primo?* I'm just a Gen7 clerk, no Genline, no real authority or importance to the Primo whatsoever. What in the Universe would be the use of trying to impress *me*?

As the Ascender entered the high, generous space of Level 13 and the magnetic rails of the Ascender gently brought us to a stop, the questions occupying my mind kept pounding:

Am I just being my usual paranoid self, or was I just played by the most powerful person in existence?

* * *

"I know, I know, I'm sorry," Nyasha raised his hands in defense as I stormed into the Head Archive office. "I should have anticipated Anderson's reluctance to open this can of worms in the middle of Election Week. Sorry for sending you half across the Thetis, but there had to be an official Officer of the Archive present. And," Nyasha smiled that mischievous, know-it-all smile of his, "I thought you might enjoy meeting the Thetis Primo for the first time."

Classic Nyasha, I thought. I come in fuming about some matter of dispute or injustice, and he manages to diffuse it in two seconds and a smile. I mean, can I be blamed for not being able to keep an angry face in front of this man? In what was clearly a magnificent triumph of evolution, Nyasha's entire being was anger-proof bundle-of-fuzziness. His small round glasses were pulled awkwardly over his short, curly hair. An equally curly stubble framed a dark smiley face, with sprays of white fighting their way toward eventual domination of head and face in the years to come. An old white lab robe casually pulled over a cheesy knitted sweater. Nyasha sat crossed-legged on a simple black swiveling office chair, feet swimming inside the most ugly, oversized ComfyFoam shoes I had ever seen.

"What's with the leg pillows?" I pointed my chin towards the fashion crime exhibits.

Nyasha shrugged, flashing a smile. "You know me, comfort trumps appearance. Now tell me about your exciting meeting uphill." He nodded at the folder of inksheets in my hand. "Crypcodes in order, te?" Nyasha pulled down the glasses from his head. Seven years of working in the Archive and I think I almost have enough evidence those were just for show. *I'll need to remember to roast him about it at some point,* I noted. But not now. More important things needed to be discussed. I grabbed the chair next to Nyasha and placed the signed inksheets on the long desk which ran the full length of the office wall.

"This was *way* overnuke for a simple crypsigning appointment, Nyasha," I said. "Something weird is going on there. Why would the Primo and his Communications Secundus sugar-coat me for half an hour in person? Why not just leave the signed inksheets with a secretary or something for me to pick up?"

A shadow crossed Nyasha's face. "Pakk was there too? Did he say anything?"

I shrugged. "No, not really. He just came up with the forms and shoved them into my face. Creepy *wapa* seemed mainly interested in cutting the chatter short."

Nyasha nodded. "He's a quasar, Jericho Pakk. Don't underestimate him for some bureaucrat. He can be vicious. And what was your impression of Sabi?"

"Primo Anderson — " first-nickname-basis with the Thetis Primo seemed too soon to be appropriate — "was very nice. Too nice, actually. That's what was weird about it. He even showed me the *kunye Embarkment Certificate* he holds in a safe in his quarters. I can't imagine this to be the standard treatment for every small-time visitor, is it?"

Nyasha laughed. "He's a *politician*, Sandrine! In an election campaign!" he raised his hand to accentuate the point and his deep, musical baritone softened. "He is a genuine people-lover. And yes, his mini lectures on the Grand Plan can be slightly overwhelming, but that's a forgivable sin for a leader, ne?"

"I guess it is," I shrugged.

Nyasha picked up the signed inksheets stacked on the table. "Let's get this formality settled, then."

He pulled his glasses back over his head. "I'll have one of the Juniors file this away immediately. Let me show you something."

Nyasha stood and dragged his ridiculous ComfyFoam slippers to the other side of the cramped office. A huge pile of crypto-locked inksheet folders was stacked on the large desk. I immediately understood what I was looking at.

"Data started coming in?" I asked.

"That's just the beginning," Nyasha sighed. "I've asked all seventy seven Research and Development departments to submit their entire raw research data files. Most of them are already late. In three days we need to deliver the most important work we'll ever do on the Thetis — *anyone* will ever do, for this matter — and I already see us sleeping on the floor here to make it in time because of those lazy *kunyos*."

"The Final Call," I said.

"The Final Call. The fork in the road. The waveform function collapse," Nyasha rolled his eyes to the ceiling, "*La Grande Décision*: which plan do we instruct the Thetis to initiate? Do we go for Plan A — resettling Humanity on 9 Ceti Gamma in two generations time? Or do we extend the journey by two more generations and aim for Gnosis Zeta, our second option? Which home planet shall fare better to our future Genline, oh dear Sandrine?"

"Some decision," I admitted.

"Irreversible," Nyasha's voice hardened. "Which is why we need our official Archive recommendation to be ironclad. Comprehensive. Based on all the gathered data since Embarkment, and skip no detail. The individual departments have been working on organizing their historical data sets for *months*."

"And your name on such a critical, public recommendation document", I said. "Can't say I'd trade places with you on this one."

"Well at least I'm not the one eventually pushing the button. That responsibility lies with the Primo".

"Wait, there's a *button?*"

"It's an expression," Nyasha didn't bite.

"Phew. For a moment I thought there's an actual initiate-forty-year-long-sequence-for-sending-Humanity's-last-survivors-to-the-chosen-planet button. Something a certain clumsy Senior Archivist might accidentally trip over and push," I tried again.

Nyasha managed a tired smile. "Button or no button, come Final Call the elected Primo will have to make the hardest decision anyone on the Thetis has ever made. We should damn well make sure he and the public get the best data by which to make that decision."

Just as he was turning away from the huge collection of official inksheets piled on the desk, an Archive intern stepped in and dropped an even taller stack next to it.

"Crop Analysis from 22nd", the intern muttered, glad to dispose of the package.

Nyasha sighed again. "You see now why everything else is secondary. If Sabi wants to withdraw the complaint, that's fine by me. No complaint — no investigation — and we might actually get our *real* work done on time."

He sure looks exhausted, I thought. "OK, fine," I said, "it's just..."

"Just what, Sandrine?" Nyasha raised his hands in surrender. "What's on your mind? Because I'd really like to go for a round in the departments still owing us reports. We need to sign off on the final dataset by no later than tomorrow. Speak up and let's move on."

"It's just..." I struggled to put my unease into words, "look, my job is to represent you, right? And you are always such a stickler for proper procedure. So I can't just ignore anomalies when I encounter them."

Nyasha nodded. "Procedure is how we systemize justice." He picked up a stack of inksheets and started out of the Archive office. "Watch your head, eh?"

I hurried after him, ignoring the friendly stab. On my way out, I picked up the crypsigned inksheet signed by the Primo and carried it with me.

"You taught me how all of this works," I said, "as Head Archive, we are in charge of keeping the Code on the Thetis. If any Thetan has a problem, they report it to us. We investigate. If they want to withdraw a complaint, they issue a request. We issue the paperwork. They sign. We approve. The Archive always has the last word. We are always in control."

"Seems right," Nyasha said, turning left and away from the Ascender platform. He nodded toward the main level stairwell. "Let's walk up. I can use the exercise."

"So," I continued, trying to keep his attention on my point, "how come when I arrived to the Primo's quarters, the withdrawal inksheets were already pre-filled and crypsigned by him? Wasn't I supposed to hand him *our* documents to sign?"

Nyasha shrugged and started up the wide staircase, keeping his gaze ahead. "Well of course they were, Sandrine. He is the *Primo of the Thetis*, you don't surprise him with documents without sending them to him first for review with his own staff. Since his intention was to withdraw the procedure anyway, I sent the docs to him ahead of you so everyone's time is saved."

I thought about this for a moment. Something still didn't smell right here.

"But... how do we know that the sheets I signed off on were the original ones you sent him? He didn't crypsign them in front of me. So when I got there, the documents were already encrypted and sealed. Shouldn't we verify at least?"

Nyasha nodded tentatively, so I kept pushing. "The inksheet was encrypted with the Primo's key, so obviously I can't decrypt and validate the content with my own credentials. But as Head Archivist, I guess *you* can?"

I stretched my hand and held out the inksheet. Nyasha eyed the document hanging between us, then gave a deep sigh and snatched it out of my hand. He chipped in with his personal credentials and his eyes began running across the text.

He didn't like what he was reading. "Well, this *is* slightly off-protocol," he muttered.

"I thought it's a binary thing. Either it's on-protocol, or it's not."

"The Primo's team altered the wording a bit," he frowned and flipped the pages forward.

"A bit?"

"Basically, instead of saying Anderson is requesting to withdraw the complaint, it's the Archive closing the case for 'lack of public

Interest'. Either way, it doesn't matter. No complaint — no case."

Nyasha climbed a few steps up the staircase, then turned to me. "Politicians are sometimes sensitive to the way things are worded and logged, you know that, right?"

I was puzzled. "So he just made me crypsign my personal ID to a decision to close an Archive investigation case?" I wasn't even sure if I should be mad or not about this, that was a first for me.

"I can't say I love it either, but it's a nonissue now. Let's keep going. Focus on what's important."

We climbed the rest of the stairs up to Level 14th in silence. Somehow, I just couldn't entirely let this go just yet.

"One last thing, Nyasha — shouldn't we notify the suspect about the case closing?" I asked.

Nyasha started to lose his fatherly patience. "Sandrine. No complaint — no suspect, te? Please either join me in my round or go home. Please."

I knew I was being a pest, but I was the protocol-purist Nyasha had designed me to be. Cast in the same mold. "I *do* want to help you, boss, but we should seal this by the book, it being the Primo and all, ne? Protocol says — when the Archive closes a case, there has to be proper delivery of the closure notice to all parties or suspects involved."

I took Nyasha's silence as acceptance, so I gently pulled the decrypted inksheet back from his hand. I scrolled the text to the top of the document. In the left hand corner, the plaintiff's name was printed in all caps: MR. SEBASTIAN ANDERSON. In the right corner, a thin black box contained the name of the case single suspect.

"So, who the hell is Dr. Almaz Bashiri, and should I go and notify him?"

Nyasha raised his hands in surrender. "You're right, te?" He stopped on the landing area of level 14 before continuing the climb upwards. "We should inform Dr. Bashiri, even if to just be in compliance on this." He pulled up the personal data file on Dr. Almaz

Bashiri and scanned through it quickly. "Well, that's to say — when we locate him."

"What do you mean?" I blinked. You can't disappear on the Thetis. Every person has an encrypted chip sliced into his finger, containing his unique personal crypID and providing constant location and vital signs to the ship's systems.

"It's nothing alarming. Dr. Bashiri's work occasionally means he's offline for short periods of time. Don't worry about it, I'll have the notification delivered to his hab."

Nyasha waved his chip finger over the document and re-encrypted the case inksheet. "OK, now seriously — let's get going or we'll never get the report done in time."

I turned to join him, walking a step behind him towards the staircase up to Level 15. My head kept pounding as I tried to set aside this issue and concentrate on the job at hand. Then, suddenly — I knew exactly where I needed to go.

"Actually, Nyasha, I am not feeling my best today," I said. "I think I'll take your advice and head home. I promise to be at the Archive with my sleeping bag first thing in the morning. We'll ace this Final Call report."

Nyasha eyed me suspiciously for a moment, but relented. "Sandrine. You know I love you like my own Genline. Go rest. But I need your brain in the next two weeks, and it's going to be rough. We can't come up with anything less than perfect on this one."

He hugged me briefly and hurried away. I turned around and headed to the Ascender at the opposite direction, making sure I was out of his line of sight when I got there. Instead of taking the uphill counter-traj carriage to 19, I boarded the traj-wise Ascender going down.

I knew where to find Dr. Almaz Bashiri. And it was a place on the Thetis which I haven't visited for fifteen years.

CHAPTER FIVE

By the time the Ascender came to a delicate stop on 8th, I was the only one left in the carriage box. That was not uncommon, as people rarely went below 10th without a specific business. First, there's the double-seal procedure to go through at 10th which is an annoyance — the seal only opens a few times per hour to keep both parts of the ship separated. Second, anything below 10th is by definition non-critical or hazardous territory, so not many people *have* business there. The *Passados* planned the Thetis so that in case of an emergency in one of the Digit Levels, 10th and below would seal completely and separate the main population of the Thetis from the danger. By design, the Thetis should be able to make the journey without those sections if necessary.

The Ascender platform was eerily quiet. Only the low-frequency humming of the magrails was barely audible over the heavy silence. As I stepped toward the main level entrance gate, even that slight humming faded away. *This must be part of the plan,* I thought. *Preparing you for what's inside.*

As I moved closer to the gate I noticed the familiar overhanging sign, its simple polycast plate and embossed lettering most likely created by Thetans of over a century ago:

Sensory Farm 8

Below it, an improvised, hand-scribbled yellow note hung loosely:

Attention: closed for re-scaping

A tingle of excitement travelled down my spine as I touched my finger to the reader on the doorframe and chipped in. Throughout my entire Basic Education, we used to get two sessions in the Sensory Farm every week. Of course, most of the time I was totally *freaked out* about this place, but still — I guess that it is one of the things you learn to miss only as you get older.

As the gates to the Farm slowly slid open, I didn't know what exactly to expect — this was off-cycle times, so no Basic Education would be taking place here for at least another year. *Was the Sensory Farm even active between generation cycles, or was it temporarily decommissioned?*

I stepped through the gate and paused at the top of a short staircase leading down to the ground level of the farm. A set of thick, black curtains were installed across the staircase to block the view from the entrance. I took a deep, slow breath, centering myself. Then I brushed through the curtains and stepped into the main Farm area.

I almost dropped to my knees when the wave of sensory overload hit me.

The first thing your eyes were always drawn to in the Sensory Farm was the impossible sky. An ingenious mix of humidity-induced mist and controlled air currents conjured an illusion of a vast, open, *endless* sky stretching as far as the eye could see. Complex formations of cloud-like swirls and layers of vapor managed to completely obscure the physical ceiling of the Farm. For a Thetan, born and raised within the confined boundaries of the ship, it was a hypnotic, viscerally terrifying sensation.

The next thing you noticed was the unsettling notion of directional lighting. Outside of the Sensory Farm and across all the Thetis levels, practical and psychological reasons dictated a uniform ambient lighting all around. The light intensity and color would shift systematically between day and night and season cycles. There was also a longer arc of calculated shift through the entire multi-generational journey, but all in all illumination was pretty uniform and predictable wherever you were on the ship. The Sensory Farm, however, was designed to emulate the natural environment typical of a planetary surface. As such, intense, high-variance directional lighting was instrumental in achieving planetary-like conditions, with full sunset-sunrise and seasonal cycles. The complex interplay of light and clouds created wild patterns of shadows mesmerizing to watch.

Then there was the sheer *space* and *size* of the Sensory Farm. For structural reasons, each level on the Thetis was criss-crossed with vertical beams or walls or otherwise supportive structures to hold the tower-shaped ship together. Thetis launched at Embarkment with 0.8g acceleration, reduced gradually to 0.6g over the span of the two hundred year journey. It had to support its own weight just as a normal building would have to on a planet of similar gravity pull. The ship thrusters provided the needed gravity effect, and pressure on the ship's hull had to be dealt with by supporting each level just like the floors on a building would need to be.

But here, you could not locate a single pillar or object obstructing your view across the entire level. In what must have been clever camouflage, most likely aided by some kind of dynamic projection, the entire Farm seemed like a single, limitless space with no artificial boundaries to be seen. I remembered wondering how this was achieved when I was a kid coming here for our weekly sessions. *I could probably find the plans for that in the Archive somewhere,* I thought. *Ha, the privileges of adulthood!*

The aggregated effect of the simulated sky, light and physical space of the Sensory Farm was dizzying. I remember that for the first six months of sessions in the Farm, each child was accompanied by a psychotherapist, watching for severe stress or phobia induced by the sudden perspective and environmental shift. I could vaguely even recall some kind of hood or vision-limiting apparatus we were instructed to wear coming in through the gate for the first few times, inducing a gradual exposure to the experience.

I took a deep breath and remembered the instructions for grounding yourself when stepping into the Farm: *start with an empty spot in the sky and lower you head in a slow, steady motion until you hit a horizon.*

Beneath the magnificent pseudo-sky, a wild terrain of hills, mountains and lakes covered the whole level area. Dirt pathways cut across a dark, misty forest. The organic curves of a mountain ridge crest painted an irregular, jagged horizon line at the distance, adding to the disorientation caused by this place. Although the Thetis itself was, by design, a vertical construct, the actual levels themselves had to be kept almost entirely flat. Structural stress equalization across such a long journey in third of the speed of light required taking as little risks as possible, and structural symmetry was enforced as a guiding principle.

As such, one's eyes were deeply challenged by the spatial perception of slopes, valleys and vertical cliffs. The first all-important lesson you learned at the Sensory Farm was how ill-adapted we Thetans were to life on an actual planet. Here I was, merely standing at the entrance platform to this extremely well-emulated piece of planetary biome, and I was well ready to puke my guts out and crawl back to my very finite, walled and controlled world of the Thetis.

But instead, I recalled what had always worked for me here. It'd been fifteen years since I last set foot in the Sensory Farm, but a hundred session per year of training had apparently built some instincts after all.

I descended slowly down the metal staircase from the gate platform to the ground level of the Farm, repeating the old mantra in my head. *Ground yourself with more senses. Turn the abstract into the concrete.*

I took the final step down onto the ground, then immediately crouched and dug my fingers into the grass-covered, wet soil beneath my feet. The physical sensation of the wet grainy material, paired with the sudden, explosive aroma of wet, cut grass hit me like a fist. I closed my eyes, absorbing the sensory input firing up its way into my spacer brain. The air smelled of a thousand things I could not name, a mixture of ingredients which simultaneously felt ancient and alien and deeply like *home*.

I opened my eyes and saw the dirt trail curling away from me, sloping gently downward and disappearing into the dark shade of a small patch of cypress trees. I pulled my fingers out of the ground and stood up slowly, starting to walk towards the treeline, a path I had walked countless times as a child, first in terror, then in amazement, and eventually — with excitement. The simulated sunlight was now slowly receding toward the horizon. The dirt beneath my soles rustled, and a distant, barely perceptible trickling sound hinted of water beyond the trees.

This is real, I reminded myself as I entered the thicket. *Real soil. Real grass. Real trees.* Those were not the tree-shaped CarboFoam sculptures scattered around the Thetis for decoration. Those were real, planted, *rooted* trees with real leaves and peeling tree bark, actually nourishing off the minerals and humidity of the ground. Seeding. Growing. *Naturally.*

It was such an unconceivable oddity that this place actually existed on the Thetis, you had to ask yourself if the *Passados* who planned it were utterly mad. To a Thetan — born, living and eventually dying in a spacefaring vessel — a place like the Sensory Farm instinctively registered first and foremost as an extremely flammable hazard area. A full level-size of trees, grass, dry leaves and wood, all growing uncontrollably — what if this place catches fire? *That's probably why they placed it in the low digits*, I thought. Sealing levels 10 and below would separate it from the main body of the ship, and help suck out the oxygen to contain the spread of a fire to other parts of the ship.

A sharp chirp stopped me in my tracks near a tall, towering cypress tree. I raised my head and shot my eyes across the surrounding treetops. My heart was racing. *Was this… a bird?* A small patch of florescent-green blurred quickly between the branches of the tree above me. I held my breath, praying that it wouldn't be scared away. The chirping continued and finally, there it was, eyeing me from a safe distance — a small, green parrot! Its head bobbing around and a pinkish beak cracking open briefly with every chirp. I was transfixed, utterly captivated by the small creature's existence right there, so close to me.

"Notice anything different?" a sharp voice shot from behind me.

"*Kunye Dio!*" I jumped off my feet and turned around so quickly I almost tumbled over. The parrot jerked off its branch and vanished into the distance.

The short man standing behind me raised an apologetic hand. "So sorry. Didn't mean to scare you."

He was wearing a collared dark sweater and a short, black jacket against the chill, blending almost entirely into the dark surroundings.

"*Never* sneak up on a girl like that!" I snapped at him. My heart was trying to settle back down, and I took a moment to examine the man in front of me. He was a short, round Gen6er, with a circle of a face, thinning black hair and a short, black goatee lending his head the shape of a question mark. He was holding a thick, boxy bag in his left hand. Slowly, he lowered his hand and extended it for a handshake.

"Dr. Almaz Bashiri," he said. "Can I assume you are Sandrine Liet, the Archivist who signed off on the case dismissal forms?"

I slowly scanned the small, plump man, letting his hand hang in the air. "Do legal news travel faster than light? Or is there a special network of people trying to extort the Primo?" I asked coldly.

Dr. Almaz Bashiri dropped his hand and placed it on the soft lid of the boxy bag he was holding. He was clearly unsettled by my reply. "Is that why you've hunted me all the way down here?"

"Your chip's not registering on any of the locator grids. The Sensory Farm is the only place on the Thetis kept in radiation isolation," I shrugged. "Hardly a hunt."

"Smart," he stated dryly. "Why did you close the investigation? Were you sent here by Anderson?"

I snorted. "I don't work for Anderson. And there *was* no investigation — Anderson filed a complaint for attempted extortion. Then he withdrew it. End of story."

Dr. Bashiri's soft, warm eyes fixated on mine. "But you don't believe it. Otherwise, what would you be doing here, te?"

"I was just admiring little birdie up there, until you scared it off."

He smiled, and the glint in his eyes spoke of quiet strength, intelligence and deep weariness. "So," he said. *"Did* you notice anything different about it?"

I turned my head, searching for the parrot hovering and chirping somewhere beyond the treetops. I pinpointed the bird, cautiously circling above the thicket, its wings spread wide, effortlessly gliding the manufactured air currents.

"Well, its wings do look quite bigger than what I remember from my time here as a child," I tried. "But I imagine that the gravity drop from 0.8g to 0.6g on the Thetis after the Trajectory FLIPP would allow for birds with larger wings, ne?"

Bashiri sighed. "Actually, this is more correlated to lower air-pressure, not gravity per-se. But more importantly," he nodded and pointed his chin towards the gliding green spot in the sky, "The FLIPP was, what, 10 Light Years behind us or so, meaning approximately thirty years?"

If there's one constant about scientists across Human history, is that they will bend any formal definition if it results in a cool-sounding acronym. The Forward Linear Inversion Propulsion Pivot, or — you guessed it — the FLIPP, was a critical maneuver in the Thetis mission plan. The ship, whose thrusters propelled it forward in space, initially accelerated at a constant 0.8g, providing everyone on board a real, steady gravity pull.

When the Thetis reached a point in its trajectory where it clocked the maximum speed of 0.3 of the Speed of Light, it was programmed to execute a complete 180-degree rotation. Its thrusters would then be pushing it in the *other direction*, decelerating the ship to the near-rest speed suitable for orbiting the target planet.

This also meant that at our post-FLIPP present, the Thetis was flying through space ass-forward, with its thrusters actually positioned *in front*, pushing back against the inertia obtained by the generations of acceleration before it. The Thetis was practically pulling the brakes from 0.3C down.

Inside the ship's hull, "up" was trajectory-wise before the FLIPP and "down" was counter-traj, and those terms were switched after the FLIPP. But in all other aspects of life within the ship, everything remained the same as before. The FLIPP itself, I'm told by people who lived through it, was a week-long nightmare — the thrusters had to be idled for the maneuver, resulting in complete Zero-G weightlessness until the new position was stabilized and they could be re-ignited. I was born the year after the FLIPP, so did not get to experience any of that excitement.

The FLIPP also initiated the sequence of slowly lowering the thrusters pressure, and with it the simulated gravity they created, to 0.6g. That was part of the dynamic conditioning the Thetis was providing us toward the real conditions our future generations will face upon Resett on the destination planet.

"Is it natural, would you say," the doctor pressed on, "for evolution to accomplish such a physical adaptation in a species' body structure within a single generation?"

The *wapa* had a point there. "Probably not," I said. "So you Genegineers modify the genes of Farm animals to maintain environmental fit as the journey progresses. I still don't see the novelty." Genetic editing was a fundamental tool used to control crops, mass-clone protein layers, and for a thousand other uses supporting life onboard the Thetis. Applying targeted modifications to bird genome didn't seem like anything of note.

Dr. Bashiri frowned. He turned to look back at the Sensory Farm entrance area, then shot a measuring look at the swirling clouds visible through the overhanging foliage. It was getting darker now, as the simulated day was drawing to its end across the Thetis.

"Come," he said and started stepping deeper into the shadowy grove. "We're losing the light."

"Wait!" I called after him, "where are we going?"

"There's something I need to show you," he replied over his

shoulder, marching away. "Quickly, we can still make it!" and he disappeared into the darkness.

Mala dio! I exhaled in frustration. This was supposed to be a quick formal stop on my way to sleep off the day's drama. As Bashiri obviously already knew about the Archive case being closed, I could just turn away right now. Notice given. Protocol followed.

I didn't know who Almaz Bashiri was or what he had been clashing with the Primo about. Nor was it my job to care anymore. All I knew is that the man reeked of trouble and that was the last thing I needed to get involved with after the past few years of my life.

I caught up with Bashiri just beyond the treeline. The cypress thicket gave way to a vast field of green wheat, the cold breeze sending ripples across it in the dimming light.

"This better be good," I blurted. Dr. Bashiri didn't answer, and kept marching silently forward into the field. For the short, bulky man that he was, he carved his way through the wheat surprisingly quickly. I kept pace by his side, the waist-high stalks engulfing me, tickling and rustling over my body. I sent both my hands forward and formed a V-shape, parting the wheat as we went deeper into the field. I remembered doing this as a kid, sailing an imaginary ship exploring the endless wheat ocean.

"Why does the Sensory Farm exist on the Thetis?" Bashiri asked abruptly. I looked sideways at him, but his eyes were fixed forward, marching intently through the field.

"Sensory stimulation," I replied instinctively.

"Yes, yes, clearly," he said, dissatisfied. "But *why*? What's the point?"

Is this a trick question? "I've been to Basic Education when I was four years old, Dr. Bashiri," I said sarcastically, "got the briefing. It's a training ground for life on a planet for us spacers."

Bashiri gave a low frustrated grunt. "Again, barely scratching the surface. What point could there be in training a spacer, who will live and die in space, as will his children and theirs, for life in a planetary environment?"

"Because... it's part of the *Passados'* plan? Which no one ever questions?" I tried the cute approach.

He just continued walking in silence for a few more seconds, unamused. "How old are you?"

"Twenty nine. Gen7, second cycle."

Bashiri slowed his pace for a bit, finally turning his head to look at me. "Ah, the Lonely Generation," he said matter-of-factly.

"Haven't heard that one before," I said. "Heard worse nicks, though."

"How many of you are out there? About nine hundred?" he asked.

"Eight hundred seventy six."

Bashiri nodded to himself, affirming his internal point to himself. "When a major generation would be what?"

I knew the numbers. "Gen7 main cycle was eight thousand and nine. Gen8 nine thousand and twelve."

"Beautiful efficiency, is it not?" for the first time since we met, a hint of a smile crossed his face. "Genius plan, actually. Concentrate generational reproduction into precisely spanned, pre-determined Gen groups. All born in the same year. All go to school at the same time. No need to maintain multiple levels of education. You can plan and predict resource consumption. Timing the entrance of each generation to the general workforce, thus better retirement planning for the elderly generations. Predictable habitat space needs, water production, you name it. Admirable thinking, really, very resource-oriented. Everyone's joined in a mission. Everyone has a plan."

"Didn't feel quite like it for us," I shrugged.

"Precisely!" Bashiri switched the hand holding his boxy bag, waving the other in the air for exclamation. "Because you are where the change is starting. Why do you think they even needed a second cycle for Gen7? Why are we having a Birth Year for Generation 9 next year, when Gen8 cycle are still teenagers? Why break the perfect cycles the Thetis is tuned to so well? Oh wait —" Bashiri stopped abruptly and looked at me with an apologetic expression. "Are you planned for this Birth Year? I did not mean to be insensitive."

"No," I replied curtly. *Kilian.* "So why is it? Were we short on reproduction quotas? Is 2nd cycle a corrective measure for pop growth patterns?"

"Reproduction quotas are just fine," Bashiri lowered his voice and stepped closer to me. His small body was covered shoulder-height by the wheat stalks. "Listen, Sandrine. You were born in space. I was born in space as well. The Thetis is all we've ever known, us and the generations before us. It's very hard for us to grasp, but you must remember that the Thetis is merely a *transitory* situation. Humanity had evolved on a planet for millions of years. And, benavida, if all goes according to plan — it will continue to flourish on another planet after Resett. So the careful and meticulous planning of everything on the Thetis has been conducted with a very narrow list of priorities in mind."

"I've studied the Passados manifests," I said. "It's part of the Archivist required reading. Risk Management. Survivability. Redundancy. It's engraved on the kunye Embarkment Manifest. Where is your point in this, Almaz? What do you mean the change is starting with us?"

"Wait, wait," Bashiri's face contracted. "You'll get this. You *must* get it."

He looked back over his shoulder at the wheat field stretching ahead. A bright shimmering glint from beyond the field surfaced a long-forgotten image in my mind: A large pool of open water, a lake. I faintly remembered a swimming lesson in this lake. A horrifying, alien experience.

We exited the wheat field onto a dirt trail slanting down toward the now very evident sounds of water. It was almost completely dark by now, which brought some welcome ease. Bashiri didn't seem at all agitated by the large open space, his eyes constantly darting around cautiously, searching for something down the path.

He took my hand in his small palm, which oddly enough didn't feel obtrusive, but rather more like a teacher focusing the attention of a somewhat dim student. He talked faster now.

"You were the first generation born after the FLIPP," he said. "The first second cycle after six generations of evenly-distributed birth cycles. This was no mistake or quota correction. This, and the upcoming birth cycles until Resettlement are all part of the plan. You're a Senior Archivist, you must have access to those plans at 13."

"Most likely," I said. *He is basically telling me I can validate his story. Wherever this was going, and whoever Dr. Bashiri really was, could be confirmed later in the Archive.*

"Good," he let go of my hand and continued down the path. "So post- FLIPP, the plan mandated breaking up future generations into smaller, more frequent birth cycles. You see — one big generation every twenty years is very efficient for the space travel part of the mission, but it would never work on a planet. It's simply too risky."

"Why? What's so different about standing on solid ground?" I asked.

"We have much less control over the environmental factors on a planet, than we do on the Thetis," Bashiri said. "Imagine an epidemic, or fire, or some natural catastrophe wiping a big portion of the working generation. You'd be left with young kids and elderly people, which spells doom for the Human society. You must reach a point where births and deaths are randomly distributed, where society includes people of all age groups simultaneously. That couldn't work on the Thetis, but would be healthy and natural on a planet. So, after the FLIPP, we started implementing 2nd cycles of birth, starting small with you Gen7 2^{nd}ers, and eventually GenXers will reach Resett with no less than 4 equally-sized cycles, from which ample genetic distribution could continue freely."

"So we were planned to be the smallest generation the Human kind has ever seen," I mumbled. "No wonder I didn't have many friends to play with as a kid."

Bashiri gestured in agreement. "Thus — the Lonely Generation." He smiled. "Your group presented many problems for us we didn't foresee at first. It was the first time we only had nine years between generations, and planning for your group, as small as it was, with the older Gen7ers being still basically kids, required some flexible planning."

Bashiri pulled up the collar of his wooly jacket against the cold breeze blowing from further down the path. "So you could definitely say you and your Genmates are involved in this much more than you know."

"Involved with what exactly? And what does the Sensory Farm have to do with it?" I really struggled to follow this strange Doctor's logic pattern.

"Ha!" Dr. Bashiri let out a surprisingly loud dry bark of a laugh. "Everything! This is were it all started! But —" he motioned toward the end of the path, where a tall white fence was slowly revealing, "— I need you to see it with your own eyes. You wouldn't believe me otherwise."

And suddenly it all clicked into place. *I know where we're going.* It was, without doubt, the main attraction of the Sensory Farm.

We reached a double-gate system leading into the fenced area, the chilling night breeze of the Farm biting into my flesh. Still, I noticed I was perspiring. Bashiri chipped in and the gate clicked open.

"Here we are," his dry tone picked up a hint of excitement. "Welcome to the Animal Vivarium."

Chapter Six

As we stepped inside, I was immediately hit by a wave of heavy, moist, *organic* odor. I remembered being equally repelled and attracted by the heavy wall of aroma in my visits here as a child. Bashiri didn't seem to notice or mind the smell. He looked at me intently as he pressed his chip finger to the inner gate control box, waiting for it to buzz open.

"What do you remember about the Vivarium?" he asked.

"I remember seeing non-Human creatures for the very first time," I said. "I was four years old. I thought I would have nightmares forever after that."

Dr. Bashiri chuckled. "Yes, this is quite common," he said, "as was probably the case for you personally, the instinctual fear of other creatures dissipates over time. 7 Generations off Earth aren't enough to override millions of years of living within a fully evolved, multi-species biome. We just need a little stimulation to remember."

I nodded. "Actually I quickly learned to love the sessions and handle the mental stress of the place. The animals were always a tough bit for me, but I still felt kind of sorry we were done with the program when we turned 14."

Bashiri tensed. "Exactly! You see, the entire Sensory Farm, including the animals in it, work in cycles. Back then, we used to need the 10 years between each operation cycle of the Farm to renew it. Scrap, process, re-scape the land, re-grow the flora and fauna. Prepare it for the next generation."

"Wait," I stopped him. "You scrap everything between generation training cycles? Even the animals?"

Bashiri nodded. "Even the animals, yes. They must be evolved to newer versions along with the conditioning plan."

"But, isn't this awfully wasteful? All these resources could be reused, no?"

"Of course it's wasteful. The entire concept of the Sensory Farm is unthinkably wasteful! Think about it — tons upon tons of real soil, which needs minerals to grow vegetation and trees, which consume huge amounts of water to provide nutrition for the dogs, cows, birds and other animals grown in here. Not to mention the hazards of operating such a thing on the Thetis. Just imagine an animal virus epidemic roaming through the ship. Who in their right mind would approve such a project on a ship like the Thetis?"

I shrugged. "The *Passados* seemed to think it was important enough. Must be critical for our emotional connection to planetary life? Rolling on grass, hugging trees, these sort of things?"

"Extremely important," Dr. Bashiri agreed, "I mean, there's this whole facet of the sensory experience which is deeply rooted in our human psyche. We did not evolve to thrive in a confined artificial space. But," he shrugged, "this could probably be solved by a graphical simulation of some sort."

Bashiri touched a switch panel near the gate. A weak flow of warm ambient light illuminated the inner area just enough to make out the row of segregated compartments used to house the various animals growing in the Farm. The increased brightness drew out a few hums, bleats and moos from further down the corridor. I tensed — the combination of animal smells and sounds in my immediate vicinity brought up a very concrete feeling I hadn't felt in 15 years. Bashiri touched my arm lightly and placed the boxy bag he was carefully carrying on the ground near me.

"Wait here," he said confidently.

Bashiri disappeared behind the door to one of the inner compartments, leaving me with his heavy-looking bag at the wider reception area of the Vivarium. I looked around at the familiar, minimalistic design of the place: a few sitting benches stacked in rows for the classes of kids coming here for tutoring sessions. A First Aid box and fire extinguisher set, sealed and untouched for decades in one corner. A neatly folded black carboplast blanket, used to wrap and desensitize the occasional hysterical child, in the other.

A door clicked behind me and Dr. Almaz Bashiri was back, holding a white, fluffy-looking ball in his hands, stepping carefully to not rattle the thing. He gently lowered himself onto one of the benches, gesturing me to come closer. The fluffy ball lay motionless, balanced on Bashiri's knees. I took a seat, and he quickly passed it onto my open palms. Startled, the thing squirmed and almost jumped out of my hands.

"*Kunye Dio!*" I shouted, totally freaked out by the panicked creature on my lap. Bashiri held it down with an assured hand.

"Shh," he whispered. I wasn't sure if he was calming me or the small animal. "Stroke it gently. It's only a bunny. Harmless little creature."

A bunny? My mind raced. *I remember bunnies.* I started slowly stroking the white, silky fur of the frightened animal. I could feel its warm body trembling through the soft fluff. *Cute little thing!*

"What you are experiencing now," Bashiri said after the animal relaxed enough for me to focus, "goes beyond the emotional value of human connection to another creature. Compassion has many beneficial psychological effects, but there's a specific *physical* reason Humans must stay exposed to real, organic beings. A reason why all of this —" he spread his hands in a gesture to the entire Sensory Farm, "— is worth it."

I kept running my fingers through the white fur-ball absentmindedly. This was almost meditative, and the bunny seemed to approve.

"I should know this," I tried recalling the details of a file I had previously read at the Archive, dealing with health-related procedures on the Thetis. "Doesn't the exposure to plants and animals preserve our planetary-based immune system?"

Dr. Bashiri smiled. "You're getting very close, Arc. Liet. Indeed, if we tried to resettle on a planet after two centuries in the sterile environment of the Thetis, we would all be dead within a year. Continuous exposure to microbes, germs, pollen and similar elements is definitely beneficial for maintaining our immune system and, thus, for our survival chances. What else?"

I tried to further decipher where Dr. Bashiri was leading me, which was not an easy feat with the cute little bunny purring between my palms. I was already in love with this chubby white angel. I could stay here all night cuddling it.

I shrugged and looked up at Dr. Bashiri. I was out of ideas.

Bashiri got up and picked his bag. "Let me connect the dots for you. Bring it with you." He started walking towards the big double-door separating the main animal housing compartments area from the back part of the structure. An inscription on one of the swinging doors read: "GenLab".

The GenLab's interior space was a stark contrast to the Vivarium lobby. Sparkly clean and brightly-lit, the large room was lined up with a row of boxy CellPrinters against one wall, all humming a constant, repetitive pattern as they churned through their production blueprints. The wall facing us was one long duraglass window, overlooking the back lot of the Vivarium. A group of heavy, yellow-painted machinery and construction vehicles were parked there, strange mechanical creatures which looked very out of context sitting idle in the dark. The land around them was torn — heaps of shoveled soil and stacks of metal support beams scattered around. This whole part of the Vivarium was a construction site, paused mid-work for the night.

"The cogs in the machine," I gestured toward the gleaming, yellow metal vehicles.

Bashiri nodded. "They're just beginning re-scaping for the next cycle."

I looked at the line of blinking, humming CellPrinters. "So this is where you print the animals?" I asked as I kept stroking my new white friend.

Bashiri walked towards the wide, flat lab table at the center of the room and carefully placed his bag on it.

"Well, to be accurate, we only CellPrint the embryos. From there, we allow them to grow naturally." He motioned me to approach the table, then helped me gently place the bunny inside a translucent box at its center. The small creature's eyes darted in all directions, surprised by the sudden change from my warm embrace to the cold slab of the GenLab table.

Dr. Bashiri unbuckled the top cover of his bag, carefully exposing a bulky, metallic instrument encased in a mesh-like protective cloth. "As you know, the entire Thetis environment is pre-planned to slowly shift from conditions very similar to Earth, to conditions resembling the two potential target planets, within the course of the journey."

"The conditioning plan," I nodded. "Sure. Smart. The Resett generation will already be conditioned for optimized assimilation into the new environment."

Bashiri nodded. "Following the same logic, the entire Sensory Farm biome, including the landscape topography, flora and fauna, everything! — is recreated from scratch each generational cycle. The plan shifts everything slightly with each generation, nudging the 'nature' around us to increasingly resemble the target planets, not Earth."

Bashiri pulled out the boxy instrument and unwrapped it. "You must have noticed that some things here are not quite as you remember them from your Junior Academy lessons."

"So being post-FLIPP in our journey," I did the mental math, "What we are seeing now is already pretty far from what Earth was like, but still not quite emulating the actual conditions on either 9 Ceti

Gamma or Gnosis Zeta."

He nodded. "We're 83% into the plan, if that's of any use."

Bashiri finally exposed the entire apparatus he was carrying. It was a small device, with some control dials on one side and a round emitter dish on the opposite facet. It looked like a radiation emitter, not dissimilar to the lab equipment we used to handle in our Science studies at the Academy.

"But!" Bashiri raised a short, thick finger in the air. "Even with the most meticulously though-out plan, nature always has the last say, doesn't it?"

"This can't be good," I muttered.

"Well, that depends," he said. "You see, the main physical reason for the Sensory Farm and the exposure to the organic life in it, is not about genetics or psychology. It's something much more mundane — Bacteria."

Ahh, this makes total sense, I thought. Our microbiome — the friendly bacteria roaming our digestive system — has profound effects on many aspects of our physical and mental health.

Bashiri pointed at the line of CellPrinters filling the room. "Genetic composition is, of course, more permanent and stable, but a 10-generation journey is simply too short for meaningful evolutionary development to occur in Humans, even when we shift the living conditions on the ship in a deliberate direction." He looked to me, easily a head taller than him. "Gravity does have bone-structure effects regardless," he admitted.

I shrugged. I was tall even for the taller-than-usual Gen7 2nders. I got used to the discomfort it induced in certain people.

"Granted," Bashiri continued, "there are always small mutations in our genetic material at reproduction. However, the humans who will land on the new planet will still be very similar genetically to Earthers. But every time you stroke a bunny, walk within trees, work the Farm soil or feed the cows, you are immediately exposed to a huge culture of bacteria, mixing and influencing your body's internal microbiome.

And bacteria," he said triumphantly, "are simple enough genetically so that we *can* manipulate it!"

Bashiri smiled at me, obviously expecting some sort of supportive reaction.

"So you genegineer the Sensory Farm bacteria in order to influence the animals and the Humans who come in contact with them," I said dryly. "And this has been going on since GenZero to assist in our gradual conditioning, immunity and what not. So what's new about it that's worth butting heads with the kunye Primo?"

My remark hit Bashiri dead center. His face fell into utter seriousness and his voice lowered to a bare whisper.

"Sometimes, Nature provides one with accidental opportunities. And sometimes one is stupid enough to take them."

Bashiri raised the RadEmitter device and held it close to his chest, pointing the emitter dish in my direction.

"Hey, Hey!" I immediately recoiled and took a step back, "don't point that thing at me! Don't they teach safety regulations at GenLab 101? You trying to get me fried?"

Bashiri shook his head in dismissal. "You have nothing to worry about, Arc. Liet. The electromagnetic pulse this device is programmed to produce is strictly on the Infra Red spectrum. Completely harmless to Humans. To all organics, for that matter. This is crucial for you to understand — the process I've been designing for the past decade cannot harm Humans in any way, not on the Thetis, and not on either of the potential Resett planets we may be heading toward."

"What kunye process?" I said curtly, "what the *hell* are you talking about, doctor?"

Bashiri flipped a switch on the small device and the RadEmitter came to life, humming faintly with a distinct rise in its oscillating pitch. When the warming up phase was done, a small dot of light appeared on the box's control panel. Bashiri looked at me and gently pushed me back another step.

"I am very sorry for what's going to happen now," he said softly.

Bashiri pressed a button on the device control panel. Something clicked deep inside the metal box, but no other effect was visible. I glanced sideways at the short doctor. His head was bowed, eyes closed, waiting. *What's going on here?*

Then I saw the bunny.

"Mala dio!" I jumped forward and grabbed the duraglass box, groping for the white, fluffy creature I had just laid inside a moment ago. It was too late.

The innocent animal lay slumped on the cold bottom. It's small body was totally limp. It was not quivering or purring anymore. Within five seconds of Bashiri pressing the button on the rad emitter, the fluffy white creature was utterly and completely dead. I grabbed the doctor by his collar, towering over his small figure, fuming with a mixture of rage and stress and confusion.

"What did you do to it, *wapa*?!" I yelled, our faces almost touching. "You said the radiation was *harmless!*"

The idea of the cute little dead creature lying less than a feet from me brought tears to my eyes.

Bashiri opened his eyes and held my stare with a steady glare. "You had to see it for real. Otherwise you wouldn't have believed it."

"Believed *what* exactly?" my voice trembled with slight hysteria. "What just happened here? How could you just... just *kill* a living thing, just to make some kind of point?"

Bashiri packed the RadEmitter back into his bag with worried haste, shooting glances toward the entrance door to the GenLab.

"We don't have much time here. The moment I shot the rad beam, the Farm sensors should have picked it up as an anomaly and flagged biohazard teams to inspect. I'll explain on the way."

He grabbed his bag in one hand and pulled my sleeve with the other, and we shot out of the GenLab and into the Vivarium main area. I managed to catch a last glance at the motionless white fur ball left behind on the main lab table. My heart jerked at the poor animal's fate. Bashiri chipped out of the Vivarium and we were soon running uphill through dark bushes and scattered low trees.

"What you just saw," Bashiri was breathing heavily from the effort of running with the heavy bag in his hand, "was the operation of the switch-gene I designed."

"The *what?*" I was trying to stay calm, which took some effort. We were aiming for the exit gates out of the Sensory Farm, although Bashiri chose a long, curved kind of detour from the direct path we took to the Vivarium on our way in.

"A switch-gene is a genetic trigger, controlling some physical reaction in its host organism. It pops into action in case a specific stimulus is present, hence the name," he explained, glancing at me briefly to see if I was following the logic.

"Funny thing is that I discovered this by complete coincidence. Apparently, some purely natural mutation in the genes of a bacteria we were studying caused the development of this switch gene, but it was dormant until the exact stimulant was introduced."

"The radiation," I said between heavy breaths. The way uphill was getting steeper as we fumbled through the dark. "The Infra Red radiation didn't kill the bunny. It was the trigger for something else."

In the corner of my eye I could see Bashiri nodding. The dots still did not fully connect for me though. "But... how? How did it kill an entire animal in less than five seconds?"

"This is actually very clever near-chemistry," Bashiri said and shot a gauging look at me, assessing if I was a suitable target for high science talk.

"Give me the executive summary," I said. "It's been a weird day."

Bashiri's face stretched with a weary smile. *The wapa was proud of this thing he discovered!*

"The short version is that once the bacteria detects the trigger, it's outer capsule emits a substance which completely neutralizes the myelin sheath covering the axons and neurons of the carrier brain."

"Wow, wow," I protested, "this is the short version? Speak Thetan, please."

"Yes, yes, OK," he grunted. "Bottom line — it cancels the conductivity necessary for your brain cells to function. In simpler terms — your brain goes lights-out."

"Now you're talking my level," I blurted sarcastically. "So a tiny bit of radiation, and the entire brain is unplugged? No muscle control. No breathing. No heartbeat."

"Yes! It all goes mute." Bashiri was content he was getting through to me at last. "What a revelation! The utilization of such a simple genegineering trick is exactly what we needed when the time between Sensory Farm cycles was about to be halved with the introduction of 2nd cycle generations like yours."

"Why?" I asked, "what did you do before the mutation?"

"Each time a training cycle ends for a young student generation, the kids are 14 years old, right? So we used to have about 10 years to exterminate and process the entire living biome of the Farm, reprint and regrow the modified plants and animals according to the progression plan, and then re-scape and ready the new version of the Sensory Farm for the next generation."

"That sounds like a lot of work," I remarked. "Why not just keep the Sensory Farm operational continuously, and add modifications gradually?"

"Economics," Bashiri said matter-of-factly. "Resource management. Water and oxygen consumption. But mainly — this isn't a real, stable biome, te? We don't have nearly the diversity of species needed for such a biosphere to thrive across centuries. It is nothing more than a fleshed-out simulation, really. A spacefaring zoo. In the end it's just easier to rebuild than maintain."

I could see now where this was going. "So you unleash this bacteria carrying the modified gene into the Sensory Farm, it then transfers this gene into all the living organisms in the Farm, and you got yourselves a kill-switch for when it's time to shut down the party for renovation. Flood the farm with an IR blast — and everything is

53

exterminated within a blink. How convenient."

Bashiri shrugged. "It *is* convenient. And completely harmless in any other circumstance. The only minor cost was shielding the entire Sensory Farm against radiation leakage, so when we bombard the area, nothing affects the other levels of the ship."

I looked up into the dark, clouded sky masking the physical ceiling construct of the Sensory Farm. The whole area was now washed with a pale greenish ambient light, emulating a moonlit night. Everything looked unreal, alien. "So this is why location tracking doesn't work here? Radiation shielding?"

"Precisely," he said. "Even though Infra Red isn't harmful to humans, we try to not take any risks on the Thetis, right? Which is why —" he paused for effect, "— I was completely shocked when I found a copy of my work, with someone playing with the triggering frequency of my gene! Can you *imagine* how dangerous such a copycat gene can be? And when I tried to raise concern about this shadow work, my entire project got shut down!"

Bashiri was trembling with suppressed rage, his eyes jumping in anxiety.

"Who shut you down?" I asked.

"It had to come directly from the Primo," Dr. Bashiri whispered adamantly. "I received no explanation, just an immediate lock on my entire research materials. All the lab's quantum computing resources were reallocated to some other project, so we halted everything. I can't just *conjure* gene research without my data!"

Was this the paranoia I sensed earlier in this man popping up again? "Why would the Primo even care about some protocol for better resource management you engineered?" I asked skeptically.

In the distance, beyond the entry gate to the Sensory Farm main area, I could hear the swishing sound Ascender doors sliding. I looked at Bashiri. We both heard it. He took a few steps back, motioning me to stay where I was and not follow him.

"Listen," he said quickly. "I can't poke into this any further. My research lab was already shut down. When I tried to investigate, I got threats from very high up. I have a Genline to think about — my daughter is due for this coming Birth Year. I can't expose her to any risks."

He started stepping back

into the dark shrubbery. "I would have let it go entirely, but someone hijacked my life's work. Modified — *weaponized it!* — to operate via a different radiation trigger. Not IR frequency, but rather something *much* higher. A frequency in the Ultraviolets which I have definitely seen before."

Bashiri shook his head in frustration. "I'm not sure why and for what use-case they are aiming, but that scares the *hell* out of me. This is the reason I contacted the Primo's office, but I was ignored. But you — you have access. You can — you *must* find out what's going on!"

The Sensory Farm doors opened and hushed whispers filled the air as a group of four people ran down the dirt path toward the Vivarium. Dr. Almaz Bashiri instinctively ducked below the vegetation, a terrified look on his face.

"I'm sorry," he whispered, "This is as far as I can risk probing. Be safe!"

Bashiri disappeared into the darkness. The diminishing sounds of his footsteps quickly fell back to silence. Only the slow, repetitive chirping of some nocturnal insect filled the air. In the distance, I could see multiple strobes of flashlights advancing through the fields, approaching the Vivarium. In the greenish, simulated moonlight washing over the Sensory Farm, the only detail I could make out was a set of piercing, icy grey eyes staring directly in my direction.

Jericho Pakk! I threw myself to the ground, hopefully preventing my tall silhouette from being spotted. I started crawling up toward the Farm exit gate.

This is no Hazard Control team, I realized in growing panic. And then:

I gotta get out of here, fast.

CHAPTER SEVEN

The ride back to Level 19 was a stressful half-hour trip. The mandated stop for the double-seal procedure at Level 10 had me constantly looking over my shoulder, somehow expecting to be halted by some undefined pursuer. Once out of the digit levels, the Ascender became more crowded and I felt I could relax a bit. I welcomed the company and somehow felt more secure blending in with the general traffic up the Thetis.

When the Ascender stopped briefly at Level 13 I instinctively looked over at the entrance to the Archive. By now it was late at night and the entire office complex was dark. The only sign of activity in the entire level came from the Art Museum on the opposite side of the level, across from the now abandoned public sports park. Judging by the posh, smartly dressed couples onboarding the Ascender, it must have been opening night for some artist or another. I wasn't up to date with the latest artistic trends anymore — too much work and no love-partner made me lose touch with the hyperactive social circles of the Thetis. *Kilian would have known not only the name of the artist, but also where the best after-party would be and who you needed to know in order to get in,* I thought.

I continued upward and had a few moments to run the day's peculiar sequence of events through my exhausted mind.

The meeting at the Primo's quarters. The awkward way he and his icy-eyed hound Jericho massaged the formal protocol in order to get the complaint filed away and buried.

Dr. Almaz Bashiri and his crazy switch-gene story. He had looked genuinely scared when he talked about his invention getting poached and tampered with by someone. *How come I haven't heard about this issue before?* I thought. If it involved public health and official research labs, it had to go through the Head Archivist Office.

Then something Bashiri said popped in my mind: when we just met at the Sensory Farm, he had already known that the case had been crypsigned for closure, and that I was the one who signed it. The only explanation could be that Bashiri was talking to someone in the data chain. But if he had an accomplice, why would he need *me* to to look into the matter?

And what was the supposed communications Sec Jericho Pakk doing there? The dots just didn't connect, and I knew this meant sleep would have to wait for later.

I skipped the stop at Level 19. I pressed my back against the cold duraglass back wall of the Ascender, and continued up for six additional levels, where I hoped the answers would start.

The Woo family lived in one of the modest hab circles of Level 25, just a short walk from the Ascender platform. It was a collection of low, two-story structures conveniently arranged around a public recreation center, a library and a gym. There were dozens of similar hab circles on 25, symmetrically constructed like a giant kaleidoscope pattern. I always found this fact slightly disturbing, but I guess that to some older Genners this layout resonated as inducing tranquility and harmony.

25 in itself was the epitome of lazy comfort — a short ride to the school and academy centers of Level 24, and an equally convenient hop to the commercial districts of 26. It was the hab of choice for many Gen7ers going through their parenting years, and it was perfectly planned for that purpose — overhanging CarboFoam tree lines, children-friendly walkways and playing grounds, community-

operated grocery corners filled each morning with fresh produce from Level 26, the kunye lot.

At this hour of night the entire level was space-quiet. None of the always-on ambient music of my own Level 19, or the never-sleeping work buzz of the commercial levels above it.

In short, Level 25 was utterly kunye *boring*. I could never live in a place like this — I needed the buzzing hubbub of the younger levels. It was the only way for me to comfortably blend in and assimilate in the crowd.

Nyasha answered the gentle tap on his door immediately. He was still dressed in the same work outfit he had earlier at the Archive, minus the horrendous ComfyFoams.

"Can't sleep?" I asked. He obviously did not expect to see me here in the middle of the night.

"Sandrine! Come in, girl, come in!" He swung the door open for me to follow him inside. The cozy living room was bathed in a soft, yellowish light. A large low table dominated the space, covered almost entirely with stacks of what I could easily recognize as Archival inksheet folders.

"Concerned about the Final Call report?" I asked, gesturing toward the piling stacks.

"The amount of data we need to process is staggering," Nyasha said with a silent sigh. "Tea?"

"Yes, please." That would be welcome after the chill of the Sensory Farm.

Nyasha picked up two half emptied tea cups lying on the kitchen counter, still steaming. The delicate white vapor rising from the rims of those cups was already infusing me with warmness.

"Angelique sleeping?" I asked quietly.

Nyasha nodded. "Let's take it outside," he whispered back, carrying two newly-brewed tea cups.

We sat down on a low bench in front of the Woo family hub, in the middle of a children's playing ground. At this hour of darkness, the abandoned swing sets, climbing ladders and baby b-ball nets looked eerily out of place.

"So what are you doing still awake at this hour?" I asked as I cuddled the hot cup of tea in my freezing hands.

Nyasha shrugged. "What every parent to a Gen8 teenager is doing — waiting for my son to come back home," he said with a touch of sarcasm. Most of the 6th Generation Thetans had Gen7 kids. But due to certain medical complications, Nyasha and Angelique had to wait until Gen8 to get greenlighted for reproduction. This made Nyasha an unusually old father of almost sixty years old, to a 15 year-old Gen8er who, as all teenagers did, considered his family hub a mere formality and spent most days and nights roaming the Thetis with his friends.

"And you?" Nyasha asked with a spark of humor in his eye. "You look way too sober to be passing through on your way back from some wild party."

"Ha." I knew it was just a friendly tease — these days I was a young and boring workaholic. *Maybe I'll move here to 25 for early retirement,* I thought.

"Seriously, Nyasha," I cut the small talk short. "And you have to be straight with me on this."

Nyasha's tired smile receded and he straightened up on the uncomfortable bench. "Have I ever been anything *but* straight with you, Sandrine." There was no question in his remark, and he was right. Nyasha had taken me under his wing from a very young age and I knew he always had my best interest in heart.

Best to just spill it out and he'll help me make sense of it all. "I've just met Dr. Almaz Bashiri," I said bluntly. "I assume he came to you first with his concerns about the switch-gene protocol."

I stared at Nyasha intently, looking for any sign of recognition that my guess was accurate. "Did you order his project shut down?"

Nyasha sighed, then leaned closer to me. "Sandrine..." His hands began drawing invisible circles in the air, which was his thing when trying to simplify a complex explanation.

"Dr. Bashiri is a brilliant scientist. Brilliant. If his talents continue down his Genline, the resettling generations would be very fortunate."

"Wait," I interrupted. "So you've known him before this incident?"

"I know him very well," Nyasha said matter-of-factly. "We grew up together in Junior Academy. Our parents had all sorts of mutual hobbies so we spent quite a lot of time near each other as teens. This is the reason I am very aware of Almaz's advantages. But, also — his shortcomings."

"But don't you trust him on a claim related to his area of expertise?" I asked.

"Oh, I trust him with the science. It's the motivation I am more dubious about." Nyasha rested his hands back in his lap and started wringing them slowly. "You see, Almaz is a very ambitious man. And he did discover a marvelously useful genengineering tool which helped optimize the operation of the Sensory Farm. But let's be honest here. You know how the Thetis works — all research is for the common good, right? Not for personal credit or benefit."

Nyasha tilted his head slightly, examining me as I sipped the hot tea, pondering his remarks.

"So he didn't like some other lab repurposing his gene," I said.

"Great minds occasionally fall into patterns of overnuked paranoia," Nyasha explained in his soothing, low tone. "Bashiri did a great thing for the Sensory Farm. And that was a neat trick. But think about the opportunities in implementing such gene-carrying bacteria in other areas. Disease treatment, pest control for crops — "

"Epidemic containment," I added.

"Precisely. This could be a breakthrough in Public Health Security on the Thetis and beyond. Bashiri doesn't particularly like the fact that the reputation will lie with either the PHS office, or other researchers," Nyasha shrugged. "It boils down to scientific ego, nothing more. Nothing Anti-Thetan, just Human."

I lay the now lukewarm cup of tea on the bench between us. "That doesn't add up, Nyasha," I said softly. With Nyasha, I could always be direct. "Dr. Bashiri didn't strike me as an ego-driven nut. He has raised legitimate concerns about the gene safety, and he gets slammed with an extortion investigation by the kunye Thetis *Primo?*"

"Ahh," Nyasha waived his hand in dismissal. "Yes, so Sabi is a brute. Especially when it comes to his family. You do know that the head of the Public Health Security office is Sabi's *wife*, don't you?"

Kunye Dio, I thought. *Anderson's wife is the head of PHS? How about some basic Archivist fact checking before you jump into conclusions, Sandrine?*

"And he's extra sensitive in this period," Nyasha continued. "He's just kicking-off his re-election campaign. And right after that, Final Call — the most critical decision a leader has ever had to make since Embarkment. So he went slightly too aggressive with this. But to his credit, he backed off almost immediately and withdrew the complaint, didn't he?"

"Not if you read the case closure documents, he didn't," I mumbled in resentment.

Nyasha shrugged. "I admit — you and me may not like the style, but he's a politician. And politicians want only one thing — to keep ruling. Anyhow, the people at PHS aren't incompetent either. If they'll find anything to worry about in the gene research, they'll raise a red flag."

Nyasha raised his hands in conclusion. "Elections tend to get people off-balance."

"I wouldn't know," I said. "The previous elections for Primo were before I was born."

"Yes," Nyasha said. "The pre-FLIPP elections. And I've worked with Primo Anderson through it and for 30 years since." His shoulders slumped and he rubbed his eyebrows wearily. "But we settled it, didn't we? It's all closed and filed, thanks to your help, Sandrine. And we can now focus of the important mission at hand — delivering the Final Call report on time with no further distractions. And for that—" Nyasha tenderly covered my cold hands with his warm palms, "—We should get some sleep, ne?"

Nyasha rose from the bench with a low grunt. "Embark and Prosper, Sandrine. And good night."

I didn't reply with the customary greeting, distracted. *Something in this whole setup just doesn't feel right,* the thought kept tapping — but I couldn't point my finger at it.

I looked at Nyasha, still in his work clothes at 2am in the morning, and felt a bit guilty for dragging him out of his hab at this hour. He should be nearing sixty by now, and age — or a lifelong of responsibility — was starting to creep up on him. He picked up my half-empty tea cup and started trudging back toward his hab.

He was right. I shook my head and chased the nagging thoughts out of my mind. *Go home, Sandrine. Sleep it off. Go home.*

"Terra Firma Espera," I mumbled toward Nyasha's receding figure, then pressed my palms to my knees and grudgingly stood up to leave.

CHAPTER EIGHT

Level 19 was never really asleep. I disembarked from the Ascender and started the walk back to my hab, exhausted and freezing cold. Still, even at this hour, you could *feel* the level was still awake and breathing — the air carried the traces of music and snippets of chatter emanating from window-lit habs. The occasional walker passing by. The delicate background tune which all hab tenants voted for just recently as a cool experiment. I mean, we were still young, and we wanted to live, right? It wasn't much, but compared to Nyasha's Level 25 this was high-adrenaline life for sure.

A feeling of comfort started permeating through me as I approached my hab complex. I was on the second floor of a cool, industrial-design building inhabited mostly by singles or young couples before their parenting years. In a few years, the Gen8ers would graduate and start filling the level with their masses of stupid adolescent noise, but we still had a few good years before that invasion would take place.

I climbed the stairs to my floor slowly, already mentally playing through my go-to-sleep routine. *I'm afraid tonight is going to be the short version,* I thought — which basically meant *kick boots off, crash on bed, wake up six hours later and figure the rest out then.*

My palm was already halfway to the door panel for chipping in when a man stepped into the dim corridor light. In stark contrast to my crumpled and zombielike feeling, he looked as fresh as a newly-filled ice bath. His freaky grey eyes pierced into mine. He got straight to the point.

"What were you doing in the Sensory Farm, Liet?" Jericho Pakk demanded. "Who did you meet there?"

At that time of night, I wasn't going to take *mala* from anyone, especially not when this wapa was standing between me and my bed. So I pushed back.

"And how precisely would you get such a strange idea, Sec Pakk? I don't assume you have a warrant granting you access to location-grid data, do you? Because then it should have passed through the Head Archive for authorization, and — oops! That would be me."

Jericho didn't flinch. *Ice cold,* I thought. "You forget that the Sensory Farm doesn't register on the location-grid, Arc. Liet — so I don't need positive location data to know where you have or haven't been. The absence of it tells the story just as well."

He slanted his head and gestured toward my feet, raising his brows in attestation. "Also, the mud on your shoes kind of proves it, doesn't it?"

"Oh I just took a stroll through the crop yards," I rebuffed and whispered, "I like it moist and filthy. Don't you?"

Pakk blinked with disgust. I gave him the cutest smile I could muster in my current state. "Now back off, and let me go to sleep."

Jericho was clearly treading outside of his comfort zone which included, I was sure, power plays and intimidation on a daily basis.

He paused to consider his next move. I could read the internal struggle playing across his face: *how do I handle this brat?*

Finally, he stepped back from the door. "Listen, Liet," he said, giving up the aggressive thug tone. "I get it. You're an idealist. Shooting straight, just doing your job. That's adorable. But it's a sensitive time now to get on Primo Anderson's bad side, te?"

"Aren't we all on the same side?" I asked innocently. "*Is* there even another side?"

"Yes we are all on the same side, the side of Human survival," Jericho said. "And *after* the elections, if any claims need to be inspected, they will be. But right now," his eyes were an icy stab in mine, "I'm seeing a clerk in official position, first dismissing — by her own crypsign — a highly-concerning threat against the Primo, then independently conducting an unsanctioned investigation against his *wife*, while sneaking for secret meetings with a disgruntled researcher who's well known to be a supporter of the Eternists."

He pronounced the word 'Eternists' as if it was a vile, despicable profanity. *Which, probably, was what this man's day job was supposed to ensure all the people of the Thetis believed as well.*

Eternist. It started as just an alternative line of thought — the idea that there was a case for Humans to thrive in space habitats rather than risk resettling on another planet. A thought experiment. But once labeled, the meaning got inflated to represent anything that was contrarian to the Plan and the mainstream line Anderson was leading. And thus, a slur, a sign of dangerous opposition. Something no one would want to be called out loud.

Jericho Pakk inched closer, and his cold fingers closed around my arm. "Could all this be a personal vendetta, aimed to influence the lawful democratic election process? "

W... What?! I panicked. *Where did this come from?* I was dumbstruck. I broke eye contact and stared at the floor, feeling my forehead breaking with cold perspiration.

Jericho didn't let go. "I am very aware that you had quite a challenging year, Sandrine. Getting disqualified from your planned Birth Year, that must have been devastating for you. Nyasha made a great effort on your behalf, so you could at least keep your Archive job."

He leaned so close I could almost smell his waxy composure. "But as a Senior Archivist you also must know that all Genline-related warrants are signed by the Thetis Primo's office," his face froze with seriousness as he laid his blow, "So whether this is an attempt at payback, or a calculated bet that a woman Primo like Saugado will be more sympathetic to the idea of appealing that sanction — I fear your actions could be viewed as not merely driven by human weakness, but rather... Anti-Thetan."

This wapa! "And to think *you* were the ones to complain about extortion," I finally managed to spit out.

"Extortion implies I need something from you, Liet. I'm just here to keep a friendly channel open. No need to arm the nukes over this, is there? Unless maybe you *are* an Eternist after all?"

"I'm not!" I cried in frustration. "None of what you said is *true!* It's just a bunch of lies and exaggerations!"

Jericho sneered. "I'll leave truths and investigations to you Archivist nerds. I just handle Communications."

I couldn't take it anymore. I pushed Pakk aside and stormed toward my hab door, tears breaking as I chipped in.

I slammed the door behind me and ran to the furthest wall across the room. I leaned on it, breathing heavily, fighting the sobs I knew would eventually erupt. Finally, I collapsed on my heels, my back against the wall.

I was so alone.

Kilian.

Chapter Nine

I lay in bed, fully clothed, for what seemed like hours. The heavy blanket I crawled under provided some sense of security but still, I was trembling — with exhaustion, with frustration, with the too-familiar feeling that I was losing control over the events in my life — *again*.

Threatening my kunye *Genline?!* There was nothing more sacred on the Thetis than the concept of one's procreation. Maintaining one's Genline growth across the journey and unto the resettled planet — that was our contribution to Humanity's future. It was what we were all here for, in the deepest sense.

On the Thetis there was no monetary system, no commerce — there was simply no need for it. In a closed environment where everything was pre-planned for optimal utilization, there was little sense in creating a value system where people will compete for resources. We didn't need rich or poor, social status or privileged access to information or goods.

We Thetans worked and produced — crops, goods, art, anything of value to us — as one, in just the right amount. The Earther Passados were smart enough to prefer abundance over scarcity, so we could all participate as both producers and consumers, without inciting a competitive cycle. We were all essentially a big team playing the long game of transitioning our race between planets. And for that brief period in Human History, an egalitarian society proved to be the most stable system with the least complications.

As individuals, our overarching mission — our *job*, so to speak — was to maintain our Genline across the generations on par with the pre-planned population goals assigned to each generation. The GenZero Embarkers were selected with a very specific genetic profile in mind, so that at Resett Humanity will be able to repopulate on the chosen planet with the highest probability of success.

So, there was no higher punishment or threat to a person on the Thetis than cutting his or her Genline.

On the Thetis there was almost no crime or violence — there was no point in stealing and Human life was much too sacred. So Genline restrictions on the Thetis were what the death sentence was to people on Earth. It was the annihilation of the essence of one's life.

This, of course, was nothing but theoretical to me. The past year of my life, the year after the mess with Kilian exploded, was spent in spiraling cycles of depression I was just beginning to drag myself out of. My right to my first and highly anticipated Birth Year was revoked, and I dived nose-first into the black abyss of self-destruction.

My dark aura pushed the few friends I had away — they were all celebrating their upcoming pregnancies and the last things the soon-to-be new Genmoms needed was me and my toxic presence around. In less than a year, the entirety of level 19 will be teeming with new babies and exhausted mothers high on hormones and bliss. *Well, count me out on this one.* Only Nyasha was there for me, keeping me busy, putting up with my instability, slowly pulling me out from the pit.

I rolled in my bed, Jericho's remarks burning within me at the exact spot he intended them to. *He said that Nyasha intervened on my behalf so I would get a second chance,* I thought. Nyasha, being his gracious self, never mentioned this part to me. *Did he put himself in risk for me? Were there any consequences for him standing behind me on this?*

This was a shocking revelation. *Were they really going to issue a lifetime ban on me?* I knew the numbers. With the classic Thetis generation cycles of 20 years apart, a woman could safely expect two Birth Years: The first at age 20, and provided proper health — the second at 40. Of course, starting with us Gen7 2nd Cyclers, the cycles started to shorten and shift, but two Birth Years and 2.3 children per Genmom were the target growth pattern regardless. To keep up with this growth multiplier, twins were very common on the Thetis. Human embryos were never CellPrinted or genegineered — After how things evolved with Late Earth tech, there's a deep taboo around that stuff on the Thetis — but they *were* selected and screened for genetic mutations, gender ratios and similar safeguards. Moulding was a no-go, nudging was OK.

Consequently, skipping even a single Birth Year would severely hamper a Genmom's genetic participation down the line. Revoking *both* Birth Years would practically cut off a woman's entire Genline. And on the Thetis, if you had no Genline, you were nobody — a lopped branch waiting to whither and die, inconsequential to the mission. A waste of resources. *This was a punishment reserved for the worst of people,* I thought in horror. This was the fate of... of *traitors.* For people who were convicted of being—

Anti-Thetan. This was the word Jericho used. A word so rarely uttered it immediately sent shivers down my spine just mentally reciting it. Anti-Thetan was essentially anti-Humanity. It was the ultimate evil.

How did it even come to this so quickly? I tried to get a grasp on things. Until this morning no-one particularly noticed my existence, and now the Secundus to the Primo is waiting by my hab in the middle of the night, threatening to nuke me off the Genline? *None of this makes sense.*

My head was swirling. *Dio, I need to sleep.* But I could already tell by the feeling creeping up my head that sleep would be a futile attempt. I sighed and chipped on the nightbeam.

I knew the pattern all too well — every single failure in my life, every disappointment started exactly like this: my inability to stay calm in front of injustice. To face a possibility of inequality and resist that creeping feeling that *I must do something,* that I have to step in and fight this.

That was *my* greatest weakness, and by *dio* did I pay prices for not being able to break this pattern.

Alas — there I was, lying in bed looking into thin air with all the day's events floating in my mind. There would be no sleep for me until I put thing in order.

As far as I knew at this point, Dr. Almaz Bashiri was working on quite a useful genetic implementation of a switch-gene in the Sensory Farm CellPrinted organism pool. This gene allowed for immediate eradication of the host organism when exposed to a dose of a specific trigger-radiation. For some reason, his breakthrough was secretly copied by the PHS lab for other potential uses, a fact which alarmed Bashiri enough to raise concerns about the process safety. Then all hell broke loose — Dr. Bashiri got accused of attempting extortion on the Primo. His research was shut down. *He said he was afraid about his daughter's Birth Year — was his Genline threatened too?* If so, it had to come from way up high.

But what does all of this have to do with me? I thought. Am I a target here, or merely an accidental participant?

Clearly, sending me to crypsign the investigation dismissal inksheet forms was a ruse. *Did Nyasha know about this?* Probably not — he was as surprised as I was when I confronted him about it. *It was such a naive and stupid thing to crypsign those forms,* I thought. I just hadn't paused for a single moment to consider it, starstruck by Sebastian Anderson's presence.

But locating Almaz Bashiri in the Sensory Farm was my own move. No one coerced me to do it. Yet Jericho showed up there with his team not two minutes after Bashiri triggered the rad emitter. *Were they on the lookout for him too? Did Dr. Bashiri know he was exposing himself by showing me the gene's operation?*

There were too many question marks in this narrative. Why was this genengineering tool important enough to wrestle control over? I mean, in a way Nyasha was right — it was a presumably delicate moment with the elections and the Final Call decision just around the corner. But still — it seemed disproportionate. Elections on the Thetis were held every 25 years or so, and were regarded as such a formality that no Thetan really cared too much about it. The Primo's role was actually more of an operational role, with most factors dominating our life already pre-planned and pre-determined from the get-go. We had no wars to win, no land to conquer. Primo was, in most aspects, an even bigger clerical job than Archivist.

So why is everybody suddenly freaking out about this bacterial switch-gene? Apparently, this was not even a new invention — it started implementation with us Seveners almost 30 years ago. Nyasha's explanation of this being just a scientist's ego trip was way over-simplifying things. A quarrel over research bragging rights would never raise so many red flags, so high up the chain, as to result in Anti-Thetan threats.

I shot up in my bed. *Those words!* I swiveled and dropped my feet to the carpeted floor.

Nothing Anti-Thetan, only Human, Nyasha said. Almost the exact same words used by Jericho. *And Nyasha, fully dressed at 2am, with two half-cups of steaming hot tea on his kitchen table.*

How could I have missed this? Fully awake now, I jumped out of bed and threw my coat on. Finally, I had a thread to pull that could lead me to what was going on:

Jericho was *there*, in Nyasha's hab, just before I arrived. Which means Nyasha *knew* about me meeting Bashiri in the Sensory Farm.

Time to get some straight kunye answers.

Chapter Ten

`Hello, World.`

The two familiar words glowed brightly in the darkness of the Archive main office. It would be another two hours before the Thetis began its daylight hours sequence, so technically everything was still running on night mode.

I preferred it this way — I didn't need any attention on the fact that I was about to dig data from the main Thetis archive on an unsanctioned query. As Senior Archivist I had, of course, some allowance for private, unlogged query time on the machine, but I didn't particularly like this option either — as became evident recently, some people managed to magically have access even to unlogged data. My safest option would be to log the session as part of the Final Call report review I was supposed to work on, and not stray too far in my queries from subjects with demonstrable connection to it.

Hello, World. The terminal welcome message had always amused me. An Archivist urban legend claimed this was a joke planted by the Passados, its meaning long-lost over the generations. Still, it held some innocent appeal to me. The most powerful machine Man has ever built, with such an understated overture!

The Quantum Unentangled Broad Information Concierge, or — you guessed it — QUBIC, was one of the few mission-critical technologies on the Thetis. In general, harsh lessons learned back on Earth led the Passados to plan for as little dependency on computer-based tech as possible. It is said that at some point back in Late Earth, machine-generated video, voice and text became so perfectly indistinguishable from Human-made ones, that it had broken all trust in anything but face to face communications. On the Thetis, with its lower gravity, flat levels and smallish community, meeting in person was the norm. We didn't need any personal mobile devices ("face leeches", my father used to call them,) to talk to someone — we just walked. Relying on computers for anything beyond the absolute necessity was widely seen as distasteful.

There were, of course, obvious areas where those were crucial, such as gene labs, climate simulations and crop production facilities, but as a general rule — anything that could be managed manually, usually was.

Yet, I actually liked losing myself inside the seemingly-infinite abyss of QUBIC's data archive. Every inch of self-consciousness and social awkwardness I experienced when dealing with actual people, had vanished the second I pressed my palms on both sides of the aqua-blue tinted translucent box.

The machine immediately sensed my crypID chip and logged me into the terminal. Then came my favorite part of the boot-up sequence: the three-dimensional display-panel kicked in, and the viewport perspective suddenly stretched "inward" to fill the entire volume of the terminal cube. The effect was dizzying — I always liked to think this was what going through a wormhole would feel like. And as the transition completed, the title 'Sr. Arc. Sandrine Liet' floated inside the cube, signaling that QUBIC was logged-in to my personal profile and ready for my queries. At the bottom, a cluster of three-dimensional blobs represented QUBIC's best guesses for relevant starting points to my query session.

The concept behind QUBIC's operation was admirably simple, really. The moment a user logged into the terminal, the quantum core algorithm would get access to the entire log of their recent activities, vital signs, location and other data. Consequently, predicting the user's 'next-up information needs' with high probability has proved very effective. It wasn't perfect, but it sure beat textual querying.

The blobs whirled and rearranged themselves in the 3D space, using blob size, color and depth within the cube to signify importance and group similar subjects together. Each blob was labeled with a floating title, and a glinting web of hair-thin lines connected between some of the blobs to suggest probable connections between related data points.

At the center of my current session home-screen was a big red blob titled Final Call Data Review. Next to it was my Assigned Cases blob which was essentially my pinned to-do list. A bit further back was Primo Sebastian Anderson, with a thin line tracing to a yet-smaller blob labeled Elections. Those, I assumed, were all related to my schedule in the past twenty-four hours, so nothing out of the ordinary. As far as I could tell, my visit to the Sensory Farm remained unlogged as it seemingly did not influence the quick-options QUBIC offered. Pushed almost all the way to the back of the cube, and progressively diminishing over the past few months due to the cold algorithm assumption of decreasing relevance, was a tiny, purple spherical blob. The label above it, almost too blurry to be readable, read *Maternity Planning*.

"Final Call Data Review," I said softly, thinking it best to begin with the mundane task I would be expected to access QUBIC for. *Nothing incriminating in just doing your kunye job, is there?*

The central red blob immediately expanded and the field of view zoomed in to focus on the information. The other blob clusters shrunk and rearranged at the cube's borders, ready to be pulled up if needed.

Legal Declaration, a formal document surfaced and came into focus. This is a crypsigned task, assigned by the Thetis Archive Office, Head Archivist Woo, Nyasha. To proceed with task initiation, please sign the following paragraphs to confirm your understanding and acknowledgement. You will only have to complete this legal declaration once.

I sighed. *OK, then.* "Proceed."

The floating text scrolled away. This is a privileged-access task, QUBIC displayed. Your review and final recommendation will be logged with your crypID for compliance and documentation purposes. To acknowledge your understanding, please sign this declaration now.

I tapped my chip-finger lightly on the side of the translucent box to confirm my crypID acceptance. The text scrolled away.

A three-dimensional drawing of the Thetis flight trajectory glowed inside the cube. At about two thirds of the way, the trajectory split into two paths, each extending to a different end point just outside of the terminal boundaries.

The Archive registers you have successfully completed the Final Call Introductory Tutorial 98 days ago. Would you like to retake the tutorial now?

"Dio, no please." Who didn't know about Final Call? As Kilian once put it, Final Call was the single biggest event our generation should expect to live through. The point of no return — the moment in our journey where the Thetis has to decide whether to keep the original plan and plant Humanity's future in the 9 Ceti system, or, alternatively, keep on sailing for two extra generations, setting our target on the secondary choice of the HD1461 star system, also known as Gnosis. Each decision would take the Thetis down a different flight trajectory and initiate a sequence of events spanning decades and irreversible in nature. I had studied that plan and decision criteria as part of my Archivist training.

The neat graphics faded away and QUBIC moved on. Another block of text appeared inside the cube.

Part 1 - Intended Objective. The Final Call Data Review objective is to deliver an official recommendation to the Thetis Primo regarding the optimal Resettlement planetary system.

Available options: (a) 9 Ceti Gamma; (b) Gnosis Zeta.

In order to support such recommendation, the Head Archive shall:

1. Review the scientific reports to be submitted by all Thetis research departments.

2. Assess the current data in comparison with the original assumptions included in the Thetis Embarkment Plan.

3. Confirm 9 Ceti Gamma as the primary Resett candidate, or recommend the prioritization of Gnosis Zeta.

Legal notice — The report itself serves as an official legal opinion submitted on behalf and in trust of the Thetis Community and the Human Race. The adoption and execution of the actions recommended by the Head Archive lies within the sole responsibility of the elected Thetis Primo. Please acknowledge.

I tapped my finger again. "Acknowledged."

Part 2 - Data Inventory, QUBIC prompted in glowing, floating letters. Total count of Thetis official research institutions: 27. Total count of submitted reports assigned for review: 26.

Huh? 26 report reviews — is Nyasha trying to work me to death?

"List reports," I said and watched as over two dozen micro-blobs grew in a circle around the virtual screen borders, each one representing a research lab. A thin silver line connected each tiny blob with the main subject, suggesting a possible navigation route for me to follow.

Total reports count: 26. Research departments with submitted reports: Trajectory Planning, Climatology Simulator, Rebiome Project, Soil & Seed Lab, Raw Materials Engineering —

"OK, hold," I paused the ramble. "List pending report."

Public Health Security Institute, QUBIC listed. The blob titled PHS floated at the edge of the screen, its red color signifying the missing data.

I pressed my palms to the sides of the terminal cube and nudged it in a circular motion. The blobs inside the three-dimensional display reacted immediately and started whirling, orbiting around the main item in the direction I was pushing toward. I kept scrolling through the blobs until PHS settled in the center of the cluster. The thin silver line connecting to it glowed, and the red blob grew and expanded. Although navigating QUBIC took some learning, once you got the hang of it it was intuitive and struck a balance between minimalistic gestures and freeform voice control.

Public Health Security Institute, read the title floating above the data area. Final Call Review Report, pending.

Yeah, OK, I thought. "General info," I commanded.

QUBIC pulled up the boilerplate information brief. Public Health Security division, established as part of the Infirmary Office at Light-Year 5.14.

I grinned. Dating events by distance travelled in our journey rather than in Earth years was a unique QUBIC thing. I kind of liked it — as the Thetis was not undergoing any cyclical pattern like a planet orbiting a star, there was no real reason to use years as the measuring stick for time passage. Indicating the location of the ship along its trajectory gave a more intuitive sense of the order of things. People, of course, kept the year-count tradition for common daily usage, but at least within QUBIC the new logic ruled.

So on our 60-plus Light Year journey, LY5.14 was quite early on. I kept reading, following PHS office's evolution. For a long time, there had been no change in its status. And then:

Promoted to independent institute status LY38.02. Achieved certification for establishing a research lab LY38.13.

Nothing out of the ordinary so far, I nodded to myself. The growth of the small division into a full-fledged research institute with its own lab did seem a bit fast and ambitious, but that in itself didn't necessarily mean anything that should raise flags.

"Prerogatives."

The floating text inside the terminal box faded and a timeline infographic surfaced. Each highlighted event was marked on the timeline with a small glowing red marker.

Initial PHS prerogatives — monitoring infirmary sterilization. Testing crop samples for contaminants and microbiotic health hazards.

Added prerogative LY38.03 — vaccines and preventive medicine.

Added prerogative LY38.18 — procreation genetic screening, Genline premapping.

Now this is interesting, I thought. The PHS was established about 5 Light Years into the journey, which should mean around 20 Earth years after Embarkment. It operated continuously for seven generations on the ship, its sole purpose being keeping the public health intact from incidental germ outbreaks. Pretty mundane job, one should think, ne?

But then, within less than 18 months, this tiny division gets spun out into its own independent status as a full Institution, gets a license for a research lab, and begins attracting more and more authority over — and access to — sensitive data and operations.

Quite a long way from sampling crops to handling baby gene mapping and selective screening of Human embryos!

That also meant the PHS had to get full access privileges to the entire genome pool of the Thetis. That's quite a dramatic shift in responsibility, and likely wrested from the Healthcare office itself. *There must have been a pretty frustrated Healthcare Secundus back then,* I thought.

Inside the translucent cube, several new lines emerged and traced connections from the PHS general info tab to other relevant topics: The Final Call Report slot, still empty. The Thetis gene pool project. Health Events calendar. PHS personnel. Some other info blobs which seemed further removed from anything useful at this point.

I considered my next navigation point. I needed to connect Dr. Bashiri with Primo Anderson. The closest probable route seemed to be through Sabi's wife.

"PHS Personnel."

The information cluster whirled again and rearranged itself with the new perspective focusing on a story-line of personal profile cards.

At the top of the branching organization chart, staring directly at me, was an UltraRes image of the most striking woman I had ever seen.

Cassidi Anderson was a knockout. QUBIC listed her as Generation 6, so she should be fifty five years old, but she could have easily passed as a twenty years younger Gen7er. Her straight blond hair was cut shoulder length, and in the Archive UltraRes scan it was pulled up into a casually-made sloppy bun, giving her the look of an overworked doctor in a rush for an infirmary shift, completely unaware of and uninterested in her stunning looks. The eyes staring at me from within the cube were deep brown and mesmerizing, speaking of intelligence and compassion. I couldn't take my eyes off of Cassidi's image for several long seconds.

"Expand," I whispered finally.

A text object extended beneath the floating face image. Born LY31.14, admitted to Junior Academy when she was not even 14 years old on a GiftedStar fast-track. Finished pre-Med at 16. Volunteered for 5 year at the Astral Solace Home for the Elderly on Level 33. Was the youngest Thetan of her generation to start the Major Academy SinguLearn program for exceptional talent. Then, a ten-year grind of Main Infirmary shift work, before transferring to the PHS as Senior Analyst.

On the break of the LY38 journey distance mark, Cassidi was promoted to Head of the Public Health Security division. Within merely two months after her nomination, the PHS apparently started its accelerated ascension up the ranks and authority status.

I leaned back in my seat. *This is one impressive woman,* I thought. An all too familiar feeling of insignificance and belittlement swept over me. Cassidi Anderson was the poster-child for the New Human all Thetans aspired to become — intelligent, compassionate, morally-active yet humble, never outshining her colleagues and partners. A quick scan through the Scientific Publication Archive did not reveal a single academic or research article where she was listed as the sole author or added an administrative credit for herself on top of her subordinate scientists.

And of course, Cassidi's physical beauty made it even harder for her to blend into the shadows. She was a woman born to be noticed.

I hesitated before scrolling further down Cassidi's information tab. I was beginning to tread dangerous waters here. Linking queries of the Thetis Primo's wife personal data to the report review I was assigned to would be tricky at best. I decided to limit my search to the bare minimum so as not to raise any data-privacy flags later on. I turned my palms together to dial back the query depth indicator to the lowest setting.

"Personal Data," I instructed QUBIC.

Spouse: Sebastian Anderson. Married LY38.00

Genline: Unnamed Anderson (Deceased), female, born LY 38.20. Samuel Anderson, male, Born LY40.10.

My head shot back with utter surprise. *Sabi Anderson had a deceased daughter?* The fact that only the birth date was specified in the file with no date of death implied that the baby had passed away in labour. *Poor Cassidi,* I mouthed.

I started to feel discomfort as I had clearly delved too deep into the personal matters of the Andersons. I quickly backtracked up the navigation tree and back into the general PHS data screen.

I took a slow breath and considered the new bits of information my data journey has surfaced. Something was nudging me, some connection in the periphery of my thought focus area I could not completely put my finger on.

What I needed was a different perspective. "Arrange on timeline viewport," I tried.

The main data blob inside the terminal cube slid back and blurred into the background. A new viewport surfaced, with a linear timeline dotted with the different data points collected so far. Each data point was represented by a bright dot on the timeline. A cluster of various adjacent events was clearly forming at a specific point in time.

"LY38 was a busy time for Mrs. Anderson," I mumbled and adjusted the pressure on both sides of the cube to zoom in on the timeline. I squinted and tried to make sense of the apparently random sequence of events.

Then, after a few seconds of concentration, a story began to form. The seemingly unrelated life events and career pivots of Cassidi Anderson carried a hint of narrative as I progressed through the glowing timeline.

There she was, a young, bright analyst newly transferred to the PHS division after a decade of grinding shifts at the infirmary. She then marries Sebastian Anderson, an up-and-coming political star running for Primo in the next General Elections. She gets pregnant for a Gen7 Birth Year, but tragically loses the child at birth. A month later, Sabi is elected Primo, and then things really start picking up — within 6 months of her husband stepping into office, she gets promoted to Head of the PHS, and achieves an unheard of feat of getting the PHS recognized as a full Institute. Under its new title, new prerogatives are authorized for the PHS for handling all Thetis vaccines. Quickly after that, she gets a license for her own research lab approved, along with new areas of responsibility in genetic screening, which in effect grants her full access to the entire gene pool data of the Thetis.

Cassidi gets a second chance for Birth Year at Gen7 2nd cycle, successfully birthing Sam Anderson, or — as he would commonly be known throughout the ship — Kunye Zee. Us Gen7 2^{nd}ers are a small enough group that *everyone* knew Zee, who was without doubt the single most obnoxious person on this side of the FLIPP.

I pulled my palms back from QUBIC and rubbed my eyes. I was so tired and they burned so much I could barely see anything through the blur. But one thing was now certain — behind the picture-perfect image of Sabi and Cassidi Anderson lay a roaring ambition and a dramatic pivot in the chain of events. The GiftedStar girl who volunteered for the elderly had transformed into an ambitious beast, clearly using her husband's position to extend her access and influence in domains far from the public eye. It was astonishing that I had never previously noticed or known about Cassidi.

I turned my attention again to the terminal, curious to see where those glowing, silver lines sprouting out of the timeline will take me next.

CHAPTER ELEVEN

"Sandrine?" a gentle hand rested on my shoulder and shook it lightly. "Sandrine!"

I jerked awake. Alarmed, I shot a look at the QUBIC terminal, then sighed internally with relief — apparently, I had fallen asleep mid-session and my palms slumped just far enough from the cube to lose connection and log off. No one could see what I was working on.

I looked up. Nyasha was standing above me. It was well beyond daybreak on the Thetis. I squinted and inhaled deeply, straightening up in my chair.

"I couldn't sleep, so I thought I might as well get an early start on the reports," I mumbled, evading direct eye contact. He grabbed a rolling chair from one of the desks and sat beside me.

"Listen, Sandrine, there's something I need to tell you," he said bluntly. What with his soft and humane manner, he was never one to beat around the bush when something had to be dealt with.

He leaned forward in his chair and slowly ran his hand through his salt and pepper curls.

"I was not completely honest with you last night when you came to my hab," he said.

I sprang awake — now *this* got my attention all right. "Truth is,"

Nyasha continued, "I was a bit surprised to see you there and wasn't sure if I should share this, but it's important you know that Anderson's Secretary of Communications, Jericho Pakk, also paid me a visit just before you arrived."

I nodded. "I kind of figured it out already."

Nyasha smiled his fatherly, warm smile. "Of course you did. He just showed at my door without prior notice. The reason I didn't mention it when you came over was that he was actually looking for you."

I grunted. "He saw me at the Sensory Farm just a few minutes before that, but I managed to sneak out."

"So he mentioned," Nyasha eyed me closely. "I brushed him off, told him you went down there on Archive business to get some data sample for our reports."

I swiveled in my chair to face Nyasha. "Well it didn't work. He ambushed me by my hab, almost gave me a heart attack. He tried to bully me into dropping any inquiry into their fake extortion nonsense."

Nyasha's face clouded over. This worried him. "It was a mistake sending you up there."

"Oh no, quite the opposite," I said. "You know how I am with bullies. Now I *want* to know what they're hiding."

Nyasha shook his head. "I thought we agreed to move on from this matter," Nyasha paused, letting the words just hang there for a moment. "So — what *were* you doing at the Sensory Farm?" he asked flatly.

I decided to trust him with the truth. *If there's one human on the Thetis I can absolutely trust, it is Nyasha.* Well, there once was another one, but I didn't imagine I would be seeing *him* ever again.

"This is where I met Dr. Almaz Bashiri," I admitted.

Nyasha deflated in his chair. "Ah, Sandrine," he sighed.

He pulled his small, round glasses up on his head and rubbed his eyes, thinking. Dear Nyasha — wearing his signature grey sleeveless sweater over an oversized flannel shirt, and with his dense, curly hair and beard, he looked like a baby's FuzzieDoll toy. All you wanted to do was cuddle between his comforting arms.

"What aren't you telling me?" I asked firmly.

Nyasha opened his eyes. "What I *am* telling you is that all my work for the past twenty years, and all *your* work, for that matter, is culminating in the single most important decision of the entire Thetis project — do we initiate the Resett procedure on 9 Ceti or opt for Gnosis. Do Humans become Cetans or Gnosii. This decision is happening right after the upcoming elections, so a lot of power is at stake. And knowing the people at play here, the last thing I want to see is you become an itch for someone who uses a blowtorch for scratching."

I raised my hands in defense. "I am not doing anything out of line here, just asking some questions." I leaned forward and looked Nyasha in the eyes. "You taught me everything I know, Nyasha. You taught me the importance of following the truth wherever it may lead. The equality of every person before the Thetis law. I cannot ignore the questions I have just because the timing is inconvenient. This is my kunye job!"

"I have also taught you that an Archivist's value lies in being practical, not academic," Nyasha said as if explaining a trivial fact of life. "If this was an urgent matter, I could understand the haste. But all you'll be doing here is raise a dust storm that will eventually backfire. They'll say the Archive is tampering with the elections. They'll claim you are supporting the agendas of opposing factions, that the whole investigation is a political move. Believe me — you don't want to be in that position."

He took both my palms in his warm hands and almost pleaded. "You know I love you like a daughter, Sandrine. But you can't risk getting red-flagged again, and there's only so much protection I can offer you. Yes, Sabi has always been one to stretch the envelope. To test the system limits. And he is aggressive — maybe this is how leaders have always been. I agree it doesn't always leave the best taste. People like you and me — we may not always like the style, but this isn't a fashion show. And I'll tell you one thing — I have never seen him do anything overtly unlawful. Let's let the elections play out as clean as possible. We'll revisit this then, shall we?"

I pulled my hands from Nyasha and rested my chin on my palms. "I don't know, Nyasha. Someone out there is playing with a killer-gene. And the whole upper-level is freaking out when anyone is looking into it. And every stone I turn seems to reveal a connection to the Primo, or his wife. *Kunye Dio*, Nyasha, I am an Archivist — how can I *not* insist on looking into this, despite any intimidation attempts?"

Nyasha didn't like what he was hearing. "We are on a mission, Sandrine. Soldiers in a mission with zero tolerance for error. And the mission is bigger than procedure. Conducting the Final Call decision cleanly and openly is of the utmost importance, even if we have to postpone other distractions."

"No, Nyasha," I hardened. "The mission is not bigger than the values it was built to serve. Our Code, our law — we need to fight for them or we lose anyhow."

Nyasha leaned back in his seat and gave me a tired smile. "You are so young."

"Saying I am young is different than saying I am wrong."

Nyasha stood up and put his glasses back on. "As a free citizen of the Thetis, if you want to ask questions or query the open Archive in your free time, I can't stop you. But I am *not* sanctioning any official inquiry based on the current data. And not on my clock please, Sandrine."

Ahh, I just love this guy, I thought. 'Based on the current data'. He didn't say 'speculations'. Or 'nonsense', or even just plain 'no'.

He is practically teasing me to get out there and back my hunches with concrete evidence.

I felt the adrenaline rush back to my brain. Nyasha started to walk out, and I called after him. "Where's the PHS report?"

He stopped and turned back. "What do you mean?"

"I went over the submissions list. All of them are in except Cassidi's."

"Impossible."

I shrugged.

A flush bloomed on his face. "That's outrageous! I have repeatedly reminded them about it. Cassidi being the Primo's wife, I'd expect PHS to have been the first to submit! Are you certain about this? Because they *assured* me that they did finally send it."

Nyasha considered it for another moment. "Let me look into it. Now go to sleep, Sandrine, and come back this afternoon for staff meeting. Can't have you drooling over QUBIC here. Might short his quantum circuits." And he left the room, smirking to himself.

As soon as the door was closed behind him, I leaped back and woke QUBIC back into life. I swiped the event timeline aside and started a new query.

"Ledger access," I ordered impatiently, and started scrolling through an endless list of data entries floating before me, aggregated from a thousand different sources within the Thetis systems.

The user interface of QUBIC was designed for intuitive navigation and data access. But on the back-end of the system, the actual logs of database entries needed a different design, created with the utmost data integrity and durability in mind. The thing needed to keep both physically and logically intact for *centuries*.

For this task, the ancient but proven technology of a Distributed Ledger was chosen. This meant that each new data entry was stacked on top of the previous ones in a huge file which was saved simultaneously in different parts of the Thetis. This allowed for redundancy in case something went wrong with the main Archive system, and also meant that once a data item was added to the ledger, it could never be deleted — at least not without corrupting everything that came after it, like trying to pull a card from the middle of a house of cards. You could only add data on top of the pile, and since multiple copies were kept, data was never lost on the Thetis.

I scrolled through the data entries regarding submissions of Final Call Review reports. Each lab on the Thetis submitted its report directly to the Main Archive terminal.

Nyasha was right. The ledger clearly showed a submission log entry for the PHS lab from a few days ago. I opened it up, but got a NULL response code. No file was pulled from the server. The report was empty.

A few lines down the list, there was another entry with the same report code, crypsigned by the Head of PHS Cassidi Anderson. Again, the report contents were missing and the entry was empty.

I snorted — the attempt was transparent as it was naive. Submitting a second data entry using the same code as the original one was a lame attempt to override and delete the first entry. But, if you knew how ledger-based systems worked, you'd have known it was futile.

Quantum feed — built for speed. Data Ledger — built to remember, I chuckled, recalling the cheesy rhyme from the introductory Archive technical certification course.

Come on, what dirt are you trying to hide, Cassidi, I thought. Did an employee submit a report you didn't want out there? Why remove the reports file from the server and submit an empty one instead to try and hide it?

And then I remembered an ancient saying from Old Earth —

If you want to find dirt, look for the person buried underneath it.

CHAPTER TWELVE

Hugo Winkler's naked body lay motionless in the center of the spacious room. He lay raised on a divan decorated with an overflowing, silky purple cloth, and was positioned leaning on one elbow. Beneath him, soft, colorful cushions were placed for support. His eyes, glazed and static, transfixed on a distant point in the ceiling. A group of a dozen people stood around the scene in a small semi-circle, focused.

I walked into the room, trying to assess what was going on without disturbing the quiet attention that was in the air. A beam of light from a nearby projector accentuated the naked man's pale skin and wrinkled face, adding dramatic flair to the entire setting. Hugo Winkler's face wore a frozen half-smile, his head framed by the craziest, most chaotic clumpy fuzzball of bleach-white hair I have ever seen.

As I stepped hesitantly closer and got noticed by the group circling the divan, Hugo's eyes broke their frozen stare and shifted their focus to me. His smile immediately widened to reveal a perfect set of square white teeth, and he called out in pathos to the group.

"OK, pads down, artists! Let's take five — we've been blessed by a surprise visit from a sexy giant from the Seventh Generation!" he motioned to me with his free hand. "Embark and *kunye* Prosper, Aphroditus Maximus! Come closer, now — did you like my

Olympia?"

"Not a single word you've just said makes any sense to me," I said, as two other participants helped Winkler into a sitting position. "Are you sure you're still mentally stable?"

Winkler sighed. "Ahh, you young generations have no culture. We'll end up flying halfway across the galaxy only to resettle humanity as a race of *savages*."

I raised my eyebrows, motioning to his naked body sitting in front of me. "Speaking of which, maybe, er… put something on?"

Hugo laughed. "Hey — you're now within the jurisdiction of the Astral Solace Home for Elderly Farts. Our home, our rules."

He motioned, and a cherry-colored robe was produced, along with a wheeler — I just then noticed Winkler was paralyzed from the waist down. He suppressed a groan as I helped him settle into the wheeler seat.

"So," he said as his signature smile returned to his flushed face, "can I safely assume you didn't climb up here just for the fun of participating in my weekly nude painting class?"

"Very safely," I assured him.

Hugo laughed. "So it's Archive business. OK, roll with me, I have to take my kunye algae proteins now."

I accompanied him as he wheeled away from the group of elders working on their inksheet pads. "Who knew retirement could be this fun?" Winkler said with an energetic flare. "*Wapa* works his entire youth off, secures his Genline spending 40 years raising kids over two generations — wapa is washed out, exhausted, but his dues to the kunye race are paid." Winkler raised both hands and nodded in acceptance. "Time for life to reignite, ne? Nothing to worry about on this tin can but sex, art and good friends, until we all get processed back into bio-nutrients!"

Thanks for the mental image, old man. "Aren't you Gen5ers like… 75?" I asked.

Hugo opened a drawer in the nearby kitchenette, retrieved a slab of ProNori gel, then sighed with defeat and began slowly slurping on the gooey substance.

"Can you believe it, kid?" he turned his wheeler softly and faced me, gesturing toward his wrinkled, weathered body. "Can you believe that back on Earth, this magnificent body would have only been midway through its lifetime, fully operational as a young stud?"

Winkler threw the spent wrapping of the protein gel into a recycler, finger-counting as he continued his griping.

"Blood platelet replacement, bone tissue re-hiving, neural cell weaving nanobot swarms," his enthusiasm grew as the list extended. "A mean life expectancy of kunye 140 years — those *wapinyos Passados* had all the technology figured out! And they took it all away from us before kicking us off their planet. Back to apes!" he said with a bitter smile.

"Going back to basics was a safer bet," I remarked dryly.

"That logic sure hits different when you're seventy-five, dragging your ass around on wheels," Hugo blurted sarcastically. "What I wouldn't give for 70 more years, te? Such a waste."

I was really starting to like this guy with his stupid cherry robe and crazy plume of white hair. "All this talk about technology body enhancements — I might start to think you're some kind of... Adapter."

Hugo sneered at the mild tease. "Oh please. I'm too old to be intimidated by the mala politics of Thetis authorities. 'Eternist' this, 'Adapter' that — everyone is either a Sabi fan or they are the enemy now, ne?"

"Oh, and by the way," he winked, "I followed your story back then, with this guy they labeled an Adapter."

"Kilian," I mumbled.

Hugo nodded. "Very effective, the way they handled it — slapped both of you real good, now no one dares to think about improvements anymore. It's just 'make children, do your job, retire and wait it out till you drop dead.' Just trust the plan to get us to our destination, no questions asked. *Very* convenient for the Andersons of this world."

"Speaking of which…" I tried to steer the conversation away from the grim turn it was taking.

"Ahh, the Archive business," Winkler conceded. "What blessing has earned me the attention of the powers that be?"

"I am actually not here in any official capacity of the Archive," I admitted. "I just hoped to get your view on a personal matter."

"Flattering!" The smile grew on Hugo's face, "an old man's wisdom is in demand! Is it related to that Adapter guy?"

"No," I replied, "but it *is* related to the Andersons."

Winkler frowned. "You mean that *bruta.*"

"Bruta? From what I've read about Cassidi Anderson, she looks like a kunye *saint*," I said.

"More of a Fallen Angel, if you want to revert to biblical terms," Hugo Winkler grunted. His face contorted. "Any reason I should spend a single extra heartbeat out of my dwindling inventory thinking about this treacherous back-stabber, when I could be perfectly content spending the rest of the day nude-posing to my Classic Art students?"

I sat down so we would be on the same eye-level. I didn't expect to strike such an exposed nerve there. An air of seriousness descended abruptly between us.

"Dr. Winkler, something is happening on the Thetis. I have no hard evidence so far, which is why I can't take this to the Archive for official investigation yet. But I have a visceral gut feeling. There have been too many coincidences in the past 24 hours for me to ignore."

"Coincidences are the Universe's way of telling you you're just too stupid to figure out the narrative behind them," Winkler leaned forward, his eyes studying mine. "So, what's the story?"

Tread carefully here, Sandrine. That was a dangerous game, talking to people about half-baked suspicions about the leading figures of the Thetis.

"I'm not sure yet," I admitted. "But every corner I peek around or question I ask raises red flags all the way up to the Primo. And the PHS seems to also be involved in this somehow."

"Ahh, the power couple," Hugo's smile hardened.

"You were head of the PHS for over twenty years before Cassidi replaced you," I said.

Winkler coughed a hard laugh. "You don't have to be polite with me, my lady. 'Booted out with a kick in the ass and a side dish of a poison kiss' would very well be a closer description. The first thing you need to know about Cassidi Anderson is that she is all kill, no tease. If the woman ever smiled, it was probably at some poor bastard's funeral."

Hugo slanted his head, thinking. "Did you start getting threats?"

"Some," I admitted. "But not from her direction, I think. They may have more to do with the Primo's office."

Winkler's face softened. "Poor girl. Of course it does. This is how they operate. You have to understand — for the Andersons, it's all about the effective use of power and authority in service of their family. He is the public figure with the official position and power. She is the private citizen, operating behind the scenes within the Thetis institutional system. Understanding this balance has cost me ten years of social limbo after I got sacked from my job."

Winkler sighed and leaned back in his wheeler. "Thankfully, my Genline was already secure at this point so they couldn't really threaten me with anything, but they *could* make me an outcast — they made sure I was smeared in the PubSheets so badly it took me a *decade* to be able to show my face in social circles again. And my credibility as a scientist was forever ruined. Darling, are you certain you want to dip your head in this bog?"

I shook my head slowly. "What choice do I have? I'm an Archivist."

"You holy bunch. OK, then the second thing you need to understand about Cassidi is that she has no restraints. No boundaries. Sabi is a public figure — if things get muddy, he'll put his rubber boots on and flee for dry land. But Cassidi? She'll scuba-dive right through the sludge to get what she wants."

I exhaled audibly. "Holding a grudge, aren't we?"

Hugo waved his hand in dismissal. "At my age, grudges are a vanity. In a sense I should actually be grateful to the Andersons. If it wasn't for the *bruta*, I would have never retired from my job leading PHS, and as you can see — I am enjoying this side of my workforce years too much to complain."

"So help me out here, doctor," I urged him. "I'm seeing this young idealist woman. A GiftedStar laureate. Ironically, spends five years volunteering right here at the Astral Solace Home. Works for you at the PHS for a while, then all of a sudden everything explodes — you're out, she takes the helm of the division and grows a small empire out of it in no-time. In your own words — there's a narrative here, not mere coincidence."

Hugo laughed. "Smart girl. The strongest weapon Perseus ever wielded was not the sword, but the mirror. Anyhow — it all goes back to my accident."

He gestured toward his incapacitated legs. "This is back twenty something years ago, on the day we had a severe radiation leak on Level 8. But first you have to understand what PHS actually *was* back then. We were a tiny division under the Health Office. We operated under the leadership of the Health Secundus, with the very unambitious task of monitoring bio contamination, mostly in crops. To be honest, it was a quiet, relaxed job. We haven't had an outbreak or Human-related risk factor discovered in *decades*. By Generation 5 of space-born humans with no form of outside influence, the Thetis was already so sterile that we had virtually no real epidemiological challenges."

Winkler was picking up on the enthusiasm as he kept going. *A real scientist*, I thought. *All passion for his subject matter.*

"This has, by the way," he continued, "had devastating effects on our immune system. People can't Resett on an alien world with such poor resistance to diseases, which is why we invented the Dusting protocol that takes place every five years, exposing us to particles simulating foreign organisms. And this is also why they'll start the ReBiome project next generation, to get people ready for life alongside plants and animals and—"

"Wait." I stopped his digression. "I think you mentioned a radiation leak?"

"It was some scientific test in the Sensory Farm Vivarium, which emitted radiation that triggered the ship's radiation sensors. As a consequence of this event we mandated covering Level 8 with rad-shielding materials."

Bashiri, I thought.

"The thing is," he continued, "the whole Thetis went *Crazy.* The sensors detecting the radiation burst activated emergency contamination hazard protocols — it was a mess. Within five seconds, the Level 10 seal shut close, the Ion Thruster engines were cut off, and we got an unexpected Zero-g situation—"

"I *remember* that day!" I shouted. "I was just a kid, but I remember the sudden gravity loss — we were floating around the hab for *hours,* totally freaked out, trying to secure things from smashing into walls. I thought the Thetis had hit an astroid or something!"

"There was serious hysteria," Hugo agreed. "And with good reason. It was the first time in the entire journey that those emergency protocols were activated. Many people injured — present company included — and most of us were certain that the Thetis had broken or driven off-traj. It took days to reaffirm our trajectory and operational status and reassure the public that all was back to normal. It's all documented in the Archive, you can look it up, te?"

"What happened to you?" I asked, uncertain if that would be a proper topic to ponder.

Winkler laughed. "Me? Oh I was just unlucky in the most non-heroic fashion imaginable. The Zero-g kick caught me in the middle of a b-ball practice. I was in mid-leap, and just kept cruising forward, crashing directly into the goal bar. My body almost broke in half from the impact."

I winced. "Ouch."

"Lucky for me, I passed out immediately. Woke in the infirmary connected to a thousand tubes, with complete chaos all around. Something like thirty percent of the Thetis population suffered injuries of some form or another. I think I was actually labeled one of the worst cases from that incident. What can I say — drama always seems to find me."

We paused for a moment. "I have a feeling this is where Cassidi Anderson enters the picture?" I asked.

"More like *swoops in*, but yes," Hugo sighed. "I mean, she was quick to the kill! I was out of it in Intensive Care for, what — a week? And I wake up to find myself suddenly being the Thetis no. 1 public enemy! PubSheets all over the ship with my face on them, flailing accusations of negligence, blaming me for the accident. Official Archive investigators literally carrying me out of my infirmary bed for interrogations. I was still in shock from my injury, hadn't had time to process the loss of feeling in my legs, and there I was — bombarded with accusations of me being responsible for the biggest accident since Embarkment. Of endangering the entire Human race."

"Did you begin doubting yourself?" I asked.

"I honestly didn't know what to make of it at first. I mean, the PHS *is* in charge of public health hazard prevention, which one could theoretically say includes radiation hazards and containment protocols for contamination outbreaks. But... this was *way* out of our actual work scope! That's like saying the Waste Management department is accountable for a baby scribbling finger-paint all over his parents' hab wall. We *never* dealt with the Vivarium, or radiation. We worked with *crops*, with *farmers!* Thing is, Cassidi knew about it just as I did. The fact that the inquiry was even *happening* spoke parsecs about the motivation behind it. Don't forget who the Head Archivist was back then," Winkler waved his finger and tilted his head with a wry smile. "Sabi's own father, no less, te?"

"Archive investigators don't play politics, ne?" I said skeptically.

"If there was no real fault to be proven, they would have closed the case."

Hugo laughed bitterly. "But you see, that's totally *irrelevant!* This is the *essence* of how the Andersons operate. It isn't about proving something, te? Or carrying an investigation to its official conclusion. It's about sowing rumors, doubts — sending you off to fight the invisible spectres of hearsay! The investigation itself never reaches a conclusion, it just somehow dissipates. No one cares, believe me — people are too busy to follow those things closely — but everyone sees you dragged into interrogation. Everyone reads the half-truths and out-of-context facts about your professional misconduct, about your private life. And you have no platform to respond, so you find yourself constantly fighting a defensive battle, trying to deflect the venomous arrows raining on you from 34th. And the average Thetan? Well they say to themselves: 'well, it can't *all* be lies, ne? That guy must have done *something* wrong!'"

Hugo lowered his chin to his chest, calming his racing heart.

"Eventually, you just grow tired of the fight."

A quite moment passed between us, Winkler's eyes distant, revisiting the painful memory.

"So she used your accident as an excuse to boot you out of rank and position," I noted. "I thought she owed her entire career to you. Didn't you see this coming?"

"I should have, yes," Winkler shrugged. "Oh, she always had *intellectual* ambition. Talented girl — gifted, even — but she was never *self*-ambitious. Never had the vigor for it, or the vision. She got *those* from her new husband."

"So, her ambitions changed after they got married?" I asked.

"It became more evident after that. More shameless. To be honest, we were all very excited for Cassidi's marriage — remember, Sabi was a newly-minted Primo back then — a shining star. Nothing of the bitter, uptight, self-serving politician he is today. I thought this would be a great opportunity for the PHS to finally be heard, to advance our research. But I could see the ambition slowly growing within her, her energy focusing."

Hugo threw both hands in the air. "It was only a matter of time before that energy burned a hole through anything standing in her way."

I looked at Hugo Winkler and felt a wave of empathy for this crazy-haired, extravagant Scientist-Artist.

"You're not angry," I said softly, "You're disappointed with her."

"Ha!" Hugo shot out. "Oh I was *angry*! For a *long* time. And not about losing the PHS, mind you."

Winkler's outburst turned a few heads toward our direction from the group of elderly art students working on their portraits. Hugo waved his hand at them, signaling everything was under control. He leaned closer to me, his face slightly flushed with excitement.

"I loved what I was doing — I spent most of my adult life working my ass off for the Public Health Security division, but after she got married to Sabi, I quickly realized that for Cassidi, the PHS became a mere platform upon which she would build a much grander vision. So yes, I *was* angry, but mainly with myself. I was her kunye *mentor*, or so I saw myself, and that was my blind spot."

One of Hugo's group members approached us, holding his painting pad under his arm. He was a rather tall man for a Gen5er, his smooth face wearing a cautious smile as he leaned into our conversation. "All OK there, Veenk? Group's just about finished, you joining us?"

Hugo pointed at the big man. "Here, ask Armitage. We grew up in the habs together. Ask him if I could even show my face around people after this."

Armitage threw an amused look at Hugo, then at me. "Is he *boring* you with his sob stories about his old job?" he chuckled, his face wearing a warm, friendly smile.

Hugo's face contorted with frustration. "Ahh, forget it. This baboon worships the ground the Andersons walk on."

The big man shrugged. "Thetis' finest, that couple. Salt of the

Earth."

Hugo sneered. "Ahh, Armitage, you *pleb!* Do you realize that back on Old Earth, 'salting the Earth' was a ritual carried by hostile conquerers to starve the natives? That's not a compliment!"

Armitage laid a huge, soft hand on Hugo's shoulder. "Whether I'm getting my history straight or not, I still believe Sabi's the greatest leader the Thetis could hope for. He'll get us there. Now," he said good-heartedly, "can we get back to the part where you were laying dick-out on the sofa and finish our work?"

"It's a divan, *wapinyo*," Hugo tolled his eyes and started turning the wheeler around toward the group. Armitage walked beside him, his sketch under his arm. I followed behind and as they joined the group, a circle of students formed around Winkler, eager for his attention. He raised his hand in pause and turned his head to me.

"I'll tell you one more thing, Archive lady. If you are serious about fighting the Andersons, the Astral Solace is home to many friends who have spent lifetimes in many professional expertise areas, and are now sitting on their hands playing retirement. If you ever need help with anything that will hurt the *bruta*, It'll be my pleasure."

I nodded my thanks and started toward the exit. Behind me I could hear Hugo Winkler sliding back into his energetic diva skin, wheeling between inksheets and complementing the elderly students in his charming, self-absorbed way.

"Lovely perspective, Yasmina," his voice trailed off behind me, echoing in the large hall, "you were very generous with my bodily dimensions here, bless you. Expect extra points in this assignment!"

A wave of good-hearted laughter rippled through the crowd, accompanying me out of the hall.

I stepped out of the low-hung building of the Astral Solace Home and into the open area of level 33. I could feel my unease grow as I kept playing Winkler's story in my head.

Something didn't sit right. I could feel it in my body — all my senses were tingling from a dissonance I could not yet articulate.

A woman was waiting for me at the Home exit area. I immediately recognized who she was — even though we had never met in person, her face would be familiar to virtually anyone on the Thetis.

Good, I thought. *This could be where actual answers start showing up. About kunye time for that.*

CHAPTER THIRTEEN

The woman sat cross-legged on a bench in the common area, her brown eyes locked on me. Slightly older than me — so a Gen7 Main Cycler — her shoulder-length dark-brown hair framed a confident face accentuated by full, plump lips. She wore a light, white blouse tucked perfectly into a formal blue skirt and had the authoritative poise of a woman who knew you'd approach her if she just sat there looking at you. I approached.

"You're Athena Saugado," I stated, a whiff of question in my voice.

"And you, dear sister, are about to get famous," she replied and handed me a stack of inksheets.

I eyed the package suspiciously, not sure what to make of it. Athena reached out and covered the top inksheet with her palm. "Take this somewhere private. It's the draft edition of the PubSheets that will go public tonight. I'm not supposed to share it with anyone."

I felt my mouth dry as I fumbled the thick stack. "How... How come you have access to the edition beforehand?" I mumbled.

Athena Saugado gave me a stern look. "One of the perks of being an electoral candidate for Primo. A perk that would be terminated if it became known that I am in the habit of sharing it with others."

I tucked the package under my arm. "Don't worry," I tried to assure her of my discretion. "What am I looking for here? And how come I am getting this personally from you? Aren't you super busy leading an election campaign right now?"

Athena's face softened a notch. "Look, my Genmom lives here now," she pointed toward the Astral Solace building. "So, if anyone checks the location grid logs later on, I have a plausible reason for being here. Soon, you'll have to consider these types of things too, unfortunately."

I shuddered. "Why? What's going on?"

Saugado stood up and straightened her skirt, using the motion to shoot a scanning look around her. "Read this through. Then meet me on Level 13. I am planned to attend my son's PoQer tournament in the main sports arena. We can talk there. I believe you may very soon be needing a friend."

I sat in the back room of the Main Archive office with the stack of inksheets in my lap, holding my head between my hands. My elbows were drilling holes into

my kneecaps. I was methodically taking in deep, full breaths, exhaling in long, slow hisses, trying to control the surging panic. It wasn't working.

What does she want from me? The thought kept pounding in my head. *Why me?*

Was this even the real draft of tonight's PubSheet edition, or just some kind of prank meant to scare me? I reluctantly flipped open the inksheet cover and started rescanning through the pages more thoroughly, carefully reading again every single word, looking for something, *anything*, to suggest this wasn't genuine.

The first items seemed predictably mundane. The Thetis may not be the most exciting place in the Universe, but the people of the Thetis were not dissimilar to people from other historically secluded communities. We had created quite a dense culture in the century and a half spent in space.

The frontsheet items concerned mainly with art and recreation: the opening standings in today's kickoff of the Thetis Grand PoQer Tournament. A new photography installation depicting an artist's view of the Sensory Farm re-landscaping work. An announcement for a live music show by some horrible singer the stupid Gen8ers adored.

It all seemed legit. Soon enough, the front page will be overtaken by news and announcements of the Gen9 baby boom. Birth Year occurred, after all, only once per generation.

Then came the section of nitpickery, bickering editor reviews of restaurants, artisan shops and garment pick-ups that were the meat of the daily PubSheet. Every *Fashionista* or *Cuisinier* would tremble before reading the latest edition, hoping the level of viciousness in describing their art would not prove fatal to their aspirations. It was a highbrowed blood-sport of sorts which could build a man's reputation — or ruin it forever.

There may not be commercial rewards on the Thetis, but there was *prestige*. And this is what gave the PubSheets their power and influence.

Which is why the item on the rear page of the inksheet draft I was reading was so conspicuously unusual.

'Officials Close to the Primo Reject Claims of Eternist Election Tampering'.

The headline stood out like an open wound amongst the positive and good-hearted news about art, food, science and culture. But the item's subsequent body of text was where things really hit close.

'Today, an official in the Anderson administration responded to concerns raised about the purity of the upcoming election process. According to sources close to the Primo's office, claims have been received that Eternist faction extremists are covertly planning to harm the democratic process of the elections. The Eternists are allegedly supported by high-ranking officials within the Thetis scientific and Archive institutions, with the alleged purpose of aiding the election of Primo contender Athena Saugado. Asked about it, the official declared these claims "unsubstantiated", denying any knowledge of foul play. "As we near the most significant moments in human history," said the official, "it is crucial that we stay united and not let extremists and defeatists set the agenda for our entire community."'

That was a *disaster*. An Eternist *extremist?* Me, who never had a single political bone in my entire body? Where the hell did this *come from?* Granted, The article didn't mention me or Dr. Almaz Bashiri by name, but Nyasha knew about our meeting. He knew about my doubts about the process with Sabi Anderson's deposition. He'd get the implied finger-pointing here in a second. *Will he believe it? Will he think I have anything to do with the Eternist faction and any alleged schemes against the Primo?* Come to think of it, I never *did* explain to Nyasha the circumstances behind me meeting Dr. Bashiri in the Sensory Farm. Nyasha being Nyasha, he was smart enough to circumvent the conversation around this pothole when I dropped on him in his hab in the middle of the night. *Was he still trying to protect me?*

I let the inksheet stack drop to the floor between my legs and caught my head again, rubbing both temples in a slow, circular motion. Once those PubSheets were published, I am most certainly *done for*. In a few hours, every main hall and public space on every level of the Thetis will display the new daily edition for everyone to read. My team in the Archive will make the connection to me instantly. Then others will, too.

This was bad, bad, *bad*.

CHAPTER FOURTEEN

Level 13 was crammed. I stormed out of the Head Archive office toward the recreation park, and had to immediately change pace to a near-crawl. Swarms of people were making their way to the arena, erected at the center of the sports grounds for the Annual Grand PoQer Tournament. People just loved this *bafunye* — I myself never saw the appeal in watching from a distance as someone else played their cards game.

As I carved my way through the crowd, I could easily distinguish the fans of each competing player by the colorful, team-branded garments and improvised signs they were carrying. The noise was deafening — whistles, tweeters and hornukas were blown to a lung-bursting volume, above which repetitive support songs were battle-shouted by competing fans. If I didn't know my physics better, I'd worry about the excessive sound wave pressure affecting the ship's trajectory in space.

The Grand PoQer Tournament would run for three days, in which the wild celebration would pretty much go on 24/7. After each round of competition, there would be parties. There would be feasts. There would also probably be numerous future Gen9 babies conceived. Thetans just loved those things, and frankly, who can blame them? We were all living the long pause in Human development until a new planet is conquered for our species to re-thrive in. Escaping the 'Eat, drink, and be merry, for tomorrow we die' mentality was not an easy feat on the Thetis. Not many 'Grand Purposes' flying around for one to adopt.

As for the tournament per se, maybe I'm just not the fan type. According to QUBIC, an earlier version of PoQer was vastly popular on pre-Embarkment Earth. But as affordable quantum computing became a commodity, many games played for millennia simply lost their appeal, becoming "solved" with a clear winning strategy. Physical sports and ball games persisted, of course — those were always more about the players than the game rules logic.

So new versions and evolved rules emerged for some popular games, making them harder to crack algorithmically. The now-standard 17-card PoQer was widely considered unsolvable even for the most powerful quantum arrays, and so it grew in popularity on the Thetis as the go-to fanboy choice. I had nothing against the game itself — it was the tournament setting that triggered my aversion to crowded spaces packed with sweating, hornuking, shouting wapas constantly rubbing against each other.

I ran up the short flight of stairs to the spectator platform, clutching the inksheets to my chest. *I need to get in front of this, fast.* There wasn't much time until the PubSheets daily edition would get distributed to all the levels. And I couldn't afford ignoring it, either. Couldn't afford another slap to my reputation. *Not with my past.*

Could Athena possibly straighten this out quietly with the PubSheet editor? She must have enough pull up there to explain the facts properly. After all, she was a candidate running for Primo against Sebastian Anderson. She got access to draft editions of the daily PubSheet. This could all still be avoided.

Athena greeted me with a cheerful smile. "Oh, you poor girl. You look terrified!" She set aside the elongated glass of sparkling wine she was holding and waved me over to sit beside her. I could feel the heat rising in my cheeks — *is this an amusing moment to her? Are we taking the final destruction of my social and professional status lightly?*

I slammed the stack of inksheets on the table in front of her, trying to balance my fury with an attempt to avoid attracting too much attention from the surrounding crowd.

"What kunye game are you playing here?" I hissed. "How do I know this bafunye is even *real*?"

"Oh it's real," Saugado studied me with steady eyes. "If it is proof you're seeking, all you have to do is wait for a couple hours until it's published. We can have our little talk then if you prefer."

"They can't publish those lies!" I protested a little too loud, attracting a few unwanted glances from the fans around us.

Athena maintained her stoic calm. "Can you point out a clear, explicit incorrect fact in the item? As far as I can tell, the text merely quotes an Anderson official stating publicly that there was *no tampering attempt identified*. How is that a lie?"

I waved my hands in frustration. "Oh, come on!" — If there's one thing you learn being born into a tiny generation where everyone knows each other, it's the gossip playbook. Chapter 1: If you want a rumor to fly, deny it.

"Effective, isn't it? I bet that'll gain some traction with your colleagues at the Archive, te?" she muttered sarcastically. Then her expression changed, as a hint of compassion seeped into her eyes. She picked up the ambery wine glass and sipped calmly. She cast a long glance around the arena, scanning the gathering crowd, until her eyes finally rested back on me.

"The good news," she said, "is that it's not an all-out personal attack on you. Yet."

"How can this not be an attack?" I burst out. "They are blaming 'a senior official in the Archive' with — practically, political *sabotage*! That's quite a direct offense in *my* book!"

Athena leaned forward, her face inches from mine. The amusement was gone from her expression. I was seeing the business-end of her political drive now.

"Listen. My teenage Gen8er son plays an amazing PoQer. May even win something tonight. Sabi Anderson doesn't — he never goes near anything that has the slightest element of chance in it. Anderson is all Chess. And I know Jericho Pakk for years. He doesn't make mistakes, everything is a plan within a plan with this guy. Publishing this item on the Grand PoQer Tournament opening night was not an oversight."

"Meaning?" I was baffled.

Athena's stiffness relaxed a notch. "Meaning, a corner item on the graveyard page of the PubSheet, on the night of the biggest celebration on the Thetis? That spells minus two-thirds of normal readership exposure — lousy way of getting something widely noticed, don't you think?"

Athena covered my hand with her palm gently. "Honey, relax. This is just seeding. It's not for today's readership. It's for the Archive database. You now have documented, time-verified breadcrumbs trailing you, so if and when an *actual* attack on you becomes necessary, evidence will show your subversion goes back a long way."

A feeling of complete deflation washed over me. "How can I kunye *relax*," I whispered. This felt like *Kilian* all over again — the feeling that the grip I had on the events in my life was becoming progressively slippery, the control over my fate incrementally feeble.

The crowd started cheering as the contestants marched into the arena. Saugado shot up from her seat, hands flailing at her son taking his place at the tournament table. *How could she be so complacent about this?* If my identity was at least partially masked, *she* was mentioned directly and explicitly in the article. But she didn't seem the least bit concerned. *Talk about politicians growing carboskin,* I thought.

Or, it's all a ruse. A lame fabrication meant to scare me into someone's corner. After all, those inksheets weren't crypsigned or verifiable to be legit. This so-called draft could literally be produced by anyone.

But why? That was the part I couldn't yet figure out. *What do I have to offer to anyone in this game?* And why would a Primo candidate try to drag me into such a thing? If, like Athena casually mentioned outside the Astral Solace Home, there was a friendship offering here, what could be the role I was expected to play in such an arrangement?

Athena Saugado descended back into her seat as the surrounding crowd settled down for the opening ceremony. Her deep brown eyes measured me top to bottom, assessing.

I had no time to waste. This was as public a setting as was possible on the Thetis. If she was playing some dubious ploy on me, the last thing I needed was to be spotted chumming up with the leader of the Eternist opposition right here in the open.

"Come clean with me, Mrs. Saugado," I said coldly. "What do you need from me?"

If my bluntness had offended her in any way, you wouldn't be able to tell it by her expression. *This woman is a rock.*

"So we still need to work on our trust, I gather," she said matter-of-factly.

"And why would I trust you?" I held her gaze, probing for the slightest sign of an emotional response. "You're the head of the kunye Eternists."

"No, I'm not."

I blinked in surprise. "What do yo mean, you're not? I've seen your Archive file. You're running for Primo as a representative of the Eternist faction —"

Athena raised her hand for pause. "Let's defer this point for a moment and assume you're correct. What does this term — 'Eternist' — mean to you?"

I broke her gaze and leaned back against the hard carboplast back of the arena's seat, calculating my response. I wasn't sure how smart it would be to turn this into an open confrontation.

"You people are cowards," I asserted. "Defeatists. You want us to abandon the Resett plan and keep the Thetis in space for eternity. You prefer that Humanity continue living out here rather than risk planetfall. Eternists are inherently opposed to the Thetis basic *cause.*"

Athena Saugado barked out a short laugh. "And so in your head, the spooky Eternist might have put up an entire show of faking PubSheet news items just to get your attention, trying to scare you into being recruited to our evil ranks."

It did sound pretty childish when you put it that way. But it still didn't mean it wasn't true. "You tell me," I blurted.

Athena's face drained of any hint of humor or amusement. She leaned forward in her seat, dead serious.

"No one in their right mind would be unequivocally in favor of keeping the Human species in space forever. What I *am* for, however, is transparent discussion."

Saugado again took my hand in hers, which was far too intimate and unsettling for my comfort level. Her eyes didn't let go of mine as she tried to drill her reasoning into me.

"Sandrine, look. You're a Senior Archivist. A woman of study, of knowledge. You must know this to be true — there are risks in every decision we choose to make. 9 Ceti could turn out to be a death trap, or it could be everything we hoped for. Choosing to skip it and spend two additional generations to reach Gnosis instead could give us more time for study and technology research, but would also mean we won't have enough power for any Plan C. And staying in space until we can ensure higher probability for success would initially be safer, sure, but you know that space travel is terribly sensitive to sudden, unforeseeable catastrophe. We're a floating single point of failure. The point is, the people of the Thetis should be *informed* about our collective options and considerations. We should be discussing this feverishly as we are nearing Final Call. Instead, we are amusing ourselves with music and sex and PoQer and, soon, baby fever, while Sabi Anderson decides our fate for us, based on who knows what."

"Leaving Earth had its risks too," I retorted. "The *passados* had the whole plan in place before Embarkment, and 9 Ceti Gamma was the best bet out of countless candidates studied for a *Century*!"

Athena smiled. "Have you read the Embarkment Certificate? And I mean the actual historical text, not the interpretations and suggested narrative the Anderson administration has entrenched into the school study materials."

It was my turn to smile. "It just so happens that I held the original Certificate at the Primo's office quite recently."

"Bravo," Athena said. "Then you are aware that there are absolutely zero mentions of either planets, or even planetary settlement at all for that matter, in the original definition of the Thetis mission, or as you called it — the *cause*."

I was momentarily taken aback, and tried to mentally pull up the text which I have long-ago memorized by heart.

She was actually right. "Well, technically," I said hesitantly, "the mission statement talks about the Thetis being sent on a mission to save the Human race and establish a new, fertile ground for our future generations to thrive on."

Athena Saugado nodded. "Exactly. So you see — 9 Ceti and Gnosis were just options as far as the Passados were concerned. They *knew* that they could never know enough about the conditions on those planets two centuries down the line and dictate the outcome of this journey. It was *always* up to us Thetans to decide our fate based on the available information at Final Call."

I shrugged. "Maybe people just trust Anderson to make the right decision for them."

"Of course they do!" Athena whisper-shouted, "that's what they've been conditioned for. Take a look around you, Arc. Liet —"

She circled her hand in a wide sweeping arc, gesturing toward the twenty thousand Thetans crowding the arena. The excitement was at its peak —people were cheering their throats out for their candidate, munching snacks and filling their game scoresheets.

"These amazing people are farmers, artisans and resource processors. They work hard and they raise their children and they've never been taught to demand a seat at the table, to be part of the decision process for their future."

"That's quite condescending," I said.

Athena waved away my remark. "I did not risk discussing this with you to placate you with political correctness. Just the honest truth. And that is, most people will gladly delegate the control over the big decisions in their life to an external authority. Back on Earth they may have called it God. On the Thetis they call it Anderson."

"Maybe you just want to take his place," I suggested.

"Of course I do," Saugado confirmed calmly. "But not for the obvious reasons. Scientists, academics, doctors, researchers — they all come to me. They all understand that we have a hugely complex decision in front of us, that we don't have nearly the level of data we need in order to make it, and that the public is kept out of the decision making process deliberately. By denying us this data, they're forcing us to adhere to the Primo's sole verdict."

"So it *is* a recruitment attempt," I said dryly.

And there it was — the first sign of emotion to emanate out of this woman. The specific emotion at hand was irritation.

"Can you state the exact time and date of Sebastian Anderson's initial complaint to the Archive regarding the attempted extortion?" she asked.

I didn't see that one coming. "I'm... not sure?"

The irritation was all but gone from her face. She was back in her calm shell. "I thought you were leading this case. That's pretty basic information, isn't it?"

"Yes, but I wasn't the one handling it at that point," I tried to save face. "Nyasha sent me to take the Primo's deposition, that's all. Anyhow, this would be privileged information."

"But I'm sure it would just be a quick fact-check for you to find out, ne? You don't have to disclose it to me if that's your concern."

Athena stood and picked up her half-empty wine glass. "Go check it out, will you? Don't worry, I'll be here long into the night at the pace my son is scoring down there."

I felt my cheeks reddening again. *So I'm running errands for her*

111

now?

Athena Saugado touched my shoulder briefly as she turned away to face the arena below us. "Good luck, Liet. You're about to take one step deeper into the gravity well."

CHAPTER FIFTEEN

Twenty minutes later, Athena was waiting for me just outside the Head Archive office.

"I know," she said, "I must stop stalking you outside of places. But PoQer isn't really my thing, truth be told. Since they quantum-proofed it with all those new rules and extended card decks, I can hardly follow the logic. Anyhow — you, my dear, are as pale as a lunar rock!"

She inched closer, and her light demeanor vanished.

"Let me guess — it wasn't there," she whispered.

"That's *impossible!*" I shot back in frustration.

Athena pressed her palms together. "Surprise, surprise."

"No, you don't understand!" I insisted. "The entire QUBIC dataset is in a public-ledger format. You *can't* delete old entries — it's technically impossible. All you can do is add new records on top — it's like this layer cake, you see?"

Athena slanted her head tentatively. She wasn't seeing it.

"Every time a new data record is added to the ledger, it gets encrypted together with all the historical records that precede it. So if you try and remove an older record — a lower layer in the cake — everything above it collapses. Meaning, all the records newer than the one you were trying to delete? They'd be gone! corrupted. And if anything like that happened, the Archive would have noticed it. And I just checked — everything works fine."

Athena didn't seem impressed with my conviction. "And yet — it wasn't there."

I nodded, my mind racing trying to figure out what the hell was going on. *What does this woman know that she isn't telling me?*

Saugado caught me eying her and immediately raised her hands in defense. "Hey. I have nothing to do with that. The reason I came to meet you is that I searched for this exact record myself, and came up empty-handed. At first I thought I was being smoked for political reasons. Or maybe I ran the wrong query. But then I saw the PubSheet draft I showed you with the cute quotes from the Primo's desk, and the dots connected."

"Which dots?" I almost screamed at her. "Which *kunye* dots connected for you?"

Athena didn't budge. "Not every day a formal case file evaporates from the main Archive, and a Senior Archivist is being targeted by the Thetis Primo and his *wapa* goons. You, my darling, are on to something, even if you don't realize it yet. Something that scares the *mala* out of Sabi Anderson. And that," Athena Saugado paused for effect, "piques my interest."

And then, a whole other set of dots connected for me too. "I can't be seen with you," I gasped and scanned our surroundings. "I'm an Archivist. I was trying to do my job. I keep the Code, I investigate, I sometimes get people to sign stuff. But if this is some political witch-hunt, I absolutely cannot afford getting dragged further into this. I can lose everything."

I turned to leave. "I'm sorry. I should go."

Athena reached out and grabbed my wrist. "And go *where*, Sandrine? Do you think you'll still have a job at the Archive tomorrow morning? That you can just ignore this away? If they can really manipulate the Archive database, that means all of us Thetans are being fed doctored data, tailored so that we'll support whatever

114

decision Sabi *wants* to sell us."

"I really can't help you. You're the politician. You obviously have friends in the PubSheets. *You* figure this mala out."

Saugado tightened her grip on my wrist. "Do you know why I'm running for Primo against Anderson?" she asked.

"Because Eternists love losing?" I suggested.

"I already told you that I am not an Eternist. And you know why? Its quite simple actually — because there's simply *no such thing*. We're not an organized group or a formal political faction. As I also explained — we don't even necessarily believe in staying in space. The word 'Eternists' itself is nothing but an Anderson invention — a myth, a catchy word, effective for labeling anyone with a different opinion than his. No, I am running because Sebastian Anderson has to be stopped. Things don't make sense. Data is missing. Tons of scientific research critical for Resett success has not been concluded yet. And Sabi is operating with an unclear agenda no one understands. We *can't* simply let him decide the entire fate of the Thetis without proper public discourse. Look at the people he surrounds himself with — brutes and imbeciles. They won't stand up to him!"

"His wife is a SinguLearn alumni. A brute, maybe, but hardly an imbecile."

Athena's face contorted. "Don't get me started on Cassidi, please Sandrine."

A shift in Athena's eye focus and attention prompted me to turn around. On the large wall next to the Main Archive office building, the wide frames of the large format digital ink boards flickered as the updated edition of the daily PubSheet downloaded and parsed. We locked eyes briefly, then walked in silence toward the dim, black-framed screens.

What we found there was beyond my worst nightmares.

'Primo Sebastian Anderson Mulls Investigation into Eternist Election Tampering'.

This was not the headline in the draft!

'Today, Primo Anderson responded to concerns raised regarding the purity of the upcoming election process. In the past few days, claims have been received that Eternist leader Mrs. Athena Saugado is involved in a covert plan to harm the Democratic process of the elections, supported by a senior officer of the Archive previously known to be close to subversive circles on the Thetis. Primo Anderson noted that "As we are nearing the most significant moment in Human history, it is important that we stay united and not let extremists and defeatists set the agenda for our entire community. I publicly call Mrs. Saugado to cease interference with the Thetis election process immediately." The Primo is yet "undecided" on the merit of launching an official investigation of the accused supporters.'

I couldn't believe what I was reading. My eyes teared up as I turned my head to Saugado.

"That wasn't the real PubSheet draft! You manipulated me. My name is practically in here." I said.

Athena was furious. Gone were the calm, fluttering gestures and attitude - she was *fuming*. "I was manipulated myself. I have underestimated the situation."

She held my shoulders and pushed me gently away from the PubSheet screen and around the corner to the Archive doorway.

"I was wrong, Sandrine, this is not seeding or an indirect 'Back Off' message. This is a full-on assault. Don't be seen with me — go to your hab, and stay there. I'll talk to Nyasha."

A trickle of people gathered around the PubSheet wall to read the latest update. Athena held my gaze with a worried expression.

"In Sol's name, girl — what have you dug up?"

Chapter Sixteen

I ran all the way up to 19, avoiding the Ascenders and other public areas of the ship. Every person I passed seemed to be staring at me. Maybe it was just the sight of a tall girl running up the spiral stairway. *Or, maybe they've all read it.*

When I reached the corridor leading to my hab, I braced myself for another ambush, ready to push my way through whoever tried to stand in my way. When, thankfully, no Pakk or any other goon emerged from the shadows, I quickly slammed the hab door behind me and secured the lock from inside.

At least I was home.

I crashed onto the bed thinking, *I need to sleep this nightmare off.* But with my heart pumping adrenaline and paranoia into my brain, that seemed like a distant possibility at best. Hesitating, I reached for the locked drawer in my bedside stand. That particular drawer hadn't been unlocked for almost a year now, and with good reason. *Just this one time,* I told myself. I wasn't going down *that* road again — not for Athena, not for my career, not for the *kunye fate of the Human race.*

Two MjölnirX pills later, drenched in sweat and still in my boots, I passed out.

A blink later, morning hammered me awake and I was puking my guts out in the toilet. *Nice reminder of why I keep this drawer locked.* I pushed myself back to my feet and washed my face with space-cold water. It helped soothe the drug sting a bit.

I started refocusing when something bright in the corner of my eye caught my attention. It was a note, slipped under my door during the night, lying on the carpeted floor, inkside down.

I approached cautiously. *An actual, hand-written note?* I thought. This was a gesture left for romantics or professional paranoids, people seeking the dramatic flare or the non-traceability of the Earthly pen and paper.

In this case, it was both. 'Morning!' the scribbling read. 'As per the latest publications in the esteemed Thetis mass media, it seems that you too have been Winklered! I hold in the highest respect my sisters and brothers in arms fighting against the mindset moulding machine, paying the ultimate price of eternal notoriety! If you are in need of a hug, or an actual serious advice on staying sane, drop by. I'm not planning any space-walking trips soon. Have fun! — Hugo'.

Contrary to objective reason, I couldn't help the burst of laughter gurgling its way up my stomach. Hugo Winkler and his note were like a ray of sunlight inside the Thetis — bright, warming and unexpected — and alarmingly indicative of a life-threatening hull breach.

A soft knock on my door slapped me back to reality. I immediately crumpled the note into my pocket and tiptoed closer to the door.

"Open up, Liet," Athena Saugado's voice whispered, "we need to talk."

I released the internal lock and she slipped inside, still dressed in her formal attire from the evening before. For a woman with her fashion perfection sense, this could only mean she kept working through the tournament night, which was worrying. She sat herself on the small couch in the main living area, cross-legged, studying my hab casually. I moved to close the door when a firm push reopened it widely, revealing Nyasha standing in the doorway. I couldn't help avoiding direct eye contact with him as he stepped inside the room and grabbed a chair from under my desk. In all of the seven years we have worked together, Nyasha never visited my hab, and this was probably the worst situation I could imagine for hosting him for the first time. I locked the door and sat on the bed, gazing at the petrol-blue carpeted floor.

"I will begin," Athena finally broke the silence.

Nyasha raised his hand to stop her. "No. It is only proper that I lead this mess."

He rubbed the bridge of his nose and pulled his glasses up on his head, then exchanged a questioning look with Athena.

"What?" I almost exploded with impatience. "Spit it out, then!"

"If a legal line is ever crossed by anyone," Nyasha started slowly, "the Archive must investigate, no VIP treatment. You understand this of course."

"Of course," I said cautiously.

Nyasha raised his eyes to meet mine. "Even if it is a senior member of the Archive itself."

My jaw almost dropped to the floor. "Wh— what?" was all I could manage.

Nyasha raised his hand again to calm me back down. "Throughout my career heading the Main Archive, I have had a very clear position on the values defining our policies on lawmaking and enforcement. My understanding was that we are living in a very unique condition — for perhaps the first time in Human history, our society is not shaped to encourage growth and prosperity, but rather to support preservation. This crucial need for unity and stability required compromises and political flexibility on behalf of the greater mission."

Now I *was* worried — Nyasha was circling the ring, which meant a punch was coming. *And isn't 'Unity and Stability' Anderson's election slogan?* I hugged my knees and waited for the sting.

"But some lines simply cannot be crossed," Nyasha continued. "And one such line is the Archive database. We simply cannot tolerate any manipulation of the single most important body of knowledge and the major decision-making resource at our disposal. If what Athena has brought to my attention is indeed true —" Nyasha gestured toward Saugado and a serious look passed between them, "— and Sabi Anderson is somehow re-editing Archive entries on the public ledger, I will have no choice in the matter. Even though we are at an extremely delicate moment where decisions unparalleled in their importance to our future have to be made. Even though we are on the verge of a general elections for Primo. If this information is valid, the Code requires me to issue a formal investigation."

Athena leaned forward on the couch. "The problem is, you too have conducted some non-commissioned digging in the QUBIC database and elsewhere. Cassidi, PHS, Bashiri — all the wrong topics for this matter."

"It thought my private query history was actually, you know, *private*," I said.

No, it wasn't, stupid. Of course — just as with the location markers in the Sensory Farm, it seemed that access to personal data was one of those political flexibilities we now apparently tolerated on the Thetis. In good times, extreme transparency was an effective way to ensure stability. In turbulent times, its creepy nature quickly overshadowed those benefits.

Athena Saugado frowned. "If things get serious with Anderson, you can bet this will come out. And it will play right into their hands. They will claim political persecution, unjust process by the Archive, a personal vendetta — you name it. They will *drown* the investigation with this mala until it's tainted beyond any ability to reach a publicly accepted conclusion."

"So I won't get near this case," I offered. "Nyasha can lead it with other team members in the Archive. This will only be appropriate, ne?"

Nyasha and Athena exchanged looks again. "Nyasha can't touch this," said Athena. "Not without digging up a pile of skeletons you don't want walking around the Thetis. Not without proof. Perma-kunye-steel proof. That's what you should focus on, Sandrine."

I retracted and pulled my legs up on the bed, boots still on. "No way," I said. "My name is practically on the kunye PubSheets. I already told you at the arena — count me out."

Nyasha leaned forward on the chair, elbows rested on his knees. His fingers plowed absent-mindedly through his short curly hair in a distracting, repetitive motion. He didn't seem to have heard my reply nor accept my clearly stated position on the matter.

"We are fully aware what a daunting ask this is of you. You're young. No Genline. I am not naive, Sandrine — going against the Primo could spin up an ugly fight. Yesterday's PubSheet was a mere teaser. There will be dirt — lots of it, and your reputation will suffer, yes. But you know better than anyone — I cannot move an inch without solid, undisputed evidence."

"I don't give a qubit's ass about reputation, Nyasha," I said. "That's for the popular kids to worry about. All I care about is my Genline."

I turned my head to Athena. "I've already messed up this coming Birth Year. But I still have a chance — Generation 10 is only a few years away. I can't risk this over politics. Can't risk not being a mother. You should understand me."

Athena tensed. She was ready to spring from her sofa, but Nyasha gestured for her to back off.

"Sadly," Nyasha sighed, "we have to consider that if the suspicions about Sebastian Anderson have merit — if his administration is tampering with Archive data to influence the Final Call decision — then *all* our Genlines may be at risk. We haven't come this far from Earth to fail due to lack of determination to enforce a clean process."

"Don't forget I am running for Primo," Athena added. "That doesn't mean I can assure full protection, but I can provide cover. I have my own outlets in the media, and I won't let Sabi drown the people with his narrative. He needs to be stopped, Sandrine. Or we will all be slaves to his hidden agendas."

"Then why me?" I resisted. "Just get some other Archivist to dig into whatever you need."

"I can't!" Nyasha cracked. Small beads of sweat clung to his forehead. "For one, I don't trust anyone outside of this room with this information. But more importantly, you're the only one who can get us the evidence we need."

Nyasha's voice softened, and his eyes glistened with remorse. "Sandrine, you know I love you like a daughter. It breaks my heart to put you in this position. And you can still say no — at this point, the PubSheets are only a slight inconvenience. Walk away, and Anderson will lose interest in you. You're smart, you'll find another job, stay low, grow a family. But here's the honest truth — without you, we have no chance. There's only one man in the entire Thetis who has the knowledge and skills needed to identify a breach into the QUBIC ledger. Unfortunately, he won't cooperate and I can't summon him since this is not part of a formal case yet so I have no jurisdiction over him. Chicken and egg, as the *Passados* used to say. We believe you're the only person who may have influence on him."

I felt the blood draining from my face. "Oh no—"

Nyasha nodded slowly. "I'm afraid so. We need you to get Kilian Ngo."

PART TWO

CHAPTER SEVENTEEN

This is just crazy, I thought as I walked around the ship, taking the longest route possible to Level 25. *Kilian will never talk to me — that was made quite clear in our last conversation almost a year ago, when he expressed he no longer wanted anything to do with me.* I'd be surprised if he'd even open the door.

And what was Athena's angle here anyway? As a political rival to Sabi, any attack coming from her would just be seen as an election play. But an official investigation by the Archive would give it legitimacy, as long as she stayed behind the scenes. She was the one to gain from forcing Anderson to run a campaign under legal suspicion, I could see that — but why was Nyasha so eager to cooperate with her on this? My logic reasoned that if it came to prosecuting Sabi, I was the ideal operator for him: my rank as Senior Archivist made me a suitable choice to lead the case, I had no history or political allegiance with Anderson or Athena, and I was smart enough to actually get results in the investigation should it lead to anything of substance. Sending me to take Anderson's deposition and having my name crypsigned on the related documentation would tie me into the case and allow Nyasha to stay officially unattached.

Nyasha would never be so utilitarian — not with me, I thought. There was a long history between us, back to when my father was still alive. Nyasha Woo was probably the only living person on the Thetis I could

125

trust with no reserve.

I stepped off the Ascender at the maintenance terminal of Level 25. Better to stick with less crowded areas for now, at least until the effect of the PubSheet item cooled off. I really couldn't deal with any further exposure and I didn't mind the extra travel time.

Ironically, Level 25 seemed even more quiet at this time of morning than it was in the middle of the night. This must be the most boring part of the Thetis — identical family habs efficiently clustered in flower-shaped arrangements, harmoniously baking in the silence of the artificial light cycles and napping mothers. *Kilian sure has mellowed down to be living here*, I thought. *After our party-crib on 19*.

I started walking toward the hab circles. The brownish pathways were covered with granulated polyflex, which I guess was meant to protect playing children and strolling elders from injuries in case of a fall. The comfy-bouncy feeling of each step was getting on my nerves, as were the repetitive patterns of carbofoam pseudo-trees decorating every corner of the level in a lame effort to instill a calming, friendly environment. I guess I was still under the influence of my visit to the Sensory Farm, because everything around me just seemed depressingly *fake*.

Suddenly, I remembered Athena's advice back at the Astral Solace Home. This was not the Sensory Farm — location grid trackers were registering my presence here on 25. Visiting the Ngo hab will just tie me further into any conspiracy theory Sabi's troops will try to involve me in. There's no plausible reason for me to even get *near* Kilian, and I am not on any official Archive task either.

I threw my hands up in frustration — every move I made, every query I ran, every kunye breath I took was aggregated and logged somewhere. I was drowning in a quicksand of data I couldn't control, feeding a narrative I couldn't influence.

I started running off the pathway and across the level to the Nyasha's hab circle. I wasn't sure how frequently the location trackers registered each Thetan's position in the ship, but it most likely wasn't every minute — after all, this wasn't mission-critical information requiring real-time data streams. So, I'd hang around Nyasha's hab for a few minutes — registering there could be easily explained and Nyasha would back me up on this. Then I'll make a run for it to Kilian's, in and out, hoping to make it back before the next tracking ping.

I was calming down my panting as I knocked impatiently on Kilian's hab door. *Settle down, Sandrine,* I commanded myself. *Be cool.*

Soft steps approached from the other side. The door slid open and a long, honey-haired young woman appeared in the doorway, leaning against the doorframe. She was wearing a bright, silky-smooth robe which struck me as a bit intimate for this time of day. She was gorgeous. I knew her.

"You're Heleni," I said.

"I know you," she said. "From school. We're both Gen7 2nders." She started reaching out for a handshake, then realized midway it was probably not that appropriate and retracted slowly. "You're Kilian's former—"

"Yes. So is he in?"

Heleni's shoulders tensed. She folded her hands below her small, perfect breasts. "No, actually he isn't."

I peeked over her shoulder to the inside of the hab. The entire living area was decorated with fashionable, soulless furniture. Not a trace of Kilian's bell-drums and wild artistic taste. I sighed quietly — you can always tell who is the controlling half of a couple by the internal design of their home. The first thing the weaker part is surrendering is personal identity.

Heleni saw the look on my face. "Is there a problem?"

"Sorry, I just could never imagine Kilian settling down in a place like 25," I said. "He used to say this is the place old Genners and sexless souls come to wither. You must have a very... calming influence on him."

Heleni's shoulders stiffened, then relaxed as an invisible smile appeared in the corner of her red mouth. She switched her weight to the other leg, the motion accentuating the small belly-bump underneath her folded arms.

"Maybe we're planning a family," she said.

Ah, bruta. A cramp in my lower stomach stabbed me as I fought the instinct to punch the smile off her smug face. *Get it together, Sandrine.* I forced the best impression of an unaffected smile I could muster.

"Embark and Prosper. Now, I need to speak to Kilian. This is official Archive business," I lied.

Heleni shrugged. "Like I said — he isn't here. He's at the Nebula on 19. They're having the Alternative History Party today — isn't it a tradition you two started back then, holding it on the day after the GPT tournament?"

Kunye mala, of course. How could I forget?

I stuck my hands into my pockets and turned to leave. "You do realize that 'GPT' already includes the word 'tournament' in it? 'GPT tournament' is duplicative."

Heleni's smile widened into a whole-hearted laugh. "You were always so smart, Sandrine." She corrected the wrapping of the shiny robe around her curvy waist. "I bet men find it such an attractive feature in you, ne?"

As the door slid shut, I could still imagine hearing her laughter echoing behind the nanofoam seal.

CHAPTER EIGHTEEN

I took the main Ascender back down to 19. I didn't care anymore about getting noticed, being recognized or what any wapa on this ship was or might be thinking about me. I mean, I *knew* that Kilian was seeing someone — people are all too generous in delivering such bits of information to you when you're heart-broken, aren't they? — But I never imagined he'd be back on the Birth Year roster so quickly.

How was this even possible? If anything, *I* was the one who did the right thing and *he* was the one who broke the Thetis Code, exposed of being an illegal Adapter! Even legally-speaking, how come I was skipped on Birth Year and he was genlining with that *bruta?*

My head was spinning. I got off on Level 19 and sat on a bench near the platform to straighten my thoughts. I couldn't go meet Kilian like this — *that was a mistake,* I thought. *I should have never agreed to do it.* Nyasha and Athena can take care of themselves. I was humiliated enough in the past 48 hours, and meeting Kilian now after so many months would be the ultimate blow. Hell, I was still in the same outfit and boots since yesterday. After *sleeping* in them. My hab was less than five minutes walk from the Ascender platform — the least I could do is go home, wash up and think this over with a clear head, ne?

"Looking good, Liet!" a familiar voice came from behind me. "Where d'*you* come from? Level 1 radioactive dumps? Seriously, you look like something a black hole spat out."

In Sol's name, the *last* person I needed to bump into right now was Kunye Zee Anderson.

"Hello, Sam," I muttered in as offputtish tone as I could muster. *Which he wouldn't take as a hint. He never does.* "I appreciate the expert opinion, especially from someone who got spat out of the Academy — *twice,* wasn't it? — until his Daddy shoved him back into their unwilling throat."

My rant was met with two girlish giggles. I raised my eyes and was surprised to find Zee accompanied by two *very* young, *very* scantily-dressed teenage Gen8ers, one on each of his sides.

"Aren't you a bit young to be undressed like that?" I eyed the girls bottom-to-top, then turned to look at Zee. "You're down to kindergarten-scavenging now, Sam?"

The girls giggled again. The smug smile on Zee's face didn't flicker, but his eyes said *piss off.*

"Academy isn't fun, is it girls?" His puffed-up smirk returned, "but you know what *is* fun? I am taking my two new *gorginiahs* friends here —" he swung his hands over each of the girls and pressed their torsos against his hip, "— to do their first sludging!"

Both Gen8ers uttered juvenile excitement noises. I shook my head and sighed. "You're going for your maiden sludging with *this* guy?"

Both girls exchanged looks. "Te," retorted the shorter, cheekier one of the pair, "anything wrong with that, *mom?*"

"Yeah," said the other girl, "it's going to be absolutely *radiant!*"

"OK," I shrugged and raised my palms in defense. *Very little use in trying to talk sense into hormone-pumped Gen8 17-year-olds on the brink of sexual adventure, te?* "Just remember — memory-suppression pills are your friend. May want to set yourselves up with a pack or two come tomorrow morning."

"Very funny, Liet," Sam Anderson intervened, trying to save the vibe he had worked hard to build with both girls from dwindling. "We may even drop by your thing in the Nebula later on, if the girls happen to have any energy left in them, which I doubt," he winked to the short, cheeky one. Shockingly, she giggled.

"It's not *my* thing,"I grunted.

"Really? Wasn't it you and that guy who started this a while back? That hacker guy?"

"Not really," I lied.

Zee locked his eyes on mine, his smile showing more teeth as he regained his confidence. Like every insecure kid in history with a touch of cruelty in him, Zee could instantly spot an opponent's weak point. He could literally *sniff* out any vulnerability he could potentially exploit.

And when he found your wound, you knew he'll be pressing it.

"Oh, it wasn't?" Zee stretched back, relaxed in his zone. His arms asserted possession over the two poor teenagers whom he had somehow led to believe were the rare, lucky winners of the prize that was his sexual attention.

"My bad, then," he continued, smugness creeping back into his too-wide-a-smile. "It's so sad, really. I mean, the man used to be *someone*, right? Unique technical talent. Could've been Head of Quantum by now, and now he's a nothing but lowlife puppet. Working the fields, running errands for the Administration. An entertainer."

"Kilian's an artist, not an entertainer," I protested meekly.

"I fail to see the difference. Same purpose as everything else on this can — just pass the time till our children reach planetfall, ne?"

I had zero desire nor patience to get into existential musings with Kunye Zee Anderson, so I just nodded my head noncommittally, hoping he would let it go.

"Well," Zee leaned closer and dropped his voice to a whisper, "at least I hear Kilian's making progress in the children department with some new girl, isn't he? Being a puppet has its benefits, I guess — you might get lucky enough to get a King's hand up your butt."

Zee stood up and smiled triumphantly at his young escorts. "My late grandfather had a saying: 'For there to be King, tha'll ought be slaves.' I guess *someone* has to play the slave part, ne?"

A wave of deep exhaustion washed over me. "Go away, Sam," I planted my head between my hands, examining the scratches running across the nanoplast flooring. I could hear him mock a sigh above me. He wasn't about to let go.

"He reminds me a lot of you, Sandrine. So, *so* smart. And, without fail, making *all* the wrong life choices. So ultimately — so, so stupid."

I raised my head abruptly, surprised by how close to home that remark hit. "Remind me," I hissed, "what exactly is *your* actual contribution, beyond being the privileged, spoiled son of the Thetis Primo?"

Zee shot a proud, winning smile toward both girls latched onto his sides. "Why, I am an educator of the younger generation of course! *Someone* must carry the burden of initiating those fine, avid young women into the Thetis culture, ne?"

"Mercy on their poor souls," I shook my head.

"Ahh, that's not very nice of you now is it, Liet? Maybe I should take *you* sludging sometime — build some trust between us. Work on our chemistry, yes?"

I grimaced expressively. "Ooh, did the Thetis just go into zero-G, or is it the food in my stomach pushing up to a vomit from that mental image?"

Both Gen8ers burst out with a laugh. Zee's face hardened.

"Ha ha. OK, Liet. Stay off the PubSheets," he muttered and turned away down the pathway, pulling his giggling fan flock beside him.

"Kunyete," I whispered and flipped my little finger at his receding back. "You and your royal Genline." *Soon, we'll find out who's spat out of a black hole and who's the one falling into it.*

*　*　*

Why I let Kunye Zee Anderson invade my mind with that whole sludging ordeal was beyond me. But there I was, trying to take the longest route possible to the Nebula Club, telling myself that each passing minute carried a minuscule — yet accumulating — probability of an extinction-level cosmic event that would elegantly prevent the encounter with Kilian. And so, I was actually being smart in maximizing my chances by dragging things out. And all the while, my mind kept going back to my own maiden immersion with Kilian in the sludge.

Despite its somewhat repulsive nickname, sludging, if done with the right partner, could be a profound physical, emotional, even *spiritual* experience. Done with the *wrong* person, however, could be acutely terrifying.

I never even heard of the thing until Kilian — always in the know of new experimental ideas brewing in the obscure backlots of the Thetis — barged into my hab one chilly afternoon. He was all jacked-up, *insisting* that we must try this new scientific phenomenon conjured down at 14th by several of his friends. And it had to be right then and there, apparently, so I just grabbed my scarf and hurried out, trying to keep up with him down five levels of the main stairwell.

In the years since, the sludging facility had gotten itself a nice little permanent corner on 19th: proper construction, cozy atmosphere and an inviting arrangement of warm lighting and incense aromas which contributed to the popularity of the activity. But when we set foot inside the seemingly-deserted Level 14 chemical workshop on that first afternoon, all we were greeted by was a grim, semi-dark lab room, dense with the odors of fermenting concoctions. Various-sized crates and containers lined the walls, creating space for a large, bath-shaped tank in the center of the floor, occupying most of the remaining space.

The entire facility was still and quiet. I looked around casually, scanning for any clue as to what I should be expecting here.

"Are we waiting for someone, K?" I asked finally.

"Oh, no, no. Everyone's out for the day. I got some friends contribbing here to prepare it for us so we can do this in privacy. That's the whole point, San."

"What is?"

'This." Kilian pointed to the large tank. It was a flat, rectangular container about waist-high, big enough to fit several people. The tank was almost filled to the brim with a pinkish-brownish substance that looked both thick and liquid simultaneously, tiny ripple lines vibrating on its surface.

Seeing my uncomprehending expression, Kilian smiled.

"Take your clothes off."

"Wait," I said, "you don't mean—"

He nodded eagerly. "And get in."

"Are you kunye crazy? I'm not getting into that thing! What is this pink goo anyway?"

Kilian's smile just broadened. "Nothing like anything else you've ever experienced."

I held his gaze, studying his steady, golden eyes intently for a few moments. The problem, I told myself, was that I just trusted this guy to the bone. It was so easy being adventurous with Kilian — anything felt safe to try when he was around.

"Turn around," I said quietly.

"Kunyete," Kilian burst out laughing, our eyes still locked. "I'm not turning anywhere. I'm going to stand right here and adore you."

I dropped my clothes to the floor. His eyes quivered. He was a man. And he was excited by me — real, deep excitement arching from the deepest corner of my soul to the tips and toes of my body. Which, at that time, was all I ever wanted from life.

"Now," Kilian dragged in a low crate and positioned it at the tank's side, "climb in. Very, very slowly."

"Are you planning to drown me in this pink goo and get rid of my body?" I tried a nervous joke as I lifted one leg over the edge of the tank.

"Shhh," Kilian took my hand and gently guided me forward, "you'll see. You'll see."

To this day, I have a clear sensory recollection of the crisp, visceral sensation of sliding into the material in the tank.

Externally, the feeling was of very slowly sinking into a heavy, thick, plasma-like material, its consistency so dense that it wasn't actually sinking — it was more like *floating down* into the tank, the pinkish dough-like material slowly engulfing my naked body, inch by silent inch.

Internally, though, it felt surprisingly like... *nothing*. While the intense feeling of being enveloped was distinctly present, the actual sensory inputs my body was responding to were essentially nonexistent. I couldn't tell if the material was wet or dry, cold or hot. It was even hard to tell whether I was moving inside the goo or not — even the gravity directional sense was thrown off by this strange stuff.

With only my head sticking out of the tank, trying to make sense of what was going on, I raised my eyes in question to Kilian.

He moved closer and kneeled beside my ear. "NanoClay. Well, actually it's a form of polysilicate, formed into extremely tiny globules which, when acting together in a sufficiently large number, spark up a set of very interesting features. Take your hand, and *very* slowly raise it out."

I lifted my left hand inside the material. The movement was very slow — it didn't take force nor did I feel any resistance, it was more like there was a natural limit to the speed at which things could move within the thick substance. Finally, my arm emerged through the surface and hung in the air. Kilian took it gently and planted a small kiss on the back of my hand.

"The first cool feature of this sludge is that those NanoClay globules don't bond to anything. It's an exorepellent."

I examined my left arm closely and indeed — it came out of the material completely clean, no moisture or any residue of the pinkish clay caught in the cracks of my skin or underneath my fingernails. Even the fine hairs on my arm where completely dry, as if nothing has ever touched them at all.

"This is… *weird*", I said.

Kilian smiled. "It doesn't absorb anything, it can't get contaminated. In fact — it doesn't really *touch* you at all, just kind of floats around you."

I let my arm slowly sink back into the bath, watching in amusement as the material swallowed it without triggering any sense of touch whatsoever.

"The second feature of this material is a bit more intense," Kilian said, straightening up on his knees above me. "Don't freak out."

Before I could react, he raised both hands high above his head, interlocked his fingers into a tight double fist, and hurled it down with all his might in a massive blow toward my immersed body.

I freaked out.

And just as his fist broke the surface of the material and my body instinctively jerked, anticipating the blow — the entire tank of NanoClay instantaneously solidified. In what seemed like a mere microsecond, the amorphous plasma hardened around me, trapping me inside it.

I freaked out some more. Then I yelled.

"Kilian! Get me out of here! What's going on? Get me *out!*"

Every sense in my body screamed with claustrophobic terror. Every inch of every limb in my body was firing in desperate stress — it was like being cast in iron, buried alive within the solid chunk of mass, unable to move a muscle with only my head sticking out to witness the horror.

I shot a glance in Kilian's direction — his hands were caught in the solid material, both fists buried and trapped below the surface. Strangely, he was completely calm.

"The second feature of those polysilicate globules is that they exist in a non-Newtonian liquid state," he explained. "Any sudden movement or force exerted on them, any abrupt compression — and they undergo instantaneous solidification."

Then, with a very slow and measured movement, Kilian started pulling both hands out of the material.

"The trick is to relax. Minimize every movement, and it turns back to its soft form."

Inch by inch his palms slid out, leaving only a quickly-fading ripple of brownish-pink goo where his fists where buried just moments before. Like my hand before, they came out completely unscathed and dry.

"No sudden movements, got it," I tried to control my panicked breathing. "But what's the actual point of this sludge, K? Why am I in this thing, afraid to move a finger?"

Kilian lay flat on his stomach atop the rigid surface, his face touching mine. It was just then I noticed that somewhere in the process his clothes had gone off too. We were both completely naked, me inside the NanoClay and he on top of it.

"What had been the point, the use and the reason for every Human invention since the beginning of time, San?" He whispered and gave me his sly-Kilian look I knew meant nothing but trouble. "Why, for having sex, of course."

His body started slowly sinking into the goo, a trillion tiny pinkish globules making way for our bodies to float closer.

Our eyes locked. "Why did I suspect this was where this was going from the moment you snatched me out of my cozy hab?" I purred as I felt his body gradually pressing against mine, finally uniting. A small shudder of excitement went through me, triggering a wave of solidification around us. I let out a gasp of surprise. Kilian didn't budge, his eyes buried deep in mine.

"Close your eyes, Sandrine. I love you. Just let go."

What followed was indescribably dreamy. Occasionally, one of us would instinctively jerk or spasm, setting off an instantaneous solid lock around us that would take us keeping perfectly still to release. The rigid restrictions enforced by this very weird material we were immersed in dictated a very narrow set of movements conducted in an ethereal state of slow-motion.

But as we found our rhythm — slow, almost imperceptible motion, two bodies floating in tandem in round, patient movements, with no external sensory distractions except the sparks created by our unison — true spiritual revelation awaited us.

It was like making love in a cloud. It was like making love in outer space. It was like floating in an entire universe made of cotton candy feeling loved and embraced and engulfed in radiating emotions of gratitude and compassion and lust.

We floated in that tank together in what must have been an entire lifetime, and when I came out of it I was like a woman coming out of childbirth — all recollection of the physical pain and the terror of being trapped totally repressed, leaving a permanent, vivid imprint of the bliss I have experienced inside.

Sludging, naturally, very quickly became a highly popular pastime. And with the new Gen8ers entering the Thetis social scene, I imagined it would star in many a coming-of-age memory of the young generation. As for myself — some memories should remain pure, te? I've never gone sludging with anyone else. I doubted the novelty or the sensuality could be recreated sans the emotional trust factor.

Which was something I had worked hard to avoid confronting, maintaining physical distance between me and that past life in hope that emotional distance would follow.

A distance that was about to be swiftly broken as I, having eventually exhausted all possible escape-routes, found myself right in front of the Nebula Club's entrance, trembling.

CHAPTER NINETEEN

The noise inside the Nebula Club was ear-blasting, which was a welcome change after the eerie desolation of Level 25 and the memory-buzz of my own mind.

Ah, the Nebula! Despite myself, an instinctive smile crept its way to my face. This shapeshifter of a place took on many forms throughout the years, each generation imposing its own trends and tastes on the design and atmosphere of the place. The result was an eclectic, undefinable mish-mash of styles which somehow felt precisely on-point and always chic. In short, the Nebula was a bona fide institution.

I walked into the all-too-familiar entrance hall as if I were in my own hab — I've spent so much of my early twenties in this place, I could probably navigate to the bar and mix myself a Neutron Cluster blindfolded. The Nebula was always full, always dense, this time of day or late at night — 'There's a Shift for Every Affliction' was the Nebula's famous motto.

The current motif of fluorescent colors and decorative, Baroquish-style ornaments reflected the latest, up-to-date design trends on the Thetis. Ornate sofas and huge, wall-wide mirrors framed in complex decorative patterns filled the large hall. The low light was welcoming and friendly, and people filled the place in groups circled around low-standing tables — drinking, laughing and moving to the live stage music. The Nebula was the place people came to when they needed to vent.

This is such a delicate situation, I thought. Hurtling through space for centuries, confined inside a sealed bullet with no fresh air or sunlight or just the plain ability to take a break, make a change. *It's places like this we need to thank for us not being at each other's throat.* Kunye *Passados,* they sure thought things through before kicking us off their planet.

I closed my eyes and listened to the music for a few moments. The band was a group of Gen7ers famous for their acoustic reconstruction of late-Earth instruments. They were *good* — the low whistle of the monotune, mixed with the warm roundness of the silver dumbelines blended beautifully together to create a throbbing, majestic atmosphere.

Noticeably cheered up, I could feel the confidence slowly building inside me for what would come next.

All around the Nebula's main hall, the lights started to dim. A wave of pulsating, repetitive ultrasub baseline started swelling from the main stage, sending ripples of physical vibrations across the room. An additional pair of musicians appeared on stage, collaborating flawlessly on a set of striangulars, their bright-resonance pinch elevating the harmony of the moment as the Nebula dipped into total darkness. *Nice touch, K,* I thought. I leaned my shoulders against the back wall and enjoyed the all-encompassing blackness — never being the one to blend-in easily in crowds, I welcomed any opportunity for hiding in public. Especially today.

Suddenly, the Nebula's walls came to life — blinding white beams traced lines across the large space, projecting a large, bright square on each wall. The crowd cheered over the deafening music — they all knew what was coming next. A hint of pride rose within me. AltHis Night was, after all, partly my creation, even if it did feel like it belonged to another, ancient life.

The Alternative History Night opening sequence was by now a tradition: the live band erupted with a forceful, heroic theme, accompanying the huge wall projections displaying a montage of opening sequences from Old Earth science fiction teleshows. It was the grand tour of Humanity's depiction of its imagined future beyond Earth. There were space battles and laser cannons, warp speeds and wormhole travel, super intelligent androids and interplanetary empires. In those shows, spacecrafts of all kinds and sizes filled the black sky, crewed by men and women in tight uniform, ready to boldly conquer the galaxy in the name of the Human Race.

This *mala* was hilarious! Those shows were such a campy and corny entertainment for us, that an entire subculture of fans evolved around them on the Thetis.

If only those Earthers had known the real circumstances that would drive Humans off their home planet, I thought. The irony was precisely why AltHis night worked.

And as if our minds were entangled, the opening sequence video faded out, the lights on the main stage grew to a bright yellow flood, and there he was.

"Greetings, spacers!" Kilian's voice echoed around the packed hall. "Are you feeling like galactic heroes tonight?"

"No!" came the crowd's response, followed by clanking drinks and semi-drunk laughs from the surrounding tables.

"Of course you don't," Kilian smiled to the crowd from the stage, his shaved head and angular cheekbones shining in the strong spotlights. "There are no space crusaders in this room tonight, ne? No Imperial fleet admirals, no interstellar bounty hunters. Not even 3-breasted whores on their way to service rich wapas in a distant spaceport. Although if you do possess a decent pair, my hab is always open for you after the show."

A wave of laughter rose from the drinking crowd. Despite myself, I couldn't suppress a little smile too. Kilian was pure talent in almost everything he touched.

'Almost' being the crucial word here, I thought.

"No, what I see before me today, ladies and gentlemen of the esteemed Thetis trash can, are a bunch of miserable refugees, kicked off their planet fifty eight light years back with the sole hope that you'll manage to not disintegrate along the way. They didn't give you a steering wheel or a reason to believe some random space dust won't shred you to atoms, but they sure did leave a lot of loose threads for us to bust our asses trying to solve along the way, haven't they?"

High on the pathos juice tonight, eh, K? I thought. But the crowd was cheering. They all loved the drama and Kilian was providing.

The projectors went back on in preparation for the next queue of videos. Kilian stepped forward to the lip of the stage, scanning the crowd. Instinctively, I shrunk deeper into the shadows of my corner.

"We have a special night this year, people! First, I see a number of Gen8ers who are finally old enough to be joining us tonight for the first time. Welcome aboard, kids, go easy on the booze, and don't forget — you throw up, you clean up. Also this year is Birth Year!"

A thunder of cheerful clapping and whistling erupted from many tables around the room. Kilian raised his hand to calm their enthusiasm.

"Yes, most of the faces I see here tonight are of the Gen7 cycles, so many of you soon-to-be hot GenMoms will be taking part in the making of a new generation! Now don't congratulate yourselves too much, ladies and gentlemen — making the babies is all the fun, *raising* the babies is something completely different. Or so I'm told."

Some good-hearted slurs were thrown at Kilian from various females in the crowd. I couldn't shake the image of Heleni and the perfect, soft baby bump peeking out of her open robe from my mind.

"OK," Kilian drew to a close, "We started this tradition ten years ago, and we have a great evening for you tonight with some new shows we dug up. This *could* have been our future, so let's enjoy the road not taken. Have fun and don't forget—"

The crowd knew the closing line by heart, and they all joined in roaring. "— You're nothing but genetic load. They could have just sent the tubes!"

Kilian bowed, and as the lights faded out on the main stage the band broke into loud, ecstatic dance music and the main lobby space quickly filled with moving bodies. After the music and the dance party, I knew, the evening would continue with continuous screening of episodes and longvids on the main walls and in designated rooms within the Nebula, curated by genre and decade of origin on Earth. And then the evening would reach my all-time favorite finale — the AltHis famous Scifi-themed costume party.

I straightened up and started plowing my way through the crowd toward the main stage. Kilian will be at the lounge area just behind the bar, where we all used to toast the traditional cup to the success of the party.

Sol, has it been ten years already? I thought. The whole thing started so small, almost an internal joke between friends. *How naive I was back then.* I was young — just turned 18, it was my first week in the Archive, and I was immediately overwhelmed with this brilliant, outspoken — explicit, at times — QIT technician. He seemingly understood QUBIC's quantum logic inside-out, and he was funny and he spoke his mind around Nyasha without any filtering whatsoever, and I was hooked.

Beware the extrovert, I thought as I dodged a splash of drink spilled by someone around me. I didn't know what Kilian saw in me, but I quickly started to join him in social meetings with his Gen7 group, made exciting new friends and engaged with him in various cultural gatherings with new and interesting people I have never known before. I was on cluster nine.

It was the stupid party challenge that eventually led to the creation of this whole thing.

I was advancing through my Archive training cycles, when I encountered various sealed parts of the QUBIC database — entire datasets hidden and encrypted inside the Archive, which were locked to my then Junior Archivist access credentials. It didn't look particularly alarming or suspicious — just part of the pre-coded journey plan. Data, like everything else on the Thetis, was controlled by the master plan the *Earther Passados* designed, unlocking and revealing new records as certain preconditions and milestones were reached. This was an efficiency thing — having huge loads of irrelevant data as part of the constant compute tasks of QUBIC was time and energy-consuming. And so, the publicly available datasets were limited by the plan to what was relevant for each part of the journey, certain blocks opening up as the Thetis transitioned between the phases of the trip.

I had no idea why a huge library of cultural and entertainment content from Earth would be locked off, nor when it was supposed to unlock and to what use. But to my curious teenage eyes, poking to see what was there seemed entirely harmless.

When I told Kilian about it, I knew he'd immediately smoke up on the challenge. And when we managed to break the encrypted seal of the datablock, a world of amazing ancient content was revealed — teleshows, longvids, music, books, all from the pre-Embarkment Earth era. We immediately knew that we had inadvertently struck treasure.

We feasted on the vids with our close circle of Kilian's friends, and eventually started arranging 'Ancient Wisdom' watch parties (the title 'Alternative History Night' came a few years later) in our new shared hab. It was all good fun.

Technically, unlocking the crypsigned Archive datablock could get Kilian into serious trouble. But somehow, the combination of the harmless nature of the content, Kilian's charm and the fact that there simply wasn't anyone else who could match his QUBIC tech skills got him out with a mere slap on the wrist from Nyasha. It would be years later until I would discover that it was this particular prank which brought him to the attention of the Andersons as a potential threat, earning him close tracking from 34th.

Kilian was standing in the center of the small lounge, a confident glass of drink in his raised hand, surrounded by his flock of follower-friends. He was in his element, controlling the energy and the crowd. As I approached, I noted to myself that this was the closest we'd been to each other for almost a full year now.

Len, a mutual friend and a former neighbor on 19 noticed me first. She was one of the nice ones when things exploded, at least *trying* to understand my impossible position. Now she was staring at me with wide eyes, dumbfounded. Kilian noticed her reaction and turned around, a trail of his smile still hanging. His eyes widened at the instant recognition.

"No. No, no, no," Kilian raised his free palm in the air, gesturing me to stop. "No way."

"I need to talk to you, K," I said over the loud music.

"No you don't. Actually, I have an official order inksheet stating just that." Kilian took a step back. The entire group around him fell silent, all staring at me. I started feeling anger tingling its way up my spine.

"Does it look like it's fun for me being here?" I asked.

"Kunyete," he said firmly. "I mean, some girls I dated were bad news, but you, Sandrine, you come with *legal* consequences! Are you out of your mind coming here?"

"I know," I said. "It's urgent. This will only take a minute."

Kilian hesitated for a moment, his clenched jaw loosening up a bit.

"Look," I said. "It's something technical that only you can answer. I have nobody else to turn to."

"This is Archive business?"

"Not exactly," I admitted. "Someone's messing with QUBIC."

Kilian gave me a long, studying look. I could see the internal calculations playing behind his dark eyes. Everyone around were watching us breaking a legal order by talking to each other. They were friends, but it wasn't completely risk-free. On the other hand, I could tell he was complimented by me reaching out to him about this. Plus, he was curious. *Professional ego is the easiest to ignite,* I thought.

Kilian sighed. "One minute," he said and dragged me to the back part of the lounge. "Talk."

"I need to know how can a data record be completely erased from the Archive database."

Kilian's expression froze. "Sandrine, what have you done this time?"

"Not me," I nodded. "But I'm trying to find out who did."

"Impossible," Kilian blurted immediately. "QUBIC is public ledger based. You know that already."

"Well, there's a missing datablock. And it could be serious, K. So how?"

There was a shift in Kilian's face. A slight, almost unnoticeable shift, but I knew him too well. His mind was grinding.

"I can't be any part of it. I'm sorry, San, this is a sensitive time in my life."

"I know," I said and lowered my head. "I've met Heleni."

Kilian's jaw clenched. "You what?!" he suppressed a shout. "You went to my hab? Grid-located? *Wapinya*, you *are* out of your mind!"

"It's *that* important, you idiot!" I shouted back. "Can you imagine my *humiliation* standing there?"

I felt the tears swelling up. *I can't break now, in front of him*, I thought. "Kilian, all I want is a chance to get my life back in order. Start a family. I deserve it too, don't I?" Kilian lowered his head. "But something's up, K," I continued, "and if we ignore it, all of those imagined futures might just be pipe dreams. I'm not dropping any of this mala on you. What I need from you is information, nothing more. Can I count on you?"

Kilian scratched his shiny bald head. He was furious. He slid his palm down from his forehead and rubbed his eyes, nose and stubble as the apparent internal struggle was playing out over his entire face. Eventually, he met my eyes with a soft look.

"Well," he shrugged, "I'm here, ain't I?"

I smiled. Kilian was trying to make me laugh, using his signature heavy-accent imitation of an old Wild West longvid he knew I'd recognize.

Seeing my reaction, he stuck a serious finger in the air pointing at me. "I'm not getting into more trouble with them, Sandrine! I've sacrificed all I have to get my Birth Year right back. This was a once-in-a-lifetime break. I can't screw this up again. I'll draw the dots for you — you connect them, te?"

Great, more dots to connect, I thought. *This whole day is treating me like a 3-year old.*

I nodded.

"As you know, there are ten QUBIC terminals on the Thetis," Kilian said. "We call them *nodes*. Each node holds an identical copy of the entire QUBIC database. The whole thing was designed with redundancy in mind, ensuring the integrity of our information across centuries of space travel."

I nodded again. I encountered the subject in my Archive study period, and although that was seven years ago, I could pretty much recall the basics.

Kilian was loving explaining this, so I didn't interrupt. "Not only were the nodes physically placed in different parts of the ship," he continued, "they also created a simple, clever mechanism in order to approve — or reject — any changes made to the data. Imagine you are trying to add a new record to the Thetis database. If your new proposed data record is approved by the system, it is added and copied across all ten nodes so that they all hold the same updated copy. But, if the data is rejected, the node you updated with your record will simply get overwritten with the older database copy on the other nine nodes. That mechanism means that the system can self-correct in case of an inadvertent, or intentional, data manipulation."

"And how does the system determine whether to add or overwrite my new record?" I asked. "Is that the majority voting thing?"

"Exactly!" Kilian pointed a proud finger at my direction. "We call it *consensus*. Which means that your new data record gets passed around for the confirmation of all other nine nodes. If a majority of those nodes vote that your record is valid — *voilà!* You get approved and your data is added to QUBIC. If we imagine the database to be a building with the oldest records at the bottom and the newest on top — you've just added a new floor to that building."

147

I smiled. Seeing Kilian that excited definitely had its effect on me. *When was the last time we've had such an up-close conversation?* I just wanted to linger in that bittersweet moment a bit longer.

"I get it regarding adding a new data record on top," I said. "But how do you *remove* an older floor from that building? What happens to all the newer floors built on top of it?"

Kilian rubbed his chin and darted his eyes around, scanning. "Well that's a lot more complicated. And risky. Actually, most people will tell you it's impossible."

"Most. But not you, right?"

For the first time since I stepped uninvited into the lounge, Kilian laughed. "It *is* kinda impossible, under normal circumstances. See, whenever you add a new floor to our data building, you get a key. You need this key to access the data record you just created. And that key is generated through a complex mathematical calculation of *all* the previous data records in the Archive. The key to any floor in the building is dependent on all the floors below it. And so—"

"—and so, if you remove a floor somewhere in that imaginary building, all the keys to the floors above it become invalid. The database gets corrupted."

"And of course you'd get this immediately," Kilian gave me an appreciative look.

Encouraged, I tried to follow the logic to the next step. "So if Anderson wanted to delete an older record in the Archive, I mean actually remove it without trace, he'd have to then go up record-by-record, floor by floor, and encrypt each floor with a new key, and then another one for the floor above it, all the way to the present."

"So not *technically* impossible," Kilian remarked.

"Just incredibly heavy on the calculation and compute resources he'd need to achieve it," I concluded.

It was Kilian's turn to nod. "And, as we already established, that can't be done from a single QUBIC terminal. It will simply get reverted to the previous database version. They'd need a majority of the ten nodes across the Thetis to approve this manipulation. Only then it would get permanently implemented."

I was already ahead. "I guess that deleting a relatively recent record like the one I am missing wouldn't be all *that* heavy lifting, ne?"

Kilian pondered this for a moment. "Yes, it varies. The older the data you try to delete, the more layers you'd need to re-encrypt on top of it, thus — more compute resourced needed. Remember the locked records we opened with all the Old Earth vids and teleshows?"

I gestured in the general direction of the Nebula main hall behind us. "What, you mean the cultural treasure that *those* drunks are feasting on? No, can't say I recall any of it."

"Ha ha," Kilian replied. "But really — the exact lesson learned from that incident was that because I was decrypting records from the oldest layers of the database — stuff inserted even before Embarkment — trying to conceal and re-encrypt them required a huge amount of compute power, triggering every possible alarm in the system. This is how we got caught."

"Thank you for acknowledging my superior intellect in presenting you with a challenge you couldn't outsmart," I said.

"A fine description of our entire relationship if I ever heard one," Kilian replied.

Ouch.

"Bottom line," he continued, "check the system monitoring logs. If anyone attempted such deep manipulation, there'd be a spike in compute resource consumption. It should have left traces."

Suddenly, an alarming concern dawned on me. "Wait. Kilian—" I gave a studying look into his eyes, "you wouldn't be connected to this missing record file in any way, would you?"

Kilian's face froze. "Do I need to remind you that I am legally restrained from going *near* a QUBIC terminal?"

"Knowing you, that's not an answer," I persisted.

Kilian's mouth curved in a weak smile. "I'm done taking risks,

San. Life erodes bravery, I guess."

A silent moment passed between us, loaded with unspoken history.

"Well isn't that just lovely!" A familiar voice came from behind us. "An officer of the Archive breaking a formal administrative restraining order, and in a public venue of all places? This is *juice!*"

Kunye Zee Anderson, properly wasted drunk and with his punchable smug face glowing with self content, was standing right there looking at us. I shot an alarmed look at Kilian. *Have I brought this mess to his door?*

Kilian didn't flinch. "Diaper up, Zee!" he flicked on his stage-smile and stepped past me toward Sam Anderson, putting a friendly hand on his shoulder. "You look like you're pleasure-pissing yourself, my friend. Liet just came to check up on the event, nothing wrong with that, is there? This was, after all, her thing."

He gestured towards the ongoing party within the Nebula hall, gripping Zee's elbow and turning him around and back into the club. "We're all just leaving anyhow. Costume Challenge coming up! What are you going as this year? Not the Jabba thing again, I hope? We needed two days to clean after you last year!"

They both burst out laughing and disappeared into the dark dance floor.

Kilian the Great, I thought. This is what we used to call him. Always found his way out of any situation on the sole merit of his personality. *Some people are just born with that halo, I guess.*

I turned to leave out of the back exit of the lounge as Kilian returned on stage, his spirit still clicked to Eleven.

"OK get ready for the Alt His Costume Challenge, everyone!" he announced. "Time to let my inner Klingon shine!"

I used the roaring cheers of the crowd to slip out of there, as I felt a hand on my shoulder. I shuddered.

Kilian stood there in the dark, hesitating. "I saw the PubSheets, Sandrine," He finally said with soft eyes. "Just wanted to say I'm sorry."

"Poetic justice," I whispered. "Punishment for old sins eventually catches up with you in unexpected circumstances. Kilian, *I* am sorry."

I walked away, Kilian's hand sliding off my back. A few steps later I was lost in the dancing crowd again, swirling and pushing my way through in the dark. It was then, engulfed in temporary blackness, that I couldn't hold back anymore. I let go, and the tears kept flowing all the way down to 13.

CHAPTER TWENTY

Hello, world.

I chuckled at the quirky terminal prompt. Nyasha shot a look at me. "You do know this is just the default welcome message, right? You can change it in your profile settings."

"I'll never get tired of this," I said, "it's hilarious. I always imagine QUBIC waking up from a wonderful quantum nap by me disturbing it and its superior intellect with my petty Human queries."

Nyasha raised an eyebrow. "Sounds like one of your Alternative History opening ceremony installations," he said. "Speaking of which — how did it go?"

I noticed my palms pressing ever so slightly harder on the side panels of the terminal. "You knew what you were asking of me," I said.

Nyasha nodded. "Yes I did. And has it turned out to be fruitful in any way?"

I sighed. "He didn't kick me out, if that's worth anything. And he did offer some pointers to the QUBIC mechanics until Kunye Zee interrupted us."

Nyasha's face hardened. "You should be more careful, Sandrine. And so should I. So before we get anything logged on the system, I want you to walk me through everything you're planning to do, so I can find out beforehand if there's any point at which I should step out of here on some emergency."

I raised my eyes from the terminal screen to look at Nyasha. In half my adult life spent working for this man, I have never seen him paint outside the lines or make any political considerations. Nyasha was as dryly professional as toilet paper. I wasn't sure I liked this new development — actually it kunye *scared* me. I needed him to be the pillar of stability and the moral anchor I could trust. Otherwise, I'm on my own in this.

"But first," Nyasha said and gently pulled my hands off the QUBIC terminal cube, "Let's kill the Zee problem before it even happens."

Nyasha placed his elbows on the small terminal desk and pressed his palms on both sides of the translucent cube. The device immediately woke up and logged him in, a cluster of colored blobs surfacing in the three dimensional navigation panel.

Nyasha looked at me while operating the database entry process. "You came to me right after visiting the Nebula. You have self-reported a short, accidental encounter with Mr. Ngo with whom you have a standing legal restraining order. I have carried out a verification process regarding your claim — "

QUBIC's terminal swirled to display a floating wireframe 3D rendering of the Thetis. Two different-colored lines traced scribbling paths across its different levels, animated in an infinite loop.

" — By validating that the adjacency of Sr. Arc. Liet and Mr. Ngo did not surpass a mere few minutes in duration."

So this is how the Grid Locator tracking system works, I thought. It looked so simple — just two brightly-colored lines dancing their way around, above and below each other in the confined area of the Thetis. Two light rays trapped in a chase within a bottle, then briefly touching — only to separate again, each to its own arbitrary destiny.

"That should do it," Nyasha leaned back and looked up at me. "If Sam Anderson ever brings this up, you have already reported the encounter beforehand. This should get the sting out of any potential claim. Now let's move on."

"This is the first time I am seeing this system," I said as Nyasha stood up and motioned me back to the chair in front of the terminal cube.

"Very few people on the Thetis have," Nyasha stated dryly. "I'm sure you can agree it's for the best."

"The trace we're seeing right now — how far back does it go?"

"Right now we are looking at a few weeks' location data for each of you, just to cover our bases ruling out any previous encounters between you two. Let's proceed."

I sat in front of the QUBIC terminal and prepared to log in again. "OK," I pressed my palms to initiate the session. "Display QUBIC node locations," I instructed the machine.

A cluster of red dots surfaced in the cube, overlayed on top of the Thetis wireframe map. Each location hosting a QUBIC node was serving a function on the ship that required extensive computing power — research, operations, and real-time analysis of complex data.

I pointed at the dot floating at the center of the group. "This is us. Level 13. Main Archive."

Nyasha nodded and pointed at the top-most QUBIC node. "Trajectory Flight Control on Level 36. What are we looking for?"

"According to Kilian, deleting a database entry requires the cooperation of a majority of the ship's QUBIC nodes. There's a voting mechanism where most nodes need to approve such a transaction."

I tilted my palms a bit to swerve the 3D ship map to a full view. "That's Quantum Democracy for you."

Nyasha didn't respond to the tentative joke. His mind was already racing elsewhere. He dragged his chair beside me and leaned forward toward the terminal. "So from a total count of ten nodes, you'd need six to initiate such a hack. What's the compute load of such an action?"

"Apparently it depends on the recency of the target data file. If the record is old enough, there should be traces of a compute surge. Let me pull this info up."

A slight modification to the display filters and a small chart appeared near each of the ten nodes. None of them showed any significant spike in the past few weeks. All was quiet on the quantum front.

"Nothing," I murmured.

"Let's go one by one," Nyasha said. "We know that Archive and Traj are off the hook — we are monitoring those on a daily basis. Where else?"

"There's one at PHS Medical Research Lab," I pointed.

Nyasha nodded. "Cassidi Anderson's lab. An apparent suspect, of course. Keep going."

"There's one at Propulsion, Level 0."

"Unlikely. It's located on the outside shell of the ship, so good luck getting there."

I kept scrolling. "Genline Premapping, used for procreation genetic screening. It *is* riding a bit high on resources now as part of the Birth Year plan."

"And, since LY38, also a part of PHS," Nyasha remarked.

My eyes immediately jumped to a dot a few levels down. "So is Crop Control! Under permanent affiliation to the PHS, by order of the Thetis Primo!"

Nyasha rubbed his eyes. "So three nodes under potential Anderson control. Not enough, but show me six and we can talk."

I sifted through the remaining node locations, looking for anything which could strike a chord. There was Climate Control — a hugely complex system in charge of every aspect of life conditions on the Thetis. There was the Vivarium GenLab in the Sensory Farm, with its genetic research and CellPrinter array, and there was the Junior Academy Research Center. None of these seemed to be under the direct influence of either PHS or the Primo's office.

"There is, of course, the terminal within the General

Administration Office on 34th," Nyasha noted. "So let's assume Sabi controls that one too. That would be four compromised nodes. Not enough for any foul play."

I went over the list again. That sensation in the back of my mind which told me I'm missing something started tinkling again.

"Something doesn't make sense here," I said.

Nyasha turned his head toward me and waited, knowing not to interrupt my elusive trail of intuition.

"I mean, let's review the situation for a moment, te?" I was thinking aloud. "A legal file is missing. An important one, sure — a case file for an attempted extortion of the Thetis Primo — but still. We are looking at *years* of planning here. Indirect, quiet actions directed at gradually gaining control over QUBIC compute asses. All of that just to conceal one complaint file on a *closed case?* Seems like an enormous overkill if you ask me. Not to mention sending Jericho Pakk to scare me off, scare Almaz Bashiri off — why even bother? I don't buy it."

"Alleged overkill."

Nyasha rose up from his chair. "You, my dear, have so far shown me only four nodes with Anderson influence. So we're still in the *alleged* territory here. Sorry, but it doesn't compile."

He patted his pants absentmindedly, looking around the room, then set his eyes on me and raised somber eyebrows in my direction. "And I should have left the room 10 minutes ago, unless you can conjure two additional QUBIC nodes for us, te?" Nyasha slowly turned away from the terminal and toward the door.

An that's when it hit me. *Of course!* "No, wait, no — Bashiri!"

Nyasha paused.

I talked fast. "When I met him at the Sensory Farm, he told me that his entire gene research project was shut down. He was deploying some... *switch-gene* to control the animal population of the Sensory Farm between generations."

"And?" Nyasha asked tentatively.

"And he specifically complained that his quantum computing resources have been taken over without any explanation. He thought it was an act of petty revenge for his raising complaints against the PHS."

"But you see a pattern here," Nyasha stated calmly.

I was already working QUBIC as fast as I could, connecting lines and query parameters between the Vivarium GenLab, PHS, the missing file and Bashiri's personal profile. Within less than a minute, I found what I was looking for.

"There's your pattern!" I called and pushed my chair back, allowing Nyasha an unobstructed view of the screen. "'To assist in critical tasks concerning the upcoming Birth Year,'" I read aloud the formal legal directive I had just dug out, "'Thetis Public Health Service is throttling down non-time-critical Quantum compute resources and reallocating them toward essential, time-sensitive projects.'"

I shot a look at Nyasha. "And guess who's getting all the extra compute resources of the GenLab node?"

"I know exactly who," Nyasha turned back to face me, his face reddened.

"What do you mean?" I was puzzled. "Did you *know* about this?"

"I *signed off* on the kunye directive myself! It was buried in the back pages of some routine stack of procedures regarding Birth Year. I didn't think twice before signing off on the whole thing."

Nyasha was fuming. He walked back toward me and leaned close, his face breaking sweat.

"If that's true — if we are actually looking at five QUBIC nodes being operated by the Andersons for an unknown private project — then I'm worried. If I myself was manipulated by them — then I'm listening. And you, Sandrine — from now on, you only have one job: find me the sixth node!" he spat out.

The shift in him was profound. The good old Uncle figure which his chubby, awkward clothes and scruffy beard gave way to a red-cheeked, furious beast.

"Find the sixth node, or we don't have proof, and I can't act. Going after the Primo with a formal investigation — in an *election year* for Sol's sake! — without solid evidence to the node manipulation, that will be plain suicide. So I need to be a hundred percent convinced about this. Find Dr. Bashiri — he may very well hold the key."

I paused.

"Go back in," I said.

"I thought we established my need to not be involved until you get further evidence."

"Trust me on this. Just pull up Kilian's location history map again. I can't do it with my credentials."

Nyasha gave me a studying look for a long minute, then sat and fired up the QUBIC terminal.

"This better be good," he murmured to himself.

The Thetis wireframe map floated again in the terminal screen. Kilian's location history, drawn in a glowing yellow squiggly line, plotted his exact whereabouts in the past two weeks. The shape reminded me of the heated wire filament of an old incandescent light bulb, which was used long ago on Earth. It reflected a mundane daily routine, mostly revolving around his hab circle on 25th and the shopping district on 26th ,with periodic drops to his new place of work on the algae hydropharm humidors of 22nd and the Nebula on 19th.

Eventually, we are creatures of habit. Fenced and bounded by our self-inflicted task lists. Even Kilian the Great.

"Now," I turned to Nyasha, "overlay it with Dr. Almaz Bashiri's tracking data."

Nyasha took a deep breath and met my gaze. He knew he was stretching the envelope of his comfort zone.

Turning back to the terminal screen, Nyasha gave out a suppressed sigh. "I guess we're all-in on this, then."

He flipped a few queries into the system, and a glowing green line traced its wobbly trajectory through the Thetis wireframe floorplan.

We both leaned our heads in, looking for intersections of the two lines, suggesting a possible meeting between the two men. There were none.

"Stretch the timeline back to the date of Bashiri's lab takeover by the PHS," I said.

Nyasha tweaked the time period dial and both lines elongated to reflect the longer span of the represented data. Still, no evidence of any connection between the two paths. Just two random people living their life on mostly totally different parts of the ship.

"Kunye mala," I said. *I was so certain about this hunch.*

Nyasha leaned back and started logging out of the system.

"Stop!" I shouted. "Go back one day."

"Sandrine — "

"One day, Nyasha!" I put my palm over his to keep it logged into the terminal. This was completely out of line, but I just knew he would never allow me such access to this data again.

A few seconds later, I felt the slightest shift in Nyasha's fingers, and the QUBIC rendering updated to include the new time span.

And there it was.

"Kunye mala indeed," Nyasha said, astonished. "Kunye mala squared."

Inside the translucent cube of the terminal's 3D display, both of the green and yellow lines displayed a steep, abrupt drop to one of the lower levels of the Thetis, which was currently off-screen. Nyasha zoomed out to include all the ship's levels. And exactly as I suspected, both lines converged to a single location, the day before Almaz Bashiri's project takeover by the PHS.

Nyasha stared into the terminal cube. "Oh my."

"Level 2?" I hesitated. I was puzzled — I actually didn't see this one coming. I was expecting a meeting between Kilian and Bashiri to take place in the GenLab, or in some public area — but *Level 2?*

"Isn't that the radioactive zone?" I asked rhetorically.

159

Nyasha nodded. "It is."

"But— *nobody* goes there!" I said, frustrated. *This bafunye isn't helpful at all*, I thought.

"Well apparently our two mystery men have," Nyasha stated quietly, looking distracted.

"And apparently," I added, "*someone* hadn't been completely straight with me, as it turns out."

I stood up as Nyasha finally logged out of the system. He was clearly thrown off by the new piece of information we had uncovered.

I needed to get to the bottom of this, and I needed to do it *fast*. Every hour that passed seemed to bring another complication into my situation and I needed to cut through it viciously if I was to make sense of any of it.

"Looks like I need to pay another visit downstairs," I said.

CHAPTER TWENTY-ONE

Crossing the Level 10 seal downwards I could feel the fight growing in me. It was a strange feeling, almost unfamiliar even. Certainly one that I had not felt in a long time. I became very aware of my breathing, of my beating heart. Being manipulated, being threatened, and deciding to take the fight back to the aggressors was somehow... liberating. *Exciting*, even.

We had been living such an oblivious, comfy life on the Thetis! We had everything we needed, and the Passados made sure that we had redundancy safeguards up our collective asses. We knew precisely how population growth would affect resource demand, so the plan was there to ensure sufficient supply. We had no monetary system; no wars or aggressive competition — nothing was scarce enough to fight over.

The social norms on the Thetis were based on two leading pillars: extreme transparency and extreme tolerance. As kids growing up, we were consistently fed with the notion that the two concepts were inseparably entangled: conformity and intolerance toward non-mainstream ideas would lead to people keeping secrets; and the need for nonconformists to hide and protect their secrets from society would lead to prejudice and more intolerance. This was doubly true for the secluded, closed-membership club that was the Thetis.

To escape that vicious cycle, we were taught to keep no secrets, see no shame in any personal preference. Everybody knew everything about everybody else, and in a way, it was actually liberating. You were who you were, no masks — there was complete freedom of thought, sexual tolerance and creative spirit.

But the egalitarian utopia the Passados conjured for us came with a hefty price: we have simply lost the fight in us. We became mellow. There was work to be done of course: crops to grow, research to conduct, goods to produce. But our collective life didn't really *depend* on it, te? The need to ensure Humanity's survival through centuries of hazardous space travel at unprecedented speeds necessitated keeping us protected in a cotton-candy of abundance and redundancies.

This hadn't always been the situation on the Thetis. As an Archivist, I had spent a large part of my training studying the history of the mission. It began a *lot* messier. Gen Zeros, the actual people chosen to populate the ship at Embarkment, and who are essentially the ancestors of all Thetans — of all the future *Human Race*, for that matter — were very different people. They were Planetfolk — direct witnesses of the violent decay of Earth, and a direct product of it: those were rough people, consumed with existential anxiety.

Granted, Gen Zeros had the highest hurdles to cross toward adapting to life in space — from living inside a confined, claustrophobic tube with decreased gravity, to the completely new social construct they were expected to adopt.

The more I read about the events of that era, the more astounded I was with their achievements. *The sheer scope of Human progress those people had to leave behind!* Sure, by the time Humanity realized that the Thetis project was its only shot for long-term survival, Earth was already a collapsing planet. Ironically, it had also simultaneously reached what would later be called "Peak Tech" — an amazing level of co-existence between Man's natural biology and Man-made artificial enhancements. Pre-Embarkment Earthers lived to 140 years old. They had instant communication and data-hive access to every corner of the planet. Calculated by body mass contribution, the average Human had 3-7% of their body composed of artificial augmentation. They could see better, heal faster, access data, perform calculations and communicate as no Human in history ever could.

And they had to leave all of that convenience and empowerment at the Thetis door. For them, it must have felt like returning to the Stone Age; Like being sent to face the Universe naked and unarmed, stripped off of a thousand years' effort to cheat nature.

A vivid recollection of an old video interview surfaced in my mind. It was part of the ancient data-block Kilian had extracted out of the Archive. At the time, it seemed to be a lesser find — certainly paling next to the plethora of entertaining shows we uncovered — but for some reason it stuck with me.

It was a heartbreaking interview with Primo Demetrius Smoak, the Thetis first Primo. By the time the piece had been recorded, he was already a very old man. I could clearly see him in my mind's eye, lying in what would be his deathbed in an early incarnation of the Astral Solace Home. In stark contrast to his broken body, his words, carried to our screen from beyond a century, came out crisp and blunt as a punch in the face.

"As Primo of this mission, I used to say that my primary job was not flight control, but rather *fright* control."

A faint chuckle could be heard from the off-camera interviewer.

"And as a result," he continued with his impossibly heavy accent, "there wasn't a day in my life that I hadn't gone to sleep terrified."

In all the videos I watched of Gen Zeros, deciphering their accents and vocabulary was the most challenging task. It was partly physical — Earthborns were adapted to higher gravity and air pressure and certain sounds were simply easier to produce for them. But it was also partly the fact that they drew their terminology from a completely different set of Human experiences. For instance, they sure had a lot of animal-related expressions, which for us Spacers were totally enigmatic.

"Terrified for yourself, or terrified for the mission?" the unseen interviewer prompted.

"Terrified for *all* our sorry asses! They stuck us in this can, like rats in a cage, but we were still facing two dozen years of acceleration required to push this enormous chunk of metal beyond direct visual contact with the planet. So we've spent years hovering above Earth like sitting ducks, and we could see it all — we saw the nukes, we saw the floods, we saw *everything* disintegrating like it was fucking entertainment! Unable to do anything but pray that some governmental snake won't decide to shoot us out of the sky in retaliation for some terrestrial dispute."

"Wouldn't it have been cutting Humanity's nose just to spite the face?"

It was Smoak's turn to chuckle. His entire bony, stern face threatened to crack with the muscular distortion.

"Maybe. But some people down there certainly didn't see it that way. Up here we've instilled a sense of mission, of sacrifice and of the sanctity of our survival. But to some folks on Earth, we were the lucky bastards who got a free ticket out of hell!"

The interview went on to address different subjects such as discipline and religion, which apparently was initially practiced quite rigorously on the Thetis, but had eventually fallen out of fashion for Gen1sters and 2nders.

Gen Zeros, having been carefully chosen for the mission with both physical and mental fitness in mind, had a strong bias toward military types who were also mostly people of faith. But as the first spaceborn generations appeared on the Thetis stage, a crisis of faith ensued. From my position of several generations down the Genline it was hard to interpret the exact phenomenon, but apparently the values simply didn't translate for the new *Homo Infinitus*. Maybe religion was just too local in nature, tied to places and buildings and burial grounds. It certainly seemed as if the entire Thetis needed a different, new social value-set, crafted for the realities of multi-centennial space travel.

Even through the distorted prism of 7 generations, Primo Demetrius Smoak was as impressive a leader as I could have imagined possible. He was certainly no mere glorified clerk — leading the Thetis through Embarkment, the Crop Crisis, new generations and the Gen2

Pogroms must've taken a true warrior. I've rewatched that video so many times, and I still teared up whenever Smoak, all shrunk and frail and tubed-up in his Home bed, laments the impossible cruelty of outliving both his children *and* grandchildren. Gen Zeros, having boarded the Thetis with their Earth-made augmentations and longevity treatments, famously lived to over a hundred, sometimes 140 years, while their Thetan offsprings were offered no more than the 80-something Nature had provided. So by an unimaginably dark twist of fate, the first generation to die in space was not Generation Zero — but rather their Gen1 spacer kids.

But the reason this particular interview struck a chord with me as I was descending the Thetis traj-wise and beyond the Level 10 seal, was a specific remark Primo Smoak made when asked by the interviewer to revisit the historic day of Detachment.

"Some people will claim," the interviewer said, "that the new Humanity was only really born on the day of communication Detachment from Earth."

"I disagree," Primo Smoak said. "Detachment only emphasized the worst of Humanity's traits from Old Earth. If anything, it took us *backwards*. I argue that the proverbial New Human will not enter the stage for a few more generations. Not until the FLIPP, anyway."

"That's a very interesting perspective, Primo Smoak. So what do you think happened on Earth? Do you believe anyone is still there?"

Demetrius hand-waived the question with his skinny, pale hand. "Irrelevant. We have no way of knowing the situation there. Our duty is to assume we are the only remaining survivors of our species. That was the main foundational idea I have tried to base my Primoship upon. But when, for almost two decades post Embarkment, communication from Earth still operated routinely, questions started getting asked by people, right? Will Earth survive after all? Did they find a way to heal, and most alarmingly — are we on this Galaxy-traversing, one-way ticket journey for *nothing*? For most of us original Thetans, the thought that all we had done, all the sacrifices made and the families left behind, were unnecessary — a panicked *misfire* — well, that was a very disempowering idea. But then, to go back to your

165

question, one day all the communications simply cut off."

"Detachment."

"We got nothing! One minute everything was nominal, a minute later — closed for business. No mission control. No data links, not even the laser clock sync-beam. Just like that, out of the black — it was all gone."

"There must have been panic on deck," the interviewer said softly.

Smoak chuckled coldly. "Everything I assumed would happen — and I *did* pre-plan for such a moment — worked the other way round. *Nothing* went as I fucking expected it to."

"That must have been a new experience for you."

"See, I was *expecting* panic. In my mind, such a sudden cut-off could only mean one of two things: a catastrophe on Earth, or a deliberate political act by whomever took control of the initiative Planet-side. In either case, the conclusion was the same — we were alone. Orphaned or abandoned, whatever one chose to believe. And once *that* fact sunk in, it had a devastating effect on the people."

The old Primo raised his hand again. "Now, of course this was just a psychological thing. We didn't really need Earth for any data or directions or anything crucial for the continuance of the mission. We were stocked-up, pre-programmed and self-sufficient from the get go. There was nothing we could do anyhow — we couldn't turn back or re-establish communication. But people liked the reassurance factor of having Earth at our back. So yes, I did expect panic."

"So you trace the origin of the crises that marked the second half of your career to the fallout from that day? To Detachment?"

"Look," Smoak's energy fired up for a brief moment, a reddish hue on his cheekbones hinting to the fighter he once was. "We were people of *action*. Military veterans, doctors, scientists, space program alumni, business entrepreneurs — those were people who used to live their life with a measuring stick. It was money, or it was power, or it was lives we saved, or lives we took — or the number of notches on whichever fucking achievement-belt you were wearing throughout your life.

Now, you take these types of competitive, aggressive people, they can't handle depression."

"Is that what you think Detachment created? A shipwide depression?"

"Oh boy, did it ever! Those mission-driven cats? Who treated every update from Earth as if it were some mission-critical task? Once Detachment took that away from them, they became as depressed as polar bears on Earth's last glacier! Staring into thin air, unsure what the fuck they were supposed to be doing next. Everything on the Thetis became slow motion. People needed a new purpose. We couldn't play Astronauts and Home Base any longer."

The interviewer paused. A slow rustling sound could be heard over the camera mic and a hand appeared from the right side of the frame, holding a picsheet in front of Demetrius Smoak's face.

"I guess that the pendulum did not take long for it to swing violently in the other direction," the interviewer said in a cautious tone. "For the record, I am presenting Mr. Smoak with a picture of Oscar Kohn."

Primo Smoak's entire posture deflated as if the IV tubing he was connected to suddenly reversed and began sucking the life out of his body. At that moment, he really did look 140 years old. He sighed deeply and nodded his head absent-mindedly.

"The kid."

"Yes," the interviewer noted. He did not put the picture away.

"Look," Primo Smoak was clearly irritated, "I may be 140 years old, but I don't need that picture stuck in my face. I can remember the boy perfectly fine."

"This is just for Archival purposes, Primo. I do not mean to upset you in any way."

"Oscar Kohn's brutal death is a scar on our entire generation," Smoak said firmly. "His face will follow me to the grave, or whatever-the-heck you call the process here."

Silence fell between the two men. The high-definition rendering of the vid shot seven generations ago preserved perfectly the internal turmoil playing out beneath Demetrius Smoak's frozen expression.

"Primo Smoak, let's—"

"No, wait. This is important. You were asking an important question which could be essential to prevent such atrocities in the future. So I will answer your question. Although I can't presume to assure historical objectivity in this matter, naturally."

"OK. We were addressing the changes on the Thetis after Detachment."

"Before that day, we were all one happy-sailing team. Well, to a point — there will always be assholes, yeah? But in essence, we were. Driven by a mission, keeping a disciplined reporting routine to Earth, joined at the hip to make this work. To make everyone we left behind proud. To save Humanity — no less. But after we lost Earth-comm — the realization that we were mere puppets occupying this pre-programmed projectile, unable to control our destiny — hell, we could have been flying straight into an astroid and wouldn't know it until we heard pang! That was a heavy load on people's minds. And so, all the Old Earth values we brought onto the ship with us began surfacing up." Smoak shook his head in contempt. "We were all going *backwards.*"

"I thought those were people of discipline," the interviewer said.

"Which only made it all that more difficult," Smoak offered a weak smile. "You fill a ship with Alpha dogs. If they are all aligned on the same vector — you get a Navy Seals team. But once they turn inward on each other — you get a gang war."

"So, Oscar Kohn was a victim of such a gang war?"

Smoak flailed a weak hand in frustration. "Oscar Kohn — second-born baby on the Thetis, should have been the future of everything we were meant to build here. A true marvel — a new generation for the Human race. Instead, he was a victim of all the old sins we have carried with us off the Planet. See, once the "one team" spirit started to disintegrate, the next-best instinct people had was self-preservation. On Earth, everything was a struggle for scarcity — for money. For rank. For spouses. For reputation — you name it. You bring this mindset to the ship, where there's no money, where there's no real deterrence to breaking the code — you can't fine anyone, you *certainly* can't throw anyone off-board — and there's little in the way to complete chaos."

"And then comes Zachary Anderson."

"And then comes the first Birth Year on the Thetis, and Zachary Anderson — firstborn baby in space! And then little Oscar and thousands more. What an excitement! But what else was born in that year?"

Smoak waited for the interviewer's reply, but he just let the question hang there for the Primo to pick it back up.

"Families, of course," Smoak said. "From a whole generation of single men and women in their prime, who were picked from war-zone service, from field hospitals and research centers around the globe, we suddenly transformed into family structures. You see where this is going."

"Families become gangs, power struggles grow into wars."

This part of the interview had always both fascinated and terrified me — our community has most certainly made *tremendous* progress since those wild and *barbaric* times. Listening to the first Primo continue to recount the fierce struggle between Thetans for positions, for possessions, for access to knowledge, for an *edge* — you just knew it would end in violence. And it did. Little Oscar Kohn was a symbolic victim — a 4 year old burned to death, accidentally trapped inside a crop field set purposely on fire by a rivaling family — but, sadly, many other depressingly harsh stories were documented in the Archive if one had an inclination to learn the dark history of the early days of the Thetis.

"Let me end this session by taking us back to something you mentioned earlier," the interviewer said. "You predicted that we won't see the New Humanity emerge until after the FLIPP. That's an intriguing assertion. Why the FLIPP? Do we really need three more generations to wipe out the residue of the recent events?"

169

"I hope we won't need more," Demetrius Smoak said. "History tends to punish the second and third generations after a major crisis. It was a well-documented syndrome on Earth which I can say, without much pride, seems to be equally true in interstellar space. The FLIPP is not a mere crisis — it will be a tectonic shift in Humanity's mindset."

"Most people regard it as just another waypoint in our journey, Primo. Putting aside the acrobatics, of course."

"I disagree," Smoak said. "I believe that the FLIPP will signify a profound shift in our society. It will be the point where the controlling theme of our journey transforms from *fleeing* to *approaching*. Only then will we be ready to shed our ancient roots and truly be reborn."

The words echoed in my mind as I disembarked the Ascender at Level 8 and stepped into the Sensory Farm entrance area. *We have come so far since then,* I thought. We were now much closer to the vision the Passados had in mind for us than the chaotic, racist and lawless bunch who have boarded the Thetis so long ago. After *generations* of tireless effort, we have built a society *worthy* of survival.

And if all goes according to plan, our children would be leading Resett and laying the foundation for Humanity's next home, while my generation sits in our rocking chairs in orbit, witnessing this wonder from above.

But apparently, some people were working to covertly undermine this vision, and for reasons I was just beginning to unravel. Why would anyone sabotage our mission — themselves included — was beyond me, but I was quickly running out of alternative explanations. Dr. Almaz Bashiri was clearly one of those people involved, which was why I was on my way to pay him a personal visit at his GenLab. I was yet unsure about the motive behind his actions — the extortion, Primo Anderson's involvement, and how Kilian connected to it all — but I sure intended to confront him straight-on about all of those and get some real kunye answers for once.

I was just climbing to the Sensory Farm platform when I was

abruptly and violently thrown sideways toward the protective railing, my head smashing against a hard carboplast post. The ship rattled and skidded, distant alarms blaring in a deafening cacophony. My vision started to fade and I could vaguely hear the emergency speakers droning their inappropriately calm, pre-recorded women's voice: "Debris Beam unbalanced. Trajectory drift identified."

I hugged the railing post as hard as I could, flailing around like a helpless rag doll. I could feel the sticky, warm presence of blood pressing against my cheek.

Trajectory drift? I mumbled as a blurry vail began descending over my eyes. I felt my consciousness retreating backwards into the back of my skull, its shutdown sequence almost complete.

This can't be happening.

I could make out the faint Clang-Clang-Clang of someone running up the metal staircase from the Sensory Farm ground level. Then — a warm palm in my hand, a firm arm pulling me off the railing. A grunt.

Nothing else.

CHAPTER TWENTY-TWO

"I owe you an apology, Ms. Liet."

Primo Sebastian Anderson was sitting on the edge of the standard-issue infirmary chair placed beside my bed, leaning forward. A soothing smile spread across his face as he almost hovered above me. "I'm afraid I might have some responsibility for the slight mishap you encountered today. How are you feeling?"

I fixed the position of my head against the rigid pillow. *If by 'slight mishap' you mean a concussion, twelve nano-tasers administered to heal my head cuts and a throbbing purple eye — then by all means, yes I'd like to hear the explanation.*

"What happened?" I asked. My voice was hoarse, and talking sent hot spikes through my temples. *I should keep it short.*

"Well, we experienced an interference in the balanced flow of matter through the Ionized Debris Beam—"

"The Trash Tube?"

Anderson's eyes narrowed. *He doesn't like being interrupted when he speaks.*

"Some people refer to the IDB as the 'Trash Tube', yes."

"So what happened?" I asked again. "Did something fall into it?

Was that the rattle we felt?"

Sabi's eyes darted in the direction of the door.

"Told you this one's a smart hadron," a familiar voice came from the corner. I turned my head so I could focus on the speaker, and was surprised to find Jericho Pakk standing by the closed door, his hand placed firmly on the handle.

What the hell is this? I thought. *Is this a courtesy visit, or some kind of interrogation?*

"Some...thing *did* unfortunately penetrate into the" — air quotes — "'Trash Tube'," Anderson said, "and that caused an instability that resulted in the Thetis skidding we all experienced. You are indeed as sharp as Nyasha mentioned to me many times."

No, no, no, I startled. *Smart is bad. Smart is Jericho Pakk creeping up to me in my hab at night. Smart won't get me anywhere at this point.*

"Is everyone on the ship OK?" I tried to sound as clueless as I could manage. My mind was racing against the constant, pounding throbs of pain. *If this was some random accident, the Primo and his most powerful Secundus wouldn't be here, would they?*

Anderson leaned back in his seat and shot a pleased look at Pakk. "We had some minor damage and some injuries, but the important thing is that we got this under control. Now, Sandrine—"

"How is that even possible?" I cut in. Sabi's lips clenched imperceptibly. Interruptions really *did* irritate him.

"What do you mean?" he asked.

"You said that something 'penetrated' into the Trash Tube," I tried to adopt the most innocent look I could muster. "So I assume it wasn't an external object from space, but rather something from within the Thetis. As far as I know there are only two openings into the Trash Tube. One on Level 1 for emergency dumping of radioactive materials. And another small shaft in—"

I froze as the realization dropped on me. Anderson bowed his head.

"The biological hazard chamber at the GenLab on Level 8. Yes, Sandrine, the reason both I and Sec Pakk are here today is that what got disintegrated in the Trash Tube was not a *something*, but rather — regrettably — a *someone*. Unfortunately, I am sad to share with you that Dr. Almaz Bashiri has chosen to end his life in the most horrific manner imaginable. We can only hope that it was a painless ending to such a bright mind."

What?! My mind exploded. How could this be happening? Why would Bashiri kill himself, and in such a horrible manner, endangering the whole ship? And why would the kunye Primo come all the way here to give me the news personally? Do they know I was on my way to meet Bashiri just as it happened?

Of course they know, stupid. That's the whole point here!

I started sweating. My head-pounding worsened and I felt I was going to faint again right there in my bed in front of the Primo and his ice-eyed wolf.

As if he was reading my mind, Sabi pressed his hands together and said, "there is a reason I asked to meet with you in private and deliver the news. And then we should really let you rest."

I was still too shaken to respond. Anderson threw another look at Pakk, took an audible deep breath and turned back to meet my eyes.

"We know, obviously, that you were in contact with Dr. Bashiri in regard to the nasty extortion attempt he tried to commit against my family. Apparently, Bashiri was a troubled soul, which is not uncommonly correlated with mental brilliance."

I nodded. No reason to deny what they already know.

"Now, we all have the greatest respect for the Archive and the unwavering adherence to the Code you all exemplify. And we've already established your own personal intellect. So I hoped that by now it would have dawned on you that this was always a no-case. We have tremendous and historical challenges in front of us which require all of our joint efforts. I strongly believe," — Anderson raised his eyebrows to emphasize 'strongly' — "that it would honor Almaz Bashiri and his remaining Genline if we chose to lay our probing into

174

his less luminous sides to rest."

"We were going to close the case anyway," I managed a meek reply, "until the file had inexplicably gone missing—"

"Nothing is missing," Jericho Pakk cut in, leaving his position by the door and taking a quick step in my direction. My whole body tensed. He reached into his inner jacket pocket and pulled an encrypted inksheet, flipped it open and handed it to me.

I threw a questioning look at Sabi. He nodded slowly, signaling for me to proceed. The device wouldn't unlock to my CrypID credentials, so I turned it toward Jericho.

"Chip finger, please," I said, mimicking his silky tone and using the very same words he had used to get my signature at the Primo quarters. Pakk was not amused. He pressed his finger on the inksheet sensor pad and the screen descrambled.

In a sudden hunch, I quickly pressed my own chip finger onto his, creating a digital handshake between us which would log his CrypID in my personal events log. Jericho withdrew his hand abruptly.

"What are you doing, Liet?" he barked.

"Sorry," I mumbled, "I'm still woozy from the mala they're pumping into me here."

I saw the fury in his eyes, but he was smart enough to keep his mouth shut and let it slide. Primo Anderson leaned in again with a serious expression.

"Mr. Pakk is absolutely right, Ms. Liet. The so-called missing file is right here, in your hands. You were clever enough to spot its absence, and the only way for me to explain the situation and regain your trust was to adopt the long-standing Thetis tradition of full transparency and hand it to you in full. As you will be able to see for yourself, this puts me in quite a vulnerable position as the leader of this ship, but I trust you will hear my explanation to the matter."

Anderson leaned back in his chair. Jericho Pakk returned to his spot by the locked door, his eyes never leaving me and the inksheet in my hand. I sat up in my bed and started reading.

175

It was obviously a medical file of some sort, dated a few years back. Two familiar names immediately jumped out of the screen — Cassidi and Sam Anderson. In the file were test protocols and results for bacteria pathogens, and something labeled 'polymerized protein'. Obviously, most of it was far beyond my medical literacy so I skimmed the illegible parts in search for the punch that would render this document important enough to hide.

I thought I had my answer by the bottom of the page, when the part labeled 'Result' was marked with the one word that didn't require a medical degree to decipher: 'Positive'.

I raised my head from the screen and looked at Anderson. "So, they got sick?"

"Actually, no they didn't," Sabi said and gently pulled the device out of my hands. Two seconds later it was safely tucked back inside Jericho Pakk's jacket. "Because this stuff doesn't *make* you sick. It's just... bacteria. You have trillions of those running through your body as we speak, te?"

"So," I raised a bemused eyebrow at the Primo, "what's the story?"

"Ah, the *story*. Yes, that's the whole point right there, my dear Archivist. To you and me, and anyone in their right mind, there most certainly is no story. But our dear late doctor *thought* he may have a story, and one that he figured could be used to threaten the Thetis Primo and his family into submitting to his personal whims and ambition."

Anderson had a cruel glint in his eyes when he spoke of the recently-deceased scientist. *He's unsettled*, I thought.

"So why even bother deleting the thing from the Archive database?" I asked. "I mean, if there's nothing to hide..."

"You do understand, Ms. Liet," Jericho Pakk barked at me from his position by the door, "that medical test files are strictly confidential, with any access to them by a person other than the CrypIDed patient being a serious felony? Do you imagine Almaz Bashiri being capable of performing such a decryption? Or maybe, can we imagine anyone else on the Thetis with the skillset *and* past experience of breaking the

176

crypsign print on archival files?"

Was he awkwardly referring to Kilian's break into the old Archive video library? Was this supposed to be some kind of threat to me? *Wrong leverage, wapa. Take it to his pregnant bruta.*

"And you do also understand," Pakk continued in his slightly-louder-than-necessary drone, "that Mrs. Anderson and her son are private citizens on the Thetis, neither of them holding a public position? Threatening to expose private medical data about them cannot constitute any claim of public right to know. It's just pure criminal."

"PHS is a public entity, isn't it?" I asked. "Isn't Mrs. Anderson heading that institute?"

Why can't you shut your mouth for once, Sandrine? I thought when I saw both men's face expressions following my remark. *You're hurt, dosed up in bed — the perfect excuse to shut the kunye up for five minutes, ne?*

Jericho took a step toward my direction, his eyes fuming. "Lady Anderson has recently decided to reposition herself at the private genegineering R&D lab, which is a private PHS subsidiary. So no, no public position, and don't get cute with me, Liet."

Primo Anderson raised his hand to give pause to his Secundus. Pakk retreated to his corner with a grunt.

"Good dog," I muttered.

"What the hell does that even mean?" Pakk retorted.

"Historical reference," I replied. "You wouldn't get it."

"Enough of that, please," Sebastian Anderson interrupted and leaned toward me with an impatient look. "Sandrine. The reason I am here, contrary to any logic of exposing my own indiscretions — is this: you need to put substance over procedure."

I was feeling very uncomfortable. Here I was, conducting an informal investigation into the unusual — and perhaps technically *impossible* — disappearance of a data record from the Archive database. Then, suddenly, my main source of information gets himself ionized to death, I am injured, and the kunye *Primo of the Thetis* shows up at my bed with the missing file, asking for... *what*, exactly?

"Ms. Liet," Anderson continued, "in the formal sense of things, I am most certainly guilty."

Lesson learned, I merely nodded noncommittally.

"I have used my Primo privileges to get Bashiri's meddling with my family's personal matters struck from the records. And yes, I am aware that this is... unorthodox, shall we call it?"

Borderline — if not full-on — criminal, if you ask me, I thought.

"You see, Sandrine, the Archive can certainly decide to investigate the matter. It would be entirely within its official charter to do so. In fact, we *know* you have been doing just that under Nyasha Woo's nose. Continuing down that path would be a legitimate *procedure* given what you now know."

Anderson shifted his weight on the single-mold, rigid chair. "But I've decided to help you reach the ending point of that path — the facts. And the facts are that Dr. Almaz Bashiri was nothing but a deranged narcissist. Trying to expose illegally-obtained data about my family, which doesn't show nor prove anything problematic! It merely states that at some point they were infected by a harmless bacteria which doesn't even make you sick. So, at the *substance* of what lies beneath all of this, there is clearly nothing, no *story*. I ask you — now that you have seen first-hand the actual file — to save us all the trouble and embarrassment of going through the procedure, only to reach a nonissue at the end of it. Will you, Sandrine, display such sound judgement?"

A heavy silence of anticipation hung between us like a moist cloud in the room. After Anderson's lengthy speech, the silence had an unsettling effect on me, hard to bear.

"I... I'm just an Archivist, Primo Anderson. Isn't this discussion in Nyasha's court?"

Sebastian Anderson's very audible sigh resounded trough the infirmary room.

"Nyasha Woo relies very much on your input in this matter, let me assure you that. As we all know too well, he is not entirely known for his innovative creative thinking."

"He's a procedure-junkie stick-ass!" Jericho contributed from his corner by the door.

Anderson raised his hand again to silence Pakk. "And as for that infamous medical file, *some* people will see it as a tool for attacking me. Running so close to the general Primo elections — empty allegations and scaremongering about my family's health could be enough to distract the discourse and smear people's reputations. You know Sam has his own political aspirations for the future."

Really!? Kunye Zee wants to be Primo? Well if that ever happens, consider me next-in-line into the Trash Tube please.

But in all seriousness, there was something to admire about Sebastian Anderson's courage in outing the entire ordeal in front of me. Yes, he was a calculating politician, and it may simply be that confessing about the file deletion and medical materials was the lesser evil compared to a full, public inspection of the Primo's actions. But still — there was a risk he was taking here, a risk of essentially handing the Archive the entire case against himself on a silver platter.

And as much as the Code-fanatic Archivist in me hated to admit, going through a whole formal investigation of an acting Primo would be no easy feat. There'd be a whole lot of public attention to both the Archive and me personally. There'd certainly be confrontations with the less polite members of Sabi's administration. And if it were only to reach the conclusion that nothing of consequence was hidden, that would indeed be an exercise in pointless, procedural stick-assness.

And maybe this is the man's soft spot. Going into such risks only to protect his wife and son — that only makes him human, ne? There was a bitter aftertaste to that thought, if I was completely honest.

A wave of weariness washed over me. Bashiri taking his own life, the Primo sitting with me here, the earlier encounter with Kilian at the Nebula — this was just too much to take in at the moment. I needed to rest and figure things out quietly.

"Primo," my throat was sore and dry. All I wanted was for them to get out of my room. "This is all way over my head, sir. The Archive team is super-busy with the Final Call review, to the point that a high-caliber investigation requiring more resources would be a huge distraction. So unless there is a clear evidence of conduct endangering the Mission —" both men were intently focused on my next words. I could see their mouths contorting with anticipation. *There is some fun in that,* I admitted to myself.

"— I would say that prioritizations would have to be made. Final Call is a Thetis foundational milestone. We can't screw this one up."

A contemptuous sneer came from Jericho. "Your *wapa* Doctor friend already screwed it up to the bone," he blurted. Sabi Anderson exchanged a silent look with Pakk, then pulled himself up from the chair with a low groan, straightening his collared shirt.

I looked at the Primo in question. "What does that mean?"

A subtle tapping from the other side of the door marked the cue for Anderson to wrap up his visit. Jericho pressed the door handle, opening it to a crack. Sabi was about to exit the room when he stopped at the doorway and turned his head to me with a serious nod.

"Let us all wait for the official assessment."

He walked out of the room, and a shy nurse slipped in to check and remove the tubing I had been connected to since the accident. When she was done with her bit, Pakk closed the door behind her, a smug smile smeared across his face. He waited.

"Oh, spill it already," I snapped at him, "you look like an exhilarated virgin on her deflowerment bed."

At least *that* dimmed his creepy smile a notch.

"We're all going to acknowledge that the past 24 hours have profoundly changed things on the Thetis. What your ex-scientist friend has done was not only kill himself, but he almost threw us all into the Trash Tube with him."

"He wasn't a friend," I protested.

"Well that doesn't really matter, does it?" Pakk said. "What does matter is that throwing himself in the Tube created an imbalance in the forces operating on the ship. Unfortunately, that imbalance pushed the Thetis off-course for a few minutes."

'Trajectory Drift Identified'. I could hear the PA system looping its warning message in my head.

"And at our speed, that was enough to throw us pretty far from our planned trajectory. Now — the news you and your Eternist friends will probably *love* to hear is that doing so probably delivered a death-blow to our ability to reach both our potential destination planets."

"What?" I blurted skeptically. "How far off-course could we be? Surely we can course-correct back to our original traj, ne?"

Pakk merely shrugged. "The big brains are working on it as we speak, but from what I'm hearing — Gnosis is definitely out of the question and there's a real risk that even 9 Ceti is a no-go. Course correcting simply won't leave us with enough propellant to do the required maneuver. So best case scenario — and that's if we are exceptionally lucky — we're on a one-destination mission now. We're either going to 9 Ceti or we're going nowhere."

For a few moments I simply blinked at him, trying to let this new information sink.

"The upside to all of this for you," he said, "is that there is no more Final Call. It's irrelevant, and so is the review or report or whatever you Archive rats are working on down there. You can take a vacation, heal yourself up. Maybe spend some time with Athena Saugado and Nyasha and all the other Eternist wapas whose life-mission against us just evaporated together with Bashiri's body."

"I'm not an eternist, *kunyete!*" I tried shouting at him, which brought a burst of coughing and a burnt throat. *Will he just go already and leave me alone? I have to do some thinking and make sense of this.*

"Of course you're not," he sneered and actually *winked* at me, smiling. "Because Eternist equals coward, doesn't it? And who wants to be a coward? Surely not any self-respecting Thetan, not in times of emergency like this, ne? After all, we're trying to save the Human race, aren't we? That's a job for *heroes*, not Eternists, ne?"

"Wow. That's some *Earth-Level* verbal gymnastics," I said in mock admiration.

"But it's catchy. You'll see." Jericho mockingly saluted at me and opened the door to leave.

"Take care. Don't go near railings, te?" and he walked out, leaving the door open behind him.

I was finally alone, my head exploding with panic.

I need to get out of here. Fast.

CHAPTER TWENTY-THREE

After Jericho's departure, I forced myself to count to a hundred, then quickly rolled out of bed. A second later, I was surprised to find myself on all fours, fighting a fierce urge to puke.

OK, maybe not quite that fast. I pulled on the IV tube connected to my left forearm and detached its supply bag. I then replaced it with a mobile capsule I found in the medical supply drawer. That way I could carry it around, the capsule dripping whatever it needed dripping into my blood system.

Life is sacred on the Thetis. Doubly so if you've yet to contribute to the Genline. So when it comes to medical care, your personal decision matrix is quite narrow in terms of choice of treatment. You are, in essence, a Thetis property. Not unlike a glorified, breathing inventory item, really. It did make sense, of course — if you're hurt or sick or dead beyond the ability to seed the next generation, you are basically just excess weight.

So when I sneaked out of my room and into the hallway, I was aware that I could well be escorted assertively back to bed by any passing nurse. Frankly, I was too weak and focused on avoiding vertigo to even resist.

What I wasn't prepared for was finding the infirmary hall, corridors, and atrium completely deserted. Not a single staff or patient in sight — just an eerie silence, interrupted periodically by the rhythmic humming and clicking of distant medical machinery.

Where is everybody? Spending your life in a confined spaceship with forty-something thousand people meant that an empty space was a *very* unusual experience. I peeked outside the infirmary building onto the Level 20 main area, and quickly spotted a gathering in front of the PubSheet display wall. I could definitely make out some worried faces in the small crowd.

Kunye what now? I thought. I walked out of the building, slowly dragging myself toward them.

'My dear fellow Thetans,' read the salutation of the official Primo announcement, smeared across the entire four-column layout of the PubSheet front page.

Since I can remember myself, the daily PubSheets were nothing but gossip and bulletin items — nothing anyone younger than forty ever bothered to read. Hey, if something's important enough, it'll get to you eventually, right? Our culture was about face to face dialog rather than written form. So the PubSheets were usually a tangential source of relevant news.

But not today. As I approached the group, I could sense the commotion and worried mumbling. I elbowed my way in to get to the news as quickly as possible. If my initial feeling was that Pakk was overplaying the scare-card on me back in the infirmary room, I wasn't so sure about it now.

My dear fellow Thetans,

Today marks a historic moment in the course of the Thetis mission. A mission we were entrusted with, carrying the last hopes and prayers of our Passados. They have sent us — a select few — from their dying planet to secure a new home for humans in this universe. Never was there a more critical mission in the course of our history.

I stand before you today as the carrier of that most sacred of torches, with my head bowed. For it is my duty to inform you that I have shamefully failed you.

Over the past few months, a subversive group has secretly assembled, attempting to extort and impeach me as the sitting Primo, and take control of the Thetis. That group is led by my political rivals and includes anti-Thetan collaborators from the scientific and archival institutions, relentlessly operating behind the scenes to seed lies and sow destruction of our fragile fabric of existence. Their motives are obvious — personal gain, hunger for power, and total cynicism towards our joint destiny and co-dependence.

Seeing they could not fracture my own legitimacy, the Eternists resorted to illegal actions against my family. They have manufactured information regarding my wife and son's personal life, and used it in an ugly extortion attempt. Unfortunately, the Archive itself has proven to be a stronghold for the Eternist faction, resulting in a quick cover-up and dismissal of my complaints without as much as minimal investigation.

More worrying, I recently learned that my complaint had not only been disregarded, but had in fact been completely *deleted* from the Archive database. It is an unprecedented violation of the Thetis Code and an outrageous personal and political attack on an elected Primo.

It will not stand.

Here on the Thetis, we live by the values of Transparency and Tolerance. Transparency is what keeps us united. Tolerance, apparently, is a double-edged sword when it comes to keeping public safety as first priority.

Yesterday, the initiator of the extortion attempt — a mentally unstable man by the name of Almaz Bashiri — has decided to end his own life by using his privileged lab access to the Ionized Debris Beam. As a result, the particle stream flowing through the central part of the Thetis encountered severe instability. You have all experienced the violent outcome, by which many good Thetans were injured, and significant damage has been sustained by the ship.

Dear Thetans. If that was all there was to it, we would have put the incident to rest and kept on with our mission. Unfortunately, this is not the case, and the consequences of the Eternist sabotage run deeper than what any of us could possibly imagine.

The sideways skid experienced by the Thetis, and at our current speed of 0.3 times the Speed of Light, resulted in a substantial deviation from our planned course — a drift that may prove irreversible and, potentially, lethal.

Dealing with such a catastrophic event demands the utmost in leadership, assertiveness, and execution capabilities. I am proud to assure you that the team leading the Thetis possesses all these merits and beyond. Under my direction, the best minds on the Thetis are tirelessly working to find a solution to the trajectory shift.

For now, we keep sailing. And we will — I swear by my Primoship! — find a solution. But salvation shall not be without sacrifice.

Our Earther Passados planned the Thetis mission for nearly a hundred years, attempting to anticipate every possible obstacle. Redundancies were incorporated into every facet of the ship, as well as in our choice of target planet. As you all know, there were two star systems identified for potential Human Resettlement. The plan included a decision point — the event we call Final Call — where all Thetans would collectively choose of our final destination.

We no longer possess this luxury.

In the course of searching for the mathematical solution to repositioning the ship in a new, safe trajectory, one fact quickly became very clear: our Flight Control team will have to expend a large portion of our emergency propellant tanks. If you feel slightly heavier today, it is because we will be decelerating slightly harder for the next few months, resulting in a fraction of a G higher than usual on the Thetis. Consequently, by the time we hopefully regain course, we will have depleted all our external propellant repositories and won't be able to execute another major maneuver of the ship.

We will pull through this together. But we must accept the fact that Gnosis Zeta is no longer a viable option for the Thetis. The Passados' plan to give us control over our destiny is no longer feasible.

My brothers and sisters! The urgency of the hour presents us with the opportunity to focus on who we are — Thetans are strong, resilient and creative. What we need right now is *Unity* — Democracy and a multitude of opinions are at our society's core, but the hour calls for deferring those to a later time. When we are all, Sol willing, standing on *Terra Firma*, there will be ample opportunity for open debate.

What matters now is *Stability*. We have almost met our demise today at the hands of subversive members within our own community. We cannot afford another such trial. The enemies within have chosen to target me, knowing they cannot subdue me and the spirit of us Thetans via the due process of elections. An attempt on me is an attempt on the Unity and Stability of the Thetis, and on the Human project itself. We must all stand strong in opposition of such extremist currents.

To ensure the success of our mission, and until exhaustive conclusions are drawn as to the origin and participants of the events at hand, I am declaring an emergency state on the Thetis.

This is not a measure taken lightly, but we must put our society's safety first.

And to any possible sympathizers with the destructive agenda led by the Eternists faction, I say — repent! Our forefathers built a peaceful community on the Thetis, yet we will not stand by as you jeopardize our future for your lowly and selfish political ambitions. You still have the opportunity to regain your sensibility. Fall back in line.

Embark and Prosper,

Primo Sebastian Anderson.

CHAPTER TWENTY-FOUR

For a few moments I just stood there, staring aimlessly at the large screen. *Embark and Prosper.* The closing salutation sealing the Embarkment Certificate. The most common greeting exchanged between Thetans on a daily basis. Its meaning appeared to be disintegrating before my eyes, either from the *Embark* side – the physical threat that we might not last the journey, or from the *Prosper* side — that we were facing a looming retraction into tyranny.

Demetrius Smoak was right, I thought. Refugees don't seed. People under attack don't build. They consume and move on. They run for cover, dig deep shelters, optimizing for survival rather than prosperity. They *fear.*

And how easy it is to convince people that they are under attack. Not ten minutes ago, Sebastian Anderson stood by my bed, confessing his ordering of the unlawful expurgation of Archive filings, and essentially assuring that he would not suffer any consequences from it. And still — this assault, when he could have as easily just let it all slide by quietly. Nobody would have cared.

The announcement in the PubSheets had clearly been in the works long in advance, ready to publish even as Sabi stepped into my room peddling his confession. Meticulously planned to incite the right reaction from people. *Why?* This was the bit I couldn't figure out. *What is Anderson still so intimidated by?*

"Don't turn around," a female voice whispered near my left ear. "Act natural."

I turned around. *Kunye mala. When it shines, it burns.* "Any of this seem natural to you, Heleni?"

Heleni took a step back. This was not how she'd played this in her head, which was precisely the effect I was going for. Her cheeks reddened. *Dio,* this bruta was just frustratingly gorgeous! Her pregnancy only accented her radiant beauty. If at any point in the future they would start Genegineering humans on spec, Heleni would be a Premium template.

"I'm here for tests," she said louder than necessary, pointing at her belly. Her eyes shot nervously in all directions. *Pretty, but the worst actress ever.*

"Yeah," I blurted out, "'maybe you're planning a family'. I got it the first time."

Heleni's face toughened. "Kunyete. You'll get no sympathy from me. I know you're involved in... this," she gestured toward the PubSheet wall.

"Oh, do you?" I said sarcastically.

"And I know you're trying to drag Kilian into this mess. Well, that's never going to happen. He almost lost *everything* because of you once. I'm not going to let you use him again."

"I never used Kilian!" I stuck my finger at her face. Some heads turned briefly in our direction. I took it down a notch. "I *loved* him. There's a huge difference."

"Oh, no, no, no. *Love* is coming here, risking being tracked and grid-located communicating with a kunye Eternist. Love is *protecting* your family, not betraying them! It's a very clear and simple thing. What you really loved wasn't Kilian. It was your own ideals. I know the story."

189

"You know *nothing* about the story, I can assure you that."

Heleni raised her hands in frustration. "Why am I even having this discussion with you? This is not why I came down here."

I shrugged. "Insecurity."

She laughed. "What, from you?" She placed a soft hand on her small, protruding belly and caressed it absentmindedly. "Why on Thetis would I be threatened by you, Sandrine?"

I tried to keep my cool as hard as I could. "You said it yourself," I smiled. "I'm smart. And for some people, it *is* so very attractive. And unlike physical beauty, smart has far greater lasting power."

Heleni just looked at me for a few seconds. Her voice unexpectedly softened when she spoke again. "I pity you," she whispered. "You're so analytical, you can't feel the change."

I bowed my head. This was going nowhere. "Why are you here, Heleni? What do you want? This can't be a social visit."

"Believe me, I'd rather be as far as possible from you right now, Sandrine. And I don't *want* anything from you, that's for sure. I am only doing this for him."

"K sent you here?"

Heleni sighed with controlled frustration. "He's furious. Explosive. I've never seen him like that. He wanted to come see you himself but I wouldn't hear of it. So I had to promise to talk to you myself."

"What about?"

Heleni lowered her voice and stepped closer to my ear. "All this," she gestured at Sabi's message on the display wall. "The... accident, or whatever they want to call it. He didn't want to tell me how exactly, but he's concerned he's involuntarily had a part in this. That he'd been played by the Primo's people. It drives him *mad.*"

"We should open a club," I said. *Come to think of it, we already did once.* "What does Kilian have to do with the Primo? Isn't he playing good boy now with the authorities?"

"I have no idea," Heleni said. "He wouldn't elaborate."

"Heleni, we're standing in the middle of a kunye public level platform. I just ditched my infirmary room. And we're both probably tracked. I would assume we have a limited window of time here. So let's skip the enigmas, te?"

Heleni glanced around again, nervous. The internal debate she was having was playing like a drama-vid on her face.

"He said you'd probably want to know where something called the sixth node is located," she said.

Kunye What?! "Heleni, this is important! What did he say *exactly?*" I grabbed both her forearms and dragged her away from the crowd. My head was throbbing and I could feel every single nano-taser stitch applied to my cuts. I had no more patience for this *bafunye*.

Heleni looked at me contemptuously. "Important to *whom,* Sandrine? Is it important to Kilian? Or is this whole thing just a hook that will only drag him down the spiral of your *'obsession du jour'*? I know he thinks you're onto something *Grand*," she waved her hands to mimic the word, "but aren't you *always* onto something grand? Isn't it your kunye hallmark? Am I crazy for wanting to protect Kilian from your destructive conspiracies?"

"But what if I *am* onto something?" I hissed. "And what if Kilian holds the key to information with major implications for *all* of us Thetans? With all due respect to the cuddly convenience of shooting you up with babies and living the quiet farmer life, he has a responsibility to this ship and its people. We all do."

"Not when the only *real* implications will be on him. On *us.* He's already been burnt once. You should know best, Sandrine — you were the one to kindle the fire. So with all due respect *back*, for Kilian there's absolutely no traj-side in getting involved. Any key he may be holding, he's better off swallowing it. You're just a specter from the past, trying to spook yourself back into his life."

So he does think about me, I noted. "Heleni, look. You've got to rise above this personal *bafunye*. This sixth node Kilian mentioned may be the evidence of an unheard-of criminal breaking of the Code. Manipulating the upcoming Elections, maybe. By our own leaders, probably."

Heleni crossed both arms under her breasts. Her honey-colored curls rested calmly on her shoulders, blending with her reddened, annoyed face.

"Ah, the Code!" Heleni sighed. "Grow up, Sandrine. We're no longer in Junior Academy, te? We can argue big ideals until gravity flips, but when it comes to real life, we are walking a very thin line now. You read the Primo — we need to line up in order to push through this trip to 9 Ceti."

"So nothing else matters anymore? Truth? The Code? Good people like Kilian being put under surveillance? Do you like sneaking around grid-locators, thinking up explanations if anyone inquires why you met me here?"

"I'm not sneaking around," she said defensively, "and I have nothing to hide, mind you. If you're so devoted to operating within the Code, you shouldn't mind everything being transparent too, should you? Where would I go that I'd mind the tracking? Only people with something to hide would be against that, ne?"

"So that's it? We just give everything up? All our privacy rights? All the balances our Passados have built into the Thetis system?"

"Did they anticipate an Eternist wapa walking into the Trash Tube and destabilizing the ship to the point where we don't even know if we can physically make it? Things *change*, Sandrine, and we need experienced people to deal with it now, even if you and me, the common spacers, need to snail-in and accept some restrictions."

"Wow," I sneered, "how such a small baby can suck out an entire woman's courage. Its all self-preservation for you now, te?"

"Maybe it's called caring for someone other than yourself. You should try it too sometime."

Against every resisting bone in my body, that stung. Heleni noticed it too. I saw remorse in her eyes as she lowered her hands to her sides and sighed.

"It's all just very scary, all this *mala*."

"I won't drag K into this, Heleni, I can promise you that. You may not believe me when I say it — but I'm really relieved things have worked out for him."

A tired smile formed at the corner of her red mouth. "It's not like I have any coherent information for you, anyhow. Kilian was pretty… upset. All he said is that you need to find the sixth node and for that you need to go back to the origin. That you'll find what you are looking for at the origin."

"The origin?" I looked at her impatiently. "The origin of *what?*"

Heleni shook her head apologetically. "I don't know. Kilian probably figured you'd get it."

We both just stood there for a few more moments, until it was clear that there was nothing else to say and the momentary connection faded off. Without any further words, Heleni simply shrugged away the awkwardness and started walking toward the Ascenders.

I pulled away from the commotion by the PubSheet wall. I needed to get to my hab and think.

CHAPTER TWENTY-FIVE

Twenty minutes later I was safely back in my hab on 19th, and by that time it was already crystal clear that Heleni was right. I took the long, backlot route down, trying to avoid meeting anyone who might have an urge to comment on my newly-acquired stardom or the fact that I was walking around bleeding from my head. Even though I was mostly successful in that endeavor, I couldn't miss the profound change in the air. Just like Heleni said, it was not something you could exactly define. You had to *feel* it.

The Thetis was quiet, but not the night kind of quiet. Not the happy-stress quiet that would engulf the ship before public events such as the Birth Year Rights announcements. Not even the exhausted, hung-over quiet of post-celebration mornings or public holidays. This kind of quiet was different, one I had never experienced before. It was the damp stillness of a *depressed* Thetis, trying to come to terms with an existential threat none of us could do anything about.

Anywhere you looked, the appearance of life in its usual pace was still there, albeit misleading. People were still engaged in heated conversations, still traversing the ship on their daily errands, still working their work and playing their play. But, if you observed closely, you couldn't miss the thin, misty layer of melancholy hovering lightly in the air, touching everything and everyone on the ship.

They were all still faking it with all their might, but the truth was that every single one of us was *terrified*.

And it is only going to get worse, I told myself. What was the phrase Heleni used? 'Snail-in'. A weird but seemingly proper metaphor relating, ironically enough, to an organism long-extinct when its environment had, too, exhausted its propellant and ran out of solutions. And the reason it was only going to get worse was because it was Birth Year.

This most sacred of Thetis rituals originally occurred once in every twenty years. And even with the cycles growing more frequent, it's been seventeen years since Gen8 was born. It was easy to forget how profound a change a Birth Year creates on the ship. The past few years had been an adult-centered heaven: Gen8ers were entering their Junior Academy years, and their parents — Gen7ers still in their thirties and a smaller group of Gen6ers kissing fifty years-old — were finally getting their freedom back. Cultural activities, sports, social events — we were all living in abundance, both spiritually and substantially. Every facility in the ship was ramping up its production and inventory in preparation for the several thousands new mouths expected to arrive with Generation 9, so there was never shortage of any conceivable resource. It was Work Hard, Play Hard — the Thetis was a Happy Hour frozen in time, and we thought it would last forever.

But the cyclical nature of life would soon dim the lights on this era on behalf of the big change that was eminently coming with Birth Year. If anything, one thing was consistent throughout Human procreation history — paternal instincts turned people inwards into the domestics of their own habs. Instead of reform, new parents sought safety. Instead of change and progress, they preferred the mental convenience of the tried and tested. *Who cares about politics when you hardly sleep at night, te?*

And soon, a whole generation of snails will emerge on the Thetis. I knew I was biased in this respect by my own situation, but I couldn't help the realization of how perfectly this would play into the hands of anyone trying to manipulate delicate matters without public attention. Half-dazed Genmoms present no opposition, and an all-encompassing existential threat plays perfectly to their weak spots.

I spent about half an hour showering and slipping into my own clothes. With my head trickling blood nonstop and my balance still recuperating, I expended several minutes on my knees scraping the small shower basin clean of red trails. By now, the infirmary personnel must have noticed my absence, and I fully expected to have someone at my door escorting me back any moment.

The quick, dry knocks on my hab door a few minutes later found me ready, if unwilling, to take the short trip upward. To my surprise, the man on the other side of the door wore no medical attire, nor expressed any desire to move me anywhere.

"Hello, Sandrine."

"Nyasha. What are you doing here?" I shot a brief look behind his shoulder for any other companions. They were none.

Nyasha stepped in and looked at me with deep compassion. This was not the middle-of-the-night sneak visit he paid me with Athena Saugado. He was here for personal reasons.

"Don't worry about the infirmary. I just came down from there. You can stay here until you get better."

"Thanks," I said and sat heavily on the bed. "I do feel a lot safer here."

He grabbed a chair and sat in front of me, leaning to get a better look at my head. "How are you feeling, Sandrine? That looks like quite a mess, to be honest with you. I've arranged medications to be delivered to your hab. Do you need anything else?"

"It's fine," I said. "Those NanoTasers hurt, but that's their job I guess, ne? Tomorrow I'll be all stitched up and ready to beam."

Nyasha smiled. He could easily see through my act, but appreciated the gesture all the same. He leaned back in his chair, and for a few moments we just sat together, sharing an unawkward silence. Something was clearly on Nyasha's mind, and I waited patiently for him to bring it forward.

"I am worried," he finally said with an accepting nod.

"You should have seen the railing."

Nyasha brushed my lame attempt at humor with another nod. "Our due date for publishing the Final Call report to the public is tomorrow. We are still lacking material information."

"Ah, Nyasha, I know I have some unfinished reports—"

Nyasha shook his head. "It's not your reports. Those have already been taken care of by Thahliya and her team." He raised his glasses onto his head and let out a short sigh. "I am being kept in the dark, Sandrine, and that puts me in a very delicate position."

This time, I knew better than to interrupt. Nyasha sharing his concerns and confiding in anyone was a rarity.

"You see," Nyasha continued, "we haven't received anything from any of Cassidi's departments. Zero data, or access, or even a formal response to our inquiry about the delivery schedule. This could hamper my ability to publish the report by the time limit dictated in the Code."

"And that would open all sorts of opportunities for interested parties to come up with inadmissibility claims," I nodded, then shrugged. "Nyasha, is this a protocol thing? Because for all other matters isn't the report and the whole concept of Final Call a pointless exercise now?"

Nyasha raised a silver eyebrow. "Is it?"

I raised my hands in frustration. "Unless that head-butt I got was *way* harder than I thought — didn't we just read that the whole plan just got flushed down the Trash Tube? We'll be extremely lucky to even be able to get to 9 Ceti and not remain stranded in space for eternity. You saw it, ne? It was all over the PubSheets."

"It must be true, then."

I eyed Nyasha suspiciously. "They ran the calculations, didn't they? If QUBIC didn't find a solution in the first few hours, the odds keep decreasing pretty fast after that."

Nyasha politely waited for me to cool off. He didn't push back or argue. In fact, he barely moved at all, his eyes planted on the floor.

"There are differing opinions," he said quietly.

That took me like a punch to the gut. *"Kei?"* I suppressed a shout. Nyasha didn't budge. I desperately waited for him to fill the silence and when he didn't, I couldn't hold back my confusion any longer.

"By *whom?* What do you mean by 'opinions'? Are those so-called opinions something you would voice out loud?" I was rambling, I knew it, but I just couldn't stand the series of laconic, insinuating replies Nyasha was serving.

Nyasha smiled again, and this time his signature weary grin was seasoned with a glint of mischievous confidence.

"It's not what you write on the wall, Sandrine. It's what you *do* behind it that matters. Sabi deeply understands that too. Which is what makes him an... efficient leader. And which is also why working on the Final Call report is more important now than ever."

Nyasha's choice of words was revealing to me. Where he said 'efficient', I heard 'dangerous'. This was a harsh concept to swallow — in a transparent and collaborative society such as existed on the Thetis, if saying one thing and doing another could so calmly be called efficiency, what's to become of us?

And then, like the layers of manufactured mist creating the illusion of clouds in the Sensory Farm dissipating, I could see it. "Kunye mala," I locked eyes with Nyasha, then clapped my hands in astonishment.

This man is the smartest, most humble man I know, I thought in awe. When anyone would expect the Final Call procedures to be dropped entirely or at least paused in light of the recent events; when the newly-declared Emergency status gave Anderson a de-facto monopoly on QUBIC resources; when no one else could get access to even remotely sufficient compute power for attempting their own calculations — the *only play* was to keep going as usual. To do the illogical thing of sticking with the plan.

Being a Code-stickler was the perfect cover for Nyasha to maintain his freedom of operation. His un-charismatic, introvert, *geeky* persona was the ultimate protection from any accusations of biased political agenda or personal ambition.

"Sticking with the Final Call report retains the Archive's top priority access to QUBIC nodes," I announced proudly.

Nyasha nodded. "Temporarily."

"When is the Emergency status entering into force?"

"Tomorrow, 5pm."

And then they will have full control over all Thetis resources for the duration of the Emergency Act. Which means they can change anything, delete anything, recrypt and no one could ever disprove them.

I sat back on the bed, deflated. "That's not a lot of time."

Nyasha pushed himself up from the chair. He straightened his grey sweater with one hand and looked around the room, his face now somber.

"What did Kilian say?"

"Nothing gets past you, does it?"

Nyasha shrugged.

"Some cryptic mala," I said. "About going back to the origin to find the sixth QUBIC node."

Nyasha pondered the words for a moment, then refocused. "You take the night to heal, Sandrine," he said, affection seeping into his voice. "Take the meds. Let the Tasers do their work, vape some algae if you need to. But come to work tomorrow morning. Cracked or not, I need your head."

CHAPTER TWENTY-SIX

As if I could even hope for a single minute of sleep that night.

I suffered through the hours, letting the tasers perform their tissue-welding and cell-regeneration. Lying in bed, staring at the ceiling and feeling every single sting of the microelectric shocks, I kept telling myself that at least in terms of life-supporting healthcare, the Thetis greatly benefited from the availability of Pre-Embarkment Earth technologies.

It was a stripped-down suite of technologies, to be certain. None of the lifestyle design augmentations of Late Earth Tech which you could apparently buy at the time were authorized on board, so all the super-power Augs had to go at the gate. Thinking about what had been achieved on Earth and readily available for any person to use was mind blowing: enhanced vision through retina-bypass implants. Cognitive enrichment through sub-scalp cerebral induction mesh. Hyper-sense and hyper-muscular performance boosters operating on gene-modded supercells. Crazy stuff in Thetis terms. And that's before even getting into longevity enhancements, bodymorphing and cultural-oriented Augs. The more extreme utilizations of those technologies were on the verge of creepiness, eventually resulting in the decision to adopt a much earlier reference point as what the Thetis project toolset would look like. Too much tech was seen as risky and prone to destabilize equality on board.

Luckily, as far as Intensive Care and trauma response, the decision went for adopting the most advanced tech of the time. And so, as painful and unrelenting those NanoTasers were working their way though my torn tissue, they did get me reasonably functional and unscarred as morning crept in.

Still, sleep was a hopeful stretch at best. It wasn't the physical discomfort keeping me up — it was the endless, torturing thought cycles carving crevasses of self-doubt in my exhausted mind. It was the self-torment and the 'what-if's and the 'why's that were multiplying within me by the second.

"Everything is real, except your thoughts," I mumbled into the darkness. That was a grounding mantra I learned from a very special woman once, which often helped me in times of mental chaos.

It didn't help this time. I was cold and I was lonely and for the first time in my life — I was truly afraid. I felt caged-in in my own hab — the one place which had always been my sanctuary, my safe recharging spot.

I strongly needed to get out. To find some comfort in the presence of other people. When I was younger, this would often mean a lightrise visit to the Nebula, resulting in the inevitable mix of hangover and bad judgement. Tonight, however, I was in no shape to handle the downward mental spiral, and that stuff would only escalate it. I needed something positive. Something tender.

She opened the door — as she always does — with a smile. Violet. *Sunny Violet*, I used to call her. Even in this illogical hour, her eyes were warm, her smile inviting. I showed up unannounced, obviously waking her up, but she was all kindness. The load on my chest was already beginning to dissipate, and I could finally breathe.

She hugged me briskly, her eyes gently searching mine for my intentions. For which type of loneliness I was there to allay. For what comes next.

"Can I come in?" I whispered into her hug.

She closed the door behind us and led me into the dark room. At the center of the small space, backed against the main wall decorated with tapestry of dark-colored patterns, Violet's bed looked wide and soft and welcoming. Without hesitation, I slid beneath the heavy, puffy blanket and curled to one side, basking in the warmth still trapped in it from her interrupted night's sleep.

A moment later, Violet's weight shifted near behind my back, her chin lightly prodding my shoulder. Her voice was warm and still half-dazed and airy.

"If we're having sex, can I jump in for a quick shower first? Unless this is a hornmergency."

I chuckled. We had, on occasion, enjoyed the spontaneous roll or two in the sheets whenever mood and inspiration aligned. I mean — *reproduction* was a planned, serious matter on the Thetis. Much more of a mission than a spontaneous occurrence. But for fun, for companionship, for seeking comfort from this life's random harshnesses — why would gender, or age, or any other rigid confinement be a limiting factor? If one found solace or thrill in another — that was a blessing, we believed.

I pressed by back against her. I closed me eyes, feeling her warm breath on my neck. A memory flashed within me:

Kilian's breath on my neck. We're lying in bed, he's hugging me from behind. We are both drifting off, drained after a long day in the squeeze.

"Good night," he whispers into my hair. He starts to disengage and roll away to the other side of the bed.

"Night," I reach my hand behind my back and lay in on the small of his back. "Unless… you want to have sex?"

I can feel him stop mid-roll, turning his head back, hesitantly gauging if I was serious.

I look back into his eyes with my best effort of a mischievous smile. I am.

Kilian inches closer tentatively, nods. "OK, let us discuss this fair proposition," he mocks a formal tone.

"There's nothing to discuss," I mock back a caricature sexy voice. "You get your body over here, strong and hard, and I'll ride it till I'm done with you. Then you can go to sleep."

Kilian stops, seemingly pondering the concept for a few seconds.

"Good talk," he concludes eventually and jumps all over me. I shriek with laughter.

This is how simple things were, I sighed.

We were in the golden phase of our time together back then. Long term, it's never healthy for a relationship to be based on too wide a gap between the participating personalities. When one side disproportionally adores the other, superiority becomes a foundational element in everything they build together. It's a powerful aphrodisiac, but in absence of reciprocity it quickly turns corrosive.

Ironically, the tables tend to turn at some point in a long relationship. Each partner's imperfections and flaws and intricacies play out to their inevitable outcome where it is impossible to adore any longer, only to carry on with a mixture of comfort and quiet disappointment.

But there, in the middle, there is a magical moment of equilibrium. The idol having descended to human. The fan having risen to worthy partner. And there, a wave of electricity ignites between two equals bonded tight by the confidence of their mutual revelations in each other.

That magic, that intoxicating confidence was me and Kilian right before everything blew up in our face.

I sighed again. "I just need a cuddle tonight, Vi. I think I may be lost."

"Well, first of all, it's morning already," Violet tucked the thick blanket around me and stroked my hair gently. "And second, Sandrine

Liet, I know you since before either of us could even speak properly. You're *never* lost. Maybe you just still haven't found your internal map for this specific journey you're on."

A moment of silence passed between us. Then I chuckled. "Kunyete. Take this cheesy bafunye to your patients, Vi, not me. Te?"

She smiled at me affectionately. I knew she was just trying to make me laugh, and somehow — strangely — it did make me feel a little better. Some people have this energy to them — they have such a stable center, that simply being in their orbit gives you calm and confidence that everything will be all right.

I lifted my hand and caressed her warm cheek. "I'm sorry, Vi, for barging in here like that. I just didn't know where to go."

"You know you're always welcome here," she said, "no matter what happens."

I nodded. "I'm afraid," I said. "I'm afraid that I am starting a war with the most powerful people on the Thetis. And I am afraid that if I'm wrong, I'd be throwing away my last remaining chance to get my life back. My Genline."

Violet just nodded slowly in silence.

"But I know that I can't just let it go. That if I'm *right*, there's some sinister mala going on which endangers all of us."

I closed my eyes again and exhaled deeply. "I just wish someone else would deal with it instead of me."

Violet rose on one elbow and looked me with soft eyes. "You know I can't give you professional advice. I'm just a mediocre therapist slash failed poet with zero notable achievements in her life —" She raised her palm to stop any protest I may be trying to express.

"But I will tell you this: you are by far the person with the best intuitions I have ever met in my entire life. After all," she smiled mischievously, "you did choose me as your best friend out of a whole generation, ne? And you being a tough and uncompromising *bruta* had caused you to sacrifice everything you had in your life, that's true. But that's who you are, and that's why there *is* no one else who can wage this war in your stead."

I felt a warm tear roll down my cheek. I shuddered and curled deeper into the blanket, looking at Violet in silence. She lay back at my side, her voice a low hum in the dark.

"All I can tell you is to follow the truth in you. If that means backing off and looking after your interests — that's totally fine. If that means going to battle in spite of all the risks, I would trust you with my life to be the best kunye fighter on this ship."

There was nothing else to be said, so we stayed together, laying in silence in the dark hab, Violet's words floating in the air and in my thoughts.

CHAPTER TWENTY-SEVEN

I must have eventually dozed off for an hour or two, because when I opened my eyes Violet was already gone. I dragged myself into the shower, rinsing off the traces of dry blood and the NanoTaser dust-like particles. I then dressed in the previous day's clothes and went straight to the Archive. There was something, a hunch, I needed to validate before anyone arrived to the office today.

Hello, World.
I sighed as the familiar text floated inside QUBIC's terminal. *So few things are constant in a woman's life,* I thought. The fact that this reliable welcome message was one of them — from a machine built around the very theory eliminating anything constant for a cloud of probabilities — was surely some divine creature's idea of irony.

It was slightly after 5am, so I figured I had at least an hour before Nyasha would come in for his early workday start. You'd find us workaholics on both ends of the spectrum — when we're young and pre-kids, or after they've grown up to leave you with a vacuum time-bubble to fill. For everyone else, office was merely a second job.

I flexed my fingers and started navigating my way through the machine's assisted decision trees. Within minutes, relaxation came over me. This was *home.* I could spend hours and days working on the terminal in a complete state of flow. I felt secure exploring its depths and data structures. With QUBIC I *understood* the causality matrix between input and output. The intricate leverages and sensitivities influencing the algorithmic decision process. With people? Not so much.

Finally, the system was ready for the data-dive I needed. *I need to tread carefully here,* I noted to myself. If what I was looking for confirmed my hunch, I would be entering the ring against some very powerful people. So I'd better take a completely admissible process — they will surely try to crack down on the legitimacy of my actions.

After a moment of inserting the search queries, the personal file I was looking for pulled up and unfolded inside the translucent terminal cube. I couldn't help but squint at the profile picture decorating the file header.

"Kunyeme, I look young," I mumbled. That particular photo had been taken not more than a year ago, but this year had certainly taken its toll on my complexion.

I swiped the profile summary page away, and navigated into the Medical History folder. *Now comes the fun part.*

It took me no more than two minutes to find, compare and validate the data I was looking for. I sat back in my chair, staring at thin air, completely astonished.

Most people don't believe in conspiracy theories because for such a theory to be true, the involved person or authority would need to have crossed deeply-rooted norms or taboos or moral boundaries to their furthest extremes. And most people are not ready to believe such behavior to be plausible, or even *possible*, coming from a public figure. So ironically, when it does, the conspiracy usually operates undetected for a *very* long time under everyone's noses.

Petty criminals go to jail, evil masterminds get parks named after them.

And in this case, I was beginning to realize, the worst possible boundaries were being crossed right in the open. And the people crossing it knew that they were protected by the sheer enormity of the treacherous act. That some crimes are, in fact, too big to fail.

What they didn't take into account was me. No one could have anticipated me being in the Sensory Farm at that precise moment. And the Thetis drift throwing me off to smash into the hard railing. And the esoteric, geeky fact that I never forget a number once I've seen it. More specifically in this case — a certain person's CrypId repeating twice in my medical events log.

I immediately understood the story emerging behind the repeating CrypId and the leverage that understanding offered me. If I acted fast enough.

It was not yet 6am. I rushed off out of the Archive office, leaving a copy of the data log on Nyasha's desk. *Necessary insurance,* I told myself. If I could pay the visit I needed and return quickly enough, Nyasha and I could have a very fruitful conversation when he showed up for work that morning.

CHAPTER TWENTY-EIGHT

With his rough-skinned palms wrapped tight around my throat, Jericho Pakk pushed and slammed me against the wall opposite his hab door. He was a good eight inches shorter than me, but his aggressiveness more than compensated for his disadvantage in size.

"You kunye wapinya," he growled, his red face so close to mine he was merely a defocused blur. "You come to my hab, to my *family*, interrupting our morning circle, with these bafunye accusations? This is a self-destructive life you are leading, Liet."

Most people will threaten you, even *hurt* you, but there's always a line they wouldn't cross. A point of real, material or physical damage. A point of no return. If you endure their storm long enough, they will escalate but, eventually, fold. But once in every while a true sociopath is born. Someone for whom total annihilation isn't an empty threat, but merely another plausible outcome in the branching narrative tree of the situation.

"Hands off, Pakk," I croaked. His grip only tightened. A speckle of black dots began floating in front of my eyes. "...biotracking..."

He knew what that meant, of course. Since I was newly-released from the infirmary, my vitals would be tracked for a few additional days to ensure the healing process stayed on track. Any major drop in Oxygen levels or a spike in blood pressure would trigger alarm bells, and an IC team would immediately rush to my location for support. For all Pakk knew, they might already be on their way.

He dropped his hands, and as the blood rushed back to my head I had to fight the vomiting reflex pulsating up my chest. After a few seconds of rebalancing, I took a deep breath and stared directly into Jericho's icy eyes.

"Touch me again, and I file for assault," I said.

Jericho stepped back and suppressed a laugh. "Oh will you? How's it been working out for you so far? I hear your filings have a tendency to mysteriously disappear." He stared back at me with an unblinking gaze. "How many more of those until your credibility is completely thrashed, eh?"

"It's not about my credibility here, Pakk," I said. "The data from the Thetis grid-locators is not a matter of opinion or popularity. It's fact. And that data puts only three people in the entire Thetis inside the Sensory Farm's zone at the time of Bashiri's death: Dr. Almaz Bashiri himself, me — and you. That was no accident or suicide, wapa. It was kunye *murder*!"

If my attempt to startle Jericho with a direct accusation had hit anywhere close to home, then I was witnessing the greatest display of self control I'd ever seen in a human being. He didn't as much as flinch.

"What data, *bruta*?" he took a threatening step closer. "If you were stupid enough to extract specific personal grid-location data without an explicit warrant, then not only is anything you think you have completely inadmissible, but I will *personally* make sure you are accused of illegal access to personal information, Archival tampering, obstruction of justice and a dozen other violations of your formal duty. So off you go, little starlet. I have a morning circle to get back to. Right *now*."

So, that's how you want to play it? Oh, I can play stupid. There was an expression back on Earth I came across in one of Demetrius Smoak's early interviews: When rock meets rock, the harder rock triumphs. When rock meets water, time shall let no rock prevail. Aggressiveness vs. erosion. What made the Thetis such a peaceful, conflict-free society was that we had all the time in the world. Ten generations worth of time to address and solve any given problem.

That was not the case here. Time for a bit of a rock fight.

"Oh my," I did my best imitation of a squeaky, girlish voice, "I wasn't a bad girly prying through your secret private data, I swear! I am too simple to understand such grown-up words like 'medical information rights' and 'data sovereignty' and all those complicated Legal Code terms. But hey — *someone* picked me up at the Sensory Farm. And *you* handed me the crypsheet in the infirmary room. Both those events are considered my personal information, aren't they? And I *do* have legal authority to access my own chip's log data, don't I?"

Pakk just nodded tentatively. I kept going.

"It's not *my* fault my silly brain just can't forget two identical numbers appearing in the same log, is it? Imagine my surprise when I saw the same CrypID number recorded on *both* the infirmary room *and* the Sensory Farm interactions! So I guess... it *must* have been you in the GenLab with the poor doctor. What do you say, Secundus Pakk?"

Jericho Pakk took a step back and looked at me in silence. His face remained ice-cold, but his eyes reflected a realization which was slowly sinking in. He was outmaneuvered, trapped. Finally, his snowy-white eyelashes blinked.

"I saved your *life* there, wapinya," he whispered.

I took a step closer to him and dropped the girlish tone, looking down right into his pale eyes. *Here comes the hammer.* "Biggest mistake you ever made. And if you want even the slightest chance of avoiding Anti-Thetan accusations, which would be devastating to your Genline, your only traj now is through Nyasha's office and collaboration with the Archive investigation. *Today.* We need to know what Anderson is plotting and why."

It's never a pretty sight to see a hard man crack. And this particular man was being tested for his loyalty to the most powerful person in existence. People in such situations could be unpredictable, yet Jericho Pakk, in his core nature, was a rational man. *He'll do the self-*

preserving thing. And Nyasha will erode him to the bone with his endless fountain of soft empathy.

I turned to leave, still feeling the throbbing pressure of Pakk's hands on my throat. "You should have left me there to die, you know."

Jericho Pakk lowered his head and said firmly, "contrary to what you think of me, I am not a killer."

I gave him a quick look over my shoulder. "Then I'll see you at Nyasha's."

The after-effect of the confrontation with Jericho Pakk vibrated through me as I descended back to Level 13. It was a sheer physical, sensual thrill, born from a feeling of power, of forcefully and effectively deploying leverage, of being on top. There was an undeniable magic in exerting dominance, especially when opposing a powerful and vicious person such as the Secundus. *We own you now.*

That primal feeling was new to me. We were living in a civilized, co-dependent society, and so had very intricate rituals for conflict management. *You don't barge hands flailing into a glass shop,* my mom always taught me. Bless her soul.

But this — this was not the mere sweet taste of winning. It was the intoxicating elixir of *crushing,* and I could see how it immediately hijacked my entire sense of perspective.

They say power is addictive. At those moments, I could clearly feel the tendrils of that adrenaline rush gripping my mind, seeding the longing for a second shot of the poison. And as the excitement started to subside, fear seeped in to fill the cracks in my euphoria. The fear of how overpowering that feeling had been, how easy it was to abandon one's cognitive and moral guards.

I dropped off at Level 13 exhausted and panting. The Thetis was fully awake and on the go by then, people traversing to their appointed workplaces, schools, and routine errands that fill a Thetan's day. All I hoped for now was that Nyasha was already at the office. I needed his calming presence to straighten out my thoughts and focus on the one thing that will demystify all this kunye mess. *Origin,* the word pounded in my head repeatedly. *Where do we find the Origin?*

As I aimed for a quick dash toward the Main Archive office, I noticed an unusual crowd gathering in the public park corner just outside the Archive entrance. I slowed down and stepped closer, carefully navigating through the sports park to remain unobserved. In the center of the crowd, standing atop one of the park's benches, Zee Anderson faced the Archive's main door. He was energizing the crowd with one of his pathos-filled speeches, occasionally earning waves of clapping from the two dozen people gathered around him in support of whatever his current cause was.

Kunye Zee's public performances of minuscule political tantrums were something of a legendary ritual on the Thetis. Not unlike the cyclical nature of harvest, Sam Anderson's loudly-acted speeches — complaining about the 'Legal Elite', the 'Scientific Clique', the educational system or a dozen other subjects — had their own form of seasonality. *Apparently,* I thought as I backtracked slowly out of sight, *we are entering the Zee Ranting Season again.* And it appeared that this time, the Archive was at the center of his relentless attention.

Wanting no part in his party, I quickly faded away from the area and back onto the Ascender platform. The conversation with Nyasha would have to wait until the coast was clear, but I had an idea for another source of valuable information. If I could not use Nyasha's experience in cracking Kilian's elusive Origin just yet, I may be able to benefit from an alternative source of experience, albeit admittedly much more... *colorful* of a source, if you will.

CHAPTER TWENTY-NINE

The entrance hall to the Astral Solace Home was unusually silent. Instead of the typical hubbub of social activity of Thetans enjoying their post-duty years, a single young receptionist was idling at the front desk. She raised her head as I approached, noticed my confusion, then shrugged and pointed toward a corridor leading into the innards of the building complex.

"It's just one of those days, I suppose," she said. "They're in Memorial Loop. I think it's that dead scientist thing."

I hesitated. Mourning rituals were a sacred thing on the Thetis. "May I join?" I asked.

The receptionist shot a look toward the corridor, then slanted her head sideways and whispered as loud as she could, punctuating every word with a timed raise of her eyebrows. "I don't suppose there's a lot of mourning going on in this particular case, you know? Everyone's pretty pissed off. You go right in, dear."

Memorial Loop was situated in the inner parts of the Astral Solace building complex. The name suggestively described the long, tubular passage built around the center part of the ship's hull. Behind the triple-layered bulkhead was the void of the Trash Tube piercing through the Thetis tip to toe.

That inner bulkhead was filled with memorial slates engraved with the names of deceased Thetans going all the way back Gen Zeros. By now, those slates filled well over half the circumference of the loop. Knowing the scrupulous planning habits of the *Passados* in those types of things, I was willing to bet that the last slate before Resett would fit perfectly into the last rectangular depression molded into the wall.

As I walked down the dark corridor leading into the Memorial Loop area, I could hear the distant hum of the assembly gathered for the ceremony. Even to my untrained ear, it sounded like an unusually large audience. With the Thetis strict population growth planning, controlling for when a new generation was brought into existence was simple and straightforward. The departure of a generation was a much more distributed affair, resulting in a parting ceremony being held on an almost daily basis in Memorial Loop.

With the rare occasion of a fatal accident, the departed were Thetans who have lived their term to its full extent. The ceremonies were usually small, attended by direct Genline and the occasional Astral Solace friend who, more often than not, was there scouting for vacant slate spots for their own eventual Day in the Loop.

There was no physical aspect to a parting ceremony — worshipping decaying bodies was a thing of our species' ghastly primitive past. And as the Thetis was a self-relying closed ecosystem, the biological body of the departed would anyway have already been processed for raw materials. The ceremony was a bonding ritual with the deceased Thetan spirit and legacy, and as such was usually a private, intimate function.

Not today. The commotion of noises pouring out of the Loop indicated a full house of elders packed inside the cramped tube. They were all here for Dr. Almaz Bashiri's ceremony, although I strongly doubted that more than a handful of them had actually known the introvert scientist when he was still alive.

As I entered the the Loop's entrance area, I couldn't miss the glowing-white flare of Hugo Winkler's hairdo, shaking in the dim light of the hall like an open phosphorous flame. Winkler was leading a feverish argument with a small group of people circled around his wheeler. I navigated to him and, as he spotted me approaching, his face brightened with a smile and he signaled me to join the group.

"Ah, Sandrine!" Hugo wheeled toward me and raised his hands in an extravagant flair. "Not one to miss a celebrity funeral, are you? Oh my!" he gasped as he noticed the swelling, purple Rorschach blot that was my bruised neck. "What on Sol's Eight Moons happened to you, girl?"

"Just a matter of slight miscommunication," I muttered. "But it's all solved now."

"I remember those types of games," said an elderly blond woman who sat by Winkler with a suggestive wink. "Too old for it now, thank you very much!"

The whole group burst in a good-hearted laughter. Not interested in any further discussion about the source of the bruise, I let it slide and turned to Winkler.

"Actually, I came here looking for you," I said. "I need to pick your brain for a bit, Doctor."

"An easy task, it being already mighty spongy with age, my dear." Winkler laughed, and weak, tedious smiles registered on the faces of the four other elders. Armitage was there, flanked on both sides by two women whom I've briefly spotted at the art class but whose names I did not register. The fourth man was decidedly older than the others, similarly assisted by a wheeler, his slouch and slightly puffed face indicating he was frail and probably not far from his own day in the Loop.

"We're confused," Winkler said as I took a seat and joined the small group. "Not only did we not have this kind of attendance to a parting ceremony since maybe Anderson's father—"

"—Bless his soul—" Armitage added.

"—But the specific situation we are facing here has caused us to run into certain… complications."

"What's up?" I asked.

Hugo tipped his head to indicate he was speaking on behalf of the group. "Well, we made a point to hold this ceremony as close to tradition as possible. Or at least try, te? True — this isn't the traditional scenario, and the audience is decidedly larger than we are accustomed to — but it is also not unprecedented."

Nods of approval passed around the small circle.

"There were initially a few grunts and gripes from certain people about paying respects to the deceased Doctor, what with the gloomy consequences of his chosen manner of departure, but we had none of it. For better or worse, the man was a brother Thetan. So we proceeded with the traditional sequence of the ceremony. We've said Contribution, and were about to move on to Passage when we entered into a bit of an ethical argument, if you'd like to call it that."

"There's nothing ethical about it!" Armitage turned his heavy-set torso toward Winkler, waving his meaty palms to support his argument. Winkler closed his eyes as if saying: *see?*

"Contribution is *specifically* divided into two parts: the factual and the symbolic," Armitage blared on in his basso voice, as if he were explaining something trivial to a thick child. "We express gratitude on behalf of the living to the lifelong contribution the deceased has made to the Thetis — that's the practical part, yes? So far — no problem. But then you're supposed to thank the departed for his last act of grace — contributing his biological material back to the Thetis and the resource-cycle of life. The text distinctly describes how, in our human body, we are mere temporary borrowers of substance from our shared resource pool. Our final duty in this life being paying back that debt by feeding it back in our passing. It's quite beautiful, really, if you think about it."

The blond woman with the slightly-overdone-face to the right of Armitage laid a soft hand on his big shoulder. "All heart, this big ape," she commented with sparkling eyes.

"Salt of the Earth!" Winkler announced. Armitage winked at him, acknowledging the friendly stab.

"Long story short," he continued, "as we all know, the good doctor has elected to not grace us with his personal biological matter. Instead, his precious atoms now trace a nice little trail a hundred and fifty thousand miles long behind the Thetis."

"Thief!" the old man on the wheeler suddenly jerked to life. "Take take all your life and not give back? Shame on his Genline!"

Hugo Winkler placed a calming hand on the man's knee. "You're upsetting your father," he said to Armitage.

"*Kei* else is new!" Armitage said defensively. "So I'm not allowed to speak my mind anymore?"

"Wait," I interrupted, "that's your *dad?*" I shifted an amazed look between Armitage, still towering and physically fit at seventy five years old, and the shrunken, feeble man slumped in the wheeler. Somehow I just couldn't imagine the genline connection there.

Hugo Winkler smiled. "Quite amazing, ne? Papa Louis is the last living remnant of Generation 4. And at 95, he tends to be rather opinionated."

"The point," Armitage regained control of the conversation, "is that you can't conclude Contribution without a body. And it only gets worse - how can you say Passage, blessing the departed soul into the new form his material may take in the Thetis ecosystem, when that too isn't going to actually happen? There's no precedent for what we're dealing with here, you see?"

All throughout Armitage's argument, the woman sitting to his left was continuously shaking her head in disbelief, her silver, short-trimmed hair quivering slightly with each shake of her head. She slapped both palms on her thighs, letting out a loud grunt. "It's just tradition, for Sol's sake! It's not a law of nature. With all due respect to the ceremonial customs, I say we just skip the problematic parts or we stick with the original text and don't make a fuss of it."

"*Just tradition!*" Papa Louis spat out. "Ha!"

Armitage raised his palm for pause. "I'm with dad on this one, Gahlia. Those traditions have been carried on for generations. I'd say they define who we are. It isn't merely a semantic argument. Without the values inherent to our traditions, what will we become?"

"*Animals,* is what!" Papa Louis cracked.

The silver-haired woman, whose name was apparently Gahlia, leaned forward toward Papa Louis and said calmly, "Traditions are just made-up boundaries. What may have fit a thousand generations on Earth might not hold up in space. And whichever new traditions help protect us through our journey — those too will need to be rethought in the new planet environment. Everything evolves, even human values."

The circle fell quiet. For some reason, all eyes were set on me. I shot a look at Hugo Winkler.

"So, what's the young generation's take on this, Sandrine?" he asked.

"Me?" I tried to buy time so I could come up with a passable deflection. With all due respect to departure ceremony procedures, the need to validate my suspicion that Bashiri's death did not play out as advertised in the official version seemed more pressing.

"Yes dear," said the blond woman to the right of Armitage. "After all, you kids will be the ones passing those traditions down the Genline, long after we've had our day in the Loop."

"I... hardly qualify as the voice of my generation," I said. "An irritating squeak, maybe."

"Are you... decently committed?" the woman asked through her pursed, red-colored lips.

I raised my head in surprise. "Do you mean am I sexually exclusive?" I asked. "Like, to a single partner?"

Armitage raised his hands in despair. "Does anyone even understand the language of these young generations anymore?" he sighed.

"Well, no," I continued and looked the blond woman in the eyes. "I mean, what's the upside, really?"

The elderly woman's cheeks immediately shot up with a blush. On my left side, Winkler burst out laughing his extravagant roar. "Way to go, girl!" he patted me on the back of my hand. "Someone sticks their nose in your bed, you give them a sniff under the blanket!"

"Listen," I took the opportunity to bring up what I was actually here for. "I came up here to ask Dr. Winkler for his advice on something. But I think you can all be helpful with this specific question."

The blond woman raised her brows. "You need *our* help? When have the young generations ever asked for *our* advice? Don't you simply know *everything*, dear?"

Armitage laughed and squeezed her thigh with his big palm. There was definitely sexual tension between those two. "We're just the Old Farts whose only purpose of existence is to politely fill the waiting line to the Loop, aren't we?"

"*Elderly* Farts, please, mind your language," the blond woman pushed Armitage's hand off her thigh.

Armitage laughed. "Ahh yes. We're from a time when euphemisms still existed, you see. With you young people's transparency trends these days, nobody cares to protect your feelings. It's all in your face, zero class. Can't imagine what they're calling us down there."

"Protein Fertilizer, that's what!" Papa Louis shouted from his wheeler.

"Let the girl speak," Gahlia hushed the group. Her short silver hair framed a stern face pierced by intelligent, pale eyes. You could tell she was exceptionally beautiful in her younger years. Still was, actually.

"But I must warn you," Armitage leaned toward me, "don't think we don't read the PubSheets up here. If this is part of any Eternist campaign against Sabi Anderson, I'll have no part in it."

"Always the Anderson fanboy," Hugo Winkler sighed.

"Proud of it!" Armitage boomed confidently, "I knew his father since we were kids. Never met a smarter, humbler, more righteous man than Benjamin Anderson, I'll tell you that much." He raised a pointed finger at me, "you should be the one to know — after all, he was Head Archivist before this Woo guy, ne?"

"Before my time, old man," I said, "I only ever worked for Nyasha since I was assigned to the Archive a few years ago. And I don't lead any personal campaign against Sebastian Anderson — that is the *last* thing I want to get my head into, as I'm sure you can imagine. But my job is to investigate potential foul play, and you must agree that the fact that the father was a saint doesn't mean the son was born with wings."

"Ha!" Papa Louis jerked again in his seat. "Same old story — far from the tree the apple rolls. Surprise, surprise!"

Armitage's face reddened with suppressed fury, but he managed to recollect himself and refrain from retorting. Watching the bickering between those two old men was a wonder unto itself, but as much as I was enjoying the show, I had come here for the knowledge these senior Thetans may possess, not for the socializing peculiarities of the Astral Solace clique.

"Dr. Winkler," I leaned toward Hugo and gave him the full focus of my attention, knowing how'd he appreciate the gesture. "I came looking for you to ask your assistance in locating something."

Winkler threw a contented look at the other group members sitting around him. "Well that's mighty flattering, my dear! Tell me — what would we be looking for?"

"The Origin," I said.

Winkler paused for a moment, waiting to hear if there was more to it. When it was clear there wasn't, he slanted his head sideways, brows raised in question. "The origin of... what, exactly? The Universe? Mankind? Babies? I'm afraid you'd have to try and be a bit more specific, darling."

"Babies!" Armitage roared in his belly-tumbling laughter, elbowing the blond woman who quickly got caught up in his infectious guffaw. "We may definitely be able to help on this one from the apex of our experience, wouldn't we, Viv?" he squeezed the plump, exposed thighs of the blonde named Viv. "*L'Origine du Monde!*" he announced, throwing a hand in the air for decoration and rewarding him with a burst of laughter from Viv and a roll of the eyes from Gahlia.

"I don't think it would be anything quite as metaphysical," I said dryly. "I can't get into too much detail, but I am looking for some kind of computer system. So it's clearly something to do with the Thetis. I was told I'd find that system at the Origin."

"It's that hacker guy of yours, isn't it?" Winkler asked disapprovingly. When he caught my involuntary nodding, he added, "why not just ask him? Why the walk-around?"

I shook my head. "We're both tracked, and I don't know where and how K got his information on this. I trust him, but if he's being cryptic, I have to assume this is for his own protection."

I looked around the small group to see if the question registered any kind of sense in any of them. "He must've thought I could easily follow his line of thought. Which — clearly — I can't." *Anymore*, I managed to suppress. "So," I forced a smile, "this is where you all come in. You've been here way longer than I have, so where would you look for the Origin?"

The group fell silent, save for the periodic murmuring sounds coming from Papa Louis who was humming himself to sleep in his wheeler. Hugo Winkler clapped his hands conclusively.

"Well, Sandrine, there's only one Origin to be spoken of, and that is Embarkment."

"Well, Clearly!" Armitage blared, unready to relinquish credit for being the one to decipher the mystery. "*Kei* other Origin can there be in our story?"

Embarkment *was* the quintessential origin story for all of us Thetans. We knew, of course, the history of *before*. Of our Earth origin and our ancestors. But after so may generations in space, it was hard to relate to that history as anything other than a peculiarly elaborate fable. For a Thetan to be able to imagine living on a planet populated by *Billions* of people, with different nations and languages, commerce, transportation... that was simply a stretch of imagination few could handle. After all, a *whole level* of the Thetis was dedicated to the Sensory Farm's premise of keeping this connecting thread between Human and Planet from being terminally severed.

So, for all practical matters, Embarkment was *our* origin, the birth of a new kind of Man — the *Homo Infinitus.*

"Obviously, that was my initial hunch too," I nodded. "As a part of my job, I am highly familiar with the Embarkment Certificate text, including the lesser-known United Nations version before the corporations got in. I've also studied the original launch plans, the mission statements, you name it. But I have a feeling this clue won't be something simply sitting in the paperwork."

Embarkment. That word still sent shivers down my spine. The biggest, most pivotal moment in human history. It also was a kind of *Rashomon* — a shapeshifting entity, its backstory, significance and historical interpretation changing as per one's inclination.

The agreed-upon facts are few and far between: The Thetis was initially conceived as a vanity project by the late-Earth United States, meant to glorify the country's economic and scientific supremacy on Land, Sea, Air and Space. But, as the Universal Law of Irony often demonstrates, it quickly ran out of budget and the country's attention was caught by the more immediate issues of climate catastrophes, struggling global economy and rising worries of an all-out global war between the starving nations.

Unleashing a devastating attack that would cripple an entire population was an alarmingly easy feat in those days of total technological dependency and cyber warfare — faceless, emotionless, push-button Armageddon. Billions of people became susceptible to the childish temper tantrum of hollow leaders quibbling over petty control in a reality quickly spinning out of one.

To us Thetans, such a self-destructive down spiral seems utterly unimaginable, even with the clarity of more than two centuries of hindsight.

To be fair, other theories for Earth's decline existed in the Thetis market of free conspiracies. Some narratives put the blame on God's wrath, the religious establishment, Democracy, money, sexual moral decay or the grand kunye lizard in the sky. It really doesn't matter.

Whatever the backstory, the consequential events leading up to where we are now are well documented.

In the two decades after the project was shelved by the US, the Thetis changed hands between a volatile mess of alternating patron states. Initially, it was hailed as the crown jewel and the hope of Humanity floating in the sky, lending its current proprietor the prestige of owning an exit strategy from Earth's inevitable demise. But soon enough, it became the White Elephant no country seemed to be able to bring to a valid, operational status. The huge construct in the sky transformed into a doomsday deterrence weapon, which could be made to drop on any stubborn enemy like a small astroid.

It was then sixty years into the building of the Thetis that the realization crystallized that no nation state could be trusted with such a devastating toy — and the large technology corporations took over the project.

It wasn't an easy transition. People hated the Techs almost as much as they'd become addicted to the convenience the products they peddled provided. Despite endless efforts and turf wars between nations, Space was still a legal regulation gray-zone which the private corporations notoriously exploited to conduct dubious data manipulations, privacy violations and unsupervised genetic engineering developments. There was zero trust in their motives and conduct, and no one knew what those companies planned to make of the huge shiny station they were building above the planet.

The truth was, of course, that it was the very fact that those companies had controlled the largest data sets on Humanity, the environment, the economy and everything else in-between, that gave them the analytic advantage of prediction. They knew where Earth was heading, they were fed-up with the incompetence of the elected governments to act, so they acquired the assets of the failing project and went to work.

And they moved fast. The Tech giants had the benefit of employing the smartest people on the planet, they had the bias for action of commercially-competitive entities, and the methodologies and efficient project management culture to get the job done. Within fifteen years of taking over, the team we now admirably call the

Passados — the mission planners and our de-facto cultural ancestors — had declared the Thetis project operational ready.

Throughout history, some of the most ambitious human projects — architectural monuments, magnificent paintings — had taken the entire lifetimes of their artists to complete. The Thetis, seventy five years into the making, was by no means a work of art — the clunky patchwork of metal hovering above Earth was literally scarred by the random whims of each of its previous owners to make their mark on it. And yet, countless scientists, engineers and designers had devoted their entire careers to bring this monumental project to fruition. And perhaps no other object in history may have had such an inspirational impact on a decaying population looking up to the sky. For the suffering people on Earth, the Thetis was the Chariot of Redemption.

The reason that the *Passados* are still admired to such an extent today is that their ingenuity and vision far exceeded the mere task of building the ship. Their ultimate mission was not building a spacecraft — it was creating a platform upon which to save Humanity itself. That meant locating alternative homes for Humans in space; instilling the mechanisms which would support such a massive transition of humans across centuries of space travel; and ensuring that the physical, emotional and social needs of such transiting population are met. So that come Resett, there will actually *exist* a population capable of re-establishing Human or Human-like life on a new planet.

Thinking about the enormity and complexity of approaching such a task still fills me with mind-blowing awe. I guess that's why I became an Archivist — I had always been drawn to the bigger questions of our mission, and digging through decades of knowledge was my way of seeking answers.

And then, while all that research and planning was going on, the Thetis was done. Operational. Tested. Ready to go. A loaded gun hanging in the sky with an unclear target and no definite rulebook. And in the trigger-thirsty atmosphere that dominated Earth at that time, it took nothing more to ignite the biggest chaos the planet had ever seen.

CHAPTER THIRTY

The Archive records get particularly messy at that point in time. I suspected it was either different parties trying to imprint their own historical narrative by controlling the formal records, or a deliberate attempt by the *Passados* to protect us future Thetans from the baggage of old alliances and social polarization. Probably a combination of both.

I could see how they'd have thought it would be better for us to have restarted from a clean slate rather than meddle in a past we would not possibly be able to comprehend in its intricacies.

One thing was certain, though — the Thetis was a lifeboat fit for an extremely limited group of people, and the decision of who would be the lucky ones chosen to board the ship became the Question of Questions — burning a hole in any discourse between the nation-states and the Big Techs who were still trying to find a way to uphold Earth's ecosystem.

It was unclear if the Thetis was ever anything more than a suicide mission — the farthest Humanity had ventured at that point was a manned slingshot mission around Saturn, which didn't really say much about the prospects of multi-generational survival in interplanetary space. But as the planet's vital signs kept degrading, it started to become clear that the actual prison was Earth itself, Thetis being the only escape strategy left. This is also where the whole situation turned dangerous, and after a shockingly close attempt by a state-backed nationalist group to shoot the Thetis out of the sky, it became clear to all the global powers involved that launching the mission was a matter of urgency. Much of the science, technology and data presumed critical for the mission's success were still missing, but those would have to be worked on and figured out by the Thetans themselves along the journey.

There were very few reliable details and quite a lot of conflicting evidence around the crew selection process (or, as it was referred to in documents originating from the Russ-Asian bloc — the Selectiva.) It seemed that the major factors in compiling the passenger list were maintaining diversity levels in areas such as genetics, trained professions, intelligence, medical and fertility conditions. They also sought candidates accustomed to a discipline-led environment. Smart, healthy professionals with a natural affinity for following instructions and functioning within rigid social structures.

Not surprisingly, the vast majority of recruits originated from military and law enforcement backgrounds. None came from government bodies or politics.

Embarkment itself was a black hole in QUBIC's data archives. By error or intentional omission, the events around the actual departure of Thetis from Earth were completely missing from the public ledger holding Humanity's entire knowledge base. Trying to reconstruct the facts from ancillary records painted a rather bleak picture of a stealthy operation of boarding the ship, sealing all bays and receiving the ignition codes and trajectory flight plans. The Thetis Embarkment was not a triumphant moment in Human space exploration history — it was an almost shameful escape in the dark of night by a privileged few, leaving a hateful, condemned Humanity sloshing in a boiling pool of rage and despair. When I imagined that moment in time I often pictured the two groups of people — the passengers of the Thetis and the citizens of Earth — facing each other, forever disconnected, the distance between them slowly and irreversibly growing, each of them terrified by the respective destiny it was bound to face. I selfishly hoped that we Thetans got the better end of the deal, but there was no way to ever tell now, was there? Earth is fifty-something light years away and had gone silent on us for generations.

"Do you ever wonder if they're still there?" I glanced around the group, searching for any hint of kindred-spirit recognition. "I mean, either they're not, and we are truly the last standing saviors of our species, or they have somehow been able to mend the planet and stop the cascade — which makes us the biggest, most pathetic laughing stock in Human history."

A moment of puzzled looks passed between the five elders, quickly followed by a forgiving group chuckle.

"Oh, honey," Viv leaned toward me, her eyes glittering with a soft pity, "we just want to dance!"

Papa Louis jerked in his wheeler and shouted in no specific direction, "we'll worry about planetfolk when we're standing on our own planet!"

"Oh, come now," Hugo Winkler came to my aid, "this is unfair to the lady here. Don't forget she is, what? Gen7?"

"2nd cycle," I confirmed.

"Practically a baby!" Winkler asserted.

"Well aren't you a rarity," Armitage declared.

"Sandrine," Hugo turned to me, "Please understand that people our age are very far beyond the existential search for our place in the universe. We've all been there, sure — we've lived through the FLIPP and many other hardships on the way to where we all are. But as you'll eventually discover too when your time comes, we have little interest in the speculative past. All we care about is securing our collective Genline on its path to Resett, and making the most of what remaining time we have until our day in the Loop. That's not a terrible sin, is it?" He looked around, his question received with supportive nods from the group.

Winkler's face sombered. He leaned a notch closer to me and his voice dropped a tone softer. "Let me put this as... delicately as I can, te? Look," Winkler passed his wiry fingers through his white hair, weighing his next words. "It's easy to disregard us Old Farts, amusing ourselves to death out of sight for most people on the Thetis. We've made our contribution. Expanded the Genline. Job done, thank you and goodbye. But what people tend to forget is that we've all been top professionals in our respective fields, and our minds are still as sharp as ever. Well, most of us."

"Hey, that was unnecessary!" Armitage protested on behalf of his father, drowsing in his wheeler.

"What he means to say," Gahlia stated pointedly, "is that we recognize when we're being used."

"What *we* mean to say, love," Viv concluded, "is that we're worried."

And just like that, all the good-hearted lightness radiating from the elderly group instantly evaporated.

I opened my mouth to respond when Winkler raised his hand to stop me. "Why did you come here, Sandrine? What knowledge can we possibly offer you that's not easily extractable from QUBIC itself?"

I knew damn well what this was. I needed to win their trust. And to do that, I'd have to offer a level of transparency which could seriously bite me in the ass if it went the wrong way. Sharing details on a covert investigation was a serious matter in my line of work. This would be a leap of faith in these people. Time to place your bets.

"I… came here," I stuttered, "because I don't think I can even trust QUBIC's data anymore." A quick look passed between Hugo and Gahlia.

"And?" Winkler prompted.

"And every kunye thread I pull, somehow traces back to the Anderson family."

Armitage grunted in protest. Winkler hushed him and gestured me to continue.

I hesitated. "I don't have the 'Why', but I have strong suspicions as to the 'What' and 'How'. Problem is, I can't mess up the future of the people who could possibly have the clues to where this path is leading."

"And that would be Kilian," Gahlia said matter-of-factly.

"Yes." *Who is this woman, exactly?* I thought.

Winkler quietly studied me for an uncomfortable number of seconds, then straightened back in his seat.

"The short answer is no."

"No?" I asked, puzzled.

"No, you can't trust any of the Archive data by now," he said. "The long answer is that you came here because you desperately need an ally. Someone whose interests are in the open. Someone who can't be pressured or leveraged upon, and who's capable of working unnoticed, with zero PubSheet value."

The group of elders nodded in unison. Winkler scanned each of them recording their unspoken approval, then set his gaze back on me, a hint of warmth creeping to the deep wrinkles around his eyes.

"You came to the right place, Arc. Liet. We'll trust you with what we know."

I suddenly shivered as a momentary wave of paranoia took over me. *What am I getting myself into here?*

"Wait," I said, "Maybe I should involve Nyasha at this point. Make this part of the formal chain of evidence."

The group chuckled.

"Nyasha Woo won't help you here, dear," Viv sighed. "He'll never go against Anderson, not really. Owes too much to Sabi's dead father."

"Bless his soul!" Armitage added.

That turn of the conversation took me by surprise.

"Viv's right," Winkler said, reading my nonplused expression. "Back when old Benjamin Anderson was about to retire and pass the Archival wand, you must imagine there were other candidates for the job of Head Arc. Not bad ones, either, te? Nyasha wasn't even the leading option."

"So how did he get chosen over the others then?" I asked.

"Back then, Sabi was running his first campaign for Primo. Certain allegations were raised against him on matters relating to illegal conduct of the elections. Let's say that Nyasha's attitude and mild response to those allegations garnered him the support of Sabi's father. And won Sabi the Primoship, of course. Nyasha owes his entire career to the Andersons, you see."

This didn't sound at all like the Nyasha I spent the past seven years with. The picture of his reddened, angry face when he sent me off to locate the 6th QUBIC node surfaced in my head. *That was genuine anger*, I thought. *To think Nyasha was faking it is insane.* But was it the righteous anger of the Code-enforcer encountering manipulation, or the burning humiliation of a person betrayed by a trusted partner?

I was not ready to believe the latter, but I could also not risk taking any chances in this matter. So I would defer judgement until I dug a bit deeper.

"OK," I finally said. "I'll keep this unofficial for now. What's on your mind, and how is it going to help me get to the Origin?"

Again, Hugo and Gahlia exchanged a silent look. Around us, people were already dispersing from Memorial Loop, having apparently solved the ceremonial dilemma with some compromise or other. Hugo nodded and pointed his chin toward the entrance to the Loop's dimmed corridor.

"Maybe let's go for a little walk," he said and gestured for Gahlia to take hold of his wheeler's handles. "Or, in my case, a little ride, te?"

"We'll let you speak privately," Armitage supported Viv's shoulders as they both rose to leave. "We'll take Papa Louis back to his hab and make sure the Loop's empty on our way out."

I followed Gahlia and Winkler into Memorial Loop. By now it was deserted, with only the slight, almost imperceptible background hum of the ship audible over the eery silence. We started the circular, mile and a half long walk around the Thetis center. I tried to listen for any hint to the torrent of particles shooting their way through the Trash Tube just behind the Loop's inner bulkhead, but I could hear nothing. I studied the walls on both sides of the corridor, noticing how in the first part of the Loop Gen1 and Gen2 memorial plates vastly outnumbered GenZeros, a silent evidence to the tragedy of an entire generation of parents outliving their own sons and daughters.

"There he is," Hugo Winkler signaled Gahlia to stop the wheeler in front of a simple plate, identical in all aspects to any of the adjacent metal rectangles. "The Dread Pirate."

Gahlia smiled wryly. Demetrius Smoak, the Thetis first Primo, enjoyed a long life to the point that his plate was one of the very last GenZeros on the wall. The fact that the nickname "Dread Pirate Smoak" was attached to the man's legacy only post-mortem tells you something about how much he was feared back in his day. The records from that era paint post-Embarkment Thetis as a harsh, high stress environment in a way us Spacers can hardly imagine, let alone empathize with, almost two centuries into the mission.

Somewhat ironically for a ship fleeing an increasingly hostile Earth into interplanetary space, the Thetis, accelerating slowly and building the velocity needed to push its huge mass beyond the Solar System, spent more than a year in full view of Planet Earth.

While technically sealed and detached from any possible connection to the planet, the slow departure created a grinding sense of anxiety on the Thetis — of being nuked from the ground, of having its systems hacked remotely, of not being able to reach escape velocity with a ship several times heavier than the original plan, of a thousand other reasons which kept the Thetans on their toes. Fearful, yet helpless in face of any malintent from the boiling, polluted and desperate planet below. Even after Earth became just another distant blue dot in the sky — and soon thereafter, invisible altogether — the fear of a sudden focused laser beam shot from Earth to annihilate the ship persisted. 'Don't get beamed out' was a popular casual salutation, recurring in many interviews and records of that time. Black humor, apparently, had kept being an effective coping mechanism even for post-planetary Man.

In an attempt to mitigate that risk, rigorous efforts were made to keep communication with Earth alive and follow the evolving situation on the planet. In any practical aspect, those early Thetans were people controlled by their past, much more than they were building their future.

And in their core nature, GenZeros were still planetfolk. Their most basic instincts, when faced with such encompassing existential threats, were to try and rebuild the foundation elements they had known from Earth: commerce, social hierarchies, religion, even militaristic law enforcement. They did not understand nor accept the *Passados* Code and rules, and the Embarkment Certificate emblem 'Embark and Prosper' never looked more detached and out-of-context from the actual life on GenZero Thetis.

Embarkment had been such a shock to the people on board, it would take another two generations for the collective adrenaline rush to subside and for a new, profoundly different Humanity to sprout. Gen1ers were the 'Wonder Generation', first generation born on the Thetis, and thus celebrated as the Savior Angels of Mankind — an attitude that would spoil any child to the bone. Their children, 'The Neglected' Gen2ers, grew in the deep shadows of their narcissist parents and their Titan, long-living grandparents, left to prove their worth through endless battles over territory, resources and meaningless lifestyle privileges.

It would take the iron fist of Primo Demetrius Smoak — and, admittedly, the later shocking death of poor Oscar Kohn — to force down the chaotic whirlwind they were all sweeping into, and reinstate the Passados plan.

"There we are," Hugo Winkler said as he looked up from his wheeler at the Primo's memorial plate. "A century and a half later, and the Pirate still may be the one to save us all."

I blinked. "So Primo Smoak is the Origin? Or is it something he created? How is that connected to Embarkment?"

Gahlia caught my arm and locked her eyes onto mine. "He didn't create it, Sandrine. But he managed to hide its existence cleverly enough that it is still a trustworthy source for us eight generations later. The Origin Kilian sent you to locate dates back far earlier than

Embarkment. Almost a century before."

I looked deep into the woman's eyes, trying to let her words sink and find meaning within me.

"How the hell do you know what Kilian meant?" I asked.

"Because I was the one who took him there," she said dryly.

A moment of panic caught me and I struggled to free my arm from her grip. I took a step back, feeling perspiration breaking across my hairline.

"Who *are* you?" I muttered.

Winkler chuckled in his seat. "Gahlia, let me break it to you gently — I suspect Ms. Liet here doesn't recognize you one bit. No offense to your ego intended, of course."

"What's the connection between you two?" I asked. "Besides the Astral Solace Home, that is."

Hugo shrugged. "We go way back. Gahlia was one of the few good souls who stood up for me when I was fighting for my PHS position with the 'Royal Missis'. And she too felt the heat of standing up against the monarchy." He blurted out a short laugh. "You could say we were both sent to our early retirement on account of 'unfavorable Cassidian conditions.'"

Hugo stretched a half-turn toward me with a ceremonial wave of his hand. "Sandrine, may I introduce you to my sister in arms — Doctor Gahlia Roskov, Senior Systems IT-something or the other. Retired, mind you."

Gahlia was unmoved. "I was Kilian's mentor all throughout the Academy. I took him in to train as QUBIC IT specialist. He was a brilliant, brilliant boy. Had a bright future ahead of him."

Until you came and put an end to it, was the subtext.

"So you're Dr. Roskov," I mumbled. "Funny we've never met before. Kilian adores you."

If the compliment had any effect on the woman, it wasn't apparent from her stone-frozen expression.

"I'm here because I am trying to protect him,' I said. "I could easily issue a subpoena and get what I need, but that would severely implicate Kilian."

"Once bitten, twice shy?" Gahlia asked sarcastically.

I sighed. "I'm trying to avoid making the same mistake again. Keep him away from any official proceedings. And, if it's any consolation to you, as a reward for doing the right legal thing back then, I got skipped on Birth Year rights."

To that, Gahlia's face defrosted and her eyes twitched momentarily. "I'm sorry to hear that," she said, her voice softer. She then reached into her inner jacket pocket and pulled out a small pad.

"Let's keep walking." She handed the pad to Winkler. The wheeler started rolling slowly down the corridor, and Gahlia fell quiet as Hugo scanned the pad's content for a few seconds before handing it to me.

"We all got this MiniSheet delivered to our habs this morning. Take a look."

I flipped the MiniSheet open. It was a formal notice from the General Infirmary.

"Dusting Protocol Initiation Notice," I read. "For tomorrow. What's so urgent about it that they had to issue a special notice to every single hab on the Thetis? Why not just post it on the daily PubSheet edition this evening? Dusting dates are set way in advance. Like, *years* in advance."

"And even more peculiarly," Winkler said, "What does the Astral Solace Home have to do with Dusting at all? We were always an off-limits zone in this matter. No need to waste that precious dust on us geezers!"

That was, in fact, true. A crucial milestone in the plan toward Resett was the ReBiome project. Set to begin after Generation 7, it set in motion various gradual shifts in the ship's environment, aimed to prepare the physique of us Spacers to life back on a planet.

It included gradual habitation to the temperature, humidity, gravity and light quality expected on the chosen planet for resettlement. That part was supposed to kick in after Final Call and the choice of a target-planet. Other aspects of the ReBiome plan were emotional/psychological — for example, GenXers would be required to keep a real pet animal in their habs, CellPrinted from the GenLab genpool archive!

An additional aspect of this acclimatization process was the toughening-up of the Thetans' physical tolerance and immune system. After almost two centuries in space living in a hyper-controlled and mostly sterile environment, we were in no shape to survive life on a open planet. Uncontrolled climate conditions and exposure to germs and bacteria would quickly cripple any Thetan setting foot on the ground.

So, the plan included a process spanning 3-generations for waking up our internal defense systems. Every five years, the Thetis underwent a day of 'Stimulus Particle Seeding' — essentially, filling the ship's atmosphere with minuscule particles designed to stimulate our body's immune and respiratory systems. Those days were commonly known as "Dusting Days", because that's exactly how it felt.

The procedure was a nightmare. Come Dusting Day morning, the whole ship would fill with a heavy yellowish-orange haze. The air would thicken to the point that visibility was limited to just a few meters. Air circulation would slow down and humidity levels would rise, smothering everyone and everything with the damp, yellow mist.

Dusting days took a heavy toll on the Thetis infirmary — before getting sucked out by the air circulation systems, the artificial dust would fire up a multitude of physical and psychological reactions. Some people would suffer respiratory difficulties, others — severe anxiety induced by feelings of suffocation. There would be claustrophobic reactions, eye-irritations, skin allergies and a kunye dozen other symptoms from the foreign substance filling the air. If there ever was a good time to lay low, keep to your hab and just pass a lazy day in bed — Dusting Day was it.

The relative harshness of this stimulation procedure dictated that Dusting Days were set years in advance, so every Thetan could properly plan for it. It was also customary for the Astral Solace Home to be exempt from participating — having already secured their Genline, there was no benefit in exposing the elders to the unnecessary health risks of the Dust and its side effects.

Which is why the MiniSheet notice Hugo Winkler handed me made no sense at all. The next designated Dusting Day was a few months ahead of us at least, and in any case should not involve the Home and its residents.

I was perplexed. "What's the rush to push up Dusting Day to a 24-hour notice?"

"We asked the same question," Gahlia said. "In fact, we issued a formal request to receive the recorded protocol of that decision process."

"And guess what we got in return," Hugo waved his hands in frustration as Gahlia kept wheeling him down the Loop, cruising forward in time through the monuments of our past generations. "A formally worded 'kunyete' advising us that the QUBIC systems are all occupied and prioritized to the new trajectory solution calculations. Our request 'shall be kept in queue until further resources were made available to the general public.' Lovely, ne?"

"That response came from the Archive?" I asked.

"PHS," Gahlia said. "Dusting is a PHS directive, so that's where we applied."

"Well," I said, "all the QUBIC nodes on the Thetis *have* been temporarily seized for working on the trajectory solution. That part may be true."

Gahlia snorted a laugh. It was the first time I have seen her display anything brighter than a frown. "That's utter bafunye," she proclaimed.

"What do you mean?" I asked, surprised to hear this stern woman swearing.

Gahlia stopped in her tracks and locked her gaze on me. She had this relaxed confidence emanating from her — I could easily imagine she was twenty years younger, if not more.

"Darling," she said softly, "calculating an alternative trajectory for the Thetis is such basic physics, you get me an inksheet and a pencil and I would manually calculate a solution for you in an hour."

Which means, of course, that a single QUBIC node should accomplish that same task in a few microseconds at most.

I was dumbfounded. *Kei the mala Dio was going on here?*

"So what you are saying," I hesitated, "is that either the total enlisting of all QUBIC resources for this task is a massive, unnecessary overnuke, or that it *is* utilized to the max for something different altogether — a real heavy-lifting task that is completely obscured from the public eye."

"Correct."

"One guess which option my bet's on," Winkler grunted. We were nearing the end of the Loop's mile, and slowed to a stop in front of the last column of memorial plates. The curved wall beyond this point was empty, ready to host the future names of all living and unborn Thetans right up to Resett. Dr. Almaz Bashiri's newly-minted plate was staring down at us from its position on the top row of the last populated column. An image of the Doctor's terrified, vulnerable face when he initially tracked me on the Sensory Farm surfaced in my mind. *And then he went and secretly met Kilian,* I reminded myself.

And then he died. And Kilian freaked out and went silent.

"Then the only remaining explanation for the sudden, unannounced Dusting," I said carefully, "is that someone eagerly needs us to stay inhabs tomorrow. All of us, including you Astral Solace tenants." I paused for a moment, then added, "so — what's tomorrow?"

Hugo Winkler shrugged again. "We are the last people to know about anything of significance on the ship."

"You must still have QUBIC access in the Archive, ne?" Gahlia asked. "That's an independent terminal, as far as I remember."

I pouted and shook my head slowly. "Anderson issued an

Emergency Directive. It overrides *everything*."

"Emergency Directive!" Gahlia burst through her pursed lips. "*What* emergency, exactly? This is all a manufactured crisis, so he can take control over whatever he needs. We are not under any emergency!"

"Well I guess, darling, that's a matter of perspective, isn't it?" Winkler suggested with sweet, theatrical mockery. "Maybe it is for the Andersons."

"Listen," I interrupted. "There's one thing Kilian mentioned that correlates with what we're seeing so far. He said that usage of multiple QUBIC nodes for a simultaneous, compute-intensive operation, could be a sign of tampering with the public ledger database."

That got their attention. Winkler turned his wheeler around, and Gahlia's eyes fixated on mine. The Loop's silence suddenly felt stressful — if I shared what I knew with both of them, it might risk the legal purity of my investigation. But it seemed that without the help of the few allies I've got, I won't be getting anywhere at all. Some lines needed to be — well, if not crossed, than at least stretched.

"My initial informal investigation," I began, "was about a suspected attempt for altering an Archive data set by Primo Sabi Anderson or one of his underlings."

Winkler and Dr. Roskov just looked at me with gaping eyes, silent.

"It was a stupid little hunch at first — a complaint from the Primos' office regarding an alleged extortion attempt by our respected Dr. Bashiri right here—" I nodded toward the plate in front of us, "— but which soon after got withdrawn and looked like nothing of significance, really."

I turned my eyes to Gahlia and continued. "It could have ended right there — the Archive is swamped with Final Call review tasks as it is, and Nyasha would gladly put anything else aside if it wasn't demonstrably urgent. But then, someone actually went and *erased* the whole case data-trail from the Archive, which by all accounts should have been—"

"Impossible," Gahlia whispered. I could see her mind racing forward.

Winkler sighed audibly. "Typical Anderson. The man's mind is an echo chamber for paranoia. Slightest deviation from plan, and he starts making hysterical mistakes."

"Maybe," I said, "at least insofar as it raised a red flag I couldn't easily ignore. But I still couldn't figure out *how* they were able to achieve such a clean purge of a QUBIC data file. At which point I turned to Kilian for help."

Dr. Roskov shook her head. "That was a stupid—"

"—smart move," Hugo said curtly. "What else could the girl do? I am far from being a legal expert in the Code, but I have traversed enough light years to give me some perspective. So I do know that without the 'How', she would never be able to unravel the 'What' and the 'Why'. The 'What' gives you the criminal act. The 'Why' gives you criminal intent. And as we *both* know, my dear doctor, if you're going after a high-caliber target such as Sabi Anderson, you better have both of them airtight or you've got *mala nada.*"

Gahlia's face tightened. She still didn't like this, but she kept listening. Time to get to the point.

"Kilian mentioned that a complete and non-trackable deletion of a record from the QUBIC public ledger would involve re-crypting all the records that came after it, so that a continuous stream of data is maintained as if the deleted record never existed."

"That's correct," Gahlia confirmed.

"He also said that to do that, a majority of the Thetis QUBIC nodes would need to accept the deletion, thereby preventing the simple re-writing of the deleted file back into the system. That's where things became more complicated, as we were able to track only five nodes controlled by Anderson's people. That wouldn't suffice for a majority. Unless—" I felt a slight tremble invading my voice, "unless there was a sixth node confirming the action."

"The Origin," Gahlia muttered softly.

"Yes."

She slanted her head slightly and considered her thoughts for a few seconds. "Let me guess — Kilian also told you that such an action should be relatively quick and wouldn't consume much compute power. At least as long as the deleted record is relatively recent, so there aren't many newer records on top of it."

"I see where you're going with this," I said. "Oh, Dio."

Hugo raised his palms in impatience. "Enlighten me please, ladies. In simple terms, would you?"

"The time and compute power required increase exponentially as you delve deeper into older database records," I explained. "Deleting a record that's just a few hours old would hardly create a noticeable disruption to the ship's systems."

"But manipulating records from deeper in the past..." Gahlia said.

"Would take the whole Quantum array on the ship spinning to a choke, I get it," Winkler caught on. He raised his eyes to meet Gahlia's. "This may be the FLIPP all over again."

"That's a possibility," she agreed.

"Wait. This is kunye crazy!" I whispered and shot a look around, checking for accidental visitors in the Loop. "A *massive* takeover of critical systems on the Thetis by its own Primo? Mandated by a made-up, *bafunye* Emergency Directive just to disguise it? *Why?*"

Winkler coughed a short laugh. "Why? We're barely past the 'How' phase, with hopes for a shot at the 'What' exactly is happening here. Who knows the 'Why' at this point?" He gestured toward Dr. Bashiri's plate on the wall. "Did he know the 'Why'?"

"I believe he did," I said.

He sighed wearily. "That's most unfortunate, then."

Winkler interlocked his fingers and laid his chin on both thumbs, pondering. "All of us — Primos and farmers alike — we all end up as a plate on this wall. Full name, a ten-word summary of our watch, and that's it. Why would anyone choose to occupy wall-space in here before their time eludes me."

I felt a need to come to Dr. Bashiri's defense. "There's more to it than I can safely share, but Dr. Bashiri may not have chosen to get plated any more than any other Thetan on this wall."

"Now that's something I haven't heard in my entire sorry life on this can!" Winkler turned his wheelers slowly and scanned me top to bottom, reassessing. "Sr. Archivist Liet — are you insinuating a possibility of a *murder* on the Thetis? Because that would be..."

"Unthinkable," Gahlia said.

"*Scandalous* is what I was going for," Hugo retorted.

"But not impossible," I said. "Not any more than manipulating formal Archive records. Not after what we now know."

"Sandrine," Dr. Gahlia Roskov's pale, penetrating eyes drilled into mine, "what aren't you telling us about this? If you're even remotely considering the possibility of a fellow Thetan breaking the most sacred pact we've established here — the sanctity of human life — then you must know *something* that could explain such an atrocity."

I lowered by head, breaking the eye contact. *This is a conversation I should be having with Nyasha,* I thought. His calm and structured thinking was what I needed to start making sense of this trail of crumbs.

"Nothing justifies murder," I whispered, "all I know is that Dr. Bashiri was worried that someone was manipulating his work, and when he started raising questions his whole work got shot down in an instant. When he tried to poke around for answers — with Anderson, Nyasha, and then me — he found himself on the wrong side of this very wall holding his memorial plate."

"I can't not notice one name you hadn't mentioned," Gahlia said sternly.

I didn't answer.

"You know," she continued, "there's no one more concerned than me with the safety and protection of Kilian. I practically raised this boy — professionally, formally, but I'd like to think I was more than that to him."

"You were," I whispered. "You *are*. So you must understand we can't mess up the one shot he got to rebuild his life. His Genline. We... *I* owe him at least that much."

"Let me guess," Gahlia said. "Bashiri turned to Kilian for help in investigating the alleged manipulation of his work."

I kept my head down, which she probably took as silent confirmation.

"And Kilian took him for a visit to Level 2," she concluded.

My head shot up with surprise. "*Mala Dio!* Now *you're* the one withholding crucial information. How the *hell* do you know about that meeting?"

"A simple deduction, my dear," she said calmly.

"Wait," Hugo Winkler gestured for us to keep moving down the Loop's pathway. "Level 2 has been a hazardous, radioactively contaminated space since right after the FLIPP. It was evacuated and stripped of any useful materials decades ago. What would anyone be looking for down there at all?"

"Well," Gahlia graciously caught up with Winkler's wheeler with a few long strides, "Kilian knew that if you were looking for absolutely genuine data, you go to the Origin."

I was startled. "So the Origin is an unregistered QUBIC node, hidden on Level 2. That's... *wild*." Finally, things started to connect from the scattered mess of facts I was trying to paint a sensible picture from.

Gahlia hesitated. "Yes and no, actually. The Origin is something I found. An undocumented rarity almost no one knows about. The node is something Kilian helped me build over the years, which makes us the only two people on the Thetis who know about its existence."

"With the exception of the dead doctor, of course," Winkler added, trying to lighten up the moment. It didn't quite work.

We kept walking in silence around the ship's inner torus. The walls on our left were empty now, holding vacancy for the names of the next generations to depart. Inevitably, Hugo Winkler's Generation 5 would soon occupy the next few thousand plate spaces on those walls.

Gahlia walked in silence for the remainder of the way back to the lobby. When we finally emerged from the dimly-lit corridor, she stopped in her tracks and gently covered my palm with both of hers. She seemed to have reached an internal decision about the matter.

"How certain are you about Anderson, about the murder, about all of this?"

"It's circumstantial," I admitted.

"Which means *mala nada*, like I have established earlier," Winkler noted.

Gahlia's face contorted. She spoke in an almost inaudibly-low voice, her face close to mine to the point I could actually smell her skin.

"You do realize that K was an accomplice, if not the main perpetrator, in the sabotage of the Archive files?"

I closed my eyes to avoid the hard, icy look of her eyes in that moment. "I do," I said. "If the deletion required the participation of this secretive QUBIC node, then unless it was you who gave Sabi's people access to it — it must have been Kilian."

Gahlia nodded. "Then you also understand that there's no chasing this ghost without severely implicating K. You won't be able to keep him on the sidelines when this blows up. Can you live with that?"

I took a deep breath, trying to suppress the ball of pressure knotting up my stomach.

"The real question is," I said, "can any of us live if I don't. Can we live, let alone thrive, in a society where its leaders are behind such acts as fraud, manipulation and even *murder*?"

Gahlia tipped her head sideways. "It won't be a first in Human history. Mostly, we survived. Do we really need to sacrifice Kilian on that altar?"

A hot flush flooded my face. I gritted my teeth at Dr. Roskov, trying to keep my voice down so as not to be overheard in the lobby. "Look! I can't imagine what pressure they put on him to comply, but the fact that Anderson needed to cook up this whole *bafunye* emergency situation tells me Kilian's done helping them. He wouldn't have sent me to find the Origin if he was still working with Sabi. That tells me K's heart is still in the right place. That I can trust him."

Gahlia's face brightened. If this was some kind of test, I must have passed it somehow to her liking.

"Then it's time to turn the tables on Anderson and his goons," she said. "If they're trying to keep us locked-in and suppressed with Dusting, we are going to use it to our advantage."

"How?"

"By doing the exact opposite, my dear. On Dusting Day, nobody expects you to be anywhere outside you hab, right? Infirmary goes on priority alert for taking in Dusting-related cases, so all regular appointments are canceled. All recreational activities too. And the Dusting particle cloud is notorious for throwing off the grid-locator sensors — so, in short, nobody would miss two little ladies taking a little field trip for a few hours off the grid."

I eyed Gahlia with a renewed sense of appreciation. "You're offering to take me to the Origin?"

"There's no other way of establishing what the *kunye mala* the Primo's so obsessed about hiding."

I shrugged. "We may be able to go undetected for a bit, but there's no way we can pass the Level 10 seal without getting registered."

Gahlia smiled widely. "Leave that to me. There are some secrets about this ship even Kilian isn't privy to. But we'll need help."

Hugo, who had been uncharacteristically quiet during the exchange, nodded in acknowledgement. "Let's go get Armitage. He'll have what you need."

"Wait, Armitage?" I balked. "Didn't you say he was an Anderson boy?"

"Sandrine darling," Hugo pressed his palms together, "I'm not saying it won't take some convincing, but eventually, one reaches an age when thrill trumps ideology. Let's hope Armitage is willing to flex some old muscles and be useful to anyone other than Viv's seemingly unaging Libido."

"And we have to hurry," Gahlia added, "Dusting's hitting in a few hours."

CHAPTER THIRTY-ONE

I was well ready to leave the Astral Solace Home for the Elderly — as far as I was concerned, I'd be happy to not set another foot in the entirety of Level 33 until my day in the Loop was due. What I truly needed was a small dose of reassurance that the plunge I was about to take was both smart and effective. Effective as in providing the right answers to what was happening behind the Thetis Primo curtains. Smart as in avoiding ruining my life in the process. I could still feel Jericho Pakk's hands on my neck, his icy hollow eyes piercing through me like I was nothing — a *nuisance*, nothing more. *Has he turned himself in to Nyasha yet?* I've managed to make such powerful enemies in the past few days. Stepped into so many gray areas. Unless I resurfaced from Level 2 with a coherent, legally admissible, Liquid-kunye-Diamond solid story, the personal consequences for me would undoubtedly be dire.

It would take going all-in on this one. There was simply no other choice.

Oddly enough, my 7th Sense was neither stirring up objections nor firing up warning lights. I may not exactly fit the spiritualist type you'd encounter around the more colorful parts of Level 19, but life experience had taught me to trust the 7th — The Sense of Wellbeing, more commonly referred to as Intuit.

Unlike the notorious 6th Sense — a vague term combining alleged abilities such as premonition, proximity sense, telepathy and other *bafunye*, the 7th was by now largely accepted as a proven facet of nature.

Turns out that thousands of years of reliance on the notion of Intuition were actually based on a real biochemical mechanism. Technologies developed on Late Earth, which enabled high-precision recording of neurochemical activity, revealed an intricate system of reactions in the human brain when faced with decision-making.

Apparently, our brain reacts differently to decisions it categorizes as being advantageous — or 'Good' — for us in the long term, versus decisions that the brain perceives as 'Bad' or 'Dangerous'. Be it the choice between an apple and a candy, a choice of city of residence or career path — the brain apparently reacts favorably to the option it deems as contributing to the aggregated wellbeing of the individual.

And when you learn to listen to this sense, learn to pierce the distracting veil of 'Logic', a huge guiding power unravels. I know this *can* seem on the verge of spiritualism, but there really is no easy way to explain it without reducing it to electrical brain maps and cellular chemistry. If you've ever got the advice of 'you know what feels right to you' — well, you've been asked to trust the 7th.

The important thing is that what I felt about my next step was similar to what I always felt toward Kilian and Nyasha, and toward hardly anyone else at all: the confidence and tranquility of a woman facing something that would never do her harm. I knew in my gut that this was the right thing to do, and if I go down with it — I'll have to figure out an escape maneuver before I hit the floor.

A bright movement in the corner of my eye caught my attention as it blurred past the entrance to Memorial Loop. I turned my head back quickly, only to catch a glimpse of blond disappearing into the dimly lit corridor.

Cassidi Anderson? Although I have only ever seen her in the Archive profile images and a few public vidrecords, there was no mistaking the confident stride crowned by the perfect shade of her warm and unpretentious sandy hair.

Could this really be her? What is she doing here, after the ceremony already ended?

Despite myself, I turned back on my heels and advanced slowly toward the Loop entrance. I just *had* to make sure it was really her, get a closer look at the infamous other half of the Andersons.

I stepped lightly, trying to reach the entry point to the Memorial Wall unnoticed. I could hear the woman's sharp, decisive steps echoing down the path, and I carefully ensured I stayed far back enough to remain concealed by the curvature of the inner Loop bulkhead.

We walked in tandem, oblivious leader and curious follower, for several minutes without stopping or a change of pace. Cassidi passed the sections of the Founding Generations plates, and progressed through the timeline of Thetan generations.

I remembered Cassidi's Archive profile, indicating that she'd lost her firstborn child at birth. The thought sent a shiver down my spine — *could she be here visiting the memorial plate of her departed baby?* The notion that I might be intruding on the woman's privacy during an intimate moment of grief made me deeply uncomfortable. *Do stillborn babies even get a plate on the wall?*

I slowed to a near-halt, hesitating, when suddenly the stepping sounds stopped. I froze, careful not to expose my presence.

After a few seconds of heavy silence, I started creeping forward, slowly peeking around the curve.

The blond woman was standing in front of the newly-minted memorial plate of Dr. Almaz Bashiri. And that woman was most definitely Cassidi Anderson.

Crouched on the floor of the Memorial Loop with my neck sticking out sideways, I just stared at her in disbelief for a few moments. There was no mistaking the upright, proud posture — the upward-facing chin; the drawn back shoulders creating an elongated s-curve in her lower spine; and the feeling that an invisible thread was attached to the top of the woman's head, exerting a constant, light upward pull. This *was* Cassidi all right, but the difference between the young woman recorded in the QUBIC profile images and the one standing before the Loop wall was nothing short of momentous.

Gone was the busy-nurse hair, done up absent-mindedly in a haphazard sort-of-bun, with stray golden hairs sprouting in random directions. Gone were the plain, loosely-fitting infirmary clothes designed for maximum practicality, sacrificing stylistic elegance. The Cassidi Anderson standing in front of me was wearing top-of-the-parsec garments from the in-fashion artisans of 26th. Every cut and seam in her mesmerizing high-neck, deep-green dress was custom-fitted in silent expression of the woman's favorable position in the resource distribution pecking order. Her sandy, muted hair was treated into a bright, shiny yellow tint, trimmed at shoulder length into an impeccable golden perfection.

And still, the most remarkable evidence to the change this woman had underwent in the years since her Archive photo was taken was the profound difference in her facial countenance.

Cassidi Anderson had become *hard*.

What had once been the soft, welcoming expression of an over-worked, under-rested overachiever — the sparkle in her eyes speaking of sharp intelligence and innocent curiosity — had been painted over by an impenetrable layer of self-preservation, pierced by cold, measuring eyes.

She was still breathtakingly beautiful. But the welcome had become warning.

I could see Cassidi's lips moving with a mumble I could not discern. After a few moments, she turned away from Dr. Bashiri's plate and continued slowly further down the Loop, her evenly-paced steps creating an echoing staccato reverberating through the circular tube. I raised up slowly, careful to remain unseen behind the curve, and kept following.

Cassidi exited the Astral Solace Home unto an uncharacteristically busy Level 33. People were scurrying around trying to complete their various errands before the Dusting lock-in would confine them to their habs. I made sure to keep a safe distance behind her as she proceeded toward the outer edge of the level main area. *If she got on an Ascender,* I thought, *there would be no way for me to keep following her without getting noticed.*

But when Cassidi reached the Ascender platform, she did not hop on the half-empty carriage. Instead, she headed toward the wide, spiraling open stairwell connecting to the level below us.

For multi-level trips, most Thetans prefer the Ascenders for their relative travel speed. But for a one or two-level hop, the Thetis had a massive shallowstep staircase system fit for carrying thousands of people and which was, in fact, the more popular travel method around the ship.

Cassidi started down the stairs, which took me somewhat by surprise — my assumption was that she would be taking the one level trip back up to the Primo quarters on 34th, what with the Dusting starting soon and all. *Was she heading to the PHS complex?* I kept my distance behind her — PHS was five levels down, so that shouldn't be a long hike. The relatively busy flow of people up and down the stairwell helped me blend in with the crowd, aided by Cassidi not looking back even once or appearing suspicious of being followed.

I was now full-on stalking this woman across the Thetis.

But when Cassidi reached the wide off-boarding platform connecting the large stairwell to the main area of Level 28 — the home for many of the Thetis scientific research facilities including the PHS complex — she did not as much as glance in the direction of the exit, but rather kept on descending down the levels. My internal alerts took notice — taking the stairs rather than using the Ascenders for a trip longer than a few levels was an unusual choice, especially as we were entering the more crowded parts of the Thetis during daytime hours. Nor was it characteristic of Cassidi to be taking strolls among the general Thetan public — as far as I could remember I had never seen Cassidi Anderson in public before, whether in a formal appearance or by plain chance. She was conducting the PHS management work from the Primo quarters on 34th and as far as I knew was never part of the daily commute or the nightly cultural scene on the ship.

No, I thought, *crossing the ship on the main stairwell with her striking blond and her gleaming emerald attire was the action of someone deliberately asking to be noticed.*

I could tell this was an uncomfortable situation for Cassidi. She plowed on, intently forward-focused and barely acknowledging the occasional shy nods and greetings from passers-by who recognized her with surprise as she crossed their path. The Thetis was a flat, classless society, but the Primo's wife still enjoyed a certain level of attraction power.

We descended past Level 27, home to the Thetis educational system: the schools, completing their transformation into nurseries and kindergartens in anticipation of the upcoming Generation 9; the Junior Academy, soon to be filled with Gen8er teenagers; and the main academy with its lab facilities.

As a former SinguLearn laureate — the rare case where an exceptionally sharp intelligence is identified and accelerated through the educational system — Cassidi probably had fond memories of this otherwise dull complex of grey, boxy structures. In this aspect we probably had something in common, as I always felt at my best between those walls of knowledge and exploration.

We continued downward toward the noisy hubbub that was the commercial district of Level 26. 26th was where items and ideas were exchanged on the Thetis — clothes, furniture and unsolicited opinions offered by the pound with the energetic passion of the ship's makers, bakers and gossip-mongers. Despite my intrinsic introvert nature — the social extravaganza was always Kilian's thing, not mine — 26th was one of my favorite places on the Thetis. Cleverly buffering between the somber seriousness of the Academy and research institutions of 27th and 28th and the mundane, sleepish family circles of 25th and 24th, the commercial district was a short hop from wherever most Thetans spent their day. Its myriad artisan corners and specialty shops provided a shot of friendly chaos if one ever felt ground down by the work-life routine that was being a Thetan.

To my surprise, Cassidi stepped off the main stairway and turned into the main commercial part of the level. She kept her steady, mechanical pace, focusing intently on the path in front of her, never once stopping to browse any of the shops or speak with the chatty artisans. As she continued inward, dissecting her way through the crowd, her walk became increasingly tense. *Classic social anxiety*, I thought. Takes one to know one I guess.

It was high Fabric Season on 26th. We were heading toward the cooler season cycle, so a new crop of winter garments was just hitting the commercial district floor. 'Commercial' being a slightly tongue-in-cheek reference for the Old Earth concept, of course — everything on the Thetis was free to make, use and exchange, and the balance between supply, demand, greediness and altruism was kept in check by the ultimate currency of a closed, flat society such as ours — one's reputation.

"Hey, aren't you the one they wrote about on the PubSheets?" a voice called to me from one of the open-front shops. The woman was probably a Gen7er, her hair held back with a wide red band, hands busy sewing decorations onto a baby-sized overall. Her fingers worked on auto-pilot as her curious eyes scanned me. I gave a non-committed shrug and moved along ever-so-slightly quicker to the next section, closing in a bit on Cassidi.

But that remark was far from being a singular incident. As I continued following Cassidi through the level, more eyes were raised, faces turned, remarks thrown at me to the point I was probably causing a bigger stir in the otherwise pragmatic atmosphere of the market than even the Primo's wife herself. I had to fall back to a bigger distance from Cassidi or there'd be no chance I could keep following her unnoticed.

Some remarks were the customary teasing of bored artisans on a slow pre-Dusting evening. "You Archivists simply *have* to stick your nose into anything, don't you? Just couldn't stand that *the people* were meant to choose the planet of our destination, so you made sure to sabotage it!" That one, delivered by a Gen6er moulder of kitchenware utilities, drew a resounding wave of applause from the adjacent stands.

Others were more vicious. "Why don't *you* Genless Eternists stay in space and let us, the people who actually *have* a Genline, Resett in peace?" Followed by the nasty stab of "no wonder they skipped you on Birth Year!"

Now, the Thetis being a particularly open and transparent society, I normally wouldn't have been rattled too much by those remarks. The boundaries between direct and invasive tend to blur in small, secluded groups. But the hostility underlying the verbal stabs I was getting felt *different*. Pronounced. Something fed by fear and self defense instincts.

My 7th was tingling with suspicion, aided by the fact that Cassidi Anderson, despite her obvious and almost crippling anxiety, was essentially *parading* me through the Thetis' most crowded public area. Clearly, she didn't come here for the artisan shops or for mingling with people — she walked mechanically, jaws clenched and eyes fixed forward, keeping herself in check by focusing on each next step.

She knows I'm following her, the realization hit me. *And this is a parade, meant to be witnessed by as many people as possible.*

A surprising feeling of relaxation came over me as Cassidi reached the secondary stairwell across the level and started descending again.

Wherever she was leading me, I knew, I was about to enter the boss-level of the Anderson conspiracy.

Any moment now, the punch this petite woman carried would finally be revealed.

CHAPTER THIRTY-TWO

I was standing just off the stairwell platform at the entrance to Level 21. Of all the places on the Thetis, I would have least imagined Cassidi leading us to the Crop Fields. I looked hesitantly through the narrow entrance and into the dim interior. The sliding double doors were designed to create a solid seal of the entire area, keeping precise humidity levels and temperatures for optimal crop yields and quality. The doors were wide open now, revealing the high-hanging ceiling of the level, which was almost double the height of most other levels on the Thetis. An elaborate system of pipes, valves and suction tubes hung from above on auto-moving sets of carbofoam rails.

'Crop Fields' was, of course, a joke. These weren't fields and the Thetis grew no crops. Not in the traditional sense, at least.

I carefully stepped into the entrance, facing the immense, level-sized honeycomb of hexagonal growth compartments, with their dark grey partitioning walls stretching almost to the ceiling. The air had the wet, metallic quality I knew to be the mark of early-cycle crop nutrition boosters. I tried listening for any clue as to where Cassidi might have gone, but the monotonous tapping of her shoes was lost in the noisy level ambiance.

For a place dedicated to the slow, delicate process of nanogrowing nutrients, level 21 was quite the cacophony. The entire level was divided into hundreds of hexagonal growth compartments, each approximately fifteen feet across. Each growth cell was independently connected to the feeder array — a web of tubery dangling from the ceiling, operated by an army of small units sliding back and forth on hanging rails like the scrawny fingers of a genius puppeteer.

There was the constant hushing and brushing of a thousand such units whizzing above. Certain crops needed tuning to their hydration levels. Others — a tweak to their lighting frequency mix. And at a certain point, a mature growth cell will be ready for Scraping, the process of nutrient extraction and the culmination of the growth-cycle. The raw nutrients would then travel one level up to the 22nd food processing lines, and the growth cell would be scrubbed and re-prepped for a new growth cycle.

This whole massive operation was supervised by the Thetis' very own KuberNomics system, the pride and glory of our generation. To me, it was still astonishing to realize that this whole major pivot in the way Humanity was being fed was the product of a space-born initiative of barely twenty years. I mean, I *remembered* plant-based foods when I was a kid. I *remembered* the hydro-farms and wet-walls where climber-ferns were grown to enormous sizes, their overclocked DNA maximizing their yield of legumes, fruit and grain. What was doubly astonishing was that the Thetans, with their acute tech-aversion, were willing to bet the farm — literally in this case, ha ha — on an automated, heavily technology-dependent system for all of the ship's subsistence.

The fact that the ingenious engineering which made the KuberNomics hyper-growth system possible was the brain-child of one Kilian Ngo, was the icing on the sympathy cake I had for this place.

After the malafest I inadvertently dragged him into, resulting in his demotion from his QIT position, Kilian was allocated to Crop Field work. Back then it was still a repetitive, manual, labour intensive job, with little room for innovation. Cycle after cycle, rinse and repeat, ad nauseam. That was the kind of punishment the Thetis authorities thought to be the most effective for a man like Kilian.

But talent is like a sun, shining bright on everything around it, spurring life and creation in whoever is lucky enough to be orbiting it, bathing in its light.

And you can't dim a sun by banishing it to a darker corner of space. True talent won't be suppressed — it just keeps on shining. So Kilian reinvented himself in the Crop Fields, put his engineering obsession to work and eventually conjured one of the greatest contributions to Thetan life in decades, arguably *generations*. He got zero public recognition for that, of course — but *I* noticed.

This work was probably why he was allowed to keep doing Alternative History Night, and the Nebula and all the other Kilian bafunye he was always up to. *And, eventually, get back on Birth Year queue.* The essence of Kilian Ngo was always pushing the envelope a tiny bit further, hoping for the silent confirmation of turning a blind eye, or the occasional slap on the wrist. Or, just the plain indifference of a system built on low-friction consensus rather than conflict management. Kilian was a relentless climber, and his invention of the KuberNomic system had provided him the slack he needed while still saving the establishment's face.

Oh, how I remembered the feeling of being the main planet to K's sun! The vibrance of nourishing on an endless, pulsating source of curiosity and creativity, an energy that fertilized the deepest parts of my insecurity, leaving no inner shadow unlit.

Until the orbit had deformed into a spiraling collision-course, my sole escape vector leaving me stranded in space, wandering between random gravity wells of one-night thrills and brief distractions, seeking a new star system I could call home.

I shook my head in riddance of the torrent of nonproductive thoughts. They'll be here, I knew, looming, ready to storm in if I only half-permit it.

"Kunye Kilian the Great," I mumbled as I stepped forward into the outer row of growth compartments. "You have really outdone yourself with this mala."

Walking through the Level 21 Crop Fields at the peak of a growth cycle was an experience unlike any other on the Thetis. It was an audible one, mostly — there wasn't much to note visually beyond the endless hive of grey hexagonal cells. But stepping into the main growth area, the mechanical whirring sounds of the overhanging delivery apparatus were immediately drowned by the all-encompassing, surreal symphony of the NanoDrip watering lattice. That was where the magic truly kicked in.

NanoDrip technology was the ingenious derivative of the one truly ground-breaking scientific discovery to have originated onboard the Thetis: the ability to efficiently compress water.

Water has always been a peculiar physical phenomenon. From the counter-intuitive tendency to expand when frozen, to the unpredictable crystal structure displayed in frozen-flake form, water always seemed to keep some yet-unraveled secret up its soggy sleeves.

And while its atomic elements of Hydrogen and Oxygen, in their pure form, were quite easy to compress and manipulate, their combination into the simple 3-atom water molecule had made water, for all practical purposes, very hard to compress.

But, apparently, not impossible, which is where QUBIC had the opportunity to earn its laurels.

Junior Academy, who had its own QUBIC node located at the research lab, had tasked it with re-mapping the most basic physical attraction forces under our unique conditions — high speed, high energy interstellar travel. QUBIC ran its complex simulations for *years* on end until, eventually, a true revelation appeared. It found a rare combination of energy, temperature, and pressure, where several electrons of the water molecule collapsed to a lower orbit around their atomic nucleus. Such collapse resulted in nearly a thousand-fold reduction in the repulsion forces acting between molecules, enabling them to cram closer together. For all practical purposes — a stable compression of water.

The process would not affect the huge weight of water the Thetis was carrying across space — mass was still mass, after all, compressed or not. But the ability to store and transport water around the ship via smaller, simpler systems did clear up a lot of space and had a tremendous effect on maintenance complexity and efficiency.

It would be a few years until further experiments on the effects of compression and decompression of water in organic cells unraveled the true potential of the discovery. It turned out that a tiny droplet of compressed water could penetrate the "protein factory" of Ribosome cells. Then, when the nano-droplet was decompressed within it to its original size, the energy and pressure exerted essentially hacked the Ribosome into a state of protein hyper-production. Similar processes were developed for hyper-growing carbs, fat, minerals and vitamin acids.

A new era dawned on human sustenance — you no longer needed to grow an entire tree just to get an apple. Hell — you didn't even need the apple, which was 85% water anyway — you could just cut to the chase and grow its base nutrients directly!

But for that revolution to hit mainstream and ignite the explosion of culinary inventiveness and diversity we were all enjoying on the Thetis today, it first had to move beyond the lab table.

Enter the most talented original thinker, an engineering prodigy ousted from the Quantum Information Technology unit and cast to Crop Farm work. Piece by piece, Kilian set to work translating the isolated lab experiment into the thriving, industrialized engineering marvel that were the Level 21 Crop Fields today.

One peculiarity of the NanoDrop irrigation process, an effect barely noticeable on the small-scale lab experiment level, was its audial imprint. The near-instantaneous decompression of a water droplet created an outward-moving pressure wave which created a distinct sound. Something between a 'Whizz' and a 'Pop', or the sound of a soap bubble bursting played in reverse.

That sound effect was, of course, much too subtle to be noticeable to the human ear on its own. But when Level 21 was going through a hyper-growth cycle with thousands — maybe millions! — of NanoDrip tubes working in non-stop concurrency, the aggregated effect was stunning.

Stepping into the Crop Fields' endless compartment array, the popping sounds seemed to be coming from everywhere around you. They came from above, below, echoed through the cell partition walls in all directions, multiplying into a 360-degree immersive, ethereal, bubbly ambiance. Walking through Level 21 felt like how I imagined diving into a glass of fizzy drink.

"Isn't it wonderful?" Cassidi Anderson's voice came from behind me.

I jerked with surprise, then turned slowly to face her. "It is," I eyed her, "but also freakishly disorienting."

Cassidi took a step closer. "I could have kept going till Propulsion on Zero but, frankly, these shoes are killing me." She was standing barefoot, holding her pair of spanking new heels in her right hand.

"Unnecessary," I said. "I realize that the similarity of our walking routes down 12 levels and through 26th negates all statistical probability for coincidental occurrence. Thus implies intentional stalking activity. And meaning this conversation, as the product of a non-commissioned tracking activity, would not be admissible in any future or existing investigation I may be conducting."

I lowered my head and mumbled, "not to mention the hundreds of witnesses. Well played."

Cassidi gave a tiny curtsy, the hem of her green dress pinched with one hand, heels held up in the other. "No *wonder* you made Senior Archivist at such a young age," she smiled. "Intelligence is the best perfume for a woman in my view. Very attractive."

I moved uncomfortably on my feet, trying to avoid her unblinking, direct stare. "How did you know I was following you?" I asked.

"Oh, you were not following *me*, my dear. I was leading *you*. In understanding the difference lies a profound life lesson for you. If you think you're the smartest person in the room, you either aren't — or you're in the wrong room. Now," she took another barefoot step closer to within arm's reach, her eyes soft and her posture less rigid, "Tell me a bit about yourself."

A rush of heat raced up my face, and I was suddenly very aware of the stinging, relentless NanoDrip chirping and popping sounds closing in from all directions. I tried to rebalance by finding something to hang on to, when an object dangling from Cassidi's neckline caught my attention. It was something so out of place, so completely improbable, that it completely derailed my line of thought.

"Wait, is that a…"

"Pearl, yes," she said, her eyes finally breaking contact and glancing at the grey, round object hanging from her exposed neck. "It's the only one on the Thetis. So, I guess, you could say it's the only one left in existence."

I was completely mesmerized. The pearl was flawless — a tiny ball-shaped wonder, its matte-grey surface unscarred and slightly reflective in the ambient light. It was held in place between two delicate brackets of magnetic suspension, so as to avoid the drill-hole which would have ruined its perfection. The mere presence of such a biological oddity had stirred a mixture of awe and anxiety in me. Opposing tidal forces of attraction and repulsion.

"It's perfect," I whispered.

"It has been passed down in the Anderson family for centuries now. It was a rarity even back on Earth — naturally cultivated for thirty five years in the depths of the ocean. One of Earth's random wonders. Do you like it?"

I immediately shriveled and looked away from Cassidi. The thought of such an alien artifact, born centuries ago on the ocean bed of a long-lost planet touching my skin threw a shiver down my spine.

"I don't think I could ever get over the thought that at the center of this perfect little thing lies an irregular, wet, *filthy* grain of mud," I said.

"We're Humans, Arc. Liet," Cassidi said calmly. "Everything *about* us is wet and filthy and random. If we're able to create perfection around that starting position, then we've truly transcended." After a short pause she added, "Come," and turned for the corridor leading into the deeper parts of Level 21, shoes still in her hand.

Worried I'd lose her in the maze of identical compartments, I hurriedly followed her to the cell's exit. Cassidi's imperial green dress and spot of blond hair played a striking contrast against the monochromatic surroundings. She advanced in a relaxed, elegant stride, letting me catch up to her while maintaining the impression of a leisurely walk in the park.

"It's important for me that you know," she turned her head to me when I reached her, "I think you did the right thing coming forward and exposing that Adapter. I realize how hard it must have been to betray someone you love."

I lowered my head. "His name is Kilian."

"And I know what you have risked," she continued, disregarding my comment, "you should also know that I tried to push with all my limited influence against the punishment of skipping you on Birth Year." She slowed her pace and shook her head slowly. "As a woman to a woman — it was a terrible, barbaric decision."

Cassidi caught my eyes with a soft look and rested an empathetic hand on my wrist. "But as you know, I have no administrative position on the Thetis. I'm just a scientist. There's no actual say for me in these matters." She shook her head slightly, "At least they let you keep your position in the Archive. It would have been a loss for the Thetis to let a talent such as yours go to waste."

That was only half-true, of course. If not for Nyasha's vigorous fight in my behalf, putting his entire professional reputation on the line for me, I would be hand-sorting ProteAlgae right here on Level 21 every kunye day for the rest of my life.

Still, it was nice of her to say that. The Cassidi Anderson walking by my side was definitely different than the woman I imagined her to be.

"Oh, and by the way," she turned halfway in my direction, "I know his name was Kilian. Kilian Ngo. And everything he invented around here." Cassidi slowed to a stop and a mischievous glint appeared in her eyes.

"Just as I know that KuberNomics is just a made up name. Doesn't mean anything, except carrying his own initials."

I couldn't help laughing. "And here I was, certain that this was a personal and direct wink only I would get."

Cassidi shrugged contentedly. *I wonder how this feels*, I thought. *To know your entire life that you're the smartest girl around. To have absolutely no doubt in your own abilities.*

After a brief pause, Cassidi started moving again, stepping out of the main corridor and into a different section of hexagonal growth cells. That area was dedicated to growing basic amino acids, bio-fermenting on big, horizontal mesh trays. It was on low-irrigation growth mode, thus markedly quieter and absent the constant drill of the NanoDrip.

Cassidi navigated through the near-identical chambers with confident elegance. She turned left and right with precise deliberation as if led by an internal map. I myself lost bearing quickly in what to me was nothing but a grey-walled maze. I eventually gave up on the effort and just kept following Cassidi, who was keeping a generous, slow pace.

"Looking at all this," Cassidi suddenly changed to a more serious tone, motioning to the Crop Fields hive extending in all directions, "don't you find the prejudice against Adapters to be just laughable hypocrisy?"

I almost tripped over an acid fermentation basin, too shocked to speak. *Kunye what did I just hear her say?*

"I mean," she continued, "people today fear technology so much, they regard Adapters as Earthers once treated terrorists, or... infidels, at some point? Like people undermining the fabric of our society, no less."

I was awe-struck. *No way this isn't a test of some sort.* On the Thetis, no one could get away with such words. With such *ideas*. Adapters were... *abominations*. Traitors. Being accused of supporting Adapter activities had cost Kilian his career, almost cost him his Genline. It cost *me* Birth Year for only associating with him!

Is Cassidi trying to lure me into some kind of a trap? Is it a mere chance that she started this conversation just as we stepped into the quieter part of the Crop Fields, or is someone listening in on us?

My 7th was literally screaming with paranoia. *How can she be chatting so lightly — with me of all people, an Archivist for Sol's sake! — about such perilous and taboo a subject?*

Cassidi read the distress on my face immediately and waved it away in dismissal. "Oh, calm down, Sandrine, will you? We're just talking, te? There's no punishment for just having ideas, is there?"

"Kilian Ngo might disagree with that statement."

"You know very well that if Kilian would have kept his ideas in the theoretical realm rather than manifest them into actions, he would have stayed perfectly safe," Cassidi said. "Granted —" she raised both palms in acknowledgment, "— making an example out of him in order to deter other aspiring Adapters from following his path may have played a role in the severeness of the outcome," she pressed her palms together, interlocking her fingers except both index fingers which were now pointing at me, "an outcome to which I objected, mind you."

"*I* didn't do anything, and I still got skipped," I said dryly.

"Making examples tends to create quite the debris. Otherwise it might go by unnoticed."

"So I was just collateral damage. Wrong woman at the wrong kunye place?"

"Apparently."

My arms dropped to my side, deflated. *This is utterly counter-productive*, I thought. What's the use of confronting lies told with a straight face, when the truth won't help anyway? *What's done is done.*

"If you need any further convincing about the lack of interest we have in persecuting Adapters, all you have to do is take a look around you. The Thetan people may resent technology and may be intimidated by those who seek to advance it, but aren't we *already* slaves to the technologies we invent? Humanity's entire *food supply* now depends on inventions like the NanoDrip and hyper-growth cells!"

"Slaves?" The word tasted sour in my mouth. "Adapters don't seek slavery. They seek *progress!*"

Cassidi just looked at me for a few moments, then said calmly, "what you call progress, my dear, is merely trading one slavemaster for another. First it was fire, then agriculture. Then transportation, and then communication. We tame it, only to become dependent on it to the point we no longer remember how to survive without it. Eventually, we turned inward to self-augmentation, and that's where progress became destructive. You're wise enough to know that progress is inevitable. You were just always afraid of going against the norm. Kilian wasn't."

"And here he is, miraculously forgiven, nestling his resurrected Genline with a beautiful new wife," I said sarcastically.

"And why do you think that is?" Cassidi asked quietly.

"He did something for you."

"And by 'You', shall I assume you mean the Thetis?"

"The Andersons."

She chuckled. "Quid pro quo, was it? Even if this *were* true, even if Kilian was absolved — wouldn't it be further testament to the forgiving, non-vindictive nature of the Anderson administration? That even a person so far astray could redeem oneself by virtue of her actions?"

She held my gaze firmly. *Yes, I heard the 'her' alright,* I thought. My body instinctively tensed as she added in a steady, controlled voice, "I believe that there is always a place for absolution if one can become useful to the greater mission."

And there it was. Cooked in the 34th quarters and delivered through this icon of Thetan royalty with her dark, flawless emerald dress and perfectly shaped blond hair and her Earthborn, pristine pearl necklace and her documented, superior intellect. The most perfect courier for the dish I was about to be served.

An offer.

But there would be no offer at all unless I was a perceived threat to the Andersons. Unless I had something to offer back. Quid pro quo.

I smiled. "You're afraid of me."

"Oh?" Cassidi raised a surprised brow.

"You're afraid because I am on to you."

Cassidi tilted her head slightly to the right, her eyes locked on me in her searching look. "Are we in some kind of a detective story, then? Do tell."

I had no patience for this charade. "I *know*, Cassidi. Everything you've been doing. Manipulating the Thetis archive database. Rewriting and erasing files to conceal what you've been working on for *years*. Your plan to get hold of the PHS since it was still a small, public side-office. The crawling annexation of departments with QUBIC nodes, until you had enough privileges to override anything you want. To hide the research you are working on in the PHS."

I hesitated for a second before adding, "And I am not the only one onto this. Bashiri knew, too."

The softness in Cassidi's expression evaporated immediately. Her posture stiffened, the amused brow now descended over detached, penetrating eyes. I could sense the effort of her self restraint as she muttered in a low, stern tone.

"To recite a forgotten scientist from your beloved Old Earth era, 'Extraordinary claims require extraordinary evidence', Senior Archivist Liet. I don't presume you are in possession of such, are you?"

The condescending brute!

"To recite an even older saying commonly used by planetfolk of that era: 'Fuck you, Mrs. Anderson'", I said. "I know Bashiri was killed for what he knew, so what can you *possibly* offer me, what with you being 'just a scientist with no administrative position on the Thetis'?"

Curiously, Cassidi was much less affected by my barrage than I had anticipated. Her shoulders relaxed a bit and she lowered her head slowly, shaking it in gentle disappointment.

"Your'e young," she said with a distant smile. "I still remember what that feels like — *everything's* either a conspiracy or negligence of the older generations. It's a great propellant for action when you're a teenager, before you grow up and become too busy just getting through the day. But, honestly Sandrine, at your age and status it is bordering on pathetic. Where you see a smoking gun, lie nothing but the ashes of a long-dead bonfire."

Gun. Bonfire. Words with no meaning on the Thetis. Ancient words, lost for centuries. *Who talks like that anymore?*

Cassidi sounded like an Archive rat, like, well — *me*, except she wore it with confidence whereas I always felt extremely self-conscious about my nerdness.

I guess it's easier when you're a beautiful, privileged woman, I thought. *Or is it all just another tactic to get my sympathy?*

"Oh, you'll feel the heat when you'll have to face the testimony we have," I said calmly.

Again, Cassidi was far from impressed. The amused expression returned to her face as she dropped her heeled shoes to the floor and stepped into them with effortless elegance.

"Please don't tell me you have everything hanging on Jericho Pakk's turning himself in, bearing a dramatic confession."

The shocked look on my face must have shined for parsecs.

"If he's smart he will," I managed to let out, the conviction already fading from my voice.

Cassidi couldn't help but laugh. "You didn't really think Jericho wouldn't tell us about your little meeting, te?" her laugh reverberated eerily between the hexagonal walls. "You are so delightfully naive, it's adorable. I am starting to develop a serious liking for you, Sandrine Liet."

She clicked a step closer to me and laid a friendly hand on my shoulder. She was all softness again, no trace of the dark, scorching expression on her face.

"There are no *murders* on the Thetis, dear. Is there a higher value than the sanctity of life in our society? No true Thetan could doubt that, ne?"

Her eyes bore into mine, gleaming empathy and conviction. "Jericho was not in the GenLab to kill Dr. Bashiri. He was there to *save* him. Just as he stopped on his way out of the Farm to save *you*. We are all so lucky he made it in time for you! Unfortunately," she broke the gaze and lowered her head, "in Bashiri's case he was too late. The doctor was already gone."

"By throwing himself down the *Trash Tube?*" I whispered in anger. "Into an Ion beam, shredded limb by limb by trillions of particles?"

"I know," Cassidi nodded slowly, "selfish, right? All that matter going to waste."

I shook my head in disbelief. Cassidi held both my arms in her hands.

"We are not your enemies," she said. "On the contrary, Sandrine. You deserve your Genline and your future back. And you deserve to be where you belong. And that's with the winners. Look at me. Trust your 7th."

She gave my arms a gentle shake and caught my gaze. I suddenly felt extremely tired, vulnerable and fed up with all this mala.

Was this for real? if it was, the last thing I should have listened to was my 7th sense, because it was kunye *screaming* with warning alarms.

"I belong in the Archive," I said finally, "with Nyasha. That is my home here."

"And that's a fine choice for a home," Cassidi said. "But it doesn't have to be the only one, te?"

I took a step back, breaking free from her hold of my arms. The cell compartment wall touched my back and I could feel the humidity through the fabric of my shirt.

So that's the proposition. My birth Year, a Genline, protection. Life back on course. But in exchange for what?

It didn't have to be said out loud. I knew very well where my attention would need to stay away from.

"I'm not for sale."

Cassidi was unmoved. "No one is, in a society where there's no concept of buying. What we have on the Thetis is cooperation. The pursuit of a win-win. Go home. Take a few days off. You've been under tremendous trauma from your injury. Maybe go browsing for baby clothes on 26th. We've passed some cute little stands earlier, didn't we?"

"And who is talking to me here, Mrs. Anderson?" I asked. "Is it only the two of us, or are you here on the Primo's behalf?"

Cassidi chuckled. "I am a Maker, Sandrine. Sabi is a Keeper. Do you understand the difference? Makers may create ideas and inventions, but the Keepers are the ones who manifest them into reality. That's why any great leader in Human history was a Keeper. The ideas we create are like bubbles, beautiful and fragile and short-lived. But it takes a Keeper to gather the resources, build the mechanisms and protect the growth and rooting of the idea. Creatives cannot lead efficiently — we're much too introvert and volatile for what it takes — and Keepers cannot innovate through major transformations. It's a symbiosis — the most successful teams were always the genius artist and the powerful supporting patron. So believe me when I say this — getting you what you want will be one of the easiest challenges Sabi had to deal with this past week."

So there it was. Straight from the top — a total reboot, a second chance. The dream package.

"Why?"

Cassidi tilted her head in question.

"Why?" I repeated. "Why go through all this with me? The tracking. The intimidation. The PubSheet exposure. What makes that failed experiment you had at the PHS so important to conceal?"

269

Cassidi was not fast enough to control the alarmed expression which flashed on her face.

"What are you talking about?" She said quickly.

"When I was in the infirmary, the Primo and Sec. Pakk paid me a visit. They showed me the medical file you were trying to erase from the records. The one about the bacteria infection you and your son caught."

Cassidi pressed her lips, jaw clenched, which for the first time offered a peek to a cruel, unattractive feature in her.

"That was a mistake," she muttered through her teeth. "They should not have bothered you with that, nor shall the Primo meet you again. You should forget what you saw, it's an entirely private matter."

"That still doesn't answer my question, Cassidi. That minor medical file doesn't even come close to requiring everything that's going on. All… this," I gestured to the space around us. "What is it that the Thetis shouldn't know about?"

Cassidi just looked at me for a few moments, assessing. Her face was a blank slate, but I could sense the fire raging behind those eyes.

"Sadly, that cannot be shared," she said resolutely.

"This is the Thetis," I demanded. "We feed each other. We elect our leaders. We choose our kunye species destination planet by common vote. We share *everything*."

"No!" She burst out. "We share *fate*, not means. Not skills. Not intelligence, or talent."

After calming herself, Cassidi forced a smile, then sighed. "We are two *very* different women, me and you. In fact, we are in most ways the exact opposite of one one another."

"And here I thought we were about to become friends," I retorted.

Cassidi sneered. "You are pulled by the strings of the past, what with your movies and the Archive, you see Old Earth as an era where meaning existed. I hate the past. I despise it. For me it is nothing but a crutch on which to build a better future for my Genline."

"Maybe," I said. "It doesn't mean that you or the Primo can decide what's best for all Thetans. If you found something important, good or bad, you need to share it. We all get a vote on our future."

"A vote?" Cassidi mouthed the word as if it were a stale, sour medication. "Do you know what you get when every single Human being gets a vote on critical, strategic matters?"

"Justice?"

"No, Sandrine, you get a society whose fate is decided by the rule of the average. And average doesn't meet the bar for survival. Name a great leader from Human history, and I'll show you a man who stood against the crowds, not bowed to them."

"That history also teaches us that no leader keeps positive developments secret from his people. Only the evil decisions are made in the dark."

Cassidi raised her hands in frustration. She hesitated for a moment, collected herself and said in her dry, controlled tone:

"Do you know why I brought you here?"

I looked around me. The cell we were in was identical to any other boring growth cell around us.

"I assumed that the empty space and the ambient noise would make it difficult for anyone to eavesdrop on us," I said.

Cassidi shook her head. "I am not concerned with eavesdroppers."

She took 3 steps backwards, revealing the part of the floor she was standing on. There was something there.

Carved into the dark grey material of the flooring and laid flat with the floor was a small, square metal plate. It was real metal, not made of any of the more modern carbon-based materials. From where I was standing, I could barely make an engraving of some sort on the face of the plate.

"Come closer," Cassidi said.

I stepped forward and stood over the plate. The lighting in the hypergrowth cell was dim and flat, but the large letters engraved into the metal were easily readable:

Here was lost

The light in our stars

Our son

OSCAR KOHN

My heart missed a beat. A dark lump crept its way up my throat as I raised my eyes to Cassidi.

"Is this where—"

"This is where they found him, yes," she said. "It was still an actual crop field back then, of course. They always built around the plate as the level progressed, out of respect. Are you familiar with the story?"

"The first murder on the Thetis," I said faintly.

"The *only* murder on the Thetis," she corrected. "And a borderline accident at that. The child was playing hide&seek with his friends in the field. When the arsonists set it on fire, no one knew he was still there. Found his scorched little body two days later."

My knees felt weak. "That's horrible."

"Yes," she muttered dismissively. "I'm curious — have you met any of the Kohns recently?"

I shook my head. "I don't think I know anyone from that family, no." Which wasn't saying much, me being the work-obsessed introvert that I was. I think I was familiar with more historical figures from the Archive files than I was with actual, living people on the Thetis.

"Well that's because they don't exist anymore," Cassidi said. "See — the Thetis population was much smaller at Generation 1 than it is today. The Kohns should have grown to be quite a large family by now, ne? So, tell me — where are they?"

I pondered the question for a few moments, studying Cassidi's face for clues. Eventually, I had to resign with a defeated shrug. Was there something I was missing? A story I should have known about which could explain the disappearance of an entire family from the Thetis genline?

Cassidi pressed her palms together as if proclaiming the obvious.

"Genetically diluted," she said and took one step forward toward me. "See, the Kohns had another child — little Oscar's older brother. And after losing Oscar, the family invested all they had in their only remaining son. They gave him the best education, pushed for him to get accepted to the Academy and used every political connection and guilt-ridden manipulation they could evoke in order to get him into a high-ranking job and position of influence on the Thetis. But," she opened her hands, palms up, her lips pursed, "you can't cheat the genline, you know. And it doesn't even take 8 generations for a family with a single child to get completely diluted in the collective Thetis gene pool, become indistinguishable from random genetic noise. To disappear, as if they never existed on board."

"Which is something you certainly can't say about the Andersons," I said. "What a legacy: Firstborn baby on the Thetis. Then a Head of Resource Allocation.   A Secundus Population Planning. A Head Archivist. And now — a Primo. You sure married into a family prone to being in the right place at the right time, ne?"

"Confusing luck and strategy is a loser's excuse," Cassidi sneered. "We mentioned the oh-so-sacred Thetan pursuit of a win-win earlier. Win-win, or win-lose — the Andersons always make sure they're secured on the win side. The rest is optional. And you, my dear, are in that rare position of being invited to choose that side."

I now knew exactly where this conversation was going. Why we were here.

I lowered my head. "You want me to drop the case," I said dryly.

"What case?" She asked cheerfully, "from my understanding, there *is* no case. The only official case on record was Sabi's complaint about the late Doctor, which was withdrawn and permanently closed. Now there's only you keeping yourself busy with an unofficial and unhealthy habit of poking around other people's matters. Maybe you have too much time on your hands. Maybe you need a more… productive occupation for that time. A baby is a lot of work, Sandrine, wouldn't you say?"

I took a step back and turned my head to the side, reluctant to let Cassidi see my eyes tearing up. I looked up at the elaborate railing and tubing apparatus hanging over us. Small units kept whizzing around, relentlessly busy fixing, nurturing, tweaking something in this giant hive of dizzyingly identical hexagons, maddeningly drowning in the monotonous popping cacophony of the decompressing NanoDrips. My mouth turned dry, and I focused my gaze on the simple metal plate fastened to the flooring seven generations ago.

"I can't do that," I whispered.

"We are on a *mission*, you fool!" Cassidi snapped, her voice eerily amplified by the reverberation in the damp cell. "This is Birth Year! The next one will be 15 years from now. Are you kunye *stupid*, or were you just not paying attention in the last ten minutes? You have one chance to secure your genline, and that is *now*. If you don't take it, even if by some magic you'll manage to get selected for the next Birth Year, it will never be enough. You are sentencing yourself, your future only child and your future genline for *extinction*! For Sol's sake, girl, if you have the slightest amount of self-worth, you'll do anything in your power to prevent it."

"I'm not Kilian," I shook my head as the meaning of her words sank in and detonated within me like subterranean nukes. "I don't have the moral flexibility. There has to be right and wrong."

Cassidi winced in repulsion. "Right and wrong? Like, for example, using your Senior Archivist credentials to pull private medical records from the Archive directory? Like illegally accessing grid-locator data on private Thetans who are under no official investigation? Or is your 'higher cause' somehow superior to everyone else's, Liet?"

274

I shriveled and raised my eyes to meet her hard, ruthless gaze. I physically felt small and exposed standing in front of that woman, her stiff, upright figure and the cramped growth-cell around us looming over me with claustrophobic effect.

Cassidi dropped her hands to her sides with a disappointed expression.

"Don't lecture me about right and wrong, Archivist. If you should have learnt anything from Human history, it is that the meaning of both are defined retroactively by the hindsight of the winners. You've been offered a seat at the future winner's table, but you insist on standing. You say you're not for sale, but when Humans finally reach planetfall again, anyone who wants to prosper better either have something to sell or the means to buy. The rest will be slaves, just as it has always been since the dawn of Man."

"I believe we've evolved since then," I said.

Cassidi sneered again. "Sadly, evolution doesn't work on such short timescales. Even in space, we're still humans. Now, my dear, you have a choice to make —"

Cassidi stepped close to me, her harsh, perfect brown eyes drilling holes into mine. My head spun as her voice softened again and her complexion relaxed into a friendly smile.

"Resign," she said lightly, "hand back your Archive credentials, and go live a comfortable life with your future family. You're an intelligent young woman, you'll find interesting roles to undertake when you feel ready for it. Or, stand trial for your abuse of position. Again. And you'll be done."

I studied her face for a few seconds, hovering mere inches from mine. That stone of a woman, unintimidated by anything this world could attempt to throw at her.

"You'll just destroy anything and anyone standing in your path, won't you?"

"The ants don't matter," she said, "it's all about the nest."

As long as you're the Queen Ant, I added internally.

"So either way — the Anderson's always win," I whispered sarcastically.

Cassidi shrugged. "You have until the end of Dusting to straighten up your priorities, or don't bother showing up for work in the Archive the next day," Cassidi said. "Oh, and one other thing — if you're thinking Jericho Pakk will save the day for you, let me offer a free tip on scare tactics: it's an intensity-level game. It only works if you're scarier than the alternative."

Cassidi stepped back and scanned me top to bottom. She let out an almost inaudible sigh as she straightened her dress and turned to leave.

"Ultimately, this is a sad day," she muttered quietly, either to me or to herself.

The clicking of Cassidi's heels could be heard long after she had left the cell we were in. Soon enough, they too drowned in the industrial symphony of the Crop Fields — the pinnacle of Kilian's creation after he'd presumably made his peace with the choices handed to him by the forming Thetis Elite.

CHAPTER THIRTY-THREE

Dusting protocol kicked in at midnight. I had reached my hab almost two hours earlier, exhausted and dripping sweat from wandering through the Crop Fields maze in search of an exit path. I then hurried down two levels to the rapidly emptying Level 19, where people were already retreating to their habs where they would normally spend Dusting Day. Unless you were designated to an essential role on the Thetis, or were caring for some emergency, the general directive was stay inside, maintain minimal physical activity, watch for any abnormal side effects in yourself and people dependent on you.

Since I met none of the above, I simply lay sprawled on my bed, my mind racing, calculating, searching for a solution to my own trajectory drift. Trying to think up a way out of the kunye mess I had gotten myself into without sacrificing my morals, or my job, and without bending the knee to the Andersons.

Two hours of turning the problem in my head and examining it from every possible angle, and I was yet to come up with one.

In times like these, perhaps morals are a luxury. And Cassidi's offer sure was tempting.

One thing was clear — the Andersons were playing on a whole different level. When most people on the Thetis were making plans for tomorrow, the weekend, *maybe* a week ahead — they had been

277

working for *generations* on post-Resett plans. Their legacy. Building the infrastructure and the competitive landscape for lasting dominance in a society yet to be established several generations down the genline.

What kunye chance do I even have fighting this kind of power? I thought.

The meeting with Cassidi was obviously a pre-designed ploy. The delivered ultimatum was quite clear-cut: drop my inquiries into the Andersons' actions. Resign from the Archive, meaning my high-status QUBIC credentials would get revoked, serving as insurance that I would never be able to go back digging. In return, I would regain my place in the Birth Year queue. Get my life, future and genline back on track. Fulfill the Thetis grander Mission — by letting them fulfill their own private one, whatever it was.

The alternative? Total elimination. Be it via finding myself on the stinging side of the Trash Tube like poor Dr. Bashiri, or by the slower, painful grind of endless legal proceedings: they'd drown me in multiple complaints of illegal tracking, unauthorized access to personal data and a dozen other manufactured claims designed to trash my reputation. And then — the inevitable erasure from the Human gene pool a Genless woman would eventually suffer.

But why? The question kept pounding in my head as I began to taste the metallic tinge of Dusting particles flowing in through the ceiling air ducts. What could possibly justify that level of obsession for Dr. Bashiri's work? I mean, Almaz was a gifted scientist and had contributed significantly to the Thetis mission, but to be honest — he mainly worked around the Sensory Farm and the optimization of its ecosystem. He *did* come up with a clever use of a bacteria-delivered gene to control animal extermination, but that's hardly worth the concern of the Primo's circle, ne? Bashiri was a pure scientist — all profession, zero politics.

So is Kilian, and so is Nyasha. So why do I feel like I'm the only one not on the Anderson leash? What kunye knowledge do I possess that stresses them out so much?

And when so much effort is invested in camouflaging their plan —

potentially lying to the whole Thetis about the accident trajectory solution and the ability to reach Final Call and our destination planets! — how *can* I sit this one out and concentrate on my selfish goals?

The haze of the Dusting particles in my hab started thickening and I was getting lightheaded by the minute. The threads of logical thinking I was trying to hold on to were slowly untwining, and I felt my limbs loosen, a massive blanket of exhaustion pressing down on me.

Before drifting to a heavy, forced sleep, the image of Oscar Kohn's surreal memorial plaque bolted into the ground surfaced in my mind. The mute testament to the ultimate sacrifice of a family who had lost a child, and then was forever lost altogether.

A fluttering realization tingled on the edges of my consciousness: *she had lost a child too. She, too, is fighting for the prevailing of her genline.*

And then, finally, sleep consumed me.

And I was back at the shore.

It was the summer we all turned fifteen. 'The Summer of Roaming', people sometimes called it with a tinge of nostalgia. The summer before all of us would commence our Junior Academy years, and so — to our young minds — the last chance we'd ever have to roam carelessly about the ship, get into trouble and be a general nuisance to the public for a whole two months.

Feeling every bit the newly-minted adults, yet lacking the maturity associated with that prestigious status, there was no experiment we wouldn't get ourselves into, no restricted area on the Thetis we wouldn't set out to explore.

Some of us got heavily into fizzing, and would regularly sneak into the Junior Academy chemlabs and throw secret all-night fizzfests. Those were early days of the NanoDrip technology invention, still under research at the Academy labs and still, older siblings had already been whispering about the newfound potential of loading the NanoDrip sprinklers with a mixture of diluted alcohol. The effect of the nanobubble spray decompressing in one's mouth, the rumor went, would deliver an alcohol-infused punch unparalleled by any other intoxication means yet known to Man.

What other motivation, really, does a fifteen year old kid need to deploy a new and untested technology directly on his own brain, te? Thank Sol, the vacation wrapped up quickly enough so that apart for one or two alarming near-misses, everyone came through it unscathed.

My own poison was of a much calmer nature. I was a pretty stressed-out kid at the time, and the Thetis was going through the noisy, crowded, suffocating phase of four-year-old Gen8ers and their sleep-deprived, red-shot-eyed mums running throughout the ship. There was no peace to be found.

I had a friend at the time. A boy kind of friend, Marco Berlin. It was a mostly platonic friendship, barring the incidental exploration of mutual curiosities, as Marco increasingly focused his romantic and physical interest on other boys. And on that summer of changes and adolescent confusion, we found refuge from the ship's chaos in each other.

The shore was our place.

We would sneak into the Level 8 Sensory Farm just as the simulated daylight began its slow dimming sequence, moving quickly to reach the small body of water at the Farm's center before nightfall overtook the pseudo-skies.

Side by side, we would lie on the fine-grained pebble beach surrounding the small artificial pond, the cool water lapping at our bare feet. There was no operational atmospheric simulation to conjure swirling vapor-clouds, no lighting mechanism to project sunset and moonlight from above. The ceiling we were staring at was bare industrial grayness, criss-crossed with exposed sprinkler piping and power grid connectors.

We didn't care. In our imagination, we were lying on a vast ocean shore, gazing up at the infinite marvels of the star-sprinkled night sky of our future home planet.

"Imagine a vast galaxy stretching across the sky, each twinkle — a whole new star system!" Marco whispered in my ear.

"Imagine a warm breeze," I said softly, "caressing your cheeks, carrying the scents of fresh grass and open fire and cooking from a nearby village."

I could feel Marco smiling besides me. "Imagine tiny, yellow fish brushing against your feet, tickling your toes."

I smiled too, then inhaled deeply through my nose and closed my eyes.

"Imagine rain."

We just lay there, silent, for a few long minutes, lost in imagination. We had so much yet to relearn.

CHAPTER THIRTY-FOUR

"Sandrine, wake up!" A firm hand on my shoulder shook me and I threw my eyes open to find two freakish creatures leaning above my bed.

"Kunye mala!" I shouted, jumping up with my back pressed against the bed's headboard. The two figures were completely covered in face masks and wide goggles, the bigger of them standing by the bedside with the other sitting on its edge. Judging by the shape, the sitter was most likely a woman.

Surprised by my reaction, she took off her goggles in one swift motion. The eyes were unmistakeable.

"Gahlia!" I exhaled in relief, "what's going on here?"

"Quick! We've got to move as long as Dusting provides us cover," she said and threw a set of mask and goggles in my lap. "Put these on. We'll do the explaining on the way down."

"What do you mean, *down*?" I asked, slipping on the flexible mask that immediately adapted to my face. "And who's *that*?"

Gahlia motioned the standing guy to get moving toward the hab door. His distinct limp left no doubt as to who he was. "*Armitage?*" I called in surprise. "So you're helping us with the case on Sabi Anderson?"

"Tentatively," Armitage grunted from beneath his face gear. "I'll defer judgement to when I actually see anything beyond gossip."

Gahlia tugged my arm. "Put on your good boots. We're taking you to the Origin. And it's going to be quite the climb."

Level 19 was deserted, which was a very unusual sight even at this hour. Middle of the night or not, there was *always* something going on, some people awake on 19th. After all, this was where the young and Genless roamed, dedicating their hormonal, creative prime years to making art, fun and love — before the next Birth Year would mark the beginning of the hatch-and-nest period of their lives.

Tonight, however, not a single soul could be seen in either the alleyways or the main level open areas. Everything had shut down for Dusting, even the always-on drinking corners and open-air social lounges spread everywhere around the level.

As the three of us exited the hab complex, we were greeted by a creepy, alien scene — a heavy, almost impenetrable haze filled the Thetis, descending from the ceiling air circulation system in a yellowish-orange gradient. The atmosphere was so thick with the Dusting cloud that merely waving a hand through it generated swirling vortices of particles. Their trails circled uninterrupted for long seconds before finally settling back into their motionless hover.

Visibility was almost non-existent, save for a few feet above the ground where the light, floating artificial dust was thinner. The bluish night-time ambient light created eerie reflections in the dust cloud, throwing off all sense of distance and direction while moving through the haze.

"Where are we going?" I heard myself shouting at the dim outlines of Gahlia and Armitage leading just a few steps ahead. My voice reverberated with a strange metallic quality in the yellow mist, its tone rendered flat and omnidirectional.

Gahlia's figure materialized before me as she slowed down to let me catch up to her. "We have to hurry," she said, her voice muffled through the mask. "The metallic particles create a kind of volumetric super-reflector, which throws off the grid locators accuracy. They can't track us while we're moving through the haze."

"At least as long as it's this dense," Armitage's voice rumbled around us from all directions. "But in a few hours they'll start sucking this mala back in."

"True," said Gahlia, urging me to keep pace with her. For a Thetan of her age, her speed and agility were surprising. "We should be good all the way down to 10th," she added. "There's no Dusting below the seal."

"So, wouldn't the locators just pick up our signals there?"

Gahlia turned her head toward me, the oversized goggles on her small face resembling some giant, alien eyes. "They would. Which is why we're taking an alternative route for that part of the way. That's what the boots are for."

Chapter Thirty-Five

Armitage was waiting for us at the lip of the main stairwell leading down from Level 19.

"I just want to make something absolutely clear," his voice boomed through the thick yellow dust, his large contour finally materializing as we approached. Armitage leaned closer, his eyes wide and unblinking behind the protective goggles.

"I know you think Sabi is orchestrating some huge, illegal conspiracy of some sort, a manipulation of the public etcetera. Now, I happen to think that on a mission like ours — democracy and law are important, but we must put survival first, te?"

"Democracy and law *are* the means to ensure survival," I said cautiously, "anything else has always ended in destruction."

Armitage frowned behind his face mask. "Maybe," he shrugged, "you're the archivist. I'm just an old piping mechanic. But these are not normal times."

"Said every tyrant in history."

Gahlia rested a firm hand on Armitage's arm before he could retort. "We have no time for this now. We need you on this."

He looked at Gahlia for a moment before meeting my eyes again.

"Look, Gahlia is the smartest person I know. Too smart to fall for me, unfortunately," he threw a playful glance at her direction, which was answered by a friendly slap on his forearm. "So if she says something's stinking here, I trust her judgement. But I'll be watching you. If I see you pulling anything that could endanger the mission — I will always put the Thetis first."

"I couldn't agree with you more on that one," I said. "I'm an Archivist. I've dedicated my life to protecting the mission."

Armitage studied me for a few more seconds, then turned to Gahlia. "I still can't tell if this girl is brilliant or plain obsessed with paranoia, but I feel her heart is in the right place."

"On the existence of a heart, I'd say the jury's still out," Gahlia responded, glancing sideways at me. *She used to be Kilian's mentor*, I reminded myself.

And without a further word, Gahlia pulled curtly on Armitage's sleeve and they both started descending the wide stairwell. I followed suit a few steps behind, trying to keep focus on the lower, more visible part of their legs. Anything above knee level blurred, then dissipated, then disappeared as a denser ripple moved through the particle cloud, engulfing them both.

Gahlia's movements were surprisingly agile and matched her slender, healthy-looking build — *that's a great shape for a Gen5er*, I thought. Armitage, on the other hand, with his heavy-set body and the slight but noticeable limp, seemed to be struggling a bit harder. *It must be quite the effort for him to be doing this — climbing down half the Thetis on foot.* They advanced steadily, helping each other through the Dusting haze, offering a silent hand and a reassuring whisper when needed. Watching those two pairs of boots engaged in a mute, harmonious dance down the ship stairs filled me with an unfamiliar mixture of calm and envy, like knowing everything will be just fine, except not necessarily for me.

When we reached Level 13, both Gahlia and Armitage needed a brief stop to catch their breath. Due to the double height of the level, the haze cloud was slightly thinner and they both took seat on one of the open park benches in front of the Main Archive entrance.

On instinct, I turned toward the familiar office doors. Gahlia raised her eyes in question.

"Insurance," I blurted behind the mask and gestured for them to wait a few moments. Armitage nodded, waving at me to hurry up.

I entered the Archive and walked directly to Nyasha's desk. I knew I had to leave some mark, a message only he would understand, in case any of Sabi's or Jericho Pakk's goons search the place for clues to my whereabouts. The last thing I wanted was to implicate Nyasha as an accomplice to my Quasar-chase.

I remembered a tale Nyasha once told me, an Old Earth fable he was fond of. It was a parable about a huge, legendary animal and several wise, blind men trying to figure out what that animal was.

I pulled a fresh inksheet from the office pile and placed it right on his desk where he'd be sure to find it first thing tomorrow morning. I wrote:

'Went on a Hail Mary to determine if this is indeed an Elephant. If a different creature emerges from the clues, or if I am trampled by the beast, please know that I did my best.'

I left the inksheet unsigned and hurried back outside.

CHAPTER THIRTY-SIX

The yellowish-orange haze of the Dusting cloud was noticeably thinner when we reached Level 10. There were no habs on this level, so no reason to deploy as much material. With the light particles' tendency to float upwards and seep through the open stairwell to the upper levels, the visibility was much better, extending to over 30 feet in each direction.

As my feet landed on the level floor, I was surprised to find not two but three masked and goggled figures waiting for me in the main gallery above the seal.

Level 10 was unique in that it was not built as a separate level like the rest of the Thetis. It was actually a gallery level, a thirty foot wide ring running full-circle around the external periphery of the ship. The ceiling hung only twelve feet high, making 10 the lowest level on the Thetis. A waist-high safety railing guarded the lip of the round gallery, allowing for a top view onto Level 9 below. That view mostly included chemplants and oxygenation pools and other raw-material processing units, their putrid fumes drifting up in waves.

The function of Level 10's unique shape was, of course, the seal.

The thinking behind the design was providing an emergency mechanism for separating the hazardous parts of the ship from the main livable areas, while ensuring the Thetis remained operational.

288

And so, every facility which could — as a result of a malfunction, human error or even malice — endanger the Thetis and its inhabitants was allocated to a level below 10th. Chemical and biological poisonous materials, radioactive waste, even the Sensory Farm and GenLab with the potential for viral outbreak — with the switch of a button, a massive iris-shaped seal would retract from beneath the gallery floor and close the gap over Level 9, creating total separation between the two parts of the ship.

Once the seal was applied, the Thetis was programmed to instantly initiate purge actions in the lower levels: releasing all atmospheric pressure to extinguish fires and prevent explosions; incineration for eliminating biological life forms such as germs and viruses (and, regrettably, all the fluffy bunnies in existence); and a host of other measures aimed at eventually releasing the seal and reconnecting the lower levels to the main Thetis body.

The Thetis was built first and foremost for durability. Designed to survive the high-risk mission of traversing interstellar space, the ship was built like a fortress — the entire bullet-shaped hull was one smooth surface. The Thetis had no windows, no fancy observation decks offering magnificent space views like those in imaginary spaceships from the Archive's old video library. Not even holes for cameras pointing outside — nothing which could shatter, break seal or deform under decades of bombardment by stray particles floating in outer space.

The outer body of the Thetis was constructed of a triple-layered shielding structure. The 3rd and outmost shield was a two feet thick NanoCeramic coating. This wonder of material engineering was the toughest protective shell Humans ever invented: designed to deflect random particles at a third of the speed of light without registering a scratch; block Cosmic and Gamma rays which are extremely harmful to Humans; and provide near-perfect insulation against both external heat and friction and internal heat leakage into the coldness of outer space.

Behind the 3rd shield, several feet of pressurized, ion-neutral argon gas provided additional heat insulation and absorbed most long-wave radiation frequencies. The gas was trapped between the outer layer and the 2nd shield, which was actually a dense mesh of thin wire made from several types of non-conductive metal. That mesh protected the internal parts of the ship from magnetic forces and electromagnetic radiation, placing the entire Thetis in the biggest Faraday Cage ever constructed.

The 1st and innermost shield was a relatively simple carbon fiber bulkhead: easy to mold and repair with the tools on the Thetis, and sturdy enough to withstand fire, explosions, or minor hull breaches. The space between the 1st and 2nd shields was mainly unpressurized utility space where various piping, structural posts and power grid infrastructure ran up and down the ship.

I raised the antidust goggles to my forehead and stepped closer to peek over the railing encircling the Level 10 gallery.

Wrong move. I immediately started feeling woozy from the overhead perspective of looking down onto Level 9 below, and my eyes began tearing up with the irritating sting of the Dusting cloud. I snapped the goggles back over my eyes and focused my gaze on the newest guest who was waiting for us in the gallery.

"Hurry," the woman said and stepped closer to us. "You have no idea what you've created, Liet."

Gahlia and Armitage walked behind us as the woman laid a guiding hand on my shoulder, leading me around the gallery ring toward an array of control units.

In an instant, I knew who the woman was. Which only made things a thousandfold more complicated.

"Athena?" I was perplexed. "Athena Saugado? What the hell are you doing here?"

Athena kept pushing forward as fast as our two elder companions could keep up, shaking her head in dismay. "You can't begin to imagine the craziness going on 34th right now. I've never seen anything like it." She turned her head and our eyes met briefly beyond the thick layers of our goggles. She was genuinely terrified.

"Cassidi is going berserk," her voice came muffled through the face mask filters. "Apparently, you weren't bought by whatever she came to offer you on Sabi's behalf. A huge miscalculation on Anderson's part."

"Kunyela," I muttered. "That *bruta* can't buy me."

Athena glanced at me again. A glint of appreciation flickered in her eyes. "No wonder they're freaking out," she said. "Problem is, they know you're out of your hab. Jericho Pakk and his people are literally turning the ship upside down looking for you."

Instinctively, I halted in my tracks and pulled Athena's shoulder to a stop. "That's not good," I said, my voice betraying a slight tremble. Athena turned around, panting silently. Before Gahlia and Armitage would be within earshot, I whispered quickly, "I suspect Pakk killed Dr. Bashiri. I confronted him about it."

"What? No way." Athena jerked with surprise, a dose of doubt now in her eyes. "I mean, don't get me wrong. I think Jericho Pakk is a self-centered, sleazy two-faced wapa. But there are no *murders* on the Thetis! That's... *unthinkable*."

I lowered my eyes to the floor. "Only until someone thinks it up."

The two others finally caught up with us, Armitage leaning slightly on Gahlia's arm. His limp seemed to have worsened a bit and he was clearly suppressing some pain.

"I haven't done this in years," he said. "Can't say I don't miss it sometimes. So — where do we suit-up?"

Athena Saugado motioned us toward a small gap near the seal control unit, where a number of equipment booths where built into the outer level bulkhead. Each booth was marked with a fluorescent red contour visible even through the thick Dusting haze.

"Emergency boxes. There'll be EVA suits inside, and oxygen tubes that should last the roundtrip. Just keep comms switched off or you'll immediately pop up."

"Wait, wait, wait!" Armitage protested, startling us with his voice booming in the space-silent level. "So that's the great plan? Stealing emergency suits?"

Gahlia's jaw clenched. She poked him with one finger, her eyes darting through her goggles. "What exactly did you think this was, Arm? You coming back from retirement for a piping maintenance job below the seal?"

Armitage burst out. "But *stealing*—"

"Hey, Hey!" Athena snapped. They both fell silent. "We're not stealing anything," she continued. "And you wouldn't be able to open the emergency repo boxes even if you wanted to. I am using my administrative credentials to access them as part of a formal safety inspection audit. That's the only way for you to get to Level 2 undetected."

Armitage coughed a short laugh. "I get it, that's smart. But for all practical purposes it's the same as stealing them. I mean, what are we doing here?" He turned to Gahlia, then to me. "Nobody's going to buy this mala! Even if we *do* find some evidence of malconduct, they'll claim it was obtained by illegal means, as part of an illegal investigation, using stolen Thetis property while tampering with Emergency equipment and defying a mandated Dusting lockdown! The Andersons will just laugh us out of sight!" He turned to face Athena again. "Maybe for you, a *politician*, running against Sabi for Primoship, this could win some points, but I've got four GrandGens and you're asking me to risk their future!"

"What do you think *this* is?" Athena waved her hand, gesturing at the heavy blanket of mist engulfing us. "A Dusting Day no one can find any mention of in the program plan? A surprise lockdown?"

She reached her hand, palm up, in my direction. "A hysterical hunt after a Senior Archivist, while trying to *bribe* her into silence? A kunye scientist *dead* after sticking his nose into PHS records? That all seem like a coincidence to you? We can discuss protocol to Andromeda and back, but this mala — whatever it is they've been scheming — happens *tonight*, Armitage. And if we don't get into the walls right now, they'll find us here. And then it really had all been for nothing."

"It's the Gordian Knot," Gahlia murmured, then met Armitage's questioning look. "QUBIC it later. But she's right."

I looked back at the opposite side of the Level gallery, where the Ascenders landing pad laid unoccupied, then back to Athena. "Your CrypID will be logged on the Emergency Box opening," I said quietly. "It will all track back to you as well."

Athena looked at me firmly. "I never said there won't be consequences for me if you're wrong."

She took a step closer to Armitage, her voice softer. "If we find nothing, and the Andersons rule forever, you'll end up the old Cuckoo who tried to relive his past with one last crazy act before his day in the Loop. I can't hide that risk from you. But if she's right —" she pointed her chin at me while keeping her eyes locked on Armitage's, "your GrandGens, *all* our GrandGens, will thank you for being the sword cutting through all this. You better be right, Sandrine," she almost pleaded.

Armitage let out a slow, deep sigh. He lowered his eyes to Gahlia. "You're at peace with this?"

"No," Gahlia said, "but she wouldn't know how to find a ball in a ballsack in that old node down there. This is pre-Embarkment tech."

"Sound like a relic. Are we even certain this thing is functioning at all?"

Gahlia smiled. "What fun would that be, ne?" She laid a gentle hand on Armitage's arm. "How's your leg? Can you handle descending eight more levels? No stairs from this point, you know."

Armitage merely grunted in dismissal. Athena looked to the opposite side of the level. The haze seemed slightly thinner now, and the stairwell landing area was barely visible from our vantage point. She scanned the three of us with a stern face.

"Once I chip the emergency booths open, the clock starts ticking. The alerts will send Jericho Pakk straight here, if they haven't already figured out what we are up to. The only thing working for us is that they probably haven't thought of checking the Astral Solace for anyone missing."

"Clearly," Armitage said sarcastically.

We stepped closer to the red pressure doors. Without ceremony, Athena chipped into each one's control box. They hissed open, revealing stacks of emergency gear which was laying there unused for generations.

"I'll buy you as much time as I can," Athena said. "Pakk can't outrank me on this, so my presence will present some administrative problem he'll have to solve with 34th. But for Sol's sake, be quick!"

She turned to me and placed both hands on my shoulders. "Listen, Sandrine. Every once in a rare while, the need arises for a hero. You are that hero today."

"What if I don't *want* to be a hero?" I whispered.

"The real ones never do."

She squeezed my shoulders lightly and broke away toward the other side of the gallery. In the distance, I could hear the quiet magnetic hum of the Ascenders awakening.

Armitage and Gahlia nodded quietly to each other, a service hatch hissed open in the outer bulkhead, and a moment later we were in the wall.

CHAPTER THIRTY-SEVEN

The climb down was excruciating. Pressed into the small space between the first and second layers of the Thetis shell, the descent to Level 2 was to be conducted along a wide structural support beam, using a set of perforations punched into the metal as gripping points for our hands and feet. We had to constantly support ourselves on that long ladder lest we drop ten levels down to the inevitable crush. And as the space around us was filled with pressurized Argon, we had to keep our helmet on for Oxygen supply, which added to the discomfort of the whole situation.

"In my time we had safety cables for in-shell grinds," Armitage grunted loudly as he started leading the way. "Climbing down half the ship's height Tarzan-style like this — that's a kunye death wish."

Gahlia threw a glance at me, meeting my eyes with a grim expression, then proceeded to descend after Armitage. I was to close the group in the rear. I lay my foot on the metal beam and peeked briefly over Gahlia's shoulder at the dark drop we were about to delve into. Luckily, the view was limited to three or four levels down due to the inward curvature of the Thetis body structure. Otherwise, I don't think I would have ever had the courage to take the first step down.

It also meant that the last couple of levels before we reached L2 would have to be climbed in a negative incline, with gravity working its best to peel us off the inner shell and hurl us down to our certain deaths.

By the time we reached the faint marking on the inner wall indicating our passing of Level 8, I was more than ready to drop out. Crammed into the airtight emergency suit, its weight working against me with every move and its faceplate fogging up with every breath, I was already dripping sweat. My eyes stung with salty drops of perspiration oozing from my forehead. It was pitch dark around us, with only the tiny suit-mounted LEDs preventing me from completely blind-guessing my next placement of a leg or a hand.

Armitage, clearly rediscovering his younger element and leading the descent in full confidence, had opened up a gap below us, his suit lights flashing and flailing around at least a full level's height beneath me and Gahlia. She was conducting her climb with meticulous precision, carefully planning the placement of each hand and foot on the thick metal beam. Which was fine by me, even though I knew Jericho Pakk's people were searching for us all over the Thetis, and that we would need all the time we could get when we'd reach the QUBIC node. I had no desire to rush it to the point where my cumbersome EVA suit, with its thick foot soles and semi-rigid glove fingers, would result in a slip or missed grip of a hand. *This is worse than the Sensory Farm*, I thought. The four-level-high stretch of blackness, randomly split by streaks of light from our suits was working its heavy load on my psyche. *I guess Thetans weren't born for large spaces.*

"We'll never make it to the bottom in one piece," I whispered to Gahlia, her helmet a few inches below my footing.

Gahlia raised her head toward me. Behind the semi-reflective faceplate, there was fear in her bright eyes. "There's no other choice," she said. "They can use grid locator tracking on us inside the ship. We won't make it halfway to 2nd before they get to us. Our only chance is to drop off the grid, and hope that they don't know where we're headed."

"So inside the shell we are going behind the sensors backs, so to speak," I completed.

Gahlia nodded. I broke my gaze from the dark abyss stretching below me and grabbed the metal beam as hard as I could. The EVA suit gloves felt cumbersome and I feared they'd slip out of the perforation I was clinging to. I reached out one leg carefully, locking it into the next hole. *This is going to take forever*, I thought. We were merely a quarter of the way down and I was already aching with exhaustion.

"Gahlia," my voice trembled. "How are you holding up?"

Gahlia grunted. "I am seventy five years old. I sometimes need help getting out of bed in cold mornings at the Solace. Believe it or not, hanging for my life trying to climb with my bare hands isn't my idea of fun. But—"

She shrieked as her left foot lost its hold and swung dangerously around the thick beam. I could only helplessly watch from above as she struggled to swing back and catch the metal column between her knees. She was groaning and panting, struggling to regain a stable hold on the beam. I looked down and she met my eyes with a terrified look, her faceplate pulsating with fogging with every breath.

"—But, the moment you mentioned Kilian talking about the Origin, I knew this was a serious matter."

"So what's the chance the Andersons aren't already on to it?" I asked carefully.

"There are things on the Thetis almost no-one knows about," she said. "Not even you Archivists. They don't exist on any record. Call it guild secrets."

Gahlia paused as she directed her suit lights to illuminate the next few feet down the descent. Then she looked up at me, her eyes hard behind the flat faceplate.

"My trust in Kilian is absolute," she said. "I trained him into what he's capable of, but what's more — I was his mentor. I can say in full confidence that his professional knowledge equals my own, if not exceeds it, and that his moral spine is second to none."

Gahlia paused her climb and leaned back against the inner shell wall, giving her hands a rest from the strain.

"Let me be blunt," she maintained her steady, harsh gaze into my eyes, "what you've imposed on Kilian doesn't spell any other word but Betrayal in my sheet."

I could feel my cheeks flush to the sound of that word. *Betrayal.* How many nights have I lost tormenting myself with that same question - *did I betray Kilian?* Did I single-handedly destroy both our futures?

"I loved Kilian," I mumbled softly into the mask.

Gahlia let out a curt laugh, her mouth blurred by the instant fogging of her faceplate. "*Love.* Probably the most common ingredient in any atrocity in Human history. At my age, I've seen them all — love, hate, revenge, plain cruelty. Love crushes the hardest. So that doesn't cut it, Sandrine. I'm willing to defer judgement, but if you want my trust, you'll have to convince me. Or, I'd be much relieved to get off this torturous ladder at the 8th Level hatch."

She nodded her head towards a horizontal silvery air duct cutting through all three layers of the Thetis hull. It took me a moment to realize what that actually was — the hatch leading from within the L8 GenLab, through the inner shields and out to the Trash Tube at the center of the Thetis. *The same hatch Dr. Almaz Bashiri was pushed through to his inevitable death.* A shudder crept up my upper back.

Below us, we could hear Armitage's heavy-set movements as he kept descending the levels, his suit lights shooting random flares through the Argon-filled space with each movement.

Gahlia seemed to be in no rush. She was waiting for my reply. I looked down beyond her and into the black drop we would have to carefully sustain for additional six levels of climb before I'd discover where Kilian meant for me to search for answers.

Finally, my eyes set back on Gahlia. "It's a long story," I said quietly. My hands were hot and sweaty inside the puffy insulating gloves. "Maybe we should do this on the way down?"

Recounting those past events, I knew, would send me down an

emotional spiral I'd much rather cope with while facing the Thetis shield wall than staring into Dr. Roskov's cold, accusing eyes.

Gahlia didn't answer. Her eyes scanned me, taking stock of the countless ways I might be trying to manipulate her.

I lowered my head, breaking away from her intense gaze. "I'm just so ashamed about that situation," I muttered. My heart was racing, beating and thumping violently with anxiety.

"There is never shame in one's situation. Only in one's actions." Gahlia straightened up from her leaning position and shook her hands, stirring up the blood circulation to her exhausted limbs. "And only you know what you did."

She lowered a careful foot and resumed her slow descent down the support beam.

"Our destination is the entrance hatch at Level 2," she called up to me. "So we are six levels away from finding out whether your feeling is justified and this had all been in vain. Let's make sure we get there feet first, te? Watch your step."

With a delicate maneuver quite impressive for Dr. Roskov's age, she slid beneath the air duct and vanished from my line of sight down the ladder. I gathered up my strength and started down after her, trying to figure out a starting point for the chain of events which started almost seven years ago, the aftermath of which I was living to this very day. How do you begin describing a connection so powerful it could never unbind, only shatter? Is there a distinct point where the story of a love's disintegration opens?

For a few minutes, neither of us spoke. We were just two women, separated by two generations and a man — a lover to one, protege to the other — grunting their way down the skeletal bones of a spaceship. There was tension in that silence, and I knew she was letting me rack up the courage at my own pace. Earning Gahlia's trust was vital for her to let me in on the secrets that were the door to unraveling the truth we were all seeking. And it was vital for me too, her being the only person on the Thetis who knew Kilian deeply enough to potentially understand what I was going through. What *we* were going through, for that matter.

Trust is transparency multiplied by time, I remembered an old proverb. And since time was something we didn't have, my only chance was to be completely open about the events leading up to Kilian's trial.

When I finally spoke, my words reverberated eerily in the dense space. "The first thing to understand is that there was no sudden, clear moment when Kilian's attraction to the Adapter way began," I started tentatively. "It was a very gradual evolution, spotted with many sobering moments of skepticism. K wasn't a fanatic in any way — he was too rational and analytical for that."

Hearing myself, it occurred to me that as public and intense as the blow-up was back then, this was actually the first time I might have had the chance to tell my side of it in complete openness. Whether Dr. Roskov accepted it or not, reminding myself why I made those choices was actually something I may have needed.

"The first thing people are struck by when meeting Kilian for the first time is his genius. You've seen that," I paused for a confirmation from Gahlia, which never arrived. "He has this childish ability to draw you into whatever he is fascinated by, and completely *drown* you in that energy of total excitement. This energy of *life* he emanates around him, and by osmosis — around *you*. And I was just this Archive nerd, te? No social life to speak of. Long, mundane nights spent at my office desk. You get the picture. And then he comes along and I was *swept away*."

We reached the top part of Level 7, where a number of slightly wider beams made for a good spot to take a breath and loosen my sore leg muscles for a minute. Gahlia was there too, leaning against the wire mesh, catching her breath in quick, shallow gasps. I avoided her eyes as best I could, focusing inward, trying to remember how it all felt in the beginning.

To be completely honest, it took a considerable effort on Kilian's part to reassure me that I was not just another *fling-du-jour* for him. At first, his energetic and confident courting played perfectly into all my

300

insecurities. He was this great-looking, brilliant guy who could — and did — take full advantage of the open fun-and-games culture of the young Thetan sex scene. And I was a too-tall, too-awkward hermit with a peculiar fascination for vintage culture and spending long nights reading historical records in the Archive. Kilian was not even on my fantasy wish-list — after all, even fantasies must have that minuscule probability of coming true for them to be exciting, ne?

What's more, Kilian's energy beam was totally binary. There were no gradients with Kilian — his love was an instant-on storm of attention. There was no getting-to-know-each-other period, none of the cautious self-questioning and careful exploration of the personality traits of the other partner. He had no interest in such boring technicalities. Kilian took me into his world with the intense confidence that I would be excited with everything he was excited about, and he showed no lesser fascination with every interest and passion of mine. He could spend entire nights listening to my ideas, asking questions and enthusiastically probing subjects he had zero interest in priorly.

Our minds and bodies melded in a fierce blast of fusion, and I loved every moment of it. At first, it was the overwhelming novelty of the possibility that someone like Kilian could be utterly, completely *into me*. Then, slowly, as that acceptance sank in, something else surfaced within me — a revelation: a dense, calm confidence in being my unguarded self with another human being. My young 21-year-old mind suddenly opened to new possibilities: maybe I *was* interesting. Maybe I *was* lovable, and sexy, and beautiful? Maybe I *did* deserve to have someone who is proud to hang out with me around the ship?

Those yet-unexplored feelings were so counter-intuitive to my normal self-speak, that for a prolonged while I just kept them on probation status, deferring judgement until the arrival of more compelling evidence.

A short chuckle echoed from below my position on the beam. "Classic Kilian," Gahlia said. "People with no inferiority complex just can't grasp their effect on the rest of us. They just plow onward, space-time is completely flat for them. No sinkholes, no gravity wells. But did he ever give you a reason to doubt his love?"

I shook my head slowly inside the helmet. "No. Not at all. Quite the contrary, if I'm honest. You know what K was like back then."

A playboy? Hyper networker? Just an energetic, healthy young Thetan enjoying his Level 19 years before the mass momification of our entire generation?

I had very little in common with that lifestyle — hell, I wasn't even *living* on 19th at that time! I was so excited with my recent recruitment as a Junior Archivist right out of the Academy that I was completely absorbed in my new job and the endless fountain of knowledge it had opened up for me via QUBIC. I had actually found a tiny, unused space on 13th and turned in it into my hab, overlooking the public park and a mere one minute walk from the Archive office.

I couldn't have been happier — or so I thought. I had my little daily routine which I was completely in love with — the short morning walk from my hab across the carbofoam garden, getting my perfectly-brewed bubble at the new café place at the park corner. They had developed this crazy process where a tiny NanoDrop of water was injected into a specially-grown bean, then decompressed within it. The sudden outward water pressure generated a fresh, potent bubble that would keep me energized for the entire day.

I'd spend the next twenty minutes sitting in the garden watching ten year old Gen8ers doing their morning gym cycles in the sports park and tuning into the day with my private morning circle ritual. Then it was into the Archive office for the day — living right nearby meant that I would be the first to show up, which allowed me some quiet time before Nyasha's morning briefing.

He would be the second one in — he too liked the tranquility of the early hours — and I'd have the chance to get his guidance on issues I found new or challenging. I think he liked the guidance part too, and we quickly became close beyond the formal working relationship and generation gap.

So when Kilian Ngo showed up one day as the freshly-minted QIT manager, reeking with talent and curious energy, Nyasha was the first to notice the sudden elevation in my facial flush levels.

"So Nyasha was supportive of the new romance?" Gahlia grunted, shaking her palms to regain blood flow after landing on the Level 6 support platform. The thick metal square bulged out into our planned downward path. We both paused for a breath before the plunge below 6.

"Well," I considered, "I was too timid at the time to ask him directly. But the long, sleepless nights of a newly-enamored couple started taking their toll, and I started to come in late. Instead of barraging me for the undisciplined brat that I was, Nyasha simply announced that for the next two months we will be holding the morning briefing an hour later."

"Ahh, and then *everyone* knew who the teacher's favorite was," Gahlia smiled.

I laughed. "He did try and come up with some lame excuse for the schedule change, but I don't think even Nyasha thought anyone from the team would buy it. His affection, by the way, did me no favors in my Senior Archivist nomination. If anything, it was the contrary — I had to be the absolute best in each and every certification test to pass the bar and get his recommendation."

"And you *were* the best," Gahlia said matter of factly, her eyes meeting mine as she started the preparations for continuing down into the Level 5 area.

Youngest Senior Archivist in Thetan history, the thought left a slight sour taste in my mouth.

Gahlia's feet disappeared beyond the rim of the platform. "The best investigator on the Thetis, yet you completely missed the Adapter in your back hab. That's one hell of a blind spot, ne?"

She lowered herself off the ledge and dropped from view, her remark still reverberating around the empty platform.

That's a fair stab, I thought — one that I couldn't easily explain away without implicating Kilian with deliberately *defrauding* me about his affiliation. Later on, when it would come to an actual legal trial, I would be pressed to do just that in order to exonerate myself from being an accomplice.

But, I reminded myself, anyone who knew Kilian was accustomed to his instantaneous zero-to-*c* acceleration when he was fired up by a new idea. That temperament also brought him dangerously close to the borders of normative Thetan playbook sometimes. As his mentor in his early professional years, Gahlia was obviously familiar with how K scrolled, ne?

"You do realize," I said as I lowered myself over the lip of the platform, "that Adapter wasn't even a negative term at that time, te? It was considered just another legitimate school of thought."

Dr. Roskov retorted with a non-committed grunt.

"I mean, I don't think Kilian even thought of himself in such definitive terms, or as belonging to any particular faction. He just had that insatiable lust for knowledge. That lust was one of the strongest things we shared, why it was so eye-opening for me to know Kilian for who he *really* was, beyond the cacophony of the social persona everyone else knew."

Knowledge. That double-edged sword the pursuit of which both defined Humanity and boded its demise.

And on the Thetis, knowledge was a controlled substance. The *Passados* who planned and launched our predecessors on this multi-generational survival trip were undoubtedly working from a very protective point of view. They've seen where Humanity and Earth ended up once the thousand-year race for Human domination over nature had finally been won. They've seen how the 'what *could* be made, *should* be made' approach of Late Earth culture resulted in a massive collapse of every single foundation supporting life on the planet. And they feared. Feared that it would happen again, that we're bound to repeat the pattern, only this time within a non-escapable capsule hurtling across the galaxy, with a hair-thin tolerance for any change in our physical, mental and social conditions.

They feared we'd follow the same trajectory leading from enlightenment to eradication that marked every Human culture in the past ten thousand years. They needed to make sure we'd make it to the other side. So they devised a plan.

Humans, being an organism feeding on problem solving, are extremely hard to tame. We will always try to hack, optimize and innovate our way up the imaginary ladder we've been cultured to believe we're on. It is, in many aspects, our defining spirit as a species. So the *Passados* decided to throttle the pace in which knowledge would be available to us at each point along the way.

And QUBIC was the enabling device at the core of the plan.

"Wizards of the Ice Cube!" Kilian used to call his QIT team, referring to the translucent, boxy QUBIC terminals.

"So how'd they let a hot *wapa* like you near it?" I used to tease him back, "could melt the entire thing into a quantum paddle."

Kilian laughed and locked me in his crushing hug. "Your flattery is futile, princess. I shall never reveal the secrets our *Passados* locked within the Ice. So I have vowed."

I pushed myself away from his hug, serving my most oh-so-innocent blinking expression I could conjure. "What better proof of one's undying love would there be, then, if not the decryption of a century-fold of dark, digitally-buried truths? What else could you possibly bring me — kunye diamonds?"

We were just being playful, of course. QITs were the few rare people skilled enough to understand the inner workings of the elaborate quantum engine behind the Thetis system. But even they could only access the open data blocks in the system. There were other layers, encrypted and blocked, which would be periodically released by the pre-set conditions of the Plan. No one could tell why and what those conditions were precisely, but as the multi-generational journey advanced, the knowledge we needed — scientific, historic or social — was made available to us.

And then came Kilian and his exceptional, once-in-a-generation talent, a talent which fed his ambitions to an extent the plan couldn't tame. Nothing could — not even me.

I just moved in to K's hab on 19th, and my world was a gushing whirlwind of excitement, new people and new ideas. Kilian's loyal entourage immediately accepted me as their own. They adored my intelligence. I felt loved, respected and, well, *seen*. After a lonely, bizarre childhood and what I jokingly called my 'hermit scholar' years at the Junior Academy, that was a revelation.

And Level 19 was where the new Thetan culture was emerging. A place solely attuned to the pleasures of the flesh, mind and spirit.

Like a chubby kid at a buffet, I was gorging on all of them. Hell, I was living with the kunye *chef de cuisine!*

"This is simply astonishing to watch," Kilian smilingly nudged me as we rolled into bed after a late-night social gathering.

"What is?" I mumbled, already drifting under.

"Your mental deflowering," he laughed and laid a tender palm on my cheek, gently stroking me to sleep, too exhausted to protest.

With Kilian, you never knew what experiences the evening might bring. One by one, people would gather at our hab. And there was always a new artist to meet, a new idea to debate or some grand philosophy to quarrel over. We were young and energetic and always absolutely right in our opinions articulately disguised as indisputable facts.

And they all despised Sebastian Anderson and what he represented.

CHAPTER THIRTY-EIGHT

"The topic on the table today, my fellow SpacerBots," Kilian announced to the circling crowd, "is equality. As you can imagine, I have a thesis about it, and you're more than welcome to try and change my mind! Who knows? Maybe today is some *wapa's* lucky day!"

Everybody laughed. It was Open Night at the Nebula, and anyone was welcome to set up shop at any of the club's corners and bring up a subject for public discussion. Well, theoretically, at least. Because whenever Kilian decided to go on stage, it was pretty much a solo act for that night.

All humans may have been created equal, but charisma is the ultimate kingmaker. Kilian's gift, or "weapon of mass distraction" as he jokingly referred to it, was the ability to hold an audience. And no one was *ever* able to win him over, to "change his mind".

"I believe," he continued, addressing the thickening crowd, "that equality on the Thetis is a fake and artificially-manufactured state. A sedative, disguised as moral value in the benefit of the powers that be, which are *way* ahead of us all in planning for the eventual domination of our future."

A strong opening if I ever saw one, I thought. Unleashing moral provocation on an unsuspecting audience was K's specialty. Oh, how he loved seeing them squirm! I snickered and winked at Kilian from across the room. Waves of murmuring protests started rising around me, proving the accuracy of his stab to the heart of social consensus. Kilian thrived at the edges.

"Bafunye!" a roaring voice rose from within the crowd. That voice belonged to a beast of a man we all knew by the name of Bøygärd. He broke out from the crowd and stepped forward to face Kilian. Bøygärd was a heavy-set, heavy-bearded blond Gen7er whose friendship with Kilian went back to their early childhood. No one was actually certain whether Bøygärd was even his first or family name. He was just Bøygärd. And he was often the counterpart in Kilian's public debates, or as he liked to scorn K by calling them — "PhilosoFarts." Watching those two get at it was like watching a duel between a scalpel and a sledgehammer.

"I say," Bøygärd announced, posing theatrically with his massive arms wide open, eying the crowd, "that in creating an equal, collaborative society, we Thetans have reached the highest achievement in Human history. I say that after five thousand years of senseless struggles between people living on the same planet, five thousand years of unproductive competition over *anything and everything* in existence — we've finally stepped up to a higher level of evolution. From a league of nations, we became a team of Humans!"

The crowd cheered. Bøygärd swiveled slowly and nodded triumphantly to the supporting audience, basking in the glow of his delivered punch.

Kilian gave a goodhearted laugh and clapped slowly. "Very astute observation, my hulking friend! And very eloquently stated."

Uh oh, I thought. As someone who watched Kilian champion dozens of such debates, I knew that flattering his opponent was a tell — K's first move in luring him into a humiliating logic trap.

This should be interesting. I stepped closer to the developing action.

"And may I ask my evolutionary-ascended Comrade here," Kilian continued smoothly, "why all of a sudden, despite every single attempt made throughout history to create an egalitarian society failing miserably, the Thetis of all places would be where it magically works?"

"Well, *maybe* because this is the first time in history where we could truly take competition for resources out of the equation, ne? We're living in a closed environment — what you see is what you get, basically. So it's a zero-sum game. The only stable way we survive is if we work together. We are all as rich and as poor as our collective abilities. And we share the benefits of our efforts — equally."

"Ahh," Kilian smiled and scanned the faces in the attentive crowd, "so in other words, the magic lies in fair, equal and *clever* allocation of our resources."

"Exactly!" Bøygärd and the crowd all burst out laughing. Anyone who knew Bøygärd — and *everybody* knew Bøygärd — knew he worked in the office of Resource Distribution. These were the people who decided how each and every resource on the Thetis would be allocated — from raw materials to hab space to people's contribution working hours. So the self-credit in attributing all of Humanity's fortune to his own work was a very much expected Bøygärdish trait.

"OK, OK now," Kilian raised his hand to calm the excitement, and I immediately noticed the minuscule way his energy shifted.

"Let's just make sure that I got this right, if you don't mind, so that I can peacefully admit to my defeat and incompetence against your solid reasoning, te?" Kilian said and carried on without waiting for a response.

"So we're agreeing that on Old Earth, people fought to get more, simply because *more* was out there — more crop, more land, more money, more computing power, more augmentations. They believed having more would protect them. After all, they lived on a huge planet, with *billions* of people and almost endless resources. The whole system was tuned to reward the gobblers and the hoarders — individuals and societies alike."

Bøygärd just nodded in impatient agreement. This was trivial stuff. Kilian smiled apologetically.

"OK, hold on," he lifted his right palm and scanned the attentive crowd, "and we're also *potentially* agreeing that on the Thetis, things changed dramatically. We don't have mansions here, and there is nothing for anyone to gain from sitting on top of a heap of grain, while the less aggressive bunch of our fellow Thetans starve to death. We have the Plan and we have a mission and our collective Genline survival relies on our co-existence."

"Fancy words, my friend," Bøygärd roared. "You could have simply gone for 'Bøygärd, oh wisest one, you are both handsome and right and I concede my childish assertations.'"

Again, the crowd laughed cheerfully. After all, Open Night wasn't a political event. It was entertainment.

Bøygärd raised a thick finger in the air. "Let me also remind you," he continued, skillfully riding the momentum of support from the audience, "that Late Earthers faced a very similar challenge — dwindling resources and nowhere to expand. Unfortunately, with their culture of winner-takes-all mentality, those *planetfolk* kept fighting for the crumbs until there were none left. The one collaboration they somehow managed to pull off, thank Sol, was our very own Thetis. And even here," Bøygärd's voice sunk to a more somber tone, "it took several generations for the clans and the families and the interest groups to unite."

"So yes," he concluded, his voice crisp as a needle in the still room, "I'd say we evolved into better, more moral humans. And equality is our only safeguard from falling back."

He's good, I thought. I was almost ready to buy the polished rhetoric.

I glanced at Kilian. He was perfectly calm, waiting out the energy drop, wearing a laser-thin grin and completely unbothered. When he spoke again, it was in a slow, hushed voice which made the entire circle of spectators lean imperceptibly closer.

"More moral Humans," Kilian mused quietly, as if to himself. "You're speaking of morality, but what you're describing is a tool — equality as a means of ensuring survival, keeping order, reducing risk. My dear Bøygärd, how much familiar are you with Human history?"

"I'm no Archivist, but I know as much as the next person, I guess."

"So you must agree that there are two levels of encoding of beneficial traits in Humans."

Kilian stepped forward closer to the crowd and gestured with his hands for emphasis. "The more hardcore traits are encoded as instincts. You put your hand in fire, you recoil. You birth a baby, you protect it, ne?"

The crowd nodded in confused agreement.

"But the more feeble traits — they were encoded as moral code, in an attempt of making them stick. Thou Shalt Not Kill. Thou Shall Not Steal. Thou Shalt Not Covet. Pretty easy to break when opportunity or adversity knocks, ne? So they were made into moral code, with the hope that when the mala hits the ion thruster, there will be an extra layer of restraint from total disintegration of society."

"I see where you're going with this!" Bøygård interrupted, "but that doesn't really make a difference to my case. Even if Thetan equality isn't any higher value, but just a tool serving our common interest — we've been at it for almost two centuries. We all benefit from this higher state of being. And that's coming from the person who's kunye making sure it stays that way!"

Bøygård burst out in his contagious belly laugh, and the whole room joined in unison. The tension finally broke.

Kilian wasn't laughing. He stood with his head low, waiting for the cheers to subside.

"So, on the Thetis, we're all equal?" He asked matter-of-factly.

"We are."

"Even the Primo?"

Bøygård tilted his head, gauging for a potential trap. "In all essence, yes. Look here, K-boy, if your whole grand rant today is about some extra perks the Primo may enjoy like extra hab space on 34th, or getting early picks on goods—"

"— I am not interested in hab space."

"— then I'm certain we can tolerate a few minor exceptions when it comes to the Primo, te? It's entirely harmless—"

"— I am not talking about his kunye hab space, or in ensuring his wife gets a guaranteed supply of her favorite ProteGel flavors!" Kilian snapped. "But it *is*, actually, interesting that you brought those up, because let me remind you that the first thing Primo Smoak did, in an attempt to end the GenZero clan wars and instill the equality you claim we all enjoy today, was cancel the 34th Primo Quarters and move to a simple hab on 24th like everyone else. Because Ladies and Gentlemen," he turned to address the crowd around him, "Entitlement is the *opposite* of Servitude. When you start to believe that being appointed by the public somehow entitles you to a preferential treatment, that's when you cease serving the public, and you expect the public to start serving *you*."

"Te, OK," Bøygärd waved his hands in dismissal, "so our equality isn't pitch-perfect. Like everything else in life, there's room for improvement. But so what? How does this actually reflect on our daily lives here, beyond the principle, theoretical level? We're all busy people, working our contributions day in and day out — we're not purists, are we?"

The crowd mumbled in acceptance.

They perform this dance so smoothly, Kilian and Bøygärd. Keeping the audience involved. Setting up each other's next serve with perfect timing, never letting the energy drift. Even I sometimes wondered if they were really debating their own opinions, or merely acting out a rehearsed stage-play. Open Night on the Nebula was definitely picking up in popularity since those two started mouth-brawling on stage here every other week.

Kilian paused for a few moments, scanning the audience with a stern expression. He tucked both hands into his pockets as his gaze hopped between the dozens of amused faces surrounding them. He frowned.

"No, my Thetan brother, we're definitely not purists. On the contrary — we are very practical people. We are people with a mission, ne? Whatever works for the mission, we are happy to adopt. In that sense, I agree with you that we *have* evolved in a century-plus of space travel. If transparency breeds mutual trust — we adopt transparency. If extreme tolerance supports social stability — we adopt tolerance. If equality is the most useful concept for aligning everyone here to the same trajectory and prevent the chaos of our earlier generations — then, by Sol, we shall swear by equality. Agreed?"

For the first time that night, the audience cheered for Kilian. Finally, he was speaking a language they could actually comprehend. Bøygärd too nodded in agreement, his face gleaming with smugness.

Kilian casually walked over to Bøygärd's side and wrapped a friendly hand around his massive shoulders. They were close, old friends, and Open Night was merely the mental equivalent of boyish wrestling — no harm meant, no offense taken.

Kilian smiled. "I love it! Fills my heart with joy to see how united we all are in agreement. So wouldn't we all *also* agree—" Kilian's eyes took a darker tone and his smile now seemed eerily out of place. It was the smallest of shifts, but my heart jerked nonetheless.

"—that if we found out that someone is breaking this sacred code... that on our enclosed board of Chess where we all play our individual parts, someone is secretly stacking queens on the sidelines, ready to deploy when we are all down to out final pawns... well, that would be — how would *you* define such a crazy conduct, Boyo?"

Bøygärd's face reddened. "Well, that would be Anti-Thetan!"

The room suddenly fell silent. The gravity of the A-word was such that it very rarely got uttered in public.

"Anti-Thetan, you say," Kilian repeated quietly and slowly shook his head in dismay.

He squeezed Bøygärd's shoulders closer, and turned his head to look into his eyes, their faces so closed they nearly touched.

Kilian spoke, his voice barely above a whisper. The audience tiptoed closer, leaning into hearing distance.

"You got family, Bøygärd, ne?"

Bøygärd gave a slight shrug. "You know my older brother. My two nephews."

"And remind me, if you don't mind — where is your brother allocated?"

"Crop control on 11th."

"So he's essentially a farmer."

"Yes," Bøygärd shrugged again.

"His wife?"

"Khristen? She's on Level 12, food processing mill."

Kilian nodded. "And the kids, they're Gen8, right? Still at school, I know, but do they already have a designated contribution field?"

Bøygärd's confused expression broke into a smile. "Beautiful kids, those two! they will both be on 14th — the boy will enter the fabric factory, and the girl is already marked for the raw material processing plant."

Kilian nodded. "All hardworking, decent contributors, te? You know I see them every morning in my Ascender ride down from 19th?"

Bøygärd gave him a questioning look, unsure where this was going.

"Now, you and I," Kilian continued, "we're no philosophers — I'm a QIT engineer, you're in Resource Distribution, we're both data people. So you know what I find peculiar to the point of statistical anomaly, Bøygärd?"

"What's that?" Bøygärd asked quietly.

"Do you know who are the people I see going *up* from 19th every morning? Up to the science labs and research centers on 28th, to PHS, to the Academy on level 27?"

Bøygärd shrugged.

Kilian took a step forward toward the encircling crowd, pulling Bøygärd alongside him. His eyes searched through the ranks until he set them on a particular member of the audience.

"Well, one example would be the distinguished Sam Anderson, who is honoring us with his presence here tonight."

All heads in the audience turned to meet an unpleasantly-surprised Zee standing amongst the group of spectators, dressed in his eternal black shirt, his eyes flaring.

Wow, I thought. *I have lived to witness Zee Anderson resent public attention. The Universe is amazing.*

"Now Sam here isn't the only Genline of a Thetis public office-holder assigned to research, science and academia positions. In fact — and I checked the records — *every* son and daughter of *every* Secundus to the Primo works above 19th at places like PHS, BioLabs, Genegineering, Material Design, you name it."

Kilian turned his gaze back to Bøygärd, lowering his voice to a whisper. "Why aren't they farmers and millworkers like your family, Boyo? Any clue?"

"Now wait a kunye minute!" Bøygärd snapped and broke off Kilian's shoulder hug. His muscles tensed, pumping blood to his reddening face. "If this is some criticism of our office decisions, let me remind you that *I* deal with *resource* allocation, not people. Contribution placement is not under my responsibility. But everyone knows the principle, ne? We all get assigned according to personal talent and Thetis needs."

"Ahh, talent," Kilian smiled. "Such an elusive concept, isn't it? It's a funny thing being a QUBIC IT — you get exposed to a lot of data. And it just so happens that Zee here," Kilian turned his head back to where Sam Anderson was standing with his jaws and fists clenched with anger, "has consistently failed every single test and certification process the PHS mandates. And the other privileged kids do not show exceptional results either. Merely on-average ranks, really. So the question stands — how come they all end up in science and knowledge-based contributions? Where are the farmers? The factory workers? The piping maintenance mechanics?"

"Does it matter, Kilian?" Bøygärd raised both palms in question.

"You're a QIT, I'm a ReDist — would it matter if our roles were switched? In the grand scheme of things, the important thing is that the accumulated knowledge on the Thetis be preserved and advanced for the benefit of our society. It really doesn't matter who does what, ne?"

Murmurs of acceptance flowed through the audience.

Kilian's confidence, however, didn't wane for a single second. In some complex manner I didn't fully grasp, he was exactly where he wanted to be in this seemingly lost debate.

"OK," he said calmly, "so before we take it to the hands, let's sum up what we've established here tonight?"

"By all means," Bøygärd said.

"So first of all we've agreed that scarcity of resources inevitably creates competitive forces — wars over dominance of land, food, shelter and other basic Human needs or, in more advances societies — over control of power, social status, money and data.

We have also agreed that on the Thetis, equality — whether true ideology or mere tool — is the reigning principle we all think will keep guiding Humanity toward the next phase in our species' destiny.

And lastly — you all seem to think that each Thetan's individual role doesn't matter too much, as long as we cumulatively keep making progress according to the Plan and don't stagnate. That about sums it up?" Kilian turned to Bøygärd for confirmation.

"You're a true poet, K-Boy," Bøygärd grunted. "Can we all drink now to my unequivocal victory?"

Bøygärd burst out in his roaring, rolling laughter, and the crowd quickly joined him. Kilian didn't flinch.

"No!" He shouted. "Because you're all pitifully wrong. And you severely endanger your genline if you don't open your eyes to the truth, *quickly.*"

"So does this mean we take it to the hands now?" Bøygärd asked.

"Take it to the hands," Kilian nodded.

Now I could see it — they were both in it together all along. Bøygärd wasn't really confronting K... This *was*, after all, just a show, and he was playing bassonet to Kilian's striangular, providing the exact level of *contrapunkt* necessary to crystallize his argument. I leaned back in my seat at the back-end of the Nebula and smiled to myself in the dark.

Bøygärd took a step backwards, leaving the center stage to Kilian, whose energy seemed to suddenly pick up as he raised his voice and addressed the thick audience.

"Oh lovely dwellers of the Nebula, let your voice be heard now! *If you believe* that almost two centuries of co-dependence in this flying box have truly transformed us, shedding our barbaric and cut-throat Human heritage in favor of an evolved, egalitarian existence — please raise your hand!"

Every single hand in the audience shot up in the air.

"And *if you believe* that we are all equal, contributing cogs in the Human machine, each doing their respective part to support the whole, and that there is no difference whatsoever in who plays what role — keep your hand in the air. Otherwise, take it down."

I could count maybe three or four hands dropping in the crowd.

Bøygärd scoffed. "Ain't your day, Kilian-the-not-so-great."

Kilian didn't budge. His voice rose up in pathos to the verge of crescendo. *"And if you believe* that when our descendants, two generations down the genline, will finally ReSett on a real planet, they will encounter abundance beyond anything we have ever known on the Thetis — fertile land to develop, water, energy — infinite potential with all Humans working together to realize it — *raise your hand in the air!"*

All hands were up again.

"Wow," Bøygärd said, "this sounds exciting, ne? Abundance?"

"Abundance!" Kilian called to the electrified audience, each syllable exploding in his mouth like he was unpacking a long-awaited present. "Can you feel it?"

"Abundance!" Roared the crowd, waving their fists in the air.

"This is what it was all about — Embark and Prosper!" Kilian hollered at the top of his lungs, his clenched fist sticking high in the air.

"Embark and Prosper!" The crowd echoed in unison.

Kilian and Bøygärd exchanged glances. Kilian dropped his hand to his side.

"Aaah, you stupid *wapas*," he said quietly, nodding his head in disappointment.

"Very discouraging," Bøygärd agreed. "Maybe the evolution thing hadn't quite yet kicked in for the dimmer subjects of our enlightened society."

"It certainly seems so," Kilian said. "So let me enlighten you, Thetan brothers and sisters, to why you're wrong and why it matters. And please — take your kunye hands down already. This place already reeks of laborer sweat. Except you, Zee. You smell like *royalty*."

"There's definitely the odor of a princess here," Bøygärd muttered in support.

I chuckled. Insulting the crowd was Kilian's signature move. He would call them SpacerBots, Lemmings, Human Organ Supply Chain — and for some reason, they loved it. It was all part of the show for them.

"So first and foremost, learn your kunye *history*. It's accessible to anyone who cares to take interest, te? You'd been led to believe that you live in terrible scarcity here on the Thetis, yes? That we should lay low until the promised planet floods us with its endless richness.

Well, let me surprise you — we are currently at the peak of living standards, quality of life and abundance of resources that our species will experience for the next 20 generations. We have plenty of food, clean water, breathable air, tremendous health and leisure time to enrich our cultural life. Population control through the Birth Year mechanism ensures we will never exceed the Thetis capabilities of maintaining those standards. The Plan made sure that we never suffer scarcity or distress, otherwise we would have already killed each other.

Oh hell, I forgot — it almost *happened* in the GenZero clan wars, ne? Lesson learned.

And on the planet? Well, what's certain is that we will *never* have it as easy as here — there will be weather, and beasts, and disease, and a thousand other struggles we never had to deal with in this hyper controlled, sterile environment. Abundance and endless resources? Ha! It's the exact opposite — Humans will be thrown back to a primitive society, and if you *do* read your history, you'll know that means people will fight for every single inch of land, every single ounce of food. And they will use every single advantage they have in order to be on top of the body heap."

The audience was quiet, taking in Kilian's barrage, unsure if he was being serious or was that still part of the tongue-in-cheek game he was playing. Bøygärd stood a step back with his massive hands crossed on his chest. His part was done.

"Now," Kilian continued softly, "that doesn't sound so egalitarian, does it?"

A few murmurs of resentment came from within the crowd.

"But wait! Won't it be the case that the simple skills — the farmers and the construction workers and the cooks — the crafts that you and your families are holding now, will be the most valued crafts in the new society? I mean, who needs QITs and ReDists when you're trying to survive on a hostile planet, right?"

"Right!" the audience cheered.

"Wrong!" Kilian raised his hands in frustration and shot a glance to Bøygärd. Bøygärd shrugged. Kilian turned back to the crowd, energized.

"Again, read you kunye history! The simpletons never win. They work themselves to death. They are replaceable. They are easy to control. *Knowledge* wins — the doctors, the scientists, the people developing technology to do everything faster and more reliably and more efficiently than any of your poor genline laborers. They win and they take control and they take first pick of *everything*, because you'll let them to — because you'll need what they have to survive.

Now, you've been taught your entire life to fear technology, to embrace equality as a moral value, to resist anything that challenges the status quo. The justifications you've been fed run from social stability to tradition to kunye fear-planting.

But, my friends, the people and families of the Anderson administration have been working all along to set their own genline's fate. They know the truth, and they plan ahead. This is why their children become scientists, ready to control the technology development roles. They go to the PHS and its research labs, ready to hold the keys to everyone's health and reproduction. They teach their kids to *rule*, when you all teach you kids to *follow*. You're all breeding ants. They're breeding lions!"

The awkward silence in the Nebula was a clear sign that even for Kilian, this night has surpassed the boundaries of people's comfort zone by a parsec or two.

For a long few seconds, no-one moved a finger in the audience. Then, with perfect timing, Bøygärd burst out laughing his huge, rumbling laugh which carried the room with him to a very welcome tension release. After a moment or so, Kilian joined in and lit the room with his shining, childish smile.

"OK, OK," Kilian said lightheartedly, "now that was quite a trip down the dark side of speculative fiction, ne? Don't take anything you've heard tonight too seriously — we're just playing a theoretical mind game here, right Boyo?"

Bøygärd bowed to the audience, still laughing his contagious belly tumbler.

"Please go back to your habs tonight remembering the important thing here: we love you all — yes, even you, Zee — and we'd happily fly across the galaxy with you filthy lot.

Embark and Prosper, for real. Good night."

CHAPTER THIRTY-NINE

"And that," I said to Gahlia, "was Kilian. You could love him or you could hate him, but you sure couldn't ignore him. Sadly," I added, "that was also when he got noticed by the Andersons for the first time. Stomping on Zee was a bad move."

Gahlia was silent. She just kept the slow, steady pace of her descent, and for a few long moments the only sounds filling the dense space were the clanks and squeaks of our boots and gloves working down the main beam.

When she finally spoke, her voice was so soft it came barely audible through the muffling of the helmet.

"And you loved him."

Her voice was tired. *Exhausted.* And I sensed it was not just the efforts of the climb.

"I loved him to the bone," I said. "Which was partly why I was so blind to the changes he was going through. And to the dangers those changes carried into our lives."

After a moment I added, "that was seven years ago. We were so much more naïve back then."

"Everything was," Gahlia said in a broken voice. "That is our generation's tragedy."

"Watch out!" Armitage hollered up at us from below. "There's damage to the Level 2 scaffolding and the mesh shield here! And for Sol's sake — hurry up! Dusting's almost over!"

I raised my head to look around for the first time in what seemed like hours. I was just passing the Level 4 mark, and Gahlia below me was halfway to the L3 crossing. This meant we would soon reach our destination.

"I miss those days," I said. "Living with Kilian was like being part of a never-ending exploration task force. So much energy, so much curiosity!"

"So," Gahlia said dryly, "you were caught up in it too."

"To a point," I admitted, "and for a while. It was very hard to keep the boundary lines in focus when you are moving that fast."

"You're an extremely smart woman, Sandrine," she muttered through her panting, "have you not for one second realized he was wandering into dangerous territory? Exploring subjects that would get him labeled as an Adapter?"

"Well eventually, of course," I said, "but remember — 'Adapter' didn't carry nearly the connotation it does today, ne? In hindsight, that was one of Sabi Anderson's evil genius moves: branding every ideology other than the one benefitting him as a negative, shameful, *anti-Thetan* vice."

Gahlia nodded. "True. And yet, you should have realized him digging into secure parts of the Archive wasn't your mundane after-hours hobby, ne?"

I felt the heat rush up my spine. "I'm not sure what you are accusing me of, Dr. Roskov!" I spat out. "Yes, of course, initially when it all began, I was fascinated by K's findings. I too couldn't fathom why such rich knowledge would be locked away from us. *Why* would the *Passados* deny our generation our history, our culture — even the dark bits which should serve as warning signs for our own future? But I was also a kunye *Archivist* — of course I knew the Code and that Kilian was cruising alarmingly close to where he could get hurt. I told him over and over: 'digging up corny teleshows from Old Earth is cute, but messing with data on augmentations? That mala's *taboo*, it's explosive material!'"

Gahlia sighed. "The perfect encouragement for someone like Kilian to keep at it."

"We got into huge fights about it," I grunted, "I mean, I was constantly worried about him, Gahlia. We just moved in together, we had plans — get committed, apply for Birth Year allocation, the whole cluster. And all the while, the public consensus regarding adapting Old Earth technologies to help us prepare for post-planetfall society was getting worse by the day!"

Gahlia nodded. "Adapters are our era's witches."

"Kilian of course resented that narrow thinking. He claimed that he wasn't actually hurting anybody. But people think it's worse — that Adapters hurt *everybody* by introducing dangerous tech into our fragile, closed system here! Can you imagine the position that situation put me in?"

"You were an Archivist. Keeper of the Code."

Gahlia lowered her leg to the final stretch of perforated beam leading down to the floor of Level 2. Step by careful step, her helmet sunk lower, only her penetrating voice echoing in the empty space.

"Was that when you decided to turn him in?"

The pain in hearing that question spoken out loud surprised me with its direct stab. I thought I would throw up, and an overwhelming claustrophobic wave washed over me. I crouched on my heels on the narrow platform, panicking, gasping for deep breaths and fighting the urge to take off my helmet.

Was that when you decided to turn him in?

I loved him! I was worried sick about what was happening to him, his obsession, the people he was drawing closer to him, to *us!* I needed advice and I had no one to turn to.

But that's exactly what you did.

"I'm an Archivist," I whispered. "This is not just a job, a

contribution — it's my identity. It's who I *am*. I took an oath to abide by the Code. And if it was any other Thetan engaged in such activities, we would have cracked down on them *long before that!*"

Gahlia just kept climbing down in silence, not looking up to my direction.

"I tried *everything*," I said, frustrated, "but Kilian wouldn't listen. I told him, 'the time for reinstating technology, for experimentation, will come — it's just not meant for *our* generations. *our* task is to sit tight. Ride it out. Just *get there.*'"

Gahlia shook her head slowly. "He wasn't convinced, I imagine."

"Do you know what he said?" I grunted. "He said that there is no such thing as sitting tight. That a society sitting tight for two centuries starts breeding children who no longer know how to stand! I was *lost*, Gahlia. He wouldn't reason."

"I know who Kilian is, Sandrine. I needed to know who *you* are."

I lowered my head, avoiding her eyes. "I had no one else I could trust. Nyasha was the only person I could turn to."

"And being the code-stickler he is, he could never placate this away."

I shook my head in silence.

"Which started the ball rolling in directions neither of you could possibly control," she whispered. "Until it backfired on both Kilian and you."

Tears were flowing down my cheeks freely now, tapping as they dripped onto the helmet's visor. I raised my head and stood up slowly, then climbed down the rest of the way to Level 2 in silence.

CHAPTER FORTY

Gahlia was already near the service hatch leading into the main level area, bent over Armitage. He was sitting on the floor, his back against the shell wall, holding his leg. He was clearly in pain from the long climb.

When she saw me land, Gahlia walked closer out of Armitage's hearing distance.

"Thank you," she said softly. "For the trust. It goes both ways."

I inhaled deeply. My chest lightened as if a ton of titanium had just been lifted off it.

"Come on," Gahlia said with a hint of a smile, "let's get this old grump on his feet. We need him intact for the next meeting."

"Meeting?" I asked, surprised. "Who the hell are we meeting on Level 2? I thought this was a radioactive no-man's zone."

Gahlia raised her eyebrows. "Not entirely. Officially, yes."

Armitage reached a hand and we both pulled him up. He was limping seriously, but he didn't complain.

"Let's go," he said and started shuffling inward.

"Where are we going?" I asked his receding back.

"Did you ever hear about the NoGen?"

I sneered. "Are you kidding me? That's a kunye kids' legend."

"Well," Armitage's basso reverberated loudly, "how'd you like to meet a legend?"

"This is a smoking disgrace, the shape the outer shells have degraded into," Armitage grunted a few moments later as we squeezed through the hatch. "You used to be able to lick ProteGel off the beams here, they were so clean. But you kids — it's all about the parties and the self expression and cultural diversity now, ne? How about some simple, honest work keeping up our only castle in the sky?"

"Hey," I raised by hands in defense, "I'm just an Archivist. The only thing I could keep up is a clean database."

Gahlia sneered. "Don't mind this *wamper*, Sandrine. He's only grumpy because his legs remind him he's not the young boy who used to climb up and down the ship anymore. Get used to it, Armi — we're Senior Generation now."

"Not quite," he insisted. "My dad's not in the Loop just yet you know."

Gahlia nodded in acknowledgment. We were all through the hatch now and out of the shell layers area. I couldn't wait to get the bulky helmet off my head and wipe my face dry of the sweat and tears and reused air circulating inside the suit.

As if reading my thoughts, Armitage held my arm down with his heavy palm.

"Not yet. Let's see how we are on radiation first. Rads should decrease as we put some distance tween us and the outer shell, so let's keep moving."

We kept moving in silence, Armitage leading the way confidently through the complicated maze of passageways.

Walking through Level 2 was an incredibly eerie experience. At the base level it was an exact replica of Level 26. But it was the ghost-town version of that level — everything was deserted, devoid of any sign of habitation. The shops had no signs, the walls had no coloring or paint over the carbofoam base material. Each step we took reverberated throughout the empty space. It was like walking through a real-scale model of the actual thing.

The entire floor was covered in a uniform layer of ultrafine powder, the result of an uninterrupted century of the steady, grinding decay Nature and its mistress Entropy enforces on anything in existence, even the most resilient artificial materials. Each step we took raised a tiny, turbulent grey puff, leaving a clear trail of footmarks and a wavy, smudged drag line where Armitage's bad leg was lugging on the surface.

The story of Level 2 is still a source of controversy on the Thetis. Planned as one of the hab and commercial expansion levels on the Thetis, it suffered an unexpected breach in its outer- shell a short time after Embarkment. The breach flooded the level with hazardous radiation levels, to the point it was declared unlivable and was never actually populated.

Various conspiracy theories thrived throughout the generations regarding the source of the hull breach: intentional sabotage by an obscure GenZero opposition group; an offensive energy beam launched at the Thetis from Earth; and other, fringier ideas. Imagination was, sometimes, all you got on the Thetis.

Level 2 was an off-zone ever since. It was plated top-to-bottom with an anti radiation mesh and used as dumping grounds for radioactive waste. Suffice to say, Level 2 was not somewhere you took your date for an evening stroll.

"Why are you helping us?" I asked Armitage. "You're clearly in pain, you are risking you life taking us through this kunye radiation-ridden wasteland, and what's more — you're helping us take down Anderson? That doesn't add up."

"I'm here for selfish reasons," Armitage admitted. "Look. My advantage was always being good with my hands. I build stuff. I fix stuff. I've always left the big thinking to the higher-ups."

"There are no higher-ups on the Thetis," I interjected.

"Yes, OK," Armitage muttered impatiently, "I got the pamphlet, as they used to say in my time. The point is — I trust Anderson. I trust him to lead us through the Plan and make the right decisions. I always have. I truly think there hasn't been any other potential leader coming *close* to his level of brains in generations."

"There better be a 'but' coming, otherwise I don't see what you're doing down here with us," I said.

"*But,*" he punctuated, "I have a GrandGen. Cute little girl, Lyra. A Gen8er. Just turned 17. *So* full of life and expectations for the future. If we don't smoke things up, *her* children will Resett on a new planet. And Gahlia here," he motioned toward Dr. Roskov, "has managed to convince me that's no longer a certainty. She knows my soft spots, that old witch."

"I'll leave the soft-spot research to Viv if that's all the same to you," Gahlia grunted through her teeth. "If we can get to the Origin before they figure out where we all disappeared, that'll be the highlight of my witching career right there."

"Speaking of which," I said cautiously, "the moment Dusting's over, won't the grid locators pick us up again? Pakk and his crew will have zero problem tracking us down here."

"We should be OK," Armitage said. "Most locators on L2 where disabled after the radiation wash that occurred when the hull breach happened. Those damaged locators injected so much noise into the system, we were sent down here to cut them off the grid. We're still as good as Dusted," he shrugged in his puffed suit, "if you ignore the massively radioactive environment we're currently walking through, of course."

Now *that* got my ears pricked up. "Wait, what? Why would there be any radiation here? I thought the waste disposal compartments were sealed and everything."

"It's not the containers. It's space radiation."

"Space radiation? As in — coming from *outside?*"

Armitage shrugged again, his voice flat and unmoved. "If you know of any space *inside*, I'd gladly reconsider my definition. You saw the huge hole in the protective mesh on shell layer 2. It means a radiation beam is washing like a flashlight through most of level 2."

"But," I grappled with this new information, "we still got these suits for protection, ne?"

Armitage gave a skeptic nod. "Hmm, not really, no, if I'm honest."

"What do you mean? They're kunye *space-suits*, aren't they? It's in the name."

"Designed originally for EVA maintenance work in Low-Earth Orbit, where most radiation particles are deflected by the planet Magnetosphere. Not designed for interstellar-space grade exposure."

"So we're essentially dressed in glorified, puffy onesies."

"That's correct. You can say we're essentially slowly cooking with every passing second."

I shot a glance backwards to Gahlia. She was dragging a few steps behind us, pushing herself hard, head down and eyes on the tips of her toes.

"So what do we do?" I asked a little louder than intended. I could feel the fear crawling up my spine as I looked around, trying to somehow *see* the invisible radiation. The walls and passageways of the bare ghost-level looked identical every which way I looked, like a huge, deserted maze.

"We hurry," Armitage grunted, dragging his limping foot as fast as he could now. "We must find the NoGen. She's our only hope for getting to the Origin while we're still pink."

'*She?*' The word startled me, instantly transforming the conceptual idea I had of the NoGen into a concrete image of a real human being. A woman.

CHAPTER FORTY-ONE

We all heard the legend of the NoGen when we were kids. But beyond a certain age, one simply dismisses such fantastic tales as being just that — a child's fable, not very different from the Tooth Fairy or the MagRail Monster.

Fables are served in two distinct flavors — scare and reward. They are an effective mental steering mechanism, harnessing our mind's fertile imagination to imprint desired traits and weed out harmful juvenile curiosities. The NoGen story was a bit of both, which is probably why it worked so well.

We were told there once was a baby, born between generations. Born out of the rigid Thetis birth cycle. Off the plan, and thus — off the Code. A baby with no name, born into a life with no future. *But if you, children, shall follow the Code and wait obediently for your assigned Birth Year — thou shalt prosper.*

That was the Reward part. Easy enough.

The Scare part of the NoGen tale was a bit more elaborate. Born in stealth and without proper medical attention to both the childbearing mother and the newborn, the NoGen was initially hidden from the Thetis authorities. Passed between a few knowing hands, fed in the shadows, tucked in thick-paneled laundry closets. A living, breathing

330

secret, in a society where total transparency was the key defining principle.

Now that couldn't last for long, could it? Babies cry. Babies consume. Babies exude. And this particular baby was showing worrying signs of sub-normal mental development. Oxygen deprivation during the unsupervised delivery, or a genetic defect which would have been detected and pruned in the formal Birth Year process, or a mythic punishment from whichever heavens one chose to believe in — the simple fact was that there was no way to keep raising the child unspotted and untaken care of.

So the administration was made aware of the problem, which, as often happens, only made things worse. A baby born out of cycle isn't only an intriguing anomaly — on the Thetis, every single resource is aligned to the twenty-year generation cycles: There would be no education facilities suited for the child's age, no production of suitable children's nutrition supplies, medical and hygienic accessories... even toys! The baby would be raised devoid of any supportive environment, which was especially crucial for a mentally or physically challenged child.

And once the existence of the NoGen became public, what could have been a community-led solution immediately became a political problem. And if there's one thing Human history is yet to show us, it is the case of an individual posing a real or imaginary threat to the reigning ideology and living to tell about it — metaphorically or physically.

Where community employs compassion, the tool of government is suppression. And on the Thetis, the most tolerant of societies in all of Human history, such a 'problem' was doubly threatening. The acceptance of an off-cycle birth would send a dangerous message to all Thetans regarding the disciplined rule of the Plan and crack the strict taboo on free, unregulated procreation.

The story doesn't elaborate on what eventually happened to the NoGen. There's a vague speculation of a special treatment center somewhere in the deeper parts of the ship or, in the scarier incarnation of the children's horror tale — a torture chamber located inside the ship's ion thruster engine complex. Whichever version you happened to hear, it always ended with a cautionary image of the NoGen: a tormented ghost roaming the Thetis at night, seeking revenge on young kids who do not listen to their moms or don't eat their ProteGel.

"Stop!" Armitage froze without warning, raising his hand abruptly.

"What's wrong?" Gahlia whispered as she caught up to us. We were just nearing a corner of two intersecting alleys leading into the Inward part of the level.

"We're smoked," Armitage said in defeat. "They got to her first."

I peeked beyond Armitage's puffy shoulders and saw it too: two distinct, clean lines of footprints in the dust, marking a confident trail from the Ascender platform, crossing our path and continuing further inward where they disappeared beyond a curve.

"They're recent," Armitage said. "Look at the sole tracks — clean, no newer dust covering the details."

I shook my head. "The disintegration of Carbofoam is very slow. Those could be from an hour ago, or they could be a few weeks old. Would look the same to the naked eye. Anyway, though, they're gone."

Armitage and Gahlia looked at me in question.

"Look closely," I continued. "There are two sets of footsteps, and they point in both directions — to and from the Ascender. They didn't even particularly try to be cautious about it, so I guess that wasn't meant to be anything covert. They came and went back up."

Armitage's face fell. His eyes ran worryingly in all directions.

"What if they've done something to her? I don't like this — my 7th sense is screaming bad news."

Another detail caught my eye. "Those footprint marks are standard shoe soles," I said. "How come they didn't need full space suits?"

Armitage looked at me for a moment, puzzled. He then reached a hand and opened his helmet visor.

"That means we're on the right path," he said. "They didn't wander here by accident. They knew the exact route leading to her. It's safe here, you can take your helmets off."

"How can you be so certain?" I asked, unconvinced.

Armitage gestured in a wide, circular motion to our surroundings. "Not all Level 2 is radioactive. There are pockets where the particle beam entering the ship doesn't reach. She lives in such a pocket. And so there are several passageways which are also clear. One thing's for smoking sure — this wasn't those people's first time here. We should hurry and check on her!"

Armitage started striding forward again, signaling us to keep up. I hesitated, carefully reaching for my helmet. I tentatively pushed the hard, translucent visor upwards. The seal surrendered and broke with a tiny hiss.

Ahh, fresh air! After what seemed like hours in the sweaty isolation of the space suit, I craved the feeling of real air on my face again. What I didn't expect was the awful, putrid smell I was greeted with. Level 2 smelled like a forgotten laundry closet opened after a decade of moisty fermentation. I immediately started to miss the metallic, artificial taste of the suit's oxygen flow.

"Come," I took Gahlia's hand and held her elbow for support, "let's hurry up."

CHAPTER FORTY-TWO

The room was like nothing I had ever seen before. 'Room' was perhaps overstating the size of the place — it was a tiny attic located up four flights of cramped stairs, at the top of a hab complex we had reached through a series of alleyways, ladders and tunnels.

The footprints we were following disappeared when we stepped off the open streets and into an internal maze of interconnected complexes. Armitage, though, didn't seem to slow down and kept navigating in confidence. After walking through what seemed like endless rows of identical streets and buildings, there was *no way* I could ever backtrack to the hatch we came in through.

"Let's go!" Armitage called and started running up the first flight of stairs.

I reached the top of the fourth floor panting. The entrance to the room was through a round opening in the floor, and Armitage was already climbing the short ladder leading up to it. I looked back at Gahlia. She was alarmingly quiet since we entered the main part of the level. She was clearly suffering, grinding through the movements. I stuck my head through the opening into the room, and was immediately flabbergasted.

"Kunye cuckoo's nest," I mumbled.

The attic was small and windowless, with a low-hanging ceiling below which I could barely stand straight. The ceiling, the floor and every inch of the room's walls were completely covered with a shiny, reflective metallic foil. What little light there was leaked into the room from the opening in the floor, dimly lighting the room with a warm, omnidirectional glow. It was like sticking your head into a giant chocolate box. The fancy ones, at least.

Armitage turned his head to me. "What nest?"

"Forget it," I said. "What are we looking for?"

Armitage raised a finger to his lips, hushing me. "She's sleeping," he whispered, a relieved smile spreading on his face.

I looked around us, puzzled — there was no one else in the tiny room. But as we both fell silent, I could faintly hear something, a repetitive expiration of air, coming from seemingly nowhere. Someone breathing hoarsely. I gave Armitage a questioning look. He signaled me to keep still and reached down the floor opening to help Gahlia with the climb into the room. She collapsed against the room wall, exhausted. Her face was shining with perspiration, and she was breathing heavily.

For a few moments the three of us just sat there on the attic's glistening foil floor, listening to both breathing rhythms dance in and out of sync.

Gahlia gradually recovered, curiously scanning the room around us. "It feels different in here," she said, "what is this place?"

"Shh!" Armitage whispered, but it was too late. Something changed in the air. The faint, steady breathing suddenly became irregular, interrupted by random, abrupt gasps.

"Rrrays," a low, strange voice mumbled. Gahlia shot an alarmed look in my direction. I looked at Armitage in question.

In the corner of my eye, something moved.

"Rrrays!" From under a perfectly camouflaged foil blanket spread on the room's floor, a woman jolted up. She was heaving and puffing heavily, her panicked eyes running between the three of us until finally landing on Armitage's soft, smiling face. That seemed to relax her, and

Noam Josephides

Armitage pushed himself closer, reaching slowly to pat her shoulder gently.

"Sandrine, Dr. Roskov," he said genially, a hint of pride in his voice, "please meet Bianca."

"Visitorrrs!" The woman's face lit up. "So many visitorrrs!"

I looked at her with complete astonishment. In a way, I knew I was now sitting across something — *someone* — that shouldn't exist.

And she has a name, I thought, *how come no one ever knew she had a name? It was always merely 'The NoGen', or — more commonly — 'it'.*

Turning people into pronouns, well, that's basic Dehumanizing Handbook, ne?

It was hard to gauge the woman's age. She seemed older than a Gen7er, but definitely younger than a Sixer. Which would put her somewhere around forty, forty-five years old? It was challenging to make an exact call, on account of her various deformations.

Her ashen-sand hair was actually a nice, quiet color, although wildly unkempt with random broken strands shooting in every possible direction. She had clearly suffered from some muscle-related development problem: her right eye and right arm were smaller than their left pairings and pulled slightly upward. The same upward twitch went for the right side of her very red mouth, lending her face a persistent smirking expression.

The most noticeable thing about the woman, however, was that every visible part of her skin was littered with badly-healed burn marks, some leaving bright scars, others reddened splotches of raw flesh.

"Hello Bianca," I said softly. "I'm Senior Archivist Sandrine Liet."

Bianca's eyes widened in awe, then shot to Armitage, seeking support. "Seniorrr Arrrchivist!" She whispered in admiration, "so many *imporrrtant* visitorrrs for the girrrl!"

I tilted my head in question. "Which visitors? Bianca, did you have

336

other people stop by before us today?"

She shriveled, planting her eyes in the floor. Armitage wrapped a gentle hand around her shoulders. His eyes pierced mine with an unexpectedly protective vigor.

"No questions, please. Questions convey a need to answer, and that's a stress factor," he hissed. Then, leaning closer to the frightened woman, his tone softened and he added: "don't worry, those women are friends. Tell me how you are feeling today, if you'd like to."

Bianca shook her head imperceptibly. "Bad day. Stinging day," she murmured, her fingers absentmindedly mulling the edges of the foil blanket covering her lower body. "Rrrays upon stinging rrrays rrradiating thrrrough me. Thrrrough all of us!"

Armitage raised his head and turned toward Gahlia and me. "Bianca has a highly unusual capability — an acute physical sensitivity to the cosmic radiation penetrating the ship. She reports feeling the actual particles flashing through her body as… internal, burning needle pricks. On some days, that could get a bit… intense."

Gahlia closed her eyes in empathy. "Poor soul, that must be torture. Armitage, we really have to —"

Armitage curtly raised his palm to reassure us he was very well aware of the time constraints we were under. When he turned back to Bianca, he was all warmth again.

"I'm so happy we were able to get our hands on this protective foil. That's quite a refuge. And you've set everything up so neatly — *very* accommodating for important guests. I'm sure our two friends who came by earlier today must have also complimented you about it. We kept looking for them but they were nowhere to be found."

Bianca's eyes glazed, lost in thought for a moment. "Sometimes you find yourself in the middle of nowherrre. And sometimes, in the middle of nowherrre, you find yourself."

The three of us exchanged puzzled looks. Bianca chuckled. "I am not crrrazy. Not today. They did not visit today. It was on a clear day, no stinging. They were verrry nice to me, those scientists. Such *smarrrt* boys!"

Armitage leaned over to Bianca. "Who where those boys, B? What did they bother you for?"

"Bashiri," I interrupted him. I looked into the woman's eyes, searching for any sign of recognition. "Was the scientist's name Bashiri? Dr. Almaz Bashiri?"

Bianca's expression remained blank. She lowered her head apologetically.

"It's so *harrrd* to keep it all in my head," she said. "If it was a clearer day today, maybe, I—"

"Kilian," I blurted and pushed myself across the floor as close as I could sit in front of her, capturing her entire attention. "The other guy. Was his name Kilian?"

Bianca's face lit up. "K-man, yes! He wanted to see the girrrl! He understands," she added proudly. "He's *hot*."

"Wait, which girl?" I said in confusion. "What are we talking about here, Bianca? Who is this girl? Where is she?"

"No, hold on," Armitage intervened, giving me a stern look. "Explain yourself, Sandrine. How did you know the visitors were Bashiri and Kilian?"

"They had a meeting here," I said. "A few days ago. The grid locators traced them going down the ship to Level 2. Obviously, since under normal circumstances their tracking data wouldn't be accessible by anyone, they didn't try to conceal it by going through the shell like we did. They just used the kunye Ascenders. Unfortunately," I added, "there is no location data about their route after disembarking on L2."

"The burnt sensors, sure," Armitage murmured.

"That's very worrying," Gahlia said in a grim tone. "If Kilian was here for the same reason we are, he'd be in a serious breach of his settlement terms. Which, to me, means he was willing to risk everything he still has."

She shook her head in dismay. "That doesn't spell any positive outcome from this little trip we're taking, I'm afraid."

"He didn't mention any of that to me when we met," I said. "And when Bashiri approached me in the Sensory Farm, he was kunye *terrified.*"

"He wanted to protect you," Gahlia said. "And himself, seeing that his trust in you is probably—"

"—and yet, here we are," I interrupted bitterly. "With Bashiri dead, and the rest of us blindly following Kilian's footsteps."

Gahlia didn't reply.

"No. Not blindly," Bianca's voice broke the silence. "K-man knew where we are going. He knew about the deserrrt."

"What desert?" I burst out and threw my hands up in frustration. "There's a girl, and now there's also a desert?"

That might have come out more sarcastic than I intended. Armitage signaled me to calm down and be patient.

Bianca looked at me with hesitation. "Do you know how on Old Earth, there were places on the planet called Deserrrts?" She asked carefully.

"Of course. Barren areas, very little water and vegetation. Extremely hard for life to survive in those conditions," I recited flatly.

Bianca's voice dropped a tone as she almost whispered, "I see them in my drrreams. All the time."

Armitage laid a hand on her knee. "Are you having some kind of nightmares, B?"

"You're walking through a desert," she ignored him, staring blankly forward, "an endless desert stretching in all directions. And in the dream, you feel very strongly that you are lost. But then, at the foot of a massive, yellow dune, you find a clock. The desert is different in each dream, but the clock is always the same."

"What's on the clock?" I asked, aware of how Bianca's speech impediment suddenly disappeared as she was reliving the dream.

"Well, the time, obviously," Bianca said like I had just asked the most stupid question in a parsec. "But you're not a fool," she continued with a hint of satisfaction, "even in the dream, you know not to trust it. You don't tell yourself: 'great! It's five thirty in the afternoon!'. Because you know a clock is just a device, and can be set to show any time. So you realize that even though you are trained to think of a clock as something displaying the objective truth, this isn't necessarily the case."

"And then?" I asked.

Bianca shrugged. "And then nothing. I wake up, feeling lost. Deprrressed, sometimes. I always thought that this drrream is haunting me because here," she gestured toward the foil-covered space of her small hab, "there is no lighting-cycle. No morrrning, no evening. But your K-man — he told me the rrreal meaning. He knew *everrrything* about the trrruth of the deserrrt!"

Gahlia gave me a cold look. A twitch in the corners of her mouth told me she was losing patience with this woman's babbling. She looked spent, and I was starting to get the feeling we should hurry up or Gahlia just might not hold up.

"Bianca," I said softly, "does this have anything to do with where Kilian and Bashiri were heading?"

"Exactly!" She replied enthusiastically. "You see, he told me the old storrry. We Thetans are the dreamers. We are all walking together through the deserrrt toward the prrromised land. But some people have an interest to contrrrol the clock. Not the clock in my drrream — our *mind clocks*. To make sure we are dependent on *them* to tell day from night!"

I leaned forward and asked in a hurried voice, "Bianca, this is very important, please try to remember — who are those people Kilian was talking about? Who's *them*?"

Gahlia and Armitage both looked at her intently, waiting for her reply. But Bianca simply nodded her head repetitively in silence. Then, the nodding shifted to a sideways swinging motion of her entire upper torso.

"It's verrry difficult," she murmured. "The stinging makes me forrrget. Wouldn't it be nice," she said, a glint of hope in her eyes, "Wouldn't it be nice to rrrest upon a planet? With its snuggly blanket of atmosphere wrrrapped around us, blocking all those stinging rrrays?"

Afraid she might be drifting off on us, I took both of Bianca's hands gently, and locked my eyes onto hers.

"Was that what Kilian and the doctor were worried about? Something about the planet? About 9 Ceti Gamma?"

"Yes..." Her face brightened in recollection. "The whale planet. There's *Dangerrr!*"

"Danger from what? Did they mention the Origin? Or Anderson?"

"Anderson!" Bianca exulted and locked our palms together. "He will put more stinging rrrays on the whale. The doctor knows. Ask the doctor!"

Gahlia sighed and rested her head back on the hab wall. "The doctor is dead," she whispered, deflated.

Bianca's eyes widened with terror. I held her wrists harder now, fighting to maintain her feeble focus.

"Why did they come to see you, Bianca? What did they need from you? There must have been a reason for the visit."

"I already told you," she murmured, almost pleading. "You don't listen, only ask questions. I *told* you," her face started reddening with anger, "they needed to see the girrrl! And nobody," her voice softened now, "nobody knows the way but me. Hey!" She called and searched Armitage's eyes for assurance, then looked back at me and Gahlia, her mouth curving on the cusp of a smile.

"Wanna see her?"

CHAPTER FORTY-THREE

The three of us followed Bianca up a steep ladder into a tight passage leading out of her secluded nest. She moved with surprising agility, and it took all our effort to keep up with her pace.

"She knows this place like the back of her hand," Armitage grunted and pushed himself up with one hand, supporting his weak leg with the other.

Moving through Level 2 felt like walking through an X-Ray scan of an actual level. "I thought I knew every nook and cranny of Level 26, but I must admit I'm completely clueless," I said. "Are you OK?"

We were now following Bianca through a series of corridors at the basement level of several interconnected complexes. Gahlia nodded. "Those suits are crap," she said. "From the moment we landed on Level 2, I could feel the radiation. Thank Sol for the rad-bunker she fixed up for herself. That protective foil was a lifesaver."

Gahlia accepted my offered hand and pulled up the few final stairs we were climbing out of the basement and back to ground level.

"I think she's taking us through a specific path of low-rad pocket areas," she said, pointing in the general direction of the alley we were walking through. "And I think we're going Outward."

We turned a corner around a low-hung complex and into a flat, featureless opening, and found Bianca and Armitage waiting for us.

Armitage looked worried.

"Listen," he whispered and pointed at his ear. We all stood still for a moment, searching the air for any unusual sound.

A distant, familiar whirr carried across the deserted level. We all recognized the source of that very distinctive sound.

"Magrails discharge," Armitage stated flatly.

"The Ascender," Gahlia whispered. "Someone's coming!"

"More visitorrrs," Bianca said with a hint of enthusiasm.

Armitage held her arm gently. "No, Bianca. *Bad* visitors. We must hurry now."

"The girrrl is close," Bianca nodded. "Come. This way. It's the only rrroute to rrreach the girrrl alive."

"Does anybody else know about this route?" I asked.

Bianca shook her head confidently. "Yearrrs and yearrrs of explorrring. Lots of stinging rrrays. But it was all worrrth it."

Bianca's expression softened. Her burnt, pockmarked skin glistened. "Because I found herrr."

Five minutes later, Gahlia was on the verge of collapsing. We were racing through Level 2, following Bianca through alleyways, corridors, basements and rooftops — she was leading us with the complete confidence of someone who had travelled that exact path countless times before.

Gahlia, on the other hand, was quickly fading away. The pace was demanding for a 75 year-old Thetan, sure, but there was more to it than just physical exertion. I was holding her hand, helping her balance and climb the staircases and ladders on our route. On random occasions, her body would tremble, and her grip would weaken in my palm. Behind the helmet visor, her face took an unnatural, sulphuric tint. Tiny, bloody cracks criss-crossed her dry lips. She noticed my worried look, but her icy-blue eyes showed nothing but clear-minded determination.

"It's the radiation," she nodded, "I know. Kunye two hundred year-old suit, right? Let's keep pushing."

"Why are you risking your life for me?" I asked in an impulse. "It's one thing to have tried to get Kilian off the hook when the whole Adapter affiliation thing blew up. I get it — you were his mentor, te? Nyasha tried to do the same for me. But K's having a nice life now. Birth Year coming up for him. You fought for him, and you won."

Gahlia chuckled. "Oh, he didn't need any fighting done. All he needed was a little leverage. You see — he had something going for him which you didn't."

I tilted my head in question. "What's that?"

"They *feared* him." Her voice was harsh and she grunted audibly. "They feared him, but they also needed him. He had dangerous ideas, but he also possessed invaluable knowledge. So they had to press on him for public visibility, but not half as much as they pressed you."

"They took my Birth Year away," I whispered in anger. "*My* Genline. *My* future."

Gahlia nodded quietly. "An effective demonstration of what he'd be in for if he strayed from their plan."

"Why spare him, and appear like a weak administration, letting an Adapter walk away with a mere slap on the wrist? They could've simply recruited another QIT engineer, no? You could've trained another Kilian."

Gahlia's lips curled up almost imperceptibly.

"Not after my dementia kicked in."

"*Kei* are you talking about?" I was baffled. "Dementia? *You?* You're the sharpest person I've ever— Oh."

Gahlia just raised her brows in an innocent expression.

"You *faked* dementia so Kilian would be protected? So he'd be the only one with the skills and knowledge to handle the QUBIC system? So they'd need him?"

"Sometimes the best fighting maneuver is simply stepping back,"

She said calmly.

"Wow," I said. "How'd you pull that off?"

She nodded her head to one side in dismissal. "Surprisingly easy, with the former head of PHS on your side, and an unrestricted access to the Archive medical records."

"So, Hugo Winkler. But I don't get it, Gahlia. You were at the pinnacle of your career, and you just... gave it all up? Retired to the Astral Solace?"

Gahlia walked in silence for a few moments. When she spoke, her voice was weary.

"You don't choose the moments when your priorities are put to test. My work had always been my entire life. But in the end, in the moment of truth — it's the people that matter, not the work. And Kilian was like a son to me. Besides," she flashed that playful smile again, "I like it in the Home. Hugo's painting classes are hugely entertaining."

We kept walking, following the trail of footsteps left by Bianca and Armitage in the white dust. That was a lot to absorb — the woman had literally sacrificed her whole career, her whole *life purpose* because of me. The way the unintended consequences of your deeds come full circle, all those years later, to face you — was mind boggling.

"That's why you're doing this," I said carefully, "you realize there was a deal. And he must have kept his end of it by giving the Andersons what they needed — something you protected your entire *life*. Your'e here because you fear Kilian may have betrayed you."

Gahlia's eyes flared at me. She was breathing fast and shallow now, and her voice was reduced to a hiss. "I always knew who Kilian is and why I trusted him," she rasped. "And I tried to give him a better bargaining position than he would have had otherwise. But," she closed her eyes for a moment, "I did have my doubts, yes. You are right about that. I know how things work — and the Andersons don't go light on anyone out of kindness, do they?"

"Not unless they get something in return, no."

"But then you came with your story, and suddenly, after all those years, the dots started connecting. So to your question — I am here because *he* was here. With the dead scientist. And that *does* tell me something important — that tells me he was smart. That tells me he knew how to sabotage the Andersons' plan when the time came. That he never betrayed my trust and my love for him. And most important, that tells me what I need to do."

"And what's that?" I whispered.

"I need to get you into that Origin node if it's the last thing I ever do. And if I'm not mistaken, our happy little friend just got us there."

I slanted my head to look over Gahlia's shoulder and saw Armitage and Bianca standing at the opening to a wide, slightly depressed area. The setting looked familiar — way up above us, in the identical setting of Level 26, this space would be occupied by an open market of hab appliance maker shoppes.

Well, almost identical.

Because the thing that filled our entire field of view was definitely one of a kind.

"Now this is a marvel for old eyes, isn't it?" Armitage muttered in awe. He climbed up a small carbofoam bench for a better view of the silvery construct in front of us.

He turned his head to me and asked, "you do know what you're looking at, right?"

I stepped forward and pushed myself up to stand on the bench beside him, never letting my eyes off the large, bulky tubular object in front of us.

"If this is what I think it is", I said, "then I am looking at something that shouldn't exist."

Armitage chuckled. "We told you there were still a few secrets to the Thetis, ne?"

I nodded. "Kilian was right," I murmured to myself. "This *is* the kunye Origin."

CHAPTER FORTY-FOUR

According to the Archive, construction of the Thetis was executed in a multi-stage, multi-layer plan. When the project was initiated by the US government, the notion of an actual emergency evacuation from Earth was merely an offshoot, theoretical exercise. Thus, it was mainly seen as an ambitious, albeit far-fetched scientific experiment, its outrageous budget approved only because it also happened to provide an extravagant political muscle-flexing opportunity.

The major technological challenge yet to be demonstrably solvable was the massive propulsion unit. Achieving reliable acceleration and navigation over two centuries of interstellar space travel required a solution an order of magnitude more advanced than anything the Human race had priorly shot at the skies.

So, the engine unit would be the first component to be built, tested, and approved. Next would be the construction of the ship's backbone and structural elements, with the actual livable areas — the levels where we Thetans have spent the past eight generations — being the last piece in the puzzle, decades down the assembly timeline.

The whole ship had to be built in orbit. Launching the fully-constructed juggernaut from Earth's surface and overcoming the planet's gravity pull would be costly and impractical. It would also be flat out suicide — the political standoff between Earth's powers was so intense at that point that such an attempt would likely be shot down before the liftoff puff cleared out.

So each component was built separately on the ground, then carried into orbit via rockets. There, a rotating crew of Space Force professionals would be waiting to intercept, off-load and assemble the parts onto the ever-growing, yet-unnamed Thetis.

For that routine to work uninterrupted for years — *decades*, really — the project managers had to come up with a plan for solving two major problems: The first — a steady platform able to host the precision work of the engine assembly and the accommodation of the operation crew itself. The second was ensuring that the platform was situated within the declared *Zona Dearmata*, an area protected by non-aggression treaties signed by the world's nations.

There was really only one reasonable candidate for the job, the name of which was plastered across the silvery construct in front of us in upside down, squarish black letters.

"The International Space Station," I said in awe, trying to place the information in my head where it might make sense. "*Kei* is this thing doing here?"

"Leftovers, I guess," Armitage laughed. "It's a beauty, isn't it?"

I caught my head between both palms. "This blows my mind. I don't understand — how come it's even here?"

He shrugged. "You're the Archivist. You tell us."

The Thetis construction plans were, of course, clearly and fully recorded in the Archive. The ISS was supposed to be just a temporary stepping stone, a convenient scaffolding on which to latch while assembling the main engine unit. It would later be dismantled and disposed of as the construction of the ship's main body would swallow and engulf it and most of its components would not be needed any longer. The only thing that was supposed to remain was the ISS main truss, which would serve as the supporting beam to what would later be the ship's Level 1.

That, apparently, was not how things actually panned out.

The outline traces of the long truss were faintly visible on the surface of the level floor. Sitting on top of it, shimmering softly in all their antiquated glory under the neutral ambient lighting, were a series of tubular components which had made the main operational body of the ISS.

"Where's the rest?" I asked.

Armitage shrugged again. "The rest were solar panels and antennas. Probably scavenged early on in the construction process. The main parts were needed for crew accommodation until late in the project, so were planned for later disassembly when things progressed further."

"And never got to that, obviously," Gahlia said in a low voice, her eyes glued to the archeological wonder standing in front of us. "Pushed the expense to the last possible moment and then, when Embarkment became an emergency — they just sealed it in and took off."

"That's... a lot to process," I said in what apparently was becoming the theme of the day. The Archive containing a completely false record of things was a first for me. And something this huge, existing in the open for almost two centuries without almost anyone knowing about it was... outrageous.

I shot a glance at Bianca. "But beyond the historical curiosity, the key question here is — what did Kilian and Bashiri find here that was so important?"

Bianca's expression flashed with a stressful twitch for a moment, her voice dry when she replied. "I... I only go to visit the girrrl there. I neverrr touch anything. I prrromise!"

"The sixth node," Gahlia grunted, tiny beads of sweat breaking over her brows. "Bianca, take us inside, please."

A distant, urgent shout echoed behind us, reverberating through the densely packed, bare alleyways of the level. We all turned our heads back and listened, trying to assess its source, but it was gone.

"Quickly, please," Gahlia whispered.

Bianca led the way, down the slight slope and into the clearing leading to the ISS main body. As we stepped nearer, it's unusual formation became clearer — a combination of seemingly unrelated compartments, attached together without any apparent organizing principle. The compartments were interconnected by short, angular black rings.

Armitage noticed my interest in the ancient construct. "They say that the nations sharing the Space Station were so out of sync with each other that even the latches they planned for connecting the units together didn't match. They had to fly up special *adapters* just so that they could attach the components to one another. Crazy, huh?"

It was my turn to shrug. "Wouldn't be the first time in history that national ego led people to protect the most foolish legacies rather than concede to the other guy's standard. I once tried to trace Old Earth's different currencies, measurement units, electricity standards, kunye *driving* directions — gave up pretty quickly. Luckily, we're past that divisive era now."

Bianca stopped. She was standing below a narrow, protruding tube in one of the ISS side arms, connected to the entire construct hanging above us. At the end of the short tube, a series of small, glass-paned apertures were fixed in a circular arrangement. In the center of that circle, a bigger porthole was missing its original glass, leaving a gaping opening into the interior of the tube.

She raised a finger to her lips and whispered, "shhh. This way in."

Sticking my head through the circular opening and into the interior of the ISS main body was like passing through a portal to a different dimension. Given that the lettering on its exterior hull were upside down when we first approached it, I half expected to find myself hanging from the interior space's ceiling. But when I set my eyes on the chaotic, cluttered arrangement of the small space station, I quickly recognized my mistake. Surprisingly, even though the station was constructed from a series of tubular modules, its interior space was actually square-shaped, with four distinct walls stretching the length of the vessel's body. There were no formal ceiling or floor planes in the ISS — every inch of each wall was crammed with instruments, cables, storage compartments and an endless array of panels, dials, gauges and LEDs — all of which were dead. The occasional hand-grip handle protruded from the walls, indicating where it was safe to grasp without tearing off any crucial part of the dense machinery.

"Yes, of course, designed for weightlessness," I mumbled to myself as I looked around. "Smart."

I pushed myself up through the opening and took a step into the main area, making way for Gahlia to climb in behind me. I could hear her grunt as she pushed herself through. Armitage was already further inside, standing in a squarish, hatch-like narrowing where two modules interconnected.

The ISS was indeed a marvel, like a packaged piece of history transported in time. Every object, every material was a novelty — from the old-fashioned aluminum metal of the grip bars to the crude yet soft fabric covering some of the instruments, down to what must have been plain, simple plastic bags containing all sorts of random supplies. Obsolete, quaint, *wonderful* findings for an Archivist geek like myself.

And somehow, somewhere within that archaic mess, lay the answer to my future. To *all* Thetan future, potentially.

"What are we looking for?" Armitage called from one of the side-branching modules deeper inside the station. For such a relatively small construct, it was surprisingly easy to get disorientated in the ISS — the absence of an 'up' and 'down' indication and the general visual overload of the cramped space created an immediate vertigo effect which made it difficult to assess direction and distance.

No wonder old people still talk about the FLIPP. They had to go through *actual* weightlessness for the better part of a week, which must have been totally disorienting.

"Where are you?" Gahlia called, "we can't see you!"

Armitage's rumbling voice seemingly came from all around us. "I followed the arrow signs on the walls to a module named 'Harmony'. That sounded promising!"

Just then I noticed the small, blue arrows painted on the walls every few feet with directional indications to the different parts of the station. *So I wasn't the only one who felt disoriented in here,* I thought.

"That's cute," Gahlia called back, "so you just passed beyond 'Destiny'. Sadly, life isn't that poetic — the node is on the other side of the station. Come back!"

Preceded by a series of loud grunts, Armitage's pressure-suited body appeared some thirty feet ahead of us, at the entrance to the corridor leading to several of the other modules. He was struggling to walk within the confined space, occasionally banging his head or toppling gear with a stray elbow.

"How did those people ever live in this place?" He grumbled as he approached.

Gahlia nodded. "Don't forget that the planetfolk who built this place grew on a planet with a gravitational pull fifty percent stronger than the Thetis. They were at least a foot shorter than the average Thetan." She eyed him sympathetically and added, "and you're not the average Thetan, te?"

"OK," I looked around to try and create a mental map of the branching module structure. "So where are we headed?"

"The other side of the station," Gahlia pointed behind me. "Look for arrows pointing toward a module called Zarya."

"And that's where the 6th node is?" I asked.

Gahlia nodded tentatively. "Assuming we can access it, yes. This is all still theoretical at this point."

"Wait — is this your first time here? You've never *actually* operated this QUBIC node?"

Gahlia turned away from me slowly and started down the path toward the passageway of intersecting modules. "I know it may sound morbid, but the fact they had to dispose of Bashiri gives me hope that he and Kilian managed to get to the data on it. Why would they bother otherwise?"

If we thought the modules we came in through were constrained, Zarya gave a whole new meaning to the word. The module was officially part of the 'Russian' side of the ISS (why two of Old Earth's leading nations could not bring themselves to share a single orbiting gizmo in peace was beyond me) — and was positioned as the natural continuation of the long tubular body of the station's main axis. But, since the connection between it and the 'American' side was a short, steeply-inclining adapter ring, the view into that part of the station was blocked until we climbed up the ramping connector and into Zarya.

The space between the opposing walls was almost too small to fit through in our pressure suits without walking sideways. The 'floor plane' we were walking on was piled waist-high with crumbling white fabric bags and soft-looking sacks strapped tight to the floor by a metal tether.

Armitage started climbing over the heap of soft sacks, grabbing a set of grip-bars attached vertically to the walls on both sides. "*Kei* are those kunye bags?" He grunted with effort. His head banged the top wall as he tried to squeeze himself past the pinnacle of the heap.

Gahlia started after him. "Who knows?" She said and pulled herself up and over to the other side. "Could be emergency parachutes. Could just as well be someone's hundred-and-eighty-year-old dirty laundry."

"Thanks for that mental image," I said in mock-disgust, "makes this climb so much more fun." I strenuously crossed my leg over the top of the bag pile, sitting on top of it for a moment before concluding the endeavor with a short slide down to the other side.

"So. Any idea how that node would look like, exactly?" I asked.

Gahlia looked around, scanning the walls around us and further into the next module ahead. "Well, this node is legacy tech. It's not even Late Earth technology — it actually dates almost a century earlier. Forget about the standard QUBIC neuro-electric cube terminal, this would be something much simpler. So I guess — a screen?"

"Oh, you mean like the million screens popping out from every inch of the walls around us?" Armitage made a wide, arching gesture, encompassing the entire space of the module. Countless flat, black slabs were hanging from metallic arms protruding in random angles from every possible surface. "They're all dead anyhow."

"Well we know the QUBIC node isn't dead, at least," Gahlia said flatly. "Why come after us if it was, ne?"

Armitage scratched his chin absentmindedly with his thick gloved hand. "OK. I guess we just go one by one then."

We worked as fast as we could, standing shoulder to shoulder in the tight space. Opening wall compartments, unlatching protective straps from sliding drawers, tracing cables to their obscure sources behind, above or below the surface of the interior bulkhead. We pressed buttons — hesitantly at first, afraid to unleash some long-hibernated electrical demon who may be dormant inside the ancient technology, then liberally — open palms squashing entire groups of squarish inanimate buttons, hoping for a spark of reaction.

There was none. The buttons, the free-hanging screens, the folding flat boxes with smaller embedded screens within them — they were all inert.

Armitage grunted with audible frustration. "As an engineer, this is highly insulting to me — pressing random buttons without the first idea of what I am doing. This is ape work!"

Gahlia nudged his shoulder to progress to the next panel. "Ape work got us this far in the galaxy, hasn't it?"

If that was supposed to cool him down, it didn't work quite as expected. "Ahh! don't get me started, Gahlia!" He grumbled. I moved further away into the entrance to the next module, which was as littered with ancient technology as the others. "What the hell is 'Zarya', anyway?" I overheard Armitage ask in a grudging tone.

"It means 'Dawn' in the language used by the Russian nation," Gahlia said.

"Ha!" His tone lightened up behind me, "life *is* poetic after all!"

I crossed over to the adjacent module and looked around. The flat surfaces of the four 'walls', the ceiling and the floor were all covered with a seemingly random arrangement of screens, key-sets, dials and other antiquated devices. I tiptoed around carefully, trying not to step on anything which looked like it might break. Anything here could prove meaningful if it could eventually be sprung to electrical life. The indication signs and labels on the various elements were mostly unhelpful, referring to unknown acronyms or vocabulary long since lost to us.

A high-pitched screeching sound pierced the air around us. It sounded like the drilling or sawing of carbofoam material you would often encounter on the Level 14 manufacturing districts. It wasn't alarmingly close, but it definitely originated somewhere within Level 2.

"What's that?" I asked and turned my head to Gahlia and Armitage.

"That's our clock," Gahlia nodded and added in a low voice, "Let's find that node. There won't be any explaining-away our being here to whomever is chasing us, so our exit strategy relies on the data we uncover."

I turned back and scanned the module, looking for a clue. A blinking LED. A button glowing dimly. A black screen ready to jolt out of hibernation. Anything.

But there was nothing. It was all dead. I started feeling the heat of frustration climbing up my neck and seeping into my cheeks.

How am I supposed to make sense of any of this ancient stuff? We're like archeologists stepping inside the excavated temple-grave of some bygone Pharaoh, trying to decipher which of the obscure glyphs on the grave walls would magically cast the spell of his resurrection!

I clenched my right hand into a fluffy, gloved fist and struck the wall in anger. Gahlia and Armitage threw their heads in my direction.

"*Kunye mala!*" I mouthed a suppressed cry.

In the corner of my eye, something bright moved. It was a tiny movement, lasting no more than a split second. A small object, let loose by the impact of my fist on the bulkhead, shifted slightly. Only a small part of the object was revealed — the corner of a rectangular, flat white card.

The card was shoved into the narrow slit between the frame of a small black screen and the bulkhead wall it was mounted on, providing easy and quick access for whomever was working on that screen.

I reached and plucked the card from behind the screen for closer examination. The material was fascinating — not an inksheet for sure, and much more flexible than a carbofoam or nanoplast mold. Its surface was bright and reflective, but not glossy or refractive. This must be some kind of... paper? I flipped the small thing around to examine its other side.

My heart missed a beat. I suppressed a gasp and instinctively shot a glance in Gahlia and Armitage's direction. My eyes were immediately drawn back to the astonishing, breathtaking discovery staring back at me from the small flat card.

* * *

It was a picture, imprinted on the card material through some arcane method of paint or dye or colorful ink of sorts. Two striking blue eyes, encased in a frame of long, straight golden hair split innocently at near-center. Stray hairs glowed fiercely, backlit by the rays of the rising Sol. A hint of light-blue, almost bleached sky in the background.

A child's face. Not older than five or six years of age. A loose smile, full of intimacy and trust.

Who is that child? A better question: who *was* that child, staring directly at me across a hundred and eighty years of time and space?

Was she the daughter of a longing-stricken astronaut, stationed on the ISS on a prolonged mission, keeping her picture close for when the endless nights of floating above the planet weighed heavy on the soul?

A beautiful daughter, her face an open map of excitement and eagerness. Was hers a life of innocence and beauty beneath the glittering Sol and open sky seen in the picture, or was it already destined to be crushed by the rising tides of pollution and warfare and the inevitable collapse that followed?

Did she know about the Thetis, being built high in those skies above her? Did she have hope for herself or her future children to be rescued from the planet? Did she ever even see her dad again?

How we take things for granted.

A shriek behind me startled me out of my spiraling thoughts. "Put the girrrl back!" Bianca was halfway up the stowage bag heap, feverishly trying to squirm her way faster into the Zarya main space, her eyes flaring in my direction. "You're rrruining her!"

I instinctively stretched my hand forward and held the small picture in front of me, quickly examining it for any damage. In the lower right corner of the card, where I was holding it between thumb and gloved finger, the color began to smear as the fabric rubbed lightly against the dye print. A small blotch of red, green and light blue stained the glove's whiteness, already setting into its dense fiber mesh. I hurriedly tried to stick the picture back behind the black screen frame, feeling like a child caught hot-handed messing with some forbidden object.

Bianca pushed urgently past Gahlia and Armitage, panting, tears welling in her eyes. She gently collected the picture from my hand and held it in front of her in both palms, barely touching the outside frame.

"You can't hurrrt her like that!" She whined. "She's irrreplaceable." Then, with glittering eyes, she added, "isn't she beautiful? I think she's an angel."

"She is," I replied, realizing after the fact how it could refer to both parts of her sentence. "Bianca — was that what Kilian and Dr. Bashiri were looking for when you led them here?"

She nodded absentmindedly, still focused on the picture in her hand. She then proceeded to tuck the card gently back into place, while I was trying to figure out how any of the instruments in front of me could be switched on. I pressed every button I could find around the screen. I pulled on a small metal lever, and a drawer with an integral keyset popped out. I tried pressing the various keys, but to no avail.

Gahlia stepped closer behind me and laid a hand on my shoulder.

"Let me try," she said.

I moved further into the Russian module to make room for Gahlia to operate the keyset. She took her helmet off and squinted at the black screen, her fingers wiggling with anticipation.

"This is certainly different from the three dimensional gesture-based interface we're used to," she mumbled as she fiddled with the keyset. A short, mechanical beep pierced the air, signaling that somehow, something Gahlia was doing was making an actual impression on the machine.

"A-ha!" Her eyes lit up as the black surface of the screen brightened slightly to a murky, dark-grey tint. "Turns out this ancient thing does respond to the crypID chip scan. Probably required QIT Engineer access permission to operate, so don't feel bad it didn't wake up for you."

Gahlia leaned forward, eyes fixated on the device. A few lines of glowing, jagged letters appeared in the corner of the screen and more started running down its left side. Gahlia clicked a few keys in succession, completely focused on the resulting flow of cryptic text in front of her.

"This is… nothing like the QUBIC terminals we have upstairs. No human interface whatsoever. You have to operate it by… pure code, it seems."

She kept operating the flat keyset below the screen, shooting her eyes back and forth between the two. A glint in her old eyes suggested she was loving it.

"Wow," she let out suddenly, "I see now why Almaz Bashiri needed to get to this node. No interface also means you have direct query access to the Thetis database. To the actual Ledger."

A short burst of shouts startled all of us. Our gazes met briefly, then we all instinctively looked towards the direction of the entrance porthole to the ISS.

"That sounded close", I whispered.

Armitage took Bianca's hand and started moving back to the other side of the station. "I'll buy you as much time as I can. But hurry up, for Sol's sake, OK?"

He pulled Bianca's hand gently to lead her after him. "I'm getting B out of here. She doesn't need to be part of this mess."

They both climbed over the bag pile and disappeared down the slope. I felt heat climbing up my neck again. Gahlia clenched her fingers in tension.

"So what now?" I urged. "What's so special about this kunye node?"

"I don't know yet," Gahlia mumbled, eyes on the screen, "but let's start with the list of recent queries processed by this terminal. Seeing the search terms Kilian and Bashiri were running on this machine may give us a clue about where to begin digging."

She punched in a few keystrokes, and the terminal spitted out a short reply message in blueish, phosphorous letters. Gahlia tilted her head slightly.

"No luck," she said. "The local queries log has been wiped clean."

Now why would they go into the trouble of doing that? No one knows about this node, much less actually comes here.

I shrugged. "Aren't all the nodes connected into one big data mesh? Even if they deleted the local logs, wouldn't they exist on the other nodes as a perfect copy?"

Gahlia hummed to herself. "Maybe, yes. But they aren't, for some reason. Oh there it is!"

"There's what?"

"I managed to find the activation command for the other screens in this module."

I raised my head — all the other black slabs around us came to life, displaying the same simplified textual sequence running down the screen.

"OK..." I said, "and that gets us... where, exactly?"

"Well, for starters it gets *you* off my back. You leaning over me like that really stresses me out, San. No offense. Now, let's work backwards here."

She resumed her quick keystroke sequence on the device, entering line after line of cryptic commands to the ancient system. I felt kind of useless, so I examined the different screens around us, trying to make sense of the different data layers starting to visualize as Gahlia progressed.

"What's working backwards mean in this context?" I asked.

"You were right. All the QUBIC nodes are connected in a consensus-driven architecture, so when a change is made — like adding another data record — regardless of which terminal was used to insert the new data, it populates onto all the other nodes so they all carry a complete and identical version of the Archive at any given time."

"Yeah, sure. So?"

"So there actually shouldn't have been any reason for Kilian and Dr. Bashiri to risk coming all this way, right? Any other QUBIC terminal would have supplied the same information."

"Maybe they needed a place where they wouldn't be spotted messing around with the Archive," I said.

Gahlia turned her head and gave me a skeptical look. "And risk radiation poisoning, or getting caught in a restricted area of the ship? With K's prior history with the Code?"

I could practically hear the sting in that remark. It hit home.

"Ne," she continued, "the only plausible reason why they would need access to this specific terminal would be that somehow, the data on this node is *different* than the others."

She kept typing, her fingers wiggling with excitement between each burst of keystrokes. She *was* loving this challenge.

I tried to catch up to her logic. "So instead of trying to figure out what they searched for, we need to find out what's here *to be searched* that's different than anywhere else."

"Precisely," she nodded absentmindedly. "Don't forget, the Thetis was built with the multi-node QUBIC architecture in mind, but the ISS wasn't. This system was designed for a small, single-purpose operation. So we start with the basics. First thing is we compare the entire ledger size and the timestamp of its latest update. Then we drill down further."

She punched in a command into her terminal screen, then leaned back in surprise.

"Aha."

"Aha what? What does it say?" I threw an instinctive cautious glance toward the entrance path.

"They're different," she said musingly. "I mean, the update timestamp isn't, it's actually identical. But the overall size of the database is slightly bigger on this node than the others."

"So there's more data on this machine? Like a hidden part of the database that doesn't exist on the other parts of the ship?"

"Unlikely," she mumbled as she continued her probing, "this isn't how it works. And when I'm compiling all the records, from the oldest to the most recent, record-by-record, they all do come out as one hundred percent identical."

"And how's that possible?"

"I... ahh, I see what it is!" Gahlia exclaimed. "Oh this is just *marvelous!*"

"What? What's going on? Tell me!" I pressed.

"Oh this is brilliant," she smiled, "see, the *Passados* used this old node as a kind of backup. An Archive of the Archive, so to speak. So it's configured to be 'write once, read many' to keep its authenticity."

"And in plain Thetan?"

"It means that regular operation, like adding a new record to the database, are carried out normally as in all the other nodes. However, operations that could alter previous data, such as DELETE or MODIFY requests, are recorded but not processed."

I nodded. "So all previous data records are kept intact, and the new data record is stored on top of them?"

"And that explains the bigger database size — all versions of the data are stored in parallel, but when you build the current state from the ground up, you get the most updated version."

"Which means Kilian and Bashiri were looking for something deliberately deleted from the main QUBIC system upstairs. The only place on the Thetis where it would still exist is here."

Gahlia stretched her fingers and turned to look at me. "It also means we don't need to know exactly what they were searching for. All we need to do is go through the list of delete requests Sabi's people ran in the system. Anything they were trying to hide will be right there in front of us."

"And we can do that?"

"We just look at the newest records in the database. Those requests should be right there at the top."

I felt my palms perspiring. *Finally!* A slight shudder shot up my spine as Gahlia swiveled back to the screen and punched in the commands.

"I'm sending the list to the screen in front of you," she said. I raised my head and one of the screens protruding from the wall woke to life and started displaying row after row of data, arranged in a table format.

My heart sank. There were hundreds, maybe *thousands* of lines running across the small screen, each of them corresponding to a different request for altering or removing data from the Archive. Anderson wasn't just trying to get rid of an inconvenient record or two. He was conducting a *massive* restructuring of the Thetis knowledge base.

"There's no way we can go through all of that," I said. "It will take us *weeks*."

"You're right," Gahlia said. She scrolled the endless list up and down the screen, then suggested, "let's start by cutting it down to the bare minimum. We don't know how far back this manipulation started, but we do know they picked up the pace when the Archive— actually, when *you* started digging into it, ne?"

I nodded. "It *was* an Archive inquiry at first, until Anderson asked to drop his complaint. Nyasha was happy to strike one case file off his list. Only after that record mysteriously disappeared, things started getting..."

"Weird, yes. OK, that's something — so whatever operation is going on, any serious attempts to cover it up began after that, so we can safely ignore all the commands predating it. And... there we go."

The list on the screen in front of me changed. The first line on the topmost position referred to the opening and closing of an extortion complaint initiated by Sebastian Anderson. Crypsigned and authorized by yours truly.

The rest of the list ran in sequence after that. It was still a few hundred records long, which was under no circumstances an amount we could divulge in the scope of time on our hands.

Gahlia fell silent, her long fingers tapping impatiently on the flat surface of the module bulkhead.

After a few seconds of pondering, she said, "maybe we can narrow the list down to several groups of data around specific areas. What do we know so far?"

"Well we certainly know that Dr. Almaz Bashiri started all of this, and that he probably had the closest understanding of what's going on. Otherwise he'd still be with us breathing Dusting smog."

Gahlia inhaled audibly and shook her head in dismay. "Every file related to Bashiri. Screen one — on your left."

A small screen woke to life and filled with several lines of data, all related to deletion and alteration requests of records crypsigned by Dr.

Bashiri.

"What else?" Gahlia pressed impatiently. "What about Sabi?"

I shrugged. "He said he tried to cover up a medical record concerning his wife. Didn't make a lot of sense to me, to be honest."

Gahlia's eyes almost popped out. "He *talked to you* about this?"

"Well, sort of. He came to visit me in the infirmary after the drift."

She threw her hands in the air in a dramatic show of frustration. "And you didn't think it was relevant information to share, you know, *before* we climbed down the ship's skeleton with our bare hands and traveled through this kunye radioactive level?"

"I'm sorry," I raised my hands in defense. "I just thought it was a *bafunye* red herring to deter me from investigating further. Paint it as being a minor, personal matter not worth my trouble."

"Well, we're certainly in the deepest trouble one could get into on the Thetis, Sandrine, so from now on — every detail matters, OK?"

Gahlia returned her hands over to the keyset and typed. "Medical records, screen number two. What else?"

The data flowed into the screen on the far right of the module. I glossed over the data lines quickly — indeed, Cassidi Anderson was mentioned in one of them, and so was their son Sam. The record titles mentioned some bacterial-related inflammation so that bit, at least, was true. There were additional records of patient names which I did not recognize.

Gahlia's voice echoed in the small space. "Think, Sandrine! This whole operation was not planned. It was a hasty reaction to your investigation and the potential public exposure it could bring with it. He must have made mistakes. For starters — why now?"

"What do you mean?" I asked.

"Why go through all of this now? What's different now that makes hiding *all of this* —" she gestured to the thousands of glowing lines on her small screen, "— so urgent?"

"The elections?" I tried.

Gahlia shook her head. "He would have won those elections in his sleep. Stirring up debate over his personal matters right now only hurts him."

"So maybe there's something he knew would pop up no matter what. Something he couldn't avoid unless he deliberately made it disappear."

"Something like what?" Gahlia pushed.

I gazed into the blackness of the screen in front of me for a few seconds, trying to refocus my thoughts. Then, something finally clicked at the back of my mind.

"The missing Final Call report!" I called.

Gahlia looked at me in question.

"We were in a terrible rush to complete the Archive Final Call report reviews of all the Thetis departments. The only report we never got, no matter how much we chased after it, was the PHS file. It almost seemed as if Cassidi was stalling with it. Maybe she hoped something will happen so she won't need to submit it for inspection."

"So Final Call related and anything from PHS, screen three. I can already see there are overlapping records between the three groups. Let's start with those, te?"

"Wait," I raised my hand. Something caught my eye on the screen she was working on. A very recent record which wasn't part of the groups Gahlia sent to the other screens. I pointed it out to her.

"Open that one up for a moment."

Gahlia clicked the keyset and the record opened up to fill the screen. I leaned closer so I could read it over her shoulder.

"That bastard," I mumbled. "He sure rushed to delete that one. But *why?*"

Gahlia didn't need me to explain what we were both looking at. It was the Trajectory and Propulsion research conducted after the drift the Thetis took when Bashiri went through the Trash Tube hatch. The one Anderson claimed was taking up all the QUBIC resources on the ship. The one he claimed called for an emergency directive on the Thetis, and the one he claimed concluded that there was no longer a viable option to reach Gnosis with the available fuel supply.

The one that gave him the excuse to call off the Final Call vote, thus rendering the Final Call report, and even the elections — irrelevant. After all, if there's no choice but to continue the journey toward 9 Ceti, then there's no point in the whole construct of auditing and publishing the entire data for the public, then electing the leader that will carry the Thetis to the chosen destination.

Sabi Anderson did not intend to win the elections in his sleep. He needed *all of us Thetans* to be asleep, hopeless and without any sense of control or choice, so he could direct the mission to his preferred destination.

But why? Why would it matter to him which planet the Thetis would orbit and Resett upon? He'll be long dead by then.

"The old engineers at the Astral were right," Gahlia said quietly, "took them five minutes to figure out this was bafunye. That we could still go either way and there's no way such heavy QUBIC resources would be needed to redo the traj plan."

I gazed at the simple, indisputable scientific conclusion displayed in glowing bluish letters on the small screen. I almost couldn't believe my eyes.

"This is the biggest, most horrible fat lie in the history of the Thetis," I whispered.

"This is the biggest, most horrible fat lie in the history of the Thetis — yet," she corrected me. "We've only just started digging."

A wave of defeat overcame me. I looked at Gahlia, my eyes tearing up with frustration.

"He's a mastermind. He buried this quickly, then masked it in a wall of noise," I said. "Made *me* the enemy. Made the Eternists the enemy. Made Bashiri an Anti-Thetan traitor. Now, people will just say thank you for some peace and quiet. Who even cares about planets and votes and Thetan-rights at this point, te?"

"He's not a mastermind, Sandrine," Gahlia shook her head, "unfortunately, he is something much more dangerous. Sebastian Anderson is the perfect opportunist. He can't foresee and plan ten moves in advance, but he seizes and reshapes an opportunity faster than anyone can blink, molding it into his narrative like it was always there. That's why some people think he's God almighty. Their Savior."

"So what's the point? Maybe he's the smartest man on the Thetis. Maybe he's just the one who wants it the most. Either way, we can't win."

Gahlia turned to me and, to my surprise, her eyes were soft and calm. She managed a weary smile.

"I was once your age, you know. So I get it — the younger you are, the faster you expect a resolution to any problem. You jump in the ring for a fight — you try to win it in the first round. You start an investigation, you expect results by the next day. Your mind is simply color-blind to longer-term processes. You'll see for yourself when you'll have children of your own. They can go through several problem-resolution cycles in a *minute*."

"Thanks for saying 'when'. It's mostly been 'if' from people recently," I said, hopefully without too much bitterness in my voice. "So what am I missing here, Dr. Roskov? Where's my blind spot?"

"Anderson didn't anticipate the drift, right? He couldn't have. So what you call the biggest lie in Thetis history — the attempt to use the current situation to push 9 Ceti as the only viable destination for the Thetis — that was not part of his plan. He's improvising now. And by the looks of all the chaos that's happening on the ship right now — he's in panic."

I nodded. "And people in panic make mistakes."

CHAPTER FORTY-FIVE

"So you have to ask yourself," Gahlia mumbled, typing on the keyset to send more data files to the screens around us, "why would someone who's clearly playing the long game feel suddenly threatened enough to throw all caution to the Tube and start covering everything up in such a sloppy manner."

I scanned the groups of records running across the screens. Something sat at the edge of my memory. Something that clearly didn't fit the picture.

"Remember what Hugo Winkler told us," I began, "he said that Cassidi and Sabi had been working for *years* to first get her to the PHS helm, then gradually appropriate more and more assets and departments under her wing."

Gahlia nodded. "I always assumed it was just her megalomaniac nature, needing to control everything she could get her hands on."

I waved my hand in dismissal. I was getting onto something here. "That's because you only got Hugo's depiction of the story."

"But now we know that taking over those departments was all about gaining majority control over the QUBIC nodes."

"Yes, but — everything has been proceeding according to their plan for years. Why start such a risky cover-up project now? I mean, the choice of 9 Ceti Gamma had always been the obvious choice.

GENERATIONS

There's no reason to think people would opt for the alternative of Gnosis Zeta, especially since it requires spending two extra generations in space. So why rock the boat when everything points to the success of their plan? That only makes sense if the cover-up was just a contingency plan. An emergency measure, in case something unexpected happens."

Gahlia considered this for a few moments. The screens covering the module's four walls were silently blinking in patient anticipation of any further commands. The hundreds of lines of data records were still there, ominously glowing at us like a multi dimensional logic puzzle.

Where is QUBIC's predictive search interface when you need it, I thought.

Gahlia turned from the main screen to face me in the small module. "So the fact that Sabi needed to improvise with the drift and the sudden data purge and the fake trajectory research, this proves that the original plan, the one he was working on all those years — that plan was about to be exposed. Something happened, and he needed to revert to the risky Plan B. OK, so," she tilted her head in tentative acceptance, "what happened?"

I pointed to the screen on my left. "Dr. Almaz Bashiri happened. There wasn't a single deletion request for any data records prior to him coming to Anderson with his information. Which Sabi then tried to label as an extortion attempt."

"And which, as we all know, resulted in Bashiri catching a ride down the Tube," Gahlia said in a humorless, grim voice.

She turned back to the terminal and began punching keystroke sequences into the machine. "Very well, let's see what you've got, *herr Doctor.*"

The raw lines of data on the left screen started shifting and reordering with every command Gahlia executed in the system. Dozens upon dozens of records scrolled briefly across the screen, then disappeared as new incoming data replaced them.

Gahlia shook her head in dissatisfaction. "They are trying to be quite thorough. There are deletion requests for most of the research

369

Bashiri was involved with. Care to direct me to where we should focus?"

I shrugged. "The only thing I can say is that when Bashiri met me at the Sensory Farm on 8th, he was totally frightened. We were followed by Secundus Pakk and his goons, and still Bashiri insisted on showing me the radiation-activated genetic mechanism he built for the Farm. In hindsight, that was a weird thing to do, wouldn't you say?"

"Not necessarily. In times of haste, people tend to cut to the chase. Did he explain how his invention worked?"

I tried to stretch my recollection. *By Sol, this feels like it happened years ago*, I thought. Blurry details from my encounter with the late doctor started to emerge.

"He said it was some kind of... bacteria? Genetically modified to react to a certain type of radiation, which he could activate from the GenLab in the Farm. The bastard eliminated the cutest furry bunny to make the point," I shuddered at the resurfacing mental image, "may his soul loop in peace, of course."

"That's interesting," Gahlia commented. "There's a lot of research in here regarding bacteria. Actually, there's some intriguing overlap between files marked as part of Bashiri's research, and other projects conducted in the PHS. Cassidi's crypsigned on most of those herself."

She continued moving data lines around and cross-comparing them — Bashiri's documents on one screen, Cassidi's documents on another. "Wow, they've sent for deletion a *lot* of work on this subject, something like twenty years worth of experiment data. This isn't a pinpoint strike, it's carpet bombing!"

Her eyes reflected the dim phosphorus glow of the various screens surrounding us. She was sitting straight with all her muscles tense — the extreme fatigue she was feeling from the radiation exposure was all but gone. She was on a *roll*.

"You'd have made a fine Head of Archive," I said.

Gahlia flicked an eye toward me for a split second, then returned her attention to the screen. "Ha. No way. Too much politicking. One advantage of having completed my Contribution years is that I get to spend my time on whatever piques my interest, with nobody controlling my time or priorities."

"Still," I replied, "I'd say — at seventy six years old, you're sharp as a liquid-diamond blade."

She let out the slightest sigh. "That blade is getting blunter by the day, sadly. It's not the age so much, I suspect — it's that retirement carries a mean punch of obsolescence. Of… irrelevance," her tone brightened, "and look now what I've found here."

Gahlia swiveled slightly to the right and pointed a finger at another screen hung near the top of the bulkhead wall. A single line of data blinked to life on the top row.

As she opened her mouth to speak, a loud, blunt thud startled us both. Gahlia jerked up from the terminal, and I instinctively grasped her shoulder in a protective gesture.

A few seconds later, Armitage's head appeared in the upward slope of the connecting sleeve to the Russian part of the station. I crossed looks with Gahlia and our hearts sank back into place.

"Don't sneak on us like that," Gahlia scolded him as he squeezed through the cramped module, "we didn't even hear you coming."

"Sorry," Armitage said. His limp was in a pretty bad shape and he was visibly clenching his jaws in pain. "I saw Bianca safely back to her hab. This level is one hell of a labyrinth! I left marks on the way so we'll be able to get out of here without her help."

"To be honest, you don't look like someone who could walk ten feet, Arm," Gahlia said in a softer voice and led Armitage to the improvised bench she was using to operate the old terminal.

"Speak for yourself," he groaned in a pained smile. "But we really should wrap this up. There are people searching the level. More than one party, too. And they don't sound very friendly, to be honest."

I exchanged worried looks with Gahlia.

Armitage groaned again and stretched his bad leg. "So — tell me something encouraging. What are we looking at here?"

He raised his chin to gesture at all the data-filled screens covering the module walls.

"We're still not completely sure," Gahlia admitted, "but I think we have an interesting direction. Remember — all we have is the list of data records Anderson is trying to delete from the Thetis Archive, so this is trying to construct a picture from what's *gone* rather than what's actually *there*."

"Sounds suspiciously like my first marriage. OK, so what's so important to hide?"

Gahlia leaned by his side and pointed at the screens to our left. "We currently have two major groups of seemingly-unrelated records. We need to figure out how and why they're connected. On the first group," she moved her finger to point at the two lower screens, "they are trying to delete a *huge* pile of research data, dating as far back as twenty years. It started with initial research conducted by Almaz Bashiri regarding the control method he developed in the Sensory Farm GenLab. Tons of experiments on molecules, CellPrinted material, and eventually wholly printed organisms—"

"A method controlling what?" Armitage interrupted.

"Basically, controlling the organism population in the Sensory Farm. Quite a clever device, really — Bashiri developed a genetic marker which, when activated, creates a reaction that results in instant neurological death."

Armitage whistled in silent appreciation. "A *killer gene*. Scary stuff. And does it actually work?"

"Sandrine witnessed its operation firsthand."

"Bashiri activated it on a live bunny in front of my eyes" I said. "It was dead within five seconds."

Armitage frowned and leaned forward, eying me with serious eyes. "How is this gene activated exactly?"

"He said it's radiation-sensitive. So it activates when exposed to a very specific wavelength. He used a custom rad emitter to beam the poor creature."

"It's all in here," Gahlia scrolled through the hundreds of data records on her screen, "years of test data using various types of radiation to calibrate the gene. The interesting bit is that at some point, we see a near-identical research — essentially a fork of Bashiri's work — emerge on the PHS record archive. *Almost* identical, because while Bashiri created a gene that activates on the very low Infra Red wavelengths — the kind that doesn't harm organisms and doesn't exist in the ambient Thetis lighting schemes — the PHS experiments show various attempts to create a similar version which reacts to higher wavelengths, even up to visible light."

Armitage moved in his seat uncomfortably. "That sounds unsafe, won't you say?"

I immediately felt the urge to step up to Bashiri's defense. "Bashiri said exactly that. He thought they were taking his research in a dangerous direction and he wanted it stopped. He flat out refused to go along with it."
"So they just copied his work and carried on by themselves," Gahlia muttered.

"We don't know that for sure," I said, "but this could be the reason he approached Sabi Anderson in the first place. Which then Anderson tried to label as an extortion attempt. We just don't know."

"OK," Armitage nodded, "so what's the second group of data?"

Gahlia gestured toward the top screen. "Well, it's actually a group of one."

She clicked and the data record opened in full on the screen. "The emergency trajectory analysis conducted after the drift. You were right, Arm — both destination planets are still within an easy correction maneuver."

Armitage raised a confused brow. "I knew all this 'single planet option' fuss was bafunye." He covered his mouth with his big palm and scratched his chin repeatedly. "Ahh, that makes me so mad. This is such an insult. OK. But what does that have to do with the other stuff? Why hide it from the public and go on that all-out effort to push the 'single planet option' narrative? Then go and bury the entire scientific proof that the Thetis — that Humanity! — still has other valid Resett options? No, this is high-risk, high-stakes play. This is *important* to him!"

"I agree," I said, "he was sweating for it to stick. Maybe he really believes we have only but one fate — and that's 9 Ceti Gamma."

Armitage sneered. "I'm an engineer, Liet. We exist on a very simplistic value-set. Very few complications in how we see the world. My mentor was a Tercero — 3rd Generation. Wonderful man. He had a saying: 'Fate is just your default factory setting'. So unless Anderson *needs* 9 Ceti to be our only fate — and then he should openly explain *why* this is the case — we still should have our say about it, *as the Passados intended.*"

I raised my hands in frustration. "The Passados, the *Passados!* Every time there's a new idea, every time someone *tries* to do something a bit differently than how things always worked around here, it's always the same story — the kunye *Passados* had their little plan *all* worked out! So if the *Passados* were so smart, and they could foresee two centuries of space travel complications and cultural shifts and social evolution and *every* kunye thing we do doesn't even matter — why did they even bother sending actual people down this miserable journey? People only mess things up. Why not just send some genetic code and a spaceload of CellPrinters and create all the humans we'll ever need when reaching the planet?"

Gahlia nudged her finger upward slightly, pointing at the screen above our heads. Her eyes were torn wide.

"Well, according to this, this is exactly what they did."

CHAPTER FORTY-SIX

Gahlia could see both our faces frozen in shock, so she continued. "That's why this record struck me as different from all the others. It's not something created on the Thetis. It's part of the pre-Embarkment data layer that was planned to unlock just before Resett. Normally we shouldn't even have access to it at this point in time, but since there was an attempt to delete it — the cypher lock had to be decrypted, so we are looking at the actual raw data. A glimpse into the future, you might say."

"No wonder they needed all that QUBIC power working on those modifications," Armitage muttered. "Records that old, that's some computational heavy lifting. Not anyway near that trajectory correction report kids' calc."

"What's in there?" I asked hurriedly. My heart was racing, equal parts excited and terrified of Gahlia's reply.

Gahlia was frantically scrolling through the huge data record, her eyes scanning the tremendous volume of text, charts, scientific formulae and large sequences of what looked like genetic code — pages and pages of highly detailed blueprints, the nature of which I had no clue.

"Well," Gahlia finally hummed, still scanning back and forth on her screen, "have any of you ever heard of the term The Probe

Generation?"

I looked at Armitage, then we both shook our heads slowly.

"Didn't think so. So according to *this*, the Thetis plan itself has a Plan B."

"We know that," I said, "that's Gnosis Zeta. There's also a list of ten additional destinations in case those two planets don't work out for Resett."

"No," Gahlia raised her palm to interrupt. "Not for planets. A plan B for *us*."

"What are you talking about?!" Armitage demanded. Gahlia raised her other hand in a gesture of defense.

"Here, see for yourself," she laid her hands back on the keyset and pushed a few keystrokes. The data record flicked open on the two screens in front of us.

"The protocol goal definition is stated very clearly in the first paragraph," Gahlia read from her screen, "'to ensure species continuity upon Planetary Resettlement in case of en-route mass biological extinction event or insufficient genetic diversity at Disembarkment.'"

"Mass biological extinction event..." I mumbled as I re-read the lines flickering on the screen.

"That means if we all dropped dead at some point along the way," Armitage explained.

"Yeah, thanks Arm, I kind of got that," I frowned at him, "what's insufficient genetic diversity though?"

Gahlia rubbed her eyes with her slim fingers. Even through the adrenaline rush and the focus required, she was noticeably weakening again. "There could be a host of reasons resulting in diminished fertility rates as the generations on the Thetis progressed. If we had failed to reach the birth rate quotas of the plan, the diversity of the collective gene pool will not have been sufficient to ensure the further evolvement of a healthy society on the new planet."

I slanted my head, unconvinced. Something didn't quite sound right about this. "But, if I remember correctly, the number of distinct genetic profiles needed to ensure the development of a diverse society isn't that high, ne? Something around... a hundred? After the upcoming Birth Year there will be over fifty thousand Thetans onboard. We're *way* past that danger by now."

"That mechanism is merely a safety measure," Gahlia said. "And you were close — there are one hundred and eighty distinct Human genetic codes in this plan here, ready to be sent to the CellPrinters if the protocol is ever activated. You could start a whole new Human race from those Probers."

"Why are they called Probers?" I asked. "And why would Anderson try to delete this plan from the Archive? It's never going to be used anyhow. We've made it intact so far."

"To your first question — once the protocol activates and the organisms are created from the enclosed genetic code, they are planned to be sent to the planet surface in a separate probe, and become the first Resettlers in the new world. Says here that the Probers will spend a minimum of a full generation on the ground before any Thetans arrive for planetfall. To your second question —"

Gahlia fell silent for a few moments and punched something into her terminal keyset. The data screens in front of us blinked out of the open record and back to the raw ledger search screen.

"— Anderson didn't try to delete this data from the Archive. He tried to modify the genetic code profiles included in it. Here, look for yourselves."

The screen was split vertically, each part filling up with the familiar and distinct coding syntax of genetic data. Both sides looked identical as they scrolled for a few seconds side by side, and then abruptly stopped as some lettering were marked in red letters, highlighting the found difference between the two versions.

"Left side is the original data. On the right are the modification requests in red."

"I can see that," I nodded. "Can't make any intelligent sense of it, though. Maybe Bashiri could have understood what that means."

"Of course he did," Gahlia said. "It's his code."

I turned my head away from the screen and caught Gahlia's eyes. She was serious.

Armitage grunted angrily, "What do you mean it's his code? So the Doctor worked *for* Sabi to create this mess?"

"Not exactly," Gahlia said. "This is why this record even surfaced in our narrowed-down list. The modification request includes inserting the exact same genetic code that appears in the PHS research records, which in itself is *almost* the exact genetic code created by Bashiri when he invented the switch-gene for the Sensory Farm."

"Except for the trigger radiation frequency," I mumbled. "He told me this was the core of the fight he had with Cassidi and her copying of his work. PHS wanted a different trigger radiation. So the PHS gene is the one they are trying to inject into the Prober code?"

Gahlia nodded. "Seems so."

"But... *why?*" I asked. I was truly dumbfounded by this whole puzzle. "What's the point in introducing such a life-threatening genetic disability to what could be the last hope for Humanity's survival? That will only make the Probers so vulnerable! They could just simply *die* from getting randomly exposed to that radiation frequency."

"No, this is genius," Armitage whispered in an appreciative tone. He turned to us, his eyes glittering. "See? I *told* you Sebastian Anderson was a once-in-a-generation leader. All of that was not about some malicious intention! All those years of work, all the sacrifices his wife made in the PHS, it was all for our *protection!*"

"Arm," Gahlia looked up at him, "what on the Thetis are you blabbering about?"

"Ha!" Armitage continued to revel in his conviction, "I knew I should have come here with you lot. By Sol! You could have put yourself in such jeopardy! To be honest, Liet — it was you who eventually got it right."

"Got *what* right, Armitage? I don't understand anything in this kunye mess!" I almost whimpered.

Armitage laid his big, bulky hand on my shoulder in a gentle gesture of calm. "Oh, but you do, Liet. You do! You said it — there was a contingency plan to spawn those artificially manufactured humans in case everything went bananas, te? Kind of a 'cast your seeds to the wind and hope for the best' last resort sort of thing."

I couldn't help chuckling. "You're such an oldie, Armitage. Love the Old Earth metaphors."

"But see," he continued enthusiastically, "we don't need it anymore, right? We've made it intact! No mass extinction event. No degraded diversity issues on the ship. We're fine, ready to Resett. So — at this point, the Prober protocol will only create complications if activated, right? So theoretically, it would be best to just delete the whole thing as if it never existed. No taking chances for any accidental activation of the protocol, or any triggered activation planted within the program which we don't know about. But!"

Armitage folded his arms across his chest and raised a finger for exclamation. He was loving this moment.

"But, of course — we're not quite there yet. We still have two generations before we reach stable orbit around 9 Ceti Gamma. We then have at least ten years of research and exploration before actually reaching final planetfall. So there are still unknowns. Accidents can happen, and we may still need the Prober Generation to salvage the mission. So a wise leader does not eliminate his contingency options. A wise leader makes sure to implement *controls* over his options in case he needs them."

Gahlia leaned back in her seat. She was silent, only her eyes running relentlessly between the glowing screens, taking in the data. I could literally feel her mind calculating, assessing.

"So what you are saying," she started slowly, as if summarizing the conclusion to herself, "is that this whole QUBIC data restructuring was intended to implement—"

"—the *same exact thing* that was developed for the Sensory Farm," Armitage completed. "A kill switch. A trigger, in case anything got out

379

of control and we had to undo the protocol for some reason!"

"'Undo the protocol'," I said. "That's a rather neutral phrasing for wiping out an entire Human generation."

"It's a safety measure! Don't be naive, Liet. You know the Code better than anyone here. We are the absolute last Humans in the entire Universe. We are on a survival mission for our entire *species* — we don't play with genengineering *people*, do we? The whole reason this was a last resort protocol is that it's a kunye dangerous game to play. Not to even speak of the moral concerns here, about which I'm not going to enter into a discussion with you right now."

Gahlia gave Armitage a stern look. "Why the secrecy, then?" She gestured to the small ISS module walls around us, all covered with screens displaying the data records we pulled from the local terminal node. "Years of planning, concealed scientific research, selling bafunye to the public — why is that necessary? If the only thing he has on his mind is public interest — why go to such lengths to hide it? That's not a very politician-y thing to be doing, ne?"

Armitage threw both hands in the air in frustration. "So we don't like the style, OK! To be honest, I don't like it either! But this man — this man is the Thetis *Primo!*" He extended a thick finger and pointed in my direction. "His wife — a *genius*, building the Thetis Public Health Service with her bare hands for years! I'm just a retired piping engineer, who am I to understand the intricacies of running the Thetis? Maybe he didn't want people to panic. Maybe he was afraid some Adapters will get funny ideas. Who knows?"

I squirmed at the obvious referral to Kilian and, by some unfathomable extension, me.

His voice softened and he lowered his hands in a calming gesture. "The fact is that we *appointed* those people to take care of us, to put our collective interests before their own. And we are — literally! — all on the same ship here, ne? What can the Andersons *possibly* be doing that will not affect them just as everyone else?"

Gahlia tapped her fingers impatiently on the plastic base of the keyset in front of her. "How did he even know about this Prober thing, or — whatever, the plan B? The protocol?"

We both looked at her in question.

"Wasn't it supposed to be locked inside the Archive until a certain time or event triggered its release to the public-access QUBIC?" She asked.

"Oh, that's actually easy to answer," I said. "Remember how Kilian and I unlocked the whole library of longvids and teleshows from the locked layer?"

Both Gahlia and Armitage looked at me numbly.

"We had this art installation going? Alternative History Night?" I tried, then waved my hand in dismissal. "OK forget it. The point is, the decryption of those locked layers is possible by access permission credentials of the Head Archivist. I guess that in certain circumstances, the Code allows for investigation into future phases of the Program and the data attached to it."

"So," Armitage hissed, "you're saying Nyasha Woo knew about this all along? Knowing you were going to risk your future, maybe your *life* in this futile pursuit — and didn't stop you?" He shrugged in disbelief. "I thought the two of you were close."

"We were. We *are*," I said unconvincingly. Nyasha was always a stickler for proper conduct when it came to classified information. But Armitage had a point there — this did seem quite extreme considering the circumstance.

This can't be, I thought. *Nyasha isn't an actor. When he and Athena appeared in my hab the other night, he was genuinely concerned. He wouldn't lie to me like that.*

"Unless," Gahlia broke my thought loop, "this discovery predates Nyasha. If this starts way back earlier, before he was even nominated as Head Archivist."

"In this case," I nodded in amazement, "the head archivist before him —"

"— was Benjamin Anderson," Gahlia completed the sentence.

"OK, hold your Ascenders," I raised both hands in the air. "This line of defense is getting shakier by the minute. Nyasha replaced Sabi Anderson's father as Head Archivist over fifteen years ago. So he and his son — now the Primo of the Thetis — sit on this Prober information for fifteen years to, what, suddenly panic about it now and take over the core kunye data system of the entire ship to erase it from existence?"

Armitage's voice hardened. "This is not a 'line of defense' and the Primo is not on trial here, Archivist Liet. In fact, with all the digging that we've done here — and I don't claim to understand every little detail of what all those genetic research papers are — I haven't seen a shred of incriminating evidence that Anderson or his family have done something to break the Code!"

"So why are they chasing us?" Gahlia said softly. She raised a finger in a minimalist gesture indicating the world outside the ISS.

Armitage bent forward and caught both of Gahlia's arms gently between his large palms. "Maybe they're not, Gahlia!" He whispered. "Maybe it's just us being paranoid. Bianca lives on this level for *years*, and she never told me about any suspicious visitors or activity around here."

I sneered in disbelief. "Except Kilian and Dr. Bashiri. *They* were both here. And now, one of them is dead and the other got a visit from the goon squad. Very reassuring."

"OK fine, youngGen," Armitage backed off from Gahlia and looked at me, "so let's try *your* story on for size, te? Let's see — our friend Bashiri invents some clever gene to help contain the Sensory Farm organism ecosystem. It's a dangerous tool, this gene — can kill any organism with a spit of the right light, te? Then, he claims that the Primo's wife snatched his invention and started modifying it against his wishes."

You condescending bastard. "That's *Doctor* Almaz Bashiri, if you don't mind," I muttered through my teeth. "And these aren't just claims. The PHS *did* secretly modify his work. We have evidence of that now," I gestured toward the screens around us, "*which they tried to erase!"*

Armitage raised his palm to pause me and continued, "So this Doctor — eventually, he got pulled off the project entirely, then went on to take his own life. Looped himself, out of professional despair. That pretty much it so far?"

"No way," I said. "There's no kunye way Almaz took his own life."

"Oh, so now we're adding murder into the story. *Murder!* An act which hadn't happened on the Thetis for almost two centuries. A concept so alien to our society that the word itself doesn't even exist anymore in formal dictionaries. And who supposedly committed this horrible, unheard-of, anti-Thetan crime? No other than the Thetis Primo himself!"

I stared at him in silence. If he was trying to make me feel crazy and stupid — well, it was working quite well.

"And why, by Sol and its carouseling planets, *why* should we assume that the most powerful person on the whole ship — the leader of Humanity, no less, would go into all of this — messing around with dangerous genetics. Hiding facts from the public. Fabricating an emergency situation. Cancelling Final Call. Trying to erase Archive records — if not out of responsibility to us Thetans? To make sure we're safe and that no dangerous tool gets into the wrong people's hands? Why would we suspect otherwise, Liet? Give us *one* reason."

"Because..." I mumbled.

"One reason to suspect malicious intent here," Armitage pressed.

My mind was racing. Something was gnawing at the edge of my consciousness. Something Sabi said. Something that didn't make sense at all.

"Because..." I heard myself repeat.

Armitage nodded in anticipation. I wanted to punch his smug face, but even at his age, that would surely send me right back to the...

Infirmary.

Anderson sitting on the edge of my bed. Same smug face. He thinks he got me on his side. The face of a man who always wins, even if it means he will change the rules on you mid-game.

"Because he has the cure," I said, gasping.

Armitage eyed me in question. Gahlia was already clicking on her keyset.

"Right?" I jumped to her side and scanned the rows of text scrolling on her small terminal screen. "He literally told me as much. When he visited me in the infirmary. He said they needed to find a cure, for his son. That *must* be it!"

"Well, sort of a cure," Gahlia punched a key and a data record shot up to the screen in front of us. "It's a temporary inhibitor. Says here it prevents the loss of conductivity in the Myelin sheath of the subject Axons and—"

"— yes, yes, I got the technical speech from Bashiri already, which was enough to crush my self-confidence, thank you very much. So basically, if you take this… inhibitor, then the radiation which was supposed to kick off the 'brain-dead-within-5-seconds' bit won't actually kill you? You'd be protected even if exposed to the exact type of electromagnetic frequency the gene was programmed for?"

Gahlia ran her eyes down the excerpt of the data file and nodded ambivalently. "Supposedly, yes. But the effectiveness decays quite quickly, it seems."

"How long would this protect you for?"

"It would inhibit the fatal neurochemical triggering for twenty four to thirty six hours," Gahlia turned her head to us in question.

"So it's not a cure. It's a drug," I said.

Gahlia nodded. "A subject carrying this gene with consistent exposure to the trigger radiation would have to be treated daily."

We fell quiet for a few long seconds, trying to process that new information.

"How come this record didn't come up in the list of PHS files we pulled up earlier?" I asked.

"Because they didn't try to delete this file from the Archive," Gahlia said. She pointed at the screen displaying the long list of modification requests.

The records all had similar data fields which included details such as their creation date, the Thetis department where each record originated, the QUBIC node which initially inserted the file, and the current modification request type. Almost all the records displayed 'Purge' as the modification request type. But the one Gahlia was pointing out had a different request type, marked as 'Access Permission Change'.

"According to this," Gahlia continued, "it was meant to remain in the system, but accessible only to specific CrypIDs rather than the general public."

"So they keep the data for the cure, but it's locked up," I said.

"Or protected, rather," Armitage added. "You could argue both ways."

"I love how optimist you manage to remain against all counter evidence," I said, trying not to sound too sarcastic.

Armitage shrugged. "I'm an engineer. We're always optimists. Don't you know that? You Archivists are the pessimist bunch."

"Why's that?"

"You just have too much knowledge, I guess. Of Human history, of everything that's ever went wrong. Legal Code. Depressing stuff. *We* simply assume we know nothing at all. We *discover*."

"That's adorable," Gahlia muttered flatly, "so do you want to know who is supposed to have access to the kill-gene inhibitor?"

"Let me guess," I said, "the access permission will be reserved to the Thetis Primo."

"Close," Gahlia nodded, "but not just any Primo. According to this request, the access will be reserved to Sebastian Anderson specifically, and to one other person."

"The Secundus?" Armitage tried.

"I say it's Cassidi," I said.

"Neither," Gahlia shook her head. "The other CrypID listed belongs to Sabi's son, Sam."

"Zee?!" I had to make sure I heard correctly. Kunye Zee holds access to the cure for the most deadly substance on the Thetis? *Who in his right mind would give Zee a key to anything more important than the kiddy's toilets?* Honestly, I didn't think even his own father trusted him enough for anything of that magnitude.

Armitage frowned. "That *is* unusual. Public transparency is a core aspect of the way things work around here. In my time we didn't have classes or preferred individuals, right Gahl?"

"I don't think it's about the Thetis at all," Gahlia whispered. Her face grew pale and she turned worrying eyes to us. "I'm afraid this is something much more sinister, Arm. Something that's planned for *after* the Thetis."

"But how, Gahlia?" Armitage resisted, "I mean — there's this risky gene invention, but there's the cure, ne? It's all under control, isn't it?"

Gahlia was very quiet. Her hands dropped from the terminal keyset to her lap and she turned around and scanned the screens surrounding us on the ISS module walls.

"Control is the key factor here," she said. "You have this innocent development meant for better risk-control." Gahlia pointed at the first screen, displaying the data records of Bashiri's original research.

"Then it gets modified, mounted on a carrier bacteria —" she pointed at the second screen listing the PHS data files, "— generalized, adapted. They develop an inhibitor to control it, but the access to it is then restricted only to the Anderson bloodline. This is almost as if someone was planning on developing —"

"— a weapon!" I heard myself shout, and I instinctively recoiled as my voice exploded in the small space of the module. "This is the word Bashiri used! I thought he was just mumbling paranoid bafunye, I mean — who would even *think* in such terms, te? But what else would you call it? A lethal device, an *engineered gene* which can kill you at the click of a rad emitter, and the inhibitor of which is held by very specific people who could give it to you."

"Or deny it," Gahlia added quietly, sinking her face into her palms, elbows resting on her knees.

"What?!" Armitage burst out, "to what purpose? Tell me! To what purpose would any normal Human being spend *decades* in developing something like this? This is preposterous! The Thetis Primo, going around pointing rad emitters at people? For *what kunye purpose*? What does anyone here possibly have that he needs so badly, for Sol's sake?"

His booming voice died down in the small, cramped module air. I looked at Gahlia. She shook her head slowly, rubbing her reddened face. I lowered my head in defeat.

"I don't know," I whispered. "And this scares the mala out of me."

Gahlia's eyes raised slowly to meet Armitage's. They both nodded in silence. Suddenly, a familiar voice shrieked behind us.

"Be carrreful!"

Armitage threw his head back at the direction of the voice and yelled, "Bianca!"

Two things then followed in quick succession: The power to the ISS was cut off, and a blinding flare exploded inside the module.

CHAPTER FORTY-SEVEN

I screamed.

"Stay back!" Armitage ran down the slope connecting our module with the entrance opening. Beyond the pile of bags blocking most of the way, Bianca's voice howled, then cut abruptly. Moving beams of light penetrated into the ISS, bouncing off the inner bulkhead walls.

After the initial blinding flash of the flare, the module was left in complete darkness. I jumped back, expecting to feel a solid wall at my back, only to bump directly into Gahlia. We both collapsed against the wall of screens, trying to regain our balance.

"What happened to the light?" I cried in her general direction.

Gahlia grunted and began pushing herself up. "They cut us down. So much for Armitage's theory, te? Here, take this!" She found my hand in the dark and I felt a small, cool, rectangular object pushed into my palm. A data chip. A loud, ear-splitting drilling noise cut through he air.

"What's on it?" I shouted over the loud noise.

"Anything I could manage to back up before the power went out!"

"Smart move!"

"We'll see," she replied and I could feel her hand on my shoulder, clasping for support. "It's also evidence against us, so be careful."

A speck of light appeared and started growing at the corner of my eye. I could barely make out the shape of the module. Several black rectangles marked the dead, useless screens, the data on them gone. The light kept jittering and flicking and creating weird, alien shadows all over the module. My eyes started adjusting to the low light and I tried to make out its source.

Then it hit me. *Mala Dio.*

"Fire!" I screamed and pushed Gahlia further into the back end of the module. "Armitage! Fire!"

I squinted hard, trying to locate him beyond the growing flames, but all I could make out was the empty descending slope into the U.S area. Beyond it was blackness, randomly pierced by strobes of white light coming from the other side of the storage bag heap.

I could still hear Bianca screaming. *Did she lead them straight to us? Or did they force her to to do it?* It didn't matter now. Loud, aggressive voices and commands were shouted over the drilling sounds. I could hear Armitage roaring, calling for Bianca.

Then there were fighting noises.

My mind was fixated on the fire, now completely blocking us from the way back to the station entrance. We were caged in.

How was this even possible? The thought kept repeating inside my head. *It's all supposed to be inflammable materials. Space-grade inflammable materials.* I couldn't think of anything else. The fire kept growing. It was starting to get hard to breathe.

Suddenly, Armitage appeared beyond the fire barrier, crawling on his knees up the connector slope. He was panting heavily.

"Quest!" he shouted at both of us. "Find the quest!"

"What?" I shouted back and shot an alarmed look at Gahlia. *What the hell is he talking about?* "We're trapped in here, Arm! Help us out!"

"No, stay back! They're armed!" he growled in pain, trying to stand up.

I gasped. Glistening in the low light of the fire, his entire leg was wet with dark, red blood.

"You're hurt!" I cried.

His face contracted in pain as he straightened up. "It was my bad leg anyhow," he gave a contorted smile and started turning back, then stopped and pointed at us.

"It's your only option! On the floor — *find the quest!*"

Armitage disappeared down the narrow corridor. A second later, a deafening sound blasted through the station, shaking the module and throwing both me and Gahlia to the floor. It was the sound of major destruction: glass shattering, metal deforming — something was tearing the station apart and grinding its construction.

We looked at each other in fear. The shouting voices grew louder now. They seemed to come from within the ISS. *What do we do now?*

Gahlia shook back into focus first. "What's the quest? Hurry! Look around us!"

We struggled to our knees. Around us, the smoke grew thicker, making it hard to see. The flames started licking the edges of the terminal screens, melting their corners into droplets of black, scorching plastic.

Above the main QUBIC terminal keyset, the burning, crippled picture of a young girl dropped to the floor. Slowly but steadily, I watched the black jagged burn line advance across the once-blue sky, the green treeline, and finally — the bright, childish smile and sparkling blue eyes. The blissful moment was consumed to ashes, and the girl's two-hundred-year journey was over.

The crumbling, burnt paper lay on the ground, and next to it — a series of blue-colored arrows, etched into the flooring material. Two arrows pointed straight ahead and were labeled 'Destiny' and 'Unity'. Another pointed to the back of the station, toward a round opening that was not blocked by the fire.

It was labeled 'Quest'.

I shot a look at Gahlia. She saw it too. "Orientation signs! Good call, Arm — let's go!"

We bolted toward the round connector behind us. We both managed to squeeze through the narrow passage and entered a tiny, cramped adapter ring connecting to two other modules.

We both looked frantically around, below and above us, trying to locate the labeled blue arrow that would reveal which was the right direction to proceed. We found it on the wall to our right, etched into the bulkhead. An arrow labeled 'Quest' pointed to the module on our left.

Another loud noise startled us. I turned my head back, but Gahlia pushed me toward the Quest module with all her strength.

"Move it, Sandrine!" she shouted. Her face was pale as the white bulkhead behind her. She had used all her energy helping us get this far. I knew she wouldn't be able to carry on much further. So I moved it.

And it was a kunye dead end.

The Quest module was shaped like a tiny, cylindrical chamber which could barely fit the two of us, and had a single enclave protruding outward from the main body of the module. The enclave was crammed with a mess of seemingly random items — from storage bags to suit gloves, boots and a variety of working tools.

What are we supposed to do now? I started panicking. Why did Armitage send us here? *Were we supposed to hide in this place?*

That was a ridiculous thought. There was no place to hide within the ISS. The station was small and had only one exit — the one we came in through, and which was now well covered by Sabi's goons. And they had made their intentions clear by trying to set us on fire and violently break into the ISS.

There has to be another way out. Armitage wouldn't send us here otherwise.

Gahlia started frantically clearing the items clogging the round, protruding enclave. I looked at her in question.

"Get in," she said flatly.

"In?" I repeated, baffled. *'In' where?*

Oh.

"No way!" I pushed her away from me, and pushed back as hard as I could against the wall. I shook my head violently, fear shooting up my spine and my entire body shaking uncontrollably.

Gahlia's face hardened. She stepped closer to me and grabbed me by the suit collar ring. "Get in!"

She pulled me toward her, our faces nearly touching. Her eyes flared. "Bashiri is dead. Bianca and Armitage too, most likely. I will probably not see the end of this, Sandrine. But you will! This is serious now. You were right all along, and only you can figure out how to stop Anderson."

She tightened her grip. "For my genline. For *all* our genlines. Get into the hatch!"

Tears began running down my cheeks. "I'm afraid," I managed a whimper. "Come with me. Please."

Gahlia shook her had. "I can't. There's only space for one."

I looked at the tiny hatch exposed by the clearing of the equipment, then back at Gahlia. I was desperate.

"What do I do?" I asked.

"First thing is you hold on to the data chip. Second thing is you breathe hard. Third thing you'll have to figure out for yourself. Nobody's been out there before."

She pulled the helmet out of my hands and quickly fitted it over my head. I could hear the latches snap into place, and she helped me climb into the small hatch. Gahlia stepped back and pushed a large button on the wall.

A thick, clear partition started sliding between us. My heart was racing. Gahlia kneeled in front of me and closed her eyes, breathing deeply.

"Embark and Prosper, Sandrine Liet."

The clear hatch door closed shut with a thud, confirming its seal. I was crammed inside, alone, knees pressed to my chest in complete isolation.

The drilling sounds disappeared. The shouts, the screams — nothing penetrated the hatch seal. I looked through the round clear partition, and the world seemed to move in slow motion.

Gahlia, looking at me with a mixture of compassion, hope and despair.

Behind her, flames advancing through the connector ring, then a massive, gray particle cloud bursting through, extinguishing the fire. Gahlia looked back.

I kept breathing fast and deep, already feeling light-headed from over-oxygenation. In the complete silence of the hatch, I could hear my own blood drumming in my ears.

Dark silhouettes emerging from the gray cloud, catching Gahlia by the shoulders, tearing her away from the partition. Away from me.

A face appeared behind the glass. A hard face. A familiar face — white, creepy eyelashes over cold icy eyes. Jericho Pakk. He was shouting, but I couldn't hear a thing.

He mouthed words with exaggerated lip and tongue movements for me to understand. That made him look like a drunk sock-puppet operated by a ventriloquist in one of the Open Theater nights we used to run at the Nebula.

I chuckled, but I could actually read his lips quite well. He was mouthing 'Come out. Everything is OK. Come out.'

I looked around at the walls of the small hatch chamber. I somehow knew what I was looking for. When I found it, I pressed it only once. And I waited.

Pakk began banging on the partition pane, hammering it with his bare fists. Again and again, he was punching the clear glass. He was shouting at me ecstatically now. No sock-puppet imitations this time.

It was quite amusing to observe the contrast between the violent pounding and the complete silence on my side of the door.

Then, a tiny sound appeared, which my ears devoured eagerly. It was a short hissing sound, followed by a fluttering feeling of decreased pressure on my skin.

On the other side of the glass, Jericho Pakk stopped his pounding. His eyes were torn wide, gaping with horror.

I closed my eyes.

Embark and Prosper.

And then I was out.

PART THREE

CHAPTER FORTY-EIGHT

I open my eyes.

Then I freeze.

Two perfectly contrasted planes fill my field of view. Behind me, the silvery-white ceramic coating of the Thetis outer hull stretches in all directions, its gentle curvature creating a glossy, bright horizon line in the distance.

Everything else is an infinite blanket of blackness, peppered with random sprinkles of bright-colored dots of light.

Stars.

Then, the realization sinks in — I am out. Out of the ISS. Out of the Thetis. Out in outer space.

Then, I panic.

Am I alive how am I alive am I breathing is the helmet leaking what am I holding in my hand what if I just let go how am I not crushed frozen suffocated drifting to the infinite depths of space —

I close my eyes again. I breathe, keeping my entire mental focus on the tactile signals of my body. Top to bottom. Bottom to top. Toes, knees, pelvis, up the spine, chin, lips, nose bridge, eyebrows, forehead, crown.

It's working. I begin to relax. I can breathe, I am not freezing to death and beside an uncomfortably growing pain in my joints, everything seems to be functioning properly.

With my eyes still closed, my attention refocuses on my left arm. Something is pulling it. Or is it me pulling something with it? Actually, it feels more like *hanging on.*

I crack my eyes open to a tiny slit, looking up toward my left hand, and I see it is gripping the hatch door handle. This brings back my directional orientation like a punch to the face, and suddenly I realize that I am hanging on for my dear life.

Of course! — my logical mind snaps back into motion — with the Thetis decelerating, thus providing the effect of gravitational pull to everything in it (or *on it*, in my sorry case), this is practically like hanging out of a window on a high floor. If I let go of the handle, I would shoot trajwise — past Level 1, past the engines truss — just like falling off a two-story hab building.

Only there's no floor at the end of the fall. Only the infinite depths of interstellar space.

I tighten my grasp on the hatch handle. I wiggle my feet around until my boots find grip on the surface of the outer hull — on the *wall*, in the current context. I am safe.

I am now ready to open my eyes again.

I remind myself of the adaptation procedure in the Sensory Farm. Start with something close, narrow field of view. Don't take it all in immediately. Control the pace of opening up your vision to the intimidating vastness of the large, open space. With the cumbersome helmet restricting my head movements, I twist my torso as far as I can so that my head half-faces the wall. I open my eyes to the plain surface lying just beyond the helmet's clear faceplate. I then force myself to maintain a steady rhythm of measured, deep breaths, and slowly turn my head back.

For a few silent moments, I just stare forward at the incomprehensible scene stretching across my entire field of view. I can hear my breathing growing heavier as I am fighting down the panic.

What seemed at first glance to be a uniform, black blanket is revealed now as an all-encompassing expanse of endlessly deep space surrounding me in all directions.

Then, an overwhelming, profound calm washes over me. I realize that I am now seeing a view no Human being has witnessed in almost two centuries: the stars and galaxies and heavenly bodies of outer space.

I take it all in. It's mesmerizing.

At the edge of my peripheral vision, I notice a movement. I turn my head ever so slowly to see what it is. Something — a small object — floats near me, then quickly accelerates away toward the engine compound. Falling down.

The data chip! By the time I realize what that object is, it is already way out of reach, sailing away for eternity, carrying with it any hope for proving the grand scale of conspiracy happening behind the Thetis scenes.

It doesn't matter. Nothing matters anymore. I turn my head back to the marvel that is portrayed in front of me — its sole spectator. I am awestruck. It is beautiful. And terrifying.

Strangely, I feel fine. I have a dim pain growing in my joints, but the real punch of the decompression effect is probably a few hours ahead. I have no idea if the oxygen supply in the suit will even last this long, but whatever comes next for me — I am quite happy spending it right here: Humanity's capsule of survival effort at my back, and the wondrous simplicity of everything else — that which was before Humanity and which shall remain after its demise — in front.

Endless worlds float around me in every direction. Each glowing dot — a star! A burning ball of inferno, its light and heat spelling life, or destruction, to the entourage of planetary bodies which may or may not be orbiting it. Its energy nurturing, or exterminating, the strange forms of life which may or may not be thriving there. Trying to cling to their home planet. To succeed where we failed.

Some of the bright ones, I know, are not stars at all. They are far-away galaxies. Each dot, when examined closely, shall reveal a billion other stars, a billion other stories. They are the fractal components of everything in existence in this universe. A dream within a dream.

For some reason, the immense vastness of outer space does not cause my mind to cripple as it does in the Sensory Farm. Perhaps it's just too surreal, too abstract. After the initial shock, I am definitely able to study the intricate structures and objects space has for me on display.

Was this star-filled view the everyday experience for Humans on Earth? Lying on grass-covered hills in their villages; looking out their high rising city windows; sailing their wide oceans across the continents. Was this irrefutable, omnipresence of the Universe and its plethora of worlds the regular, mundane backdrop of each and every human's night not so long ago?

No wonder they had such ambition — they witnessed the infinite potential of life right before their eyes.

No wonder, too, they were so consumed with fear — their insignificance in this Universe was invariably and persistently evident.

There are so many of them! I think. Dots for stars, tiny smudges for far-away galaxies and nebulas and clusters. And inbetween them all — blackness.

Blackness, but not nothingness. My mind lingers on this thought. It seems to carry some significance, hovering just below the surface of my consciousness. I focus on what I know about interstellar Space. Facts, knowledge, science — these are my mental comfort zones, so I concentrate on what I can analyze.

To begin with, the fact that I am still alive isn't at all trivial. Apart from the Oxygen supply and decent temperature control which my EVA suit is supposed to handle, the fact is that what seems to be totally empty, black space actually isn't. Even at the most vacant parts of the Galaxy, far from any star or planetary system, some matter particles do randomly float around. The *Passados* made sure to plan the trajectory of the Thetis such that it would pass through areas with the least particle density possible, but still — there's never total vacuum in space.

And with the Thetis traveling at a third of the speed of light, hitting even the tiniest particle should have cut through me like a surgical beam knife. The Thetis itself was covered with a NanoCeramic coating providing protection and deflectability, but I, sadly, did not enjoy such a luxury treatment. The EVA suit was mere clothing in that aspect and wouldn't provide any shielding whatsoever.

Luckily, both me and the ship are under the Ion Dome. Or, actually — the Ion Dome is under us. With the pseudo-gravitational pull created by the Thetis deceleration in its trajectory, directions become confusing at times. Doubly so when you're out in the open without a frame of reference.

Anyhow, the fact that the ship is constantly shooting an ionizing beam forward, magnetically sucking the ionized particles into the central Trash Tube, creates a protective umbrella-shaped dome which precedes the ship, behind which one is relatively safe from piercing stray atoms. I imagine that this protected area doesn't stretch too far away from the ship's body, so I make sure to hold myself as pressed as I can to the Thetis hull panels.

I turn my head down and to the right and try to spot the Ion Dome beyond the bulging construct of the engine compound. There, seemingly floating beneath the falling ship, an almost transparent canopy of light is shimmering. It glows faintly against the black backdrop, tiny flares sparking across it in random patterns. Each spark, I presume, marks the collision-point of a matter particle.

I observe the sparking canopy for a while, trying to gauge the current density of dangerous particles the Thetis is plowing through.

The flares occur, on average, every few seconds. That seems… I don't know, kind of medium hazard? I have zero base for comparison. And it's not like I have anywhere else to go, so I'll just have to assume I'm sufficiently protected.

Then, of course, there's radiation. *Blackness, but not nothingness.* The Ion Dome may be sweeping unsuspecting particles off my flight path, but it cannot block the waves of radiation washing over and through me.

I turn my head back to the stars. Each point of light — a powerful beam of rays in all possible parts of the spectrum. Some utterly harmless to organic life. Other will only hurt you upon excessive and long-lasting exposure. A few will kill a person on the spot. The Thetis is wrapped in multiple layers of deflecting and absorbing materials to protect the humans inside it from this torrent of radiation. I don't assume my EVA suit offers the same quality of shielding.

Everything you see, *all* you see is light. And most of what's out there — you can't even see. The Galaxy around us, like a gargantuan array of a billion rad emitters, spits its rays at us in millions of different wavelengths, only a tiny fraction of them in the range of visible light.

The divine scenery spread before my eyes, those ancient lights carried across millions and billions of years from the farthest parts of the universe, is quietly killing me with each passing second of its colorful marvel.

At least I know I'm not infected by the Anderson kill gene, I tried to humor myself. With all those stars around, at least *one* must probably include emissions in the exact wavelength which triggers the gene, right? If I had it, I'd already be brain-dead.

I look around. Everything I can see with my eyes is limited to a range of wavelengths we call 'Visible Light', which is simply those parts of the spectrum Earth's atmosphere did not filter out from the much wider gamut emitted by its sun. Those were the most beneficial wavelengths for a Human to be sensitive to — for survival, for finding food and water, for controlling the environment. Other animals, I knew, had other light sensitivities, all within the range Earth's atmosphere was kind enough to allow through.

Even in this aspect, the two target planets for the Thetis mission were different than one another, and different from Earth. Different sun emission patterns, different atmospheric composition — the sky above Humanity in its new home planet, the stars they will be marveling upon at night, the color of their sun — it will all be different from what Humanity grew under on Earth.

In time, they will have to evolve. To become true natives of their newly chosen homeworld.

Until then, we carry our ancient, Earthborn genes, perfected through millennia of iterations, into a totally alien habitat.

In that aspect, 9 Ceti Gamma isn't any better than Gnosis Zeta or vice versa. Each with its own unique characteristics, neither of them resembling Earth more closely than the other.

This is why everything Sabi Anderson was pulling behind the scenes to force the decision for 9 Ceti as Thetis' final destination is so hard for me to comprehend. There *is* no ultimate difference between the two.

Unless...

To give freedom is to love. The power to revoke it is to rule.

Unless there is.

For there to be King, tha'll ought be slaves.

Like a violent punch to the face, everything clicks into place. I scream, immediately fogging my entire faceplate. In a way that's a blessing, a temporary sanctuary from the piercing, relentless glare of the stars.

My head threatens to explode. I blindly tighten my grip on the handles, suddenly conscious of the possibility of falling off the length of the ship, beyond the sparkling glow of the Ion Dome and away into the blackness.

It all makes horrible sense now. Bashiri's research. Cassidi's move to take over it and modify the killer gene. The specific choice of triggering wavelength for the deadly effect. Developing the gene-carrier bacteria. The need to cover it all up, including locking up the access to the life-saving inhibitor. *Including getting rid of Bashiri.* Testing it all on the Prober human genetic pool.

And all that astoundingly intricate plan — *everything* the Andersons had been brewing up secretly for two generations, from Sabi's father to his inept son — all of it would only work if us Thetans chose 9 Ceti as our Resett destination. So this decision had to be ensured. There could be no risk-factors such as Democratic voting. It *had* to be The Whale, even if this meant no voting at all. Breaking the Passados Plan.

But there was a part missing. The weaponized tool was created. It was tested. And the tracks properly covered.

But for the final execution of the plan, the carrier would have to be distributed widely across the ship. To infect every single Thetan with the gene-carrying bacteria. That would be the point of no return.

And for that to happen, Anderson would need to initiate something widespread, something—

Oh my Sol.

Something like a Dusting.

CHAPTER FORTY-NINE

I close my eyes. Then I burst into laughter, which explodes and echoes ear-splittingly inside the helmet. I don't mind — I just keep laughing uncontrollably. Tears start rolling down my cheeks, laughter and sorrow mixed in salty trickles. I can't see anything now, the glowing pinpoints of the stars smeared into cross-shaped sparkles by the moisture covering my inner faceplate.

We are so naïve! We thought we managed to create a whole new society on the Thetis — egalitarian, transparent, honest. Worthy of being the Humans of the future. *Homo Infinitus!*

But it was our leaders, the few people to whom we gave power over our lives, who betrayed us.

Who tasted power, saw its potential, then harnessed everything the Thetis had to offer in order to chart their own future as our ultimate, eternal rulers. As Humanity's new *Emperors*.

Cassidi's words echo in my head, *'when Humans reach planetfall, anyone better either have something to sell or the means to buy.'*

If I am right about this, all of us and all our future Genlines will be buying our *lives* from the Andersons until the end of time, day in and day out. Humanity itself will have successfully escaped its demise on Old Earth — only to be resurrected as a society of *slaves*.

I am not laughing anymore.

I have to stop this.

But *how?* The only proof for anything — the Archive records documenting the elaborate conspiracy Sabi Anderson and his yes-men have been weaving around us for decades — were inside the old ISS QUBIC terminal. And now, it was in the hands of Jericho Pakk, likely being destroyed as we speak. Without such genuine evidence, any public accusation against the Thetis Primo, especially one of this far-reaching magnitude, will simply be laughed aside.

And in any case, there's nothing I can do while stranded outside the Thetis, spacehanging in my rapidly depleting EVA suit.

I need Kilian. He has seen some of this. He'll know what to do.

But first things first — I need to get back inside, and I can't go back through the ISS Quest hatch. Pakk will be eagerly waiting for me beyond that pressure door.

Time to break into a spaceship, I guess.

I'm not the only one recently pushed outside an exit hatch from the Thetis. I just hope my outcome will be more positive than that of the previous spacewalker.

I look up at the hatch opening leading back into the ISS. Into the Thetis. I squeeze my fingers hard, tightening my grip on the handles securing me to the ship's body.

Then I let go.

CHAPTER FIFTY

I'm falling.

Actually, I'm not falling. I'm just maintaining a constant velocity and direction, whereas the huge body of the Thetis cruising alongside me is decelerating under the steady push of its engines. So, this isn't falling — it's just inertia. Life lesson for you right there.

Physics and Enlightmentics aside, for all practical purposes the effect feels just like falling at 0.6g down the side of a gargantuan ship, hurtling toward a flaring blanket of exploding ionized particles of random space dust, beyond which — if I even make it through unscathed — awaits the endless abyss of space, ready to swallow me into oblivion.

Not ideal.

Letting go of the ISS hatch handles certainly triggered a dramatic chain of consequences.

But I have no time for planning and reflection. I have no time for panic. I need to get back into the ship, and for that I need to be very precise, and ice-bloodingly cool. The moment will come very soon.

Just imagine you are scare-diving from the jump board hanging over the Level 13 park. Save for the inflatable mattress at the bottom, granted, but just about the same height.

Somehow, the memory helps. Perhaps it triggers a muscle memory of sorts connected with the sensation of falling. I manage to calm down just enough that I can focus on locating the only potential landing spot — the engine truss platform arm. Which should, theoretically, be right below me.

Theoretically — because I assume no human eye has actually seen that truss in well over a century. The presumable location of the construct I deduct from Thetis body blueprints studied long ago in the Archive. I am betting it is still there. It would be a very awkward and unfortunate turn of events — for the Thetis and, not less importantly, for me personally — if it isn't.

I squint my eyes and try to spot the metallic arm so I could prepare for impact. The thing is — space is *very dark*. And spacecraft don't usually expend energy illuminating their exteriors. It just isn't immediately useful for a generation ship planned to spend two centuries in interstellar travel. So whatever the coating and color composition the ship is covered with, the only available light to get reflected off it is the ambient starlight from the billions of stars and galaxies surrounding us. And that illumination is very, very weak. Making everything, even a thirty-foot long construction arm coated in the purest deflective white NanoCeramic material, a very dark thing to spot. Almost indistinguishable from the backdrop of black space.

I assume the best way to locate a physical object in space would be to look for *gaps* in the random sprinkle of stars — to look for an object *blocking* the light rather than reflecting it.

That realization dawns on me in an intuitive surprise, and just in time. The moment I switch my perspective, the wide engine support truss comes swooping toward me, fast and quiet like the Universe's largest b-ball bat.

I panic, instinctively trying to wiggle my way out of the fast-growing black slab of nothingness.

Big mistake, my internal alarms blare. You *want* to be the ball right now.

Relax. This is scare diving. Only in complete darkness. And without seeing the floor, just the absence of one. Basic stuff.

At the last possible second, the surface of the truss materializes through the darkness. I barely manage to tense my muscles for impact, when the wide metal beam explodes into me. A series of utterly unhealthy cracking sounds shoot up from my legs and echo in my ears. *That can't be good,* I note to myself in a surprisingly detached observation. The truss caught me at a slight off-angle, which means I am now sliding fast down the length of the beam toward the edge of the glowing canopy of the Ion Dome. It's just one of those days.

I instinctively stretch both hands upward, blindly and frantically trying to find anything to grasp — a support rod, a protruding bolt, anything breaking the smooth deflective surface of the beam's coating.

Through the thick fabric of my left glove, I feel something, an imperfection in the surface. But I'm sliding too fast and it's beyond reach before I can react. I curl my fingers to a hook, pressing as hard as I can against the truss, trying to create more friction. Then, a second imperfection hits the tips of my fingers. Then a third, all in quick succession and at seemingly equal intervals.

I try to gauge the timing for the fourth bump, then bury my curled fingers into the ship's body with all the force I can muster. Just in time, my fingers latch into a tiny, finger-wide groove marking the connection between two body coating plates. I press hard, and I feel my arms stretching my scapulas to the point of strain. My legs are flailing, trying to find grip. Shots of extreme pain flare through my fingers, my arms, and straight into my spine. But I hold on. With everything I have got left in me, I hold on.

And then, I'm no longer sliding. I am hanging on the sloping beam with my fingers stuck into the panel connection slit, my heart pounding in my ears and my lungs panting uncontrollably.

After a few seconds the adrenaline rush subsides, my faceplate is gradually clearing up from the fogging caused by my excessive respiration, and there is silence.

And I am alone. More alone than any human has been in the past one hundred and eighty years, literally dangling from a bridge over the endless abyss. The ship above me is constantly pulling up, threatening to tear me off it if I let go of the tiny groove I am desperately hanging onto.

I have to get back inside. I have to warn everybody on the Thetis about Sabi's plan. I have to find a way.

But what's the point? Even if I survive this, even if I'm able to get back into the ship and deliver my warning, I can't even begin to prove it, can I? And even if I do, it's already too late anyway. Dusting's done, they're all already infected with the bacteria, already contaminated with the gene produced to cripple and enslave an entire population. The Andersons will be selling them their daily dose of cure forever.

What would the price be for each twenty four hours of a person's life? It would be unlimited. It would be *everything*.

There must be something we can do. Find an antidote. Develop the inhibitor into a permanent cure. *Something.*

Kilian would know. Nyasha could access the locked parts of the Archive. Something must be there — something we can use to reverse this fate imposed on us by the tyranny of a single man.

I need to get up there, I think as I raise my head and look straight into the wide, funneling opening of the Ionized Debris Beam. I have to somehow climb up the Trash Tube, up to the only other hatch I can use to enter back into the ship. The GenLab hatch on level 8. The hatch that saw Dr. Almaz Bashiri pass the other way, expelled into the torrent of magnetized ions, disintegrated and carried all the way through the Tube and out the back of the Thetis.

Which would most likely be my own ill-fated destiny should I dive into that lethal flow of particles.

I tighten my hold on the engine truss beam, trying to consider my alternative options. I have none. And as if to illustrate the point, a high-pitched chirping sound starts drilling inside my helmet. And although I have zero experience or training in anything remotely similar to operating an EVA suit, I am pretty sure that alarm means to inform me of some quickly depleting resource or another. Which can't spell anything good.

I look up and around to gauge my situation. The opening of the Trash Tube looms above me like the mouth of a gargantuan monster, and I can almost see through all its 36-level span to the other side of the Thetis. The entry hatch — *My* entry hatch — is eight levels up from my location.

That's obviously too high for a jump, even in 0.6g. And even if I could climb eight levels on the inner hull side of the ship, that would be much too long to spend within the Tube and survive the bombardment of particles flowing through it, through *me*. The EVA suit should provide a minimal amount of protection from some particles, but still, the chances of making it to 8th seem improbable if not impossible.

I look down at the glowing canopy of the Ion Dome. The closest part of its circumference is right below my legs, randomly flaring up whenever the invisible ionizing beam meets the occasional stray particle floating in the ship's path. The particle ionizes and then, magnetically charged, an array of electromagnets built into the lip of the Trash Tube attract it into the tunnel.

My eyes focus on the area stretching from the glowing canopy below me to the Tube's mouth above. Then I see it — a hazy, almost translucent stream, wide at the base of the Ion Dome, then narrowing as the rising particles accelerate and are siphoned into the Tube tunnel.

An idea starts forming in my head, and I find myself already making calculations. The rising particles. The electromagnets pulling them up into the tunnel. Could those magnets put *me* up as well?

In and of itself, that wouldn't cut it — even with all the metal parts of my EVA suit, the pull force just wouldn't be strong enough. Not to lift my entire weight 8 levels high. Not from the static position I am currently at.

But what if I wasn't static? what if I had an initial upward velocity toward the tunnel? I'd be working against the ship's deceleration, and with the added pull from the magnets I'd be essentially surfing the particle wave upward, up the funnel and, hopefully, far enough into the tunnel to reach the hatch before I slow down to a halt — or disintegrate into atoms by the particle beam.

It's a crazy kunye idea but, honestly, right now it's all I have.

If I can time my jump to a relatively quiet moment in the particle stream, my chances of surviving would increase substantially.

Unfortunately, the flaring pattern of the Dome seems completely random. There's no consistent logic to the rhythm of space particles crossing the Thetis trajectory and getting magno-sucked into the Tube. One second everything's quiet, and in the next the canopy is flaring violently all over. There's no math here, no analytical solution. The Archivist in me will have to let go. Trust my 7th and just wing it the best I can.

I scan my immediate surroundings for anything I could use to gather upward speed. The extended metal arm I am holding onto slants upward and to the center of the funnel, where it meets the circular engine platform. Following the arm will get me right to the edge of the particle ascension funnel, and should be well within the traction area of the Tube's electromagnets. If there's any merit to my improvised plan, this is where it will all test out.

I decide to make a run for it.

I press my fingers and bore hard into the metal groove, pushing myself up to a crouching position on the beam. I press my thighs together on the cool material, securing and stabilizing myself as best I can. Only now I realize that with every flare of the Ion Dome, a noticeable vibration runs through the whole construct supporting it.

I look up. The tunnel is right above me. I create a mental image of the tentative point of the 8th Level hatch.

I look down at the Ion Dome below me. The flares are relatively calm now.

This is the moment. No overthinking it. I run.

I run up the slope of the beam. I am pushing as hard as I can, my muscles straining to pump up the speed. I am halfway up the beam when I realize I am screaming my lungs out. I press on, charging all the way to the upper edge of the straight beam.

I begin to feel a slight tug around my waist. Then another one, as delicate as a tickle, around my ankles and wrists, then at the outer part of my shoulders.

The metal rings in the suit! It's working!

The magnetic pull intensifies and it becomes easier to push more for the last stretch of beam. It feels… ethereal, like a dancer on stage, pulled by invisible strings to an impossible leap above the crowd.

I reach the top of the beam and look up — I see stars twinkling on the other side of the tunnel.

Below me, the Ion Dome canopy flares and glows and bursts in activity.

This is all or nothing. Embark and Prosper.

I jump.

A million explosions detonate inside my head. I scream. I close my eyes in pain. Flashes of all shapes and colors erupt and fulminate on the inside of my eyelids.

I cross the lip of the Tube entrance. I crack my eyes open and can spot the rectangular discoloring of the hatch door on the 8th Level.

I stretch my hands forward. I press my knees to my stomach, my chin hard into my chest, bracing for impact. Then everything goes dark.

My senses numbly register the vague notion of hitting something hard, and nothing else after that.

CHAPTER FIFTY-ONE

I blinked back to existence into a fuzzy, cotton-candy covered blur. Smears of warm colors washed and moved across my entire field of vision. My body was nowhere to be felt nor operated. Like a baby born into water, I was floating, devoid of any sensory input or context.

I didn't need any senses to know exactly who was hovering above me. I could *feel* him.

"Hi, Kilian." *Was I smiling?* It felt like I was smiling but I had no idea if my face registered any expression at all. "I was *out*."

"I know you were out, you crazy *wapa*," his familiar voice washed over me, "I had to pull you back inside through that hatch. You were all but *gone*, you lunatic."

I knew he'd be proud of me, I thought.

"I'll be OK," I managed a whisper. *Am I still smiling?* "I knew you'd come to save me. It's *beautiful* out there, K."

The warm-colored blur leaned closer, almost focusing into the face I knew so well. "What were you *doing* there, San? We need to get a doctor in here, and quick."

I tried to shake my head slowly. A stab of pain sliced through my temples with every motion. I groaned, slowly willing my palm into movement, searching with my fingers until I found Kilian's arm. I giggled. It was all very hazy.

"I found the Elephant."

"What are you talking about?" I felt his warm palm on my forehead, then on my cheek. "You're not making any sense, San."

I knew I wasn't. That's what was so funny about it.

"It's an old parable," I sighed. "It's about this huge legendary animal. I *found it!*"

My vision was reigniting now, and I could make out Kilian's face almost clearly. He looked genuinely worried. It was beautiful.

"Alarms are going off all over the Thetis," he said. "Opening the hatch sent Anderson's people running for you. I had to carry you all the way up here. It's the only safe place for you now."

I painfully raised my head a notch, trying to orientate. Even through the blur, there was no mistaking where we were.

"The Archive," I mumbled. "Oh, K, of all places on the ship."

Kilian hummed in question, "what's wrong with the Archive?"

I smiled. "It's perfect. You're a genius, Kilian. Always been. Now help me up."

There would be no time for tender recovery in Kilian's arms. I needed to get the final evidence. *Fast.*

"Kunye *what?*" Kilian frowned. "Oh no you don't. You stay right here, San."

"No time," I said. "Dusting's over, so today is Final Call day. If we don't stop Anderson, in a few hours the Thetis begins its maneuver toward 9 Ceti Gamma. And then we're *doomed,* K."

The struggle played across Kilian' face, but he knew I was right.

"So, how do we stop him, San?"

I giggled as if it was the most obvious thing in the world. "We're going to have a baby."

CHAPTER FIFTY-TWO

Two minutes later, my palms dropped in exhaustion off the sides of the Archive QUBIC terminal.

With a short, mundane chirp, the machine logged off and ejected a small, flat data chip which I had just loaded with a precious array of genetic data. The data chip everything now depended on. *Everything*.

I tucked it deeply into my pocket. "Come, quick!" I grabbed Kilian's sleeve and bolted out of the Archive office. Kilian stumbled behind me, trying to keep up.

"Wait! Where are we going now?" he called from behind me.

"We got this *wapa!*" I yelled and pressed on as hard as I could toward the Level 13 Ascender platform, "we have to get to the CellPrinters, fast!"

Kilian caught up with me, and we both started cutting through the sports park, jumping over benches and fake CarboFoam decorative shrubs. We ran through groups of Gen8er teens doing their athletic sessions in the park, ignoring the disgruntled comments thrown our way.

"Move aside! Everybody move!" I shouted as the nearest Ascender platform came into view. The few people on the platform quickly stepped aside and I slammed the DuraGlass door shut so that we were alone in the translucent carriage box. The Ascender started moving down. We both panted deeply, gulping air. Instinctively, I shot a glance across the park at the Archive office complex, and there they were — Sebastian Anderson and his entourage, barging through the Head Office door. *They are closer than I'd hoped. Dio, can't this jewel box go any faster?*

"Listen," I put my hand on Kilian's arm. "This is all on me." I looked him deeply in the eyes — *my Kilian*. "Go home. You still have your chance for a Genline."

Kilian covered my hand with his warm palm. "I was down there too, San. I *know*. Bashiri had a plan."

"Yeah, well, Bashiri's *gone*, K," I said impatiently. "So we're stuck with *me*."

Kilian shook his head in dismay. "We thought we had more time. I didn't want to involve you in this *mala*. But I'm not letting you face this alone."

The Ascender passed the seal and swished to a stop at Level 8, and we were out of the box and on the move again. Kilian followed me as we both stormed right through the Sensory Farm entrance gate. *No time for spatial habituation this time,* I thought. We will just have to deal with it.

As I reached the metal platform above the Farm, I did a low-grav roll and was on the ground running in less than a second. The Sensory Farm was magnificent at this hour of simulated sunset. The artificial sky was streaked with crimson clouds, like the broad brushstrokes of a foolishly romantic painter. The side light of the setting pseudo-Sun threw long, impressive shadows across the land, which seemed to be moving to an internal clock of their own.

I noticed Kilian was having a hard time adjusting to the sensory overload of entering the Farm. "Don't look at the sky!" I shouted over my shoulder as I kept running toward the Vivarium. "Look down at the ground, limited field of view!"

"I haven't done this in twenty years," Kilian managed to mutter below his rapid breathing.

We ran through the wheat fields as fast as we could, my hand checking the bulge in my side pocket to ensure the data chip was still there. *Not losing another one.* Our bodies left a clear trail of trampled stalks tracing our path through the field. Kilian noticed it too, and gestured to me in question.

"Forget it!" I called, "nothing we can do about that now. Let's move on!"

"What's on the chip?" Kilian asked as we emerged from the wheat field. Beyond the tree line, a speck of white hinted at the location of the Vivarium fence.

"The biggest bet I'll ever make in my lifetime," I replied. "And, just maybe, our insurance policy."

CHAPTER FIFTY-THREE

Chipping through the Vivarium and GenLab doors was a breeze. *Good. They didn't revoke my access credentials yet.* I hoped that meant we still had a few minutes before Sabi's goons descended all over us.

The Vivarium was a cacophony of wild grunts, bleats and barks — the printing cycle, in full force during my last visit with Dr. Almaz Bashiri, had evidently concluded, which made the passage through the corridor a notably stinky challenge.

The large GenLab room was quiet. The CellPrinters sat motionless along the wall, and the large window overlooking the Farm was filled with a serene, calm scene of darkening nature.

I ran directly to the nearest CellPrinter and examined its tubing and supply levels. It looked in proper working condition, idling quietly. I paused for a moment — what I was about to attempt was far more complex than the machine's routine function — and was considered so taboo that I was already getting cold feet.

I am going straight to hell for this, I thought.

Well, better just me than everyone on the ship.

Distant sounds of chatter and yelling snapped me back into focus. *They're here.* "Kilian! Grab a Protein cartridge from the other machine!" I pointed. As he handed me a newly-filled box, I attached it to the back of the CellPrinter. I quickly connected the tubes to the wall sockets supplying Amino acid extract and NanoForm fluid. Everything looked in order.

I pulled the genetic data chip out of my pocket and examined it. Then I raised my eyes and looked at Kilian.

"Don't hate me for this, Kilian," I said and slapped the chip onto the front panel of the CellPrinter. It immediately snapped into place inside the machine's input slot. A blinking LED indicated that data transfer was ongoing.

Kilian eyed me suspiciously. "What are we doing here, Sandrine? Sandrine! What are we kunye doing with the CellPrinter?"

"Shh," I whispered. The voices were getting nearer. I glanced at the CellPrinter front panel. Data Transfer was complete. I took a deep breath, then another. Then quickly pressed the master switch controlling the machine's operation.

With a soft electric hum, the CellPrinter whirred to life and began printing.

"Get back," I pushed Kilian lightly, nudging him toward the lab's back exit. "Take the RadEmitter and wait for my cue behind that door."

Kilian looked at the pressure-door leading to the back yard of the building. "How are we supposed to get out of here? They're probably all over the Farm by now."

"Go to the back of the yard. There's an Emergency Ascender safebox there. Go!"

Kilian picked up the RadEmitter and retreated toward the pressure-door. I could see his hesitation in leaving me alone. I looked at the printer — it was about halfway through its process. *Just a few more minutes.* I waved Kilian to get the kunye out already — he didn't need to see this. He'd suffered enough on the account of me being part of his life. *Go on, go on!* I urged the CellPrinter. With its quiet persistence, the machine kept sucking raw materials, moulding and bioforming tissue, unimpressed by my haste.

The doors to the GeneLab burst open. My heart jerked. *Too soon!* I needed another minute. And I needed this to not happen *here*. There should be more people around. Witnesses. There was no point otherwise.

"Stop right there, Liet!" Anderson marched in flanked by his guards, pointing a commanding finger as he closed in on me.

I peeked at the printer's main panel — seventy percent.

I have to stall him for just one more minute. The machine kept humming almost unnoticeably as it continued its elaborate process. The men approaching me didn't give it any thought at all. *Good.*

"Hey. Hey!" I shouted. Anderson and his entourage stopped in their tracks, startled.

"Mr. Anderson, your charade stops right here!" I tried in the most intimidating voice I could muster.

He cocked his head to one side, trying to restrain his fury. "I would seriously reconsider your choice of tone when addressing the Thetis Primo," he said through gritted teeth.

"You and your family have been planning to contaminate the Thetis gene pool for your own Genline benefit," I shouted at him. "And I can finally prove it now."

Sabi was well into losing his temper. "Your delusions and ridiculous accusations have caused enough damage!" He waved his finger erratically, cruelty seeping into his words. "It's a good thing we won't be tolerating any more Liets down the Genline, isn't it?"

He turned to his guards. "Let's get this over with, shall we? Escort her out of here."

The guards barely started moving when a soft, friendly, musical bleep filled the air. The guards paused, puzzled, searching for the source of the sound. I, of course, knew exactly where it came from. It was the cue I've been waiting for.

I darted toward the CellPrinter.

* * *

A split-second later I was pulling on the product drawer handle so hard I almost broke the thing — no time for the 5-minute thawing period before the latch auto-releases. The drawer finally gave and I pulled out a small, red BioBox containing the newly-printed organism.

Thankfully, the translucent cover was still frosty — had I looked directly at what was inside, I'd have most likely lost my nerve. I pressed the BioBox to my chest, considering my next move. *I need witnesses. It's all useless otherwise.*

In the spur of the moment, I reached for the emergency panel on the lab's wall. It was a mandatory device in any potential hazard-zone on the Thetis. With proper CrypID credentials, one could set off alarms, activate sprinklers, even initiate a full Level 10 seal. Those won't do me any good at the moment, but maybe another feature of the system would.

I touched the panel with my chip finger. A tiny LED blinked green.

"Mr. Sebastian Anderson," I said, keeping my eyes on Sabi, "I am Senior Archivist Sandrine Liet, and this broadcast is transmitted live on the Thetis emergency public announcement channel."

My eyes ran wildly between the men in the room, watching for any unexpected movement. Sabi motioned them to keep position. I held the BioBox tighter. *Our future depends on you now, little baby,* I thought.

"Inside this BioBox, I am holding a genuinely CellPrinted, genestamp-validated First Generation Prober Human embryo."

Sabi Anderson was stunned. I could literally see the blood draining from his face. "You did *what!?*" he cried with disbelief.

My courage picked up as I mentally directed my words to the entire Thetan population listening somewhere above us.

"The gene map of this embryo was altered to carry a switch-gene created by PHS lab, headed by your wife Cassidi Anderson. That gene was reappropriated and modified from the research of the late Dr. Almaz Bashiri, with the aim of gaining control and perpetuating your rule over Humanity after Resett." I saw my words process in Sabi's mind.

"That woman is insane and dangerous!" Sabi shouted to his entourage. Then he turned his venomous eyes back to me and snarled. "But not very smart, unfortunately. Or did you neglect the fact that the Primo can override anyone's access credentials?"

His eyes rose to the lab's ceiling, as if addressing the omnipresent entity of the ship itself. "Close and lock emergency public channel," he commanded. "And revoke this woman's credentials. *All* of them!"

Oh, no.

Anderson then turned back to his guards. "Get her, now!"

The goons jumped forward to grab me. I panicked. *Time for Plan B.*

I bolted for the back-exit pressure door. "Kilian!" I screamed, "open the Emergency Ascender!"

I crashed through the door, hugging the BioBox as hard as I could. *This is my only chance.*

Kilian stood by the Emergency Ascender platform, holding the RadEmitter. He didn't need further orders — he grabbed my free hand and pulled me into the cramped emergency box.

Just then, the pressure-door burst open behind us. Sabi and his team poured out and started running toward us.

Anderson was full-on furious now. "Assist this Anti-Thetan, Mr. Ngo, and you're condemning yourself to the same fate."

Kilian pushed me deeper into the emergency box. It was designed for a single-person ride, and he had to wrap himself around me to fit both of us inside.

"There's only one Anti-Thetan here, *Primo*," Kilian spat back at Sabi, "and my bet's not on her."

Kilian slammed his fist on the emergency button and the Ascender shot up into its DuraGlass enclosure tube, a bullet within a transparent barrel. We started sliding up and away above the Sensory Farm like a rocket launching off from a malicious planet. We were both panting hard, panic taking control over my entire body.

"What were you thinking, Sandrine?" Kilian embraced me, the BioBox pressed tightly between us.

"We have to get above 10th," I whispered into his chest, "beyond the Rad block, then everyone will see. You got the RadEmitter with you, right? It's crucial — you have to dial it to 380nm frequency! You got that? 380 nanometer UVA frequency! They need to see what he tries to plant in us, Kilian."

Kilian's voice broke. "But a human baby, Sandrine? You can't possible think —"

"It's not a baby yet at this point, just a bunch of synthesized cells," I choked up, my eyes swelling with tears. "Or is it? I don't know anymore, Kilian."

Blam! A deafening explosion rattled the Emergency Ascender, nearly throwing it off its magrails. Everything around us shook violently, and the BioBox almost hurled out of my hands.

"*Kunye Mala!*" I screamed.

"What was that?" Kilian tried to stabilize both of us as the platform thankfully kept sliding up the rails. I peeked over Kilian's shoulder — on the opposite side of the level, I could clearly see Sabi Anderson and his group riding the outer-wall Ascender, about half a level below us. They were looking directly at us.

"Mala Dio, they're chasing us!" I yelled.

Two more hits impacted on the DuraGlass protection tube, the second one sending long, deep cracks further up our climb path. I squinted my eyes, trying to identify what hit us, when I suddenly realized — they had a gun! A real, actual *gun!*

"They're shooting at us, Kilian!" I cried. *What's going on here?* Guns did not exist on the Thetis. Guns were something you saw in Archival movies or history records. *Where the kunye did they get an actual gun!?*

Kilian pushed me deeper into the box. More shots erupted and the protective tube began to crack, raining tiny shards of glass with each impact. He covered me and the BioBox with his body, embracing us as tightly as he could. Sabi's Ascender rose in the distance, keeping pace below us with a clear and consistent line of sight to our tiny emergency box.

"Don't let the baby die, San," Kilian whispered. "Find a way. Remember what it means to us. What they took from us."

Kilian's expression froze as two more blasts shattered the DuraGlass protective shell. The platform came to an emergency brake and stopped violently. I shrieked. Kilian's body leaned on me heavily, pinning me into the back wall. His face touched mine, eyes fixated on me, static.

"Kilian?" a warm, wet presence spread between us as I realized something was terribly, terribly wrong.

Chapter Fifty-Four

"Kilian!" I cried. Kilian's body went limp and a fountain of dark blood gushed from his chest. The emergency box doors slid open and he collapsed onto the outer platform, his torso ripped open. Blood spewed endlessly from a hole torn by a bullet that had passed through his collarbone, crushing everything in its path.

"Kilian, no!" I fell to my knees next to him, trying for any signs of life.

There were none.

I shot my head up and immediately recognized the Level 10 platform. The area was teeming with people, drawn here by the gunfire and emergency alarms blaring across the Thetis. When they saw Kilian collapsing into a pool of blood they all backed off, unsure of what was happening and keeping a safe distance. Looking down from the Level 10 gallery, I could spot Sabi's Ascender speeding up Level 9, mere seconds from reaching us.

There weren't many options for running or hiding on Level 10. And I couldn't bring myself to leave Kilian lying there on the floor. I picked up the RadEmitter and held the BioBox in my other hand. *All I can do now is wait.* Wait for the Primo of the Thetis to catch up with me. Then publicly expose him for creating the most devastating weapon in Human history.

I shivered. Then I shot a glance at the RadEmitter — it was dialed perfectly to the 380nm UVA frequency. *Kilian's last action,* I thought. *Executed perfectly, as he always does.*

He said his bet was on me. *Now I'd better make good on that bet.*

"Sandrine!" a familiar, warm voice called out to me, and I saw Nyasha running toward me, breaking through the crowd. He was followed by Athena Saugado, who eyed me with a terrified expression.

"Are you OK?" Nyasha shouted as they drew closer. "I saw your note!"

"Stay back!" I shouted back and waved them to a stop. "They have guns! Actual guns!"

Just then, Nyasha's gaze fell on Kilian's ripped body lying at my feet. His eyes widened in terror. Nyasha stopped in his tracks and reached back to halt Athena beside him.

Sebastian Anderson burst out of the Ascender running, waving the crowd away with his pistol. His face was a sweaty, enraged death sentence, and his goon squad began spreading around us, circling us in.

"Step away from those boxes right now, Liet, and maybe I'll allow you the painless option of the Trash Tube instead of shooting you right here and now." A gasp of surprise went through the crowd. The circle of spectators withdrew a step back as they realized what Anderson was holding. Nyasha and Saugado didn't move. They were standing just slightly out of arm's reach from the Primo.

This is it, I thought. *You wanted an audience — you got it. Now, it's all-in. My very own Final Call.*

I rose slowly, clutching the BioBox and the RadEmitter firmly with both hands. I kept my fingers as far from the RadEmitter trigger as I could — *I can kill everyone here with a flick of that button,* I thought.

"Mr. Sebastian Anderson—" I started. I felt anxiety washing over me as I searched for the courage to continue.

Anderson's loud, confident voice cut in, his eyes never leaving the RadEmitter box in my hand. "This woman has broken every Thetan code and moral value possible," he addressed the thickening audience, "and we are taking her in *right now*. Remove your hands from that box, Liet." He gave his guards a silent nod, and they started closing in.

Nyasha took a step forward and stood by me. "I am the investigative authority on this ship, and *I* would like to hear what *my* Senior Archivist has to say. Or are you going to shoot me too, Sabi?"

Nyasha turned and met my gaze. "I hope you know what you're doing, Sandrine. Please continue."

I lowered my eyes and looked at Kilian. Brave, beautiful, dead Kilian. *Give me courage*, I pleaded with him. *I now have absolutely nothing else to lose.* Should this play out as me being the delusional nut who blamed the Thetis Primo with a crazy conspiracy theory, then I am done anyhow — no genline, no job, no friends. *But if I'm right.*

If I'm right, I will have saved the entire Thetis population and its future from a dire, evil plan to enslave Humanity forever. I will die in peace knowing I've stood up against Sabi's insatiable hunger for control and submission. Kilian believed me. Kilian believed *in* me.

"My name is Senior Archivist Sandrine Liet," my voice trembled. "In the past few days, I have been in the centre of a deliberate, targeted campaign of lies and fabricated pseudo-facts. That campaign had one purpose: discrediting my reputation and detract from the significance of the truth I present to you today."

I threw a hesitant glance sideways, making sure Nyasha and Athena were still there. They were my only insurance policy from getting shot by Sabi who was very quickly losing his temper.

"Bringing the truth to light had already claimed the lives of too many good people — Dr. Gahlia Roskov and Armitage, two brave Thetans who gave their lives in pursuit of that truth. Dr. Almaz Bashiri, a brilliant inventor who was brutally *murdered* for exposing the Anderson family's scheme. And here before you—" I swallowed hard, fighting the swelling emotions, "—lies Kilian Ngo, an expectant father, shot by the hand of our very own Primo."

* * *

The audience gasped. Sabi took a threatening step forward, gun pointed directly at my head. "Your *boyfriend* here was an anti-Thetan Adapter traitor. He deserves no pity for what he brought on himself. And Almaz Bashiri was a paranoid Eternist who tried to play politics for his own reputation. If you want to avoid a similar fate, I suggest you cut this show short and submit yourself peacefully to my team. Any claims you have will be investigated by the proper authorities."

Sabi put on a careful, cynical smile, his words addressed to the spectating crowd. "The Thetis will also happily provide any mental support or restitution you may need. We shouldn't attribute to malice that which could be attributed to incompetence. Or delusions."

I was furious. *Don't fall into this trap, Sandrine. He's a master in this game. Just keep going.*

I raised my left hand holding the BioBox. "I hold in my hand the proof," I continued, "the proof that you, people of the Thetis, and your entire future Genline were compromised by Primo Sebastian Anderson."

I took a deep, slow breath and held it in my lungs, trying to control my anxiety. I knew what was coming now. There was no way around it.

"This box holds a genuine Human embryo containing a malicious gene developed by the Andersons. That gene, unfortunately, was carried to all of you via infectious bacteria in last night's Dusting."

There is no turning back here. The only way out of this was plowing forward through the whole motion. *They need to see it to believe me.*

My hands gripped the BioBox handle so hard my knuckles turned inksheet-white. I fixed my eyes on Nyasha.

"This gene, this *Slave-Gene*, can kill any human carrying it in less than a minute, when exposed to a specific radiation frequency. That frequency is the trigger for the gene's horrible mechanism. Originally, it was a harmless tool, invented by Dr. Bashiri and used in the Sensory Farm for years," I found the courage to shift my eyes and meet Sabi Anderson's gaze, "but it was hijacked. Hijacked and weaponized by altering its trigger frequency to match the distinct UVA frequency existing on 9 Ceti Gamma. Anderson's preferred Resett destination. Our planned future home planet."

I paused. The crowd was silent, mesmerized. They were taking it all in. *Good.*

"Our children, and children's children, will be genetically programmed to die on this planet. And the only ones holding the treatment, the inhibitor — the people dooming our future Human society to be slaves to the medicine only *they* can supply — will be the Anderson family."

The murmur of confusion within the circling audience grew.

"What is she talking about, Anderson?" someone called at the Primo. Other protests started rising within the crowd.

Athena Saugado tried to restrain the front line of the crowd, who were trying to close in on me. *They don't believe me.*

I looked at Kilian, lying motionless at my feet, drenched in a pool of blood, his executioner standing right in front of me. *Forgive me, Kilian, I have no other choice.*

I raised my right hand holding the RadEmitter and pointed it directly at the BioBox.

"To prove my claim," I almost shouted above the crowd, "this radiation emitter is dialed to the exact frequency triggering the lethal gene. 380nm UVA — the exact frequency existing on 9 Ceti Gamma. If what I am revealing to you today is true, then the moment I activate this RadEmitter, this CellPrinted sample will react and die by the exact same biological process that would kill a grown human. That would kill *your* future children."

The crowd fell silent. I could feel my heartbeat drumming in my ears. I moved my right thumb to the RadEmitter trigger button, my palms sweating.

Remember what they took from us, I could hear Kilian's whisper. *Don't let the baby die.*

Sabi Anderson's jaw clenched. With two deliberate steps he quickly closed the distance between us, his gun now mere inches from my face. His pale eyes burned in fury as he spoke.

"You dare and push that button, that's *murder*. And I will use the full extent of my power as Primo of Humanity to execute you on the spot right here and now. There will be no second chances."

He inched forward and pressed the muzzle to my forehead. I could feel the circle of cold metal burying into skin. But I was not afraid anymore. A soothing calm spread inside me — finally, Anderson had made a crucial mistake.

"If that's murder, then you admit that the radiation does trigger the kill switch," I said calmly.

The entire level was space-silent. Sabi's brow trembled. He paused, our eyes interlocked. Then, he burst out laughing. An angry, aggressive laugh, as he took a step back, still pointing his gun at me.

"It hardly matters anymore, does it?" Anderson spat through his teeth. "You think you're so very smart, Liet. But you still can't change the outcome."

He turned to address the circling crowd. "The Thetis is a society where the Code rules above all. And that Code gives the acting Primo the sole authority over deciding on the destination planet and initiating Resett protocol. That's why it's named Final Call. Now — we face a huge challenge of preparing humanity for resettling on 9 Ceti Gamma, and no provocation from known anti-Thetan *murderers* should distract us from our cause."

Athena Saugado stepped forward. "The law also dictates a general election for Primo, letting the people of the Thetis choose which Primo will make that decision. You stole that right from our people!"

Anderson was not intimidated. "And we will hold those elections soon enough as planned. As you very well know, Sec. Saugado, the rescheduling of those elections was a necessity, mandated strictly within the limits of the Code. Sadly for you and the rest of the Eternist cowards, it will also be purely academic, as we are definitely heading to 9 Ceti, like it or not."

He pointed at Athena and Nyasha with his free hand. "Are both of you, Head Archivist and challenger for the Primo role, going to break the Thetis Code by refusing to follow a Primo's mandate?"

Nyasha joined Athena in front of the audience. His face was somber and grey with anger. "You could withdraw from the Primo role right now," he said. "No Primo means we take it to public vote. The people deserve answers."

Sabi chuckled. "And why would I ever do that, Mr. Woo?" He turned back to me. "Drop the RadEmitter, Liet. My family built this ship. The Andersons have been serving the Thetan people for *generations*. As they shall continue doing for many more."

He stepped closer and pressed the gun to my forehead again. I could smell the sweat and insane determination driving this man.

Don't let the baby die, Kilian's voice echoed in my head. *Find a way.*

Sabi's finger started moving, slowly increasing the pressure on the gun's trigger. I closed my eyes.

"Ruling is my Genline's destiny," I heard Anderson's whisper. "Do you believe in destiny?"

My eyes snapped open.

"I believe in gravity, *wapa*," I whispered back.

I swung my right hand and flung the RadEmitter as hard as I could. Just before letting go, I pressed the small trigger on its side panel. The small box hurled and tumbled through the air, drawing a long arc beyond the lip of the Level 10 gallery. As it crossed over the railing and started its plunge into Level 9, I could hear the distinctive, mechanical click confirming its activation.

CHAPTER FIFTY-FIVE

The fast sequence of events that followed was exactly as described in the Thetis Emergency Procedures guidebook:

As the RadEmitter shot its 380nm beam into the empty air of Level 9, the ship's security sensors immediately flagged it as a safety hazard and initiated the emergency seal protocol.

The first step in the protocol was an instantaneous cutoff of the Thetis thrust engines. With the loss of thrust and the gravity effect it provided, the entire ship was immediately thrown into zero-g.

To use the element of surprise, I knew I had to time my next move perfectly. I grabbed the railing with my free hand, jumped as high as I could and sent a powerful kick into Anderson's chest. His eyes filled with terror, but it was futile — he had nothing to grasp, nothing to counter the inertia from my kick. Anderson floated uncontrollably below the gallery lip and into Level 9, arms flailing, his gun drifting calmly out of reach. I held onto the metal railing as hard as I could, clutching the BioBox close with the other hand. Behind me, I could vaguely register the crowd voices. They were screaming in panic.

And then, the seal protocol initiated. With loud grunts and screeches of metal plates grinding against each other, the iris-shaped seal quickly contracted toward its centre. Sabi was well below the sealing plane, drifting downward, unable to change course.

433

As the seal drew to a close, I could see his terrified face staring directly at me. His eyes were torn wide. He too knew what was coming next.

The seal closed with an ear-popping pulse of air pressure. Immediately, red emergency lights flooded the ship. An automatic announcement blared :

Level 10 emergency seal activated.

Atmosphere purge in process.

The next step in the process was vicious. The seal protocol was designed to mitigate any fire hazard spreading from the digit levels. The fire extinguishing action was simple and brutal: emergency hatches snapped open all around the inner bulkhead, exposing the ship's interior to the Trash Tube. In all levels below the 10th, the oxygenated air — along with any unsecured objects in open areas — was immediately sucked out into space.

I should have felt sorry for Sebastian Anderson, violently thrown into the Debris Beam, shredded by the torrent of ionized particles. I have seen it with my own eyes. *So did Bashiri.* Yet, all I could think about were the innocent animals in the Sensory Farm, suffocating in their cages, completely surprised by the death sentence I had imposed on them.

A small tremor ran through the Thetis. The purge completed. The emergency hatches closed and new air started hissing back into the digit levels. Somewhere above us, the small ion cloud that was once Primo Sebastian Anderson was slowly dissipating into the emptiness of interstellar space. Another small vibration signaled the reignition of the ship's engines. The Thetis started decelerating again, and gravity slowly returned.

We were all struggling back to our feet as I met Nyasha's bewildered eyes. He was panting heavily.

I hesitated. "What's to become of me now?" I whispered. "All the evidence I had — it's gone. But Pakk knows. And Cassidi knows! They'll never—"

"—and we know too," Nyasha said and reached into his pocket. He held my gaze for a moment before continuing, "when I found the inksheet you left on my desk this morning, there was another item right there beside it."

Nyasha pulled out a small, flat data chip. Athena Saugado joined by his side, lightly massaging a bruised shoulder. "A few weeks ago, Dr. Bashiri approached us proclaiming a raging conspiracy story," she said. "We just dismissed it until he could come up with concrete data. You know how it is in election campaigns, all sorts of weirdos pop up. Turns out—"

"—turns out Kilian helped him get that data," Nyasha raised the data chip. "It's all in here."

The dots finally connected. "He took Bashiri to Level 2," I nodded. "They found the sixth node. He *knew*."

I kneeled beside Kilian's motionless body, anger filling me with overwhelming pulses. I looked up at Athena and Nyasha, eyes flaring. "This could have all been prevented!" I cried. "Kilian. Armitage. Gahlia. This... *baby!*"

With all the excitement, I almost didn't notice I was still clutching the BioBox to my chest.

"I am sorry, Sandrine," Nyasha lowered his eyes to the floor, "I just wasn't certain I could trust him. I now know I should have. Kilian was a good man. You, I never doubted."

I rose slowly back to my feet. A moment of silence passed between the three of us.

"Mrs. Saugado," I said finally, "As acting Primo of the Thetis, I believe you have an urgent decision to make. 9 Ceti Gamma is no longer a viable destination for the people of the Thetis."

Athena's eyes locked into mine. I looked back at her intently.

"Please find us a new home."

PART FOUR

Epilogue

I am standing on the main Traj Control stage at the center of Level 36. It is a relatively small space, almost at the tip of the bullet-shaped Thetis. On the main flight control telemetry display, an impressive simulation is running. It is the first render constructed from survey data of the proposed landing site chosen for the Thetis first-contact probe. The simulated views of Gnosis Zeta are colorful and mesmerizing and send shivers of hope up my spine. Primo Athena Saugado is standing in front of the screen, walking us through the details of the presentation.

It's been six months since the "Anderson Matter", as it is now somewhat neutrally referred to by most Thetans. Standing close to my right, Heleni is tenderly holding little Apollo, sleeping without a care in her arms. The baby, growing on 3 months old by now, is already sporting the dark-golden tinges of Kilian's eyes. To my initial surprise and, admittedly, against my instinctive misjudgment, Heleni proved to be a very bright woman and a key contributor to our rushed research into Gnosis Zeta's conditions. We will always be separated by our memory of Kilian, but with time eroding the crispness of conflict, that too begins to fade away, making way for common ground between us two. Anyway, Apollo is the epitome of perfection.

To my left, Nyasha sighs and slowly shakes his head in quiet appreciation. The past months haven't been kind to him — he took the entire affair very personally and seems to have aged an entire decade in that short time. He submitted his request to retire from his position as Head Archivist shortly after things settled down a bit, offering to support my nomination as his successor if I wanted the job. He thought Primo Saugado would support it too, despite my relatively young age. I still haven't given either of them an answer.

Thetis life has been very different in the past six months. Initially, the entire ship slumped into a kind of collective depression. The revelation of how close our society got to becoming subdued by our own chosen leader induced a wide soul-searching and major awakening by people across the ship. We were raised and taught to trust the basic values of the Thetan society without question. Having been so deeply duped by our very own was a scary eye-opener, leaving many people feeling deprived of their most basic frame of identity.

Adding to it, the sudden addition of two entire generations until we reach Resett in the Gnosis system meant that Gen5ers and Gen6ers, who'd spent their entire lives expecting to witness the day within their lifetimes, were robbed of that hope. Like their ancestors, they too will end their days in space.

The combination of those elements resulted in a major spiritual crisis on the Thetis.

As for Cassidi and Zee, they are rarely seen in public these days. Some people still hold the conviction that they too were misled by Sabi, and did not take personal part in the conspiracy. Some people will always do. Still others advocate that the conspiracy was on *our* part, that Athena Saugado somehow overthrew Anderson from his just reign. They do not care for the science or evidence. For their kind, narrative trumps truth. Those, too, will always exist.

It will take time. Climbing out of this crisis — healing ourselves — will most likely have to involve the emergence of a whole new value system and social contract for Humanity. We are not nearly there at this point. Suspicion, paranoia and aggression remain much too prevalent, and when trust is lost in our shared systems — well, then we are only reseeding everything that bred Old Earth's demise.

But things will eventually cool down, and we've been given a gift — two whole generations to emerge as the final and ultimate *homo infinitus* — the 10th Generation. Our GenXers.

"So, Sandrine, does this look right to you?" Athena nods at the 3D rendering on display — a simulated view from the planet's ground level looking up to the dark night sky. The image is presented in extreme fidelity on the large screen, an immense field of stars recreated in intricate detail by the simulation. An evident denser band of white wash stretches from one end of the screen to the other. *The Milky Way.* The depiction is so real I begin to feel weight building on my chest — those artificial stars filling the night sky bring back stressful moments.

But externally, I shrug. "Looks OK to me, I guess. I've only been out there for, what, a few minutes? Doesn't make me an expert."

"Ha. Kunyete *and* your humility. Even a *second* makes you an expert compared with us boxed souls."

I laugh wholeheartedly until the pressure in my belly intensifies to the point I can't laugh any longer. I breathe deeply and rest a gentle hand on the ball-shaped bump, searching for that comforting feeling of movement within. In the past months, I too have been working on my own little Gen9er. My very own genline. Well, sort of.

I throw a glance at Nyasha. *I will take you up on that offer eventually,* I think. *Sandrine Liet, Head Archivist.* I can't say I dislike the sound of that.

But Nyasha will have to wait a few more months for me. For the first time in as long as I can recall, I am taking my time for *me* now.

For me and her.

I caress the fabric covering my belly with both hands. I imagine waves of warmth pulsating from my palms, slowly engulfing the little baby, nourishing and protecting her from everything in this alien, harsh universe.

When her time comes, she will see so much more than I ever will, than *any* of us Thetans ever will. A whole new homeworld. Rebuilding a planet-based society. Our two hundred years and nine generations of accumulated experience might not even be relevant for the challenges she will have to face. Her entire generation will have to create their own reality, a new mythology, a Human genline in sync with an entirely new ecosystem.

In time, she will also need to learn about her own origin. How she came to be — the Prober gene code inside her. The CellPrinter and BioBox that sparked her to life. How her creation saved the entire Human race. How special she was. How special she *is*.

Quite a load for a young lady's shoulders, I think. This will have to be a gentle journey for both us girls.

I smile nervously and look up to the large screen, where the simulation has moved away from the star-filled sky to a rendering of Gnosis Zeta's rich aquatic bodies. Bright ripples and tiny white-capped crests fill the display. The room is quiet — every single person is mesmerized by the beauty and tranquility of our future ocean. Even within an artificial rendering, the feeling of freedom, of endless space and opportunity is hitting strong on all of us. We are looking at the best version of our future home. Before weather disasters, before diseases, before toxic grounds and everything else the planet will inevitably throw at us newcomers.

And then, suddenly, *I know her name.*

She will be named after the ocean.

She will *be* the freedom her life brought to us all.

Babies are born a blank slate. The name we give them is the first etching in the mold of history and culture we fix around them as they grow. A mold shaped by our achievements and mistakes, by the virtues and shortcomings of who we are and everyone who came before us.

The ocean waves on the screen are now lapping on the blindingly bright shores of Zeta's arctic continent. The sky is deep blue and clear above the long, flat shoreline. Swept for thousands of years by erratic freezing wind blasts, the shore is littered as far as the eye can see with crisp white frost flowers. They have crystallized here, undisturbed, on this alien beach for millennia. Each glinting frost flower is unique, its exclusive, unrepeatable shape formed by the conditions and environment surrounding it. Collectively, they fill endless fields of whiteness stretching deep into the frozen continent, reflecting the simulated sunlight in a sparkle of warm flares.

The view is breathtaking.

I feel the warmth of my palm seeping into my belly. To my right, baby Apollo is awake and quietly glued to the screen, instinctively reacting to the marvels unfolding in front of us.

Babies may be born a blank slate, but they grow to adopt the values we revere. And ours will have been given a rare opportunity — a chance for a real Resett, a new world for a new society.

I think — we're coming off the heels of a lazy century spent in transit. The first generations worked hard to adapt to living in space. To innovate. To sustain. That took *hustle*. Then, humanity took a century off with shelved ambitions and lack of pressing goals. We had it all comfortably set up for us.

Sebastian Anderson was a well-needed slap in the face. A reminder of the pitfalls of being Human.

We need to start thinking pro-actively again about how we want to shape our children's society. In life, as in space, there is no true vacuum — something, or someone, will always fill any vacancy of rules, of borders, of values. We need to set our own and stand guard over them.

We have the knowledge. We have the science. We have the tools. And we have chosen a magnificent new world for our species to prosper on.

We are the only ones who can screw this up again. It's only up to us to be worthy of a new beginning.

For our genline's sake, I hope we are.

Want more

GENERATIONS?

A special BONUS SHORT STORY about one of the novel's

characters is available to you FOR FREE.

Download it to your e-reader or read it instantly online!

Get your FREE SHORT STORY COPY here:

GENERATIONSNOVELS.COM/BONUS